W9-CNE-490

COLD AS HELL

ALSO BY RHETT C. BRUNO & JAIME CASTLE

The Black Badge Series
Dead Acre (prequel novella)
Cold as Hell

The Buried Goddess Saga
Web of Eyes
Winds of War
Will of Fire
Way of Gods
War of Men
Word of Truth

Standalone Novels
The Luna Missile Crisis

COLD AS HELL

RHETT C. BRUNO
JAIME CASTLE

**BLACK
STONE**
PUBLISHING

Copyright © 2022 by Rhett C. Bruno and Steven Beaulieu
Published in 2022 by Blackstone Publishing
Cover design by Stephen S. Gibson. Typography by Steve Beaulieu

All rights reserved. This book or any portion
thereof may not be reproduced or used in any manner
whatsoever without the express written permission
of the publisher except for the use of brief quotations
in a book review.

The characters and events in this book are fictitious.
Any similarity to real persons, living or dead, is coincidental
and not intended by the author.

Printed in the United States of America

First edition: 2022
ISBN 979-8-200-71067-6
Fiction / Fantasy / Action & Adventure

Version 1

CIP data for this book is available
from the Library of Congress

Blackstone Publishing
31 Mistletoe Rd.
Ashland, OR 97520

www.BlackstonePublishing.com

*For Oliver, who has asked about
this book every day for the past year.
For Juneau, whose joy transcends this world.
For Robyn, for whom my heart beats.
And for Steve Beaulieu, without whom
this book would not exist.*
—JC

*For Elise, who puts up with me every day.
For Aela, whose tiny smile melts my heart.
And for Raven, the inspiration for Timperina.*
—RCB

*Thanks to Josh Stanton and the Blackstone
Publishing family, our good friend Nicholas
Sansbury Smith, Steve Feldberg, Roger Clark, Ethan
Ellenberg, Diana Gil, Ananda Finwall, Hayley Stone,
Christopher Valin, Stephen S. Gibson,
and so many more.*

The Nephilim were on the earth at that time, when those divine beings were having relations with human women, who gave birth to children for them.

—Genesis 6:4a

ONE

Ash fluttered through the air of Lonely Hill, like someone left a candle burning and the cat knocked it over while they slept. But this wasn't a house fire. You'd see that plume of black for miles and miles.

This was different.

A fleck landed on my cheek before quickly melting. Not ash, but snow flurries.

A bit of good fortune for a place like Lonely Hill, I suppose, set smack dab in the middle of Satan's asshole. It was usually hot and dry in these parts. No real reason for man to be here at all, really.

Lonely Hill was just another blot on an old, weathered map. Nothing special in the natural sense of the word, but I don't get dispatched by the White Throne unless there's a "super" before the "natural." And snow in the middle of summer when the air barely had a chill on it? Ain't nothing natural about that.

So as my tawny mare, Timperina, kicked up dried mud, my proverbial hackles were right there too, waiting, expecting at any moment for some ghoul or devil to come popping out from behind the apothecary or the butcher shop, trying to make a meal of me.

Prepared as I might've been, nothing of the sort looked like it was gonna happen. I did, however, get the typical stares from locals, poking their heads from their shutters and doors and their noses where they don't belong. No matter where I went, folks mistook my unique brand of authority for that of a federal marshal. I'm not, but some people—'specially kids, animals, and anyone ultrasensitive to the spiritual realm—can sense that something ain't right about me.

Wasn't my appearance. That's pretty damn normal for a man out here. Bearded. Rugged. Too many scars to count on two hands. Nothing of my outward visage to tell the general public that I was, technically, dead. Or *undead*. I'm hazy on the exact details besides having been shot up, left for the worms, and brought back years later to find myself stuck on this side of eternity, serving the whims and fancies of angels.

I took a corner onto Lonely Hill's main avenue and saw a crowd gathered at the end of the road. More peculiar flurries swirled betwixt them on the breeze like fireflies. Judging by their faces, I knew I'd found it. Whatever *it* was.

I hitched Timp at the saloon a few doors down, choosing to take the remainder of the distance by foot. Better not to act like I was above anybody, yet. As I got closer, I realized I didn't need the expressions to tell me something disturbing had gone down.

"By all the saints and elders," I said under my breath. Had I still been alive, the smell alone would have probably knocked me on my ass. Death is a sickly sweet aroma. Even in its early stages, it's enough to overwhelm and stir up bile at the very least.

Parked along the street's edge, a few men were seated or lying down, being cared for while sucking down whiskey to drown out the pain of bullet wounds. Got a few more stares as I shoved through the rabble, hoping to get a clearer picture. To their credit, no one tried to stop me. If there was a lawman in town, he wasn't showing face yet, neither.

Parts of the West were being tamed these days, even had their hired band of Pinkertons—outlaw hunters, bounty hunters, and the like—but small towns like this would be the last to fall to law and order. Places like Lonely Hill relied upon small crews of barely trained gunmen. How would I know? These were the exact places where the old me would've ridden through with his rowdy pals, put our boots up on a saloon table, and drank for free so long as we flashed our iron.

Yeah, I took what I wanted without asking in my day, but I'd never shot up a town like this.

The word *massacre* usually speaks of dozens or hundreds dead, but there wasn't a better word for the two corpses I spotted, bloodied and broken remains strewn across the red clay streets.

Beyond them, a two-story building stood catty-corner to the others. The facade was painted a bright cherry red with big, gold letters. Frost dappled the words and made them hard to read, but I got it, eventually: DUFAUX BANK AND TRUST.

So, what was this, then? A robbery gone awry? That felt too normal for my particular talents. Angels care about many things, but the wealth of men ain't one of them.

I let my eyes wander a bit, but no one else was moving. Not an inch. Looked as if someone had snapped a photograph like them rich folk in the city are fond of, still as statues.

"Who's the stranger?" an older man finally croaked, talking about me but not to me.

"A marshal, clearly," his wife added, nudging him in the side.

"Oh, thank heavens," said another, a younger man with a clean face and a lazy eye. "Mr. Marshal, I ain't never seen anything like this."

I didn't respond—not even at the accusation of being a fed. Just let my glare pass across them, instilling silence. I always found it better to examine a situation before hearing from those around it, either their opinions or the things they pretend to have seen. Everyone always wants to feel a part of having solved a mystery.

With a sigh, I made my way to the first body. The poor bastard lay facedown in a puddle of his own blood. His dark-colored vest was so soaked in it, I couldn't determine its original color. Black? Dark blue? Some kind of maroon even? But pinned to his left breast was a silver star.

It's unclear to me how the star became the universal symbol for authority, but when I was brought back to life, it included a branding of sorts on my bare chest. Often, I consider its five points to be that of the hand behind my resuscitation. But I can't deny it looks like a black star or badge. Amongst us Hands of God, we often call ourselves just that—the Black Badges. Sounds earthlier that way. Makes it a bit easier to forget that we ain't normal.

And here it was again, a star to signify this man's position as Lonely Hill's protector. The sheriff. Dead as a doornail.

Didn't do a very good job at it—protecting. Or, I suppose, he did a fine one by some estimations. One of his deputies was the other corpse, lying across the square in a similar outfit, body bent backward over a bale of hay so I couldn't see his head. If he still had one.

"So, what is it? You some kind of marshal?" a voice asked from behind me.

Still, I didn't look or answer. Just kept my eyes trained upon the former sheriff. He was young—younger than I'd been when I bit the dust. Had a beard, but barely.

"What the hell happened here, Sheriff?" I whispered before getting to work.

As one could expect, upon my resurrection I was imbued with *otherworldly* abilities of my own—powers, some would say, and they wouldn't be wrong. Among those is the ability to see the final moments of a person's life, assuming they're fresh enough.

It's not as glamorous as it sounds. Some things I've seen simply can't be unseen, no matter how much I wish it so. I've watched as husbands strangled their wives to death through the very eyes of the woman in question. Felt his hands around my throat. Choked as those final gasps for life left my lungs.

Myself? I was shot and killed by a fellow named Ace Ryker, a man I'd called a friend.

Each time I Divine someone whose life ended violently, I not only experience their pain but mine all over again.

That's why I wasn't so eager to do what I knew needed doing.

But hell, nothing's ever easy for a Black Badge.

I dipped my finger into some of the blood, drew a wet line across my forehead, and spoke a few words in Latin. It wasn't necessary to the process, but I'd gotten used to doing it. Somehow made me feel closer to the deceased before violating the sanctity of their minds.

"*A tenebris ad lucem.*" *From darkness to light,* or close enough for a rough translation. Far as I knew, no one was grading me on my language skills.

I've encountered other Black Badges who do no ritual of the sort, but Divining is a deeply personal thing to each of us. To intrude on last moments? It ain't for the faint of heart.

I took a steadying breath, then pulled off my glove and placed my bare hand against the sheriff's sallow flesh.

A jolt of power coursed through me. My head snapped back, and my eyes shone with what I could only assume to be the light of Heaven's gate. Everything around me faded—the street, the buildings, all of Lonely Hill vanished into searing bright white and my vision settled into the mind of the deceased . . .

* * *

My ears registered the tumult of gunfire. Screams. Terror. A bullet whizzed past my head, and I cried out in a deep voice, though it wasn't me speaking.

"Watch your fire, Deputy!" I—and, by that, I mean my sheriff host—glanced back at a terrified, scrawny deputy shooting blindly from behind a barrel.

Then I looked around the town square, frantic. I knew by some insight or intuition that my host was searching for cover while more and more bullets thudded the ground around me. My hand trembled, barely able to keep my six-shooter level.

No matter how brave, burly, or manly one might be, nothing tests your mettle like a gunfight.

"Best st-st-stand down, outlaws!" my host shouted, wielding absolutely none of the bravado he hoped to convey.

Dirt sprayed up. A bird screeched—funny little detail to note in the midst of this chaos. Splinters spit outward from buildings, hitching posts, barrels, and everything else.

However, so far, I had seen no sign of said outlaws, just the twig-thick deputy, twenty paces behind me, shooting wild at something leaping and diving near the bank.

That's when I realized that that something was, in fact, someone.

She—for I believe it to have been a woman—moved like nothing I've ever seen. The only feet I'd seen that carried such catlike grace belonged to vampires, and the sun was far too high for this to be any such creature.

Rounds fired in her direction, every single one missing by what might as well've been miles. I couldn't tell if everyone in this town with a gun was a shit shot or she was just that good. Then I watched as what appeared to be a small axe flew end over end a distance of at least thirty feet before slamming home in the center of one deputy's forehead. He dropped back and into a bale of hay.

Several folks screamed, including me. "Theo!"

Before anyone could get to Theo—and truth was, it wouldn't have done a damn bit of good—the doors of the bank burst open from the inside. A gust of freezing air and flecks of ice whipped out, stinging my host's cheeks like tiny knives.

From that hellish shroud emerged a towering man. He was wearing the skin of a polar bear or some white wolf over his shoulders and chest and most of his face was covered by a mask, leaving just tanned skin and dark eyes to be seen. Shards of ice swirled around his arms.

That was all I saw before blistering, white-hot pain reverberated through me, starting in my back and spreading outward. I'd felt this pain before.

A bullet straight through my heart. Only, this time, it entered from the back . . .

* * *

My eyes shot open—or perhaps they'd never been closed at all. Divining a death that frenzied took a lot out of me. Often it left me on my knees, panting, making sense of it all as a flood of feeling and emotion came and went in a flash.

I blinked to settle my vision.

Standing before me was the scrawny deputy who'd survived the battle by hiding and shooting his gun blindly. He now had the same revolver pointed directly at my skull.

TWO

"Whatchu think you're doing, mister?" the deputy asked.

He looked like a loose thread pulled at the edge of a worn vest, or the runt of an already small litter.

As his gun swayed just inches from my face, I thought about letting him shoot me. Nothing makes a man stop and listen like watching as the person whose head you just blew a hole through starts talking like nothing even happened.

Instead, I kept my peace and waited for him to lose nerve. They always do. Not like what was left of Lonely Hill's law and order was gonna open fire and shoot a stranger on his knees in front of the whole damn town.

"We don't take kindly to defecating the dead," he said.

He meant desecrating, but I let it go. He'd had a bad enough day. So, I just glared up at him like I knew a secret. Fact was, I did. A bullet in the back had killed the sheriff, and that most likely meant friendly fire. And only one frightened deputy was shooting blindly in the sheriff's direction.

I spoke softly as to not let anyone else hear me. "Feeling guilty, Deputy?"

His eyes went wide as saucepans, and his face turned red.

"Leave the fella alone, Dale," said another voice. "Can't do worse keeping us safe than y'all done."

This one belonged to one of the townsmen. By the sound of him, he was twice Deputy Dale's age, at least.

"What'd you say?" Deputy Dale asked.

Wasn't clear if he was speaking to me or the other guy, but either way, he received no replies.

I rose, sure Dale was harmless as a dove. I brushed myself off and ignored the shaking gun. It followed me, so I gently pushed back my duster.

They say a man looking to protect himself carries a single gun, but a man looking to kill carries two. Don't know what it says about me, but I got a third strapped across my back—a Winchester repeater to complement my twin pearl-handled Peacemakers. Not to mention a silver-dusted hunting knife hidden in my boot. If things get hairy, I've also got an onyx-black lasso—which I promise you is more terrifying to monsters than the guns.

"Mind putting that thing down?" I said. "I ain't here to stir up trouble."

Deputy Dale looked me over. I know where his eyes were roaming. He was wondering if he could shoot faster than I could pull. Probably could. He just didn't know it wouldn't matter.

By now, the crowd had backed up a respectable distance, likely fearing they'd get sprayed with brain matter should Deputy Dale decide to take his second life of the day. Matter of fact, it looked like even more had now come out of their hidey-holes to watch.

"Please?" I said with very little emotion.

Dale lowered his weapon halfway. "You a fed?"

"No, sir," I replied.

"Then what? Some kind of bounty hunter?"

"Of a sort."

"Well, they long gone," Deputy Dale said, looking over my shoulder at the mob behind us. He was sweating bullets. "And you should be, too. Look at Theo, over there."

I did as he asked, not making a show of it. But just as I'd seen in my Divining with the sheriff, Theo lay baking in the sun. From here, I could now see the tomahawk sticking out of his face. Only difference was, now the haze had fallen and flies buzzed around his split skull. I could've Divined him too, but I saw him die. And honestly, a hatchet to the head was the last thing I needed to experience.

"These people need to grieve without any more hullaballoo," Dale said.

"Hullaballoo?"

"You know. Another stranger, coming in here, mucking up the place."

I grunted and turned my back on him, moving toward the entrance to the bank.

"Marshal, I'm warning you," he said.

I almost laughed.

My job as a Black Badge is a difficult one to explain. Though I have no earthly authority in the traditional sense of the word—no writs or warrants—there ain't a lawman alive who's gonna keep me from fulfilling my duties. Besides, I've been given no choice in that matter. I got debts to pay.

The White Throne sent me to Lonely Hill for a reason. I don't know what it is yet, but the Lord works in mysterious ways, and all that bullshit people say when they don't understand stuff. All I know is that whatever reason I'm here, it means this is a task for someone with a bit more experience than Deputy Dale.

And before anyone gets themselves in a state of confusion, allow me to set the record straight. I wasn't a good man in life. There was barely a sin I hadn't ticked the box off of in my day. In fact, I'd always figured I'd rub elbows with the Devil himself when I parted this Earth. Probably did during those years before I was brought back.

Yet here I am. I think even the White Throne knows well enough that good men falter when it comes time for pulling the trigger. You need a special kind of someone to shoot first and ask questions later. Or choose never to ask at all.

That fella is me.

The name's James Crowley, but most days, I'm just a goddamned Hand of God.

You might say, "My word, Mr. Crowley, that language ain't appropriate for a sentence also including the Lord's name." And hell, you might even be right. After all, the Almighty did see fit to give me another lot in life.

Revived by angels. That's a gift!

Bullshit.

This is a curse if there ever was one. I may serve Heaven as penance for a life of crime, but Heaven ain't at the end of the rainbow road for me. When—and if—the White Throne decides it's had its fill of me, I don't get Paradise. No, sir. No golden streets, pearly gates, or mansions in the sky.

The only promise is me getting spared the icy depths of Hell.

And when you find out eternal damnation—there's that "damn" word again—when you find out it's a real thing, you learn to play nice with angels. Trust me.

Deputy Dale was still spitting threats at my back as I trudged toward the bank. Puddles of what looked like blood pooled around its foundation. A lady huffed and threw a long-gloved hand over her lips when I reached down and dipped my finger in it. Heard some muttering behind me, too, like I'd just dug up the dead.

To my surprise—and dare I say relief—it appeared like nothing more than water mixing with the red clay that was so prevalent in this region. It wasn't from rain, that's for sure. This region hadn't seen rain in too many months. Might've been melted snow but those flurries couldn't have done this much. It was just too much water streaming out of the bank like a springtime creek.

A paper flyer lay in the wetness. I picked it up and squinted. Something about a Founders' Day Festival up at Revelation Springs in a week or so, hosted by Dufaux Bank and Trust. They'd be a little short on spending money, all things considered.

Leather groaned after I flicked the paper aside and stood.

I made my way up the front porch. It was dead silent but for the sound of my spurs jingling and my boots thudding. I reached for the door handle. That's when Dale's protests grew to a degree that could no longer be ignored.

"Now wait right there, Marshal!"

I spun, quick as a whip, pulling my pistol.

"I ain't a goddamned marshal!" I barked, firing two bullets at the kid's feet. Wasn't trying to hurt him, just trying to put a little bit of that fear of God in him. He danced like I wanted. Then, he dropped to his knees like his skinny legs wouldn't hold him any longer. Probably couldn't.

Bringing my arm down halfway to straight, I turned to the rest of the townsfolk who weren't already running. The injured men outside the saloon went pale, likely fearing another shootout that this time they wouldn't be lucky enough to survive.

"Now, I already said I ain't here to hurt nobody," I stated. "I'm here to find out what happened to your town. Y'all go home and let me work."

The faces staring back at me held terror in their features. Some retreated slowly. Others whispered. I raised my gun again, and they all scattered like startled crows.

When they were gone, only Deputy Dale remained nearby. He stared at me, his soft jaw set in as hard a line as it could go, trying and failing to conceal his many emotions. Anger and fear were likely to be chief among those.

"You need more convincing, Deputy?" I asked.

To my astonishment, he approached me, stopping when he saw my shooting arm twitch, and then pressed forward again. Even I had to admit the guy had some cojones on him.

He slowed his pace when he reached the porch but still climbed. A pace or two from me, he said, "Don't know who you are, mister, but I . . . I can't let you go in there unaccompanied. It's a crime scene, and if you ain't a marshal like you says you ain't, then you got no right being there."

I kept my gaze fixed squarely upon him. Then I spun my pistol once and shoved it into its holster.

"Unaccompanied, eh?"

I shouldered my way past him and down the porch stairs. I couldn't see him with my back turned as it was, but I knew he was watching, wondering what it was I was doing. Was I leaving? Was I walking ten paces before turning to send him following after the sheriff he'd likely accidentally murdered?

I stopped when I reached said former sheriff. Dale made a mono-syllabic sound like a whimper or a puff. Reaching down, I snatched the star from the sheriff's jacket and returned to Dale.

"Fine," I said, palming it against his chest. "Lead the way. Looks like you're the new sheriff anyway."

Dale grabbed it before it fell to the ground. He stuttered through an unintelligible response and then promptly plunged it into his pocket. Confused as he might've been, his back straightened, and he nodded.

"It ain't pretty in there," he said, head shaking.

"Never is."

Dale led the way toward double doors that had already been busted open. He pushed them wider, and the frost-coated brass hinges squealed in displeasure.

The moment I passed the threshold I could sense the increased fri-gidity in the air as if out of habit, though there was no gooseflesh on my skin. Part of my . . . condition is that I don't *feel* the same way as everyone else. You can shoot me, stab me, kick me—nothing.

Sounds pretty damn good, don't it? Well, it ain't exactly. That numb-ness extends to the bedroom too. And the bar. And just about anywhere else pleasure can be found.

The bank's antechamber looked like it had been nice for such a quaint town, more like the lobby of a playhouse than a bank. But now, the walls and floor were peppered with bullet holes. On the back wall, by the teller's booth, an aperture the size of a cannonball told the story of a shotgun being involved. Fragments of chewed-up wood mingled amidst the chaos, soaking in meltwater with chunks of ice still floating in it.

A high, arched ceiling proved the building's external facade was just that—not two stories, just a tall one and beautifully crafted. On that ceil-ing was painted some exaggerated scene of a man finding what appeared to be gold in a spring and hoisting it high above his head as a geyser shot up behind him—tough to tell, coated in ice as it was. Blades of light emanated from the gold as if it were holy. To some men, I suppose it is.

"Lot of money put into this place," I remarked.

"Mr. Dufaux has a dream of having a bank in every town across the nation, he does," Dale said.

"Mr. Dufaux," I said. "And who might that be?"

Dale looked as if I'd slapped him. Then, his face shone like he was telling a bedtime tale to his children.

"Why, Reginald Dufaux is a legend! The man started with just the boots on his feet and the hat on his pate. Built—from the ground up, I might add—the premier banking institution in this here region starting in Revelation Springs. Lonely Hill has never been prouder than the day Mr. Dufaux brought his bank and trust to our humble little old abode."

"Never heard of him." I shrugged. It wasn't entirely true. The name was familiar from my passings through the region, but I'd never met the man. I've never been too fond of moneybaggers who made their fortunes off someone else's hard earnings.

I know that sounds funny from a former outlaw and thief, but what we did—me and my old bandit crew, the Scuttlers, led by Ace Ryker—was an art form. Took more work than an honest day of hard work.

"He live around here?" I asked.

Dale laughed, sharp and short. "Golly, no. He's got an estate outside Revelation Springs. He's gonna be like a bull on fire when he finds out about this."

Despite it being midday, it was eerily dark inside. Flurries and dust flittered here and there like ash. Any window that hadn't been shot out remained fogged up by the thick film of rime that cast an unholy darkness throughout the place. Which answered the question: Is this why I was sent here?

The White Throne was stingy with details, expecting me to decipher things on my own. Most times, that was simple. Others, not so much. But here, standing inside this dark, wintry, cold bank, I could feel the touch of Hell. The hulking outlaw I'd seen wielding ice? Whoever he

was, however he got those powers, those sort of abilities come only one
way: communing with demons.

Most times, when folks think about Hell, images of fire and brimstone come to mind. But the cold and ice that filled the bank, those are
the true signs of Hell. And cold can be just as unforgiving as any flame.
It's really simpler than people think. The Almighty, Heaven, they're light.
The sun . . . that's fire. Old Lucifer, the Devil, Satan, the Adversary, the
Morningstar—don't matter what you call him—his heart is cold as the
darkness in which he dwells.

Whatever happened in this bank, it was hellish to the core.

"What happened here, Sheriff?" Steam swirled around my breath.

For a second, I don't think Dale knew I was talking to him, being
the first time anyone ever called him by that title.

I realized my words might have sounded like an accusation by the
way he responded.

"Oh. I. Uhm . . ." He turned toward me and continued. "Listen,
I don't know what you think you saw or know . . ." His voice got low
even though there was no one living to hear him. "But Sheriff Daniels,
he's a—was—a good man. He died protecting us like he always did.
That's it, clear and simple."

Whether or not he accidentally killed the sheriff in the firefight was
irrelevant to me. Bad things happen when bullets start getting flung
around willy-nilly.

"Just tell me what happened here and I'll be happy to pry no further," I said. After the chaos I witnessed through the sheriff's eyes, a fresh
perspective seemed necessary.

Dale swallowed the lump in his throat. "Thank you, Marshal."

"Name's Crowley. And I ain't a marshal. We clear on that?"

Dale nodded.

"What. Happened. Here?" I said each word pointedly, like I wasn't
gonna ask again.

"Wish I understood," Dale said, his gaze growing distant. "Never
seen them before, and they came in like a twister and left just as quick.
Or, like a blizzard, I reckon."

"Just took the money and split, huh?"

"Like nothing I've ever seen. Before anyone in town knew what happened, they'd already broke the safe open. Barely time to mount a defense. Look."

He gestured to the teller's desk, the bars from the counter to the ceiling offering extra protection and making it hard to see the vault beyond. So many snow eddies filled the other side, I felt like we'd entered one of those toy snow globes.

Our boots sloshed through an inch of water while he led me around. The grated door leading behind the bars lay in shards on the floor, shattered like glass. Water rippled through from my steps, and my foot hit a chunk of ice. And not just ice.

A man was frozen solid on his knees, eyes open, staring in horror at whatever had done this to him. He looked as if an avalanche had buried him. The shotgun in his hand had been stuck with him, seemingly the culprit responsible for blowing that hole in the wall.

The vault door behind him was snapped open, unnatural tendrils of ice snaking through the crank. Even from here, I could tell the inside was completely empty. A bank branch in a small town like this wouldn't house too much, but money's money, and it was gone.

"Harvey ran this branch," Dale said, barely above a whisper. "Nice fella. Bit of a drinker, though."

"No warmth in the belly could have saved him from this." I took off my glove and lay my bare hand upon the bank manager's shoulder, the ice slick as it slowly melted. Enough that some frostbit flesh poked through. While Dale was busy peeking around corners as if anyone was still around, I tried to Divine the poor sap.

Nothing happened. Well, that's not entirely accurate. But, seeing as I only get to witness the final half-a-minute or so of a life, all I saw was a dark blur—the nothingness Harvey here saw from within the ice. I felt the hellish bitter cold seeping through to his bones before numbness set in. Heard the slow *thump, thump, thumping* of his heart before it all went black.

When I came to, pulling on a glove instinctively, even my numb body gave off a shiver. What a way to go. I got thirty seconds. Only

God knows how long he lived inside his frozen tomb, wondering where it all went wrong.

"That safe was supposed to be impenetrable," Dale said, poking around the thick metal entry.

"Apparently not," I said, rising.

Incredulity racked his features. "What kind of weapon could freeze it like that? And Harvey . . . It's almost like—"

"How many were there, Sheriff?" I interrupted. I didn't want him to finish the sentence and say the word I knew was coming. The all-powerful word that can give cause for snow in a place where it doesn't snow.

Magic.

When normal people start throwing around that word, well, let's just say my job gets tougher.

"Please stop calling me that," Dale said. "I ain't proud of what happened."

"Proud or not, you're all this town's got now, son. So, tell me what you know."

It was time to pry the mind of the crime's chief witness. The dead weren't gonna show me any more secrets. But one thing was certain— things didn't add up. Not one damn bit. Demons and the like, things I usually chased after, didn't have much need for cash. And these outlaws didn't seem to be making it a goal of killing like possessed or demon hosts typically did. Sure, three were dead, but only lawmen and the teller who'd pulled a boomstick.

"Sheriff," I said. "You plan on answering?"

Dale looked like he was having a conniption. He was sweating before. Now? It was like a dam burst, and a whole ocean was pouring off him.

"It was pretty wild, Mr. Crowley."

"That ain't what I asked."

He peered out the window as if the outlaws might come back. "I counted two. Maybe three."

"Well, which was it?"

"I-I—"

"It don't matter. A crew that small robbed your town blind and got out unscathed?"

Again, Dale looked dejected. "It's a small town, Mr. Crowley. Only about a hundred or so, not counting those living close enough to use our services."

"The people of Lonely Hill ain't armed?"

"Half of us are women and children," he said.

"Still, seems easy enough to take down two or three outlaws who get themselves boxed in here when there's a dozen or more armed and knowing how to shoot."

He closed his eyes and shook his head. "You didn't see them."

Fact was, I had. Or at least two of them. But he didn't need to know the extent of it.

"One was big," he continued. "Real big, with crazy hair like . . . like snow. The other moved so fast she was a blur to my eyes. I think her skin was painted. I . . . I just kept shooting and . . ."

He paused for a moment, no doubt thinking about that stray bullet which claimed his sheriff's life.

"And the third you *maybe* saw?" I asked, hoping to break that train of thought.

"Just felt the wind when bullets whipped past from somewhere on the rooftops."

"Sharpshooter, huh?"

"Maybe. Sharpest I've ever seen."

"More would be dead if that were true," I said.

"It was probably his bullet killed Sheriff Daniels."

Dale sounded like he was trying to convince himself more than me. So, I just gave him a sidelong glare and waited for him to continue. He blinked fast a few times before he did.

"Anyway, he scared everyone away like he was herding us," he said. "Like we was sheep. Carved a path right out of the square after they broke open the vault. Sent most of us running."

I felt like that last sentence was a slip of his tongue, and his red face agreed. Then, his words did too.

"Wasn't like I ran," he said, quick. "Stayed down right outside, and I think they thought I was dead. Heard every word they said on the way out. Surviving's got to count for something."

I glared so hard at him he stopped to swallow the rock forming in his throat.

"Didn't think that was a good bit to start with?" I said.

"Forgive me, Mr. Crowley, but I still don't know who you is."

"I *is* the only damn bastard around here that ain't hiding out. I'm here to help, and you need to cooperate."

He nodded, slow. "Well, I heard them all, but it was loud. So loud with the screaming, horses, gunshots . . . I ain't even sure it was English."

I threw my hands up in frustration.

"Wait. Wait," he said, raising his own to placate me. "I *think* I heard the big one say it was time to hit the next one."

"You think?"

"He did. He said it was time to get on."

"Which way did they leave?" I asked.

"Huh?"

I slapped his arm. "When they left, which way did they go?"

He bit his lip, and I could see the gears of his mind turning.

"West," he decided, finally.

"You sure?"

He nodded. "Yeah, after they loaded everything onto a wagon, they headed west."

"What's the nearest town in that direction big enough to have a bank?"

"Well, it's Elkhart, I reckon. You don't think—"

"Of course, I think. If they're going on a spree, they'll be moving fast."

"We gotta warn them."

"I plan to do a lot more than warn." I swept out from behind the teller's station, blowing by him.

I stopped by the bank's entrance. Turning to him, I tipped my hat. "Good luck with Mr. Dufaux," I told him. Then, I headed out and back toward Timperina. She was busy nipping at a young boy trying to give her a pat. She didn't have much tolerance for anybody but me.

Shooing him off, I walked her by the saloon to see if I could get any of the injured men talking. Nobody had seen any more than I already had. Same ghost stories of a shooter on the roof, an impossibly fast woman that some were sure was a man. And a big brute with some kind of dynamite that blew ice instead of fire.

Nothing that helped more than what Dale spoke of.

Not keen on wasting any more time, I decided to leave Lonely Hill in my dust. At least I wasn't riding blind anymore. There were many ways it could come about, but someone had been entrusted with the frigid powers of Hell and was using them to get rich.

I can't say I wouldn't have done the same if I'd been so lucky back when I was an outlaw. But I wasn't anymore. And if all these years serving the White Throne had taught me anything, it was that any man or thing with abilities like this didn't usually stop at robbing and fending off lawmen.

They escalated. Innocents died.

That is, unless I stopped them first. Frozen corpses, icy black magic, hellish murder—all in a day's work.

THREE

It's hard to remember the days, crossing the wild, when I was a normal man. Not sure how people do it. Bad enough with bandits, outlaws, brigands, and loons out here—men depraved either from birth or gone nuts with their brains baking in the hot sun. Worse knowing what other monsters lurk in the forgotten corners of the world. Guess that's what makes it simple, though, ain't it? Most folks don't know any better.

But when the sun goes down in the West, and the wolves start their song, it's hard not to clench a bit tighter on the reins. People aren't afraid of being alone in the dark. They're afraid of *not* being alone in the dark.

And friend, I'll tell you one thing: you ain't never alone. Not ever.

One of my many blessings from on high is the ability to see as well at midnight as at noon. Good for spotting wicked beings that may be after me. And wicked things are always after the Black Badges. They ain't happy we escaped our fate. Ain't happy we got the second chance they never did.

So, I stick to the worn paths.

Just easier that way. And poor Timperina is getting on in years. She may be sturdy as an ox, but I feel better not pushing her to gallop unless I've got no better choice. And her ears ain't what they used to be, either. Sometimes, I feel her muscles tense over threats so distant, she need not worry at all.

Maybe it isn't age. Maybe she and I have run into one too many werewolves or shapeshifters. Hard to know the mind of a horse. Could be, she thinks every living thing her weary eyes behold might transform into something rabid and terrifying.

Shit, she's not all wrong about that. The meditation of wise men ain't always sound . . . but horses and simple things? Humans should be so lucky.

"*Crooowleeey.*"

I heard the voice of my angelic handler, Shargrafein, but it was really more like a nagging tingle in the back of my mind. I wasn't in the mood, it's not often I am.

"What do you think, girl?" I leaned over and whispered into Timp's ear. "Should I answer?"

Timp's ear twitched in response, and she released a low snort. I patted the side of her neck and snickered. "Yeah. You can say that again."

"*Crowleeey.*" My name rang again, a pinprick in my brain.

I clicked my tongue, and Timp—ever the obedient girl—slowed to a meander. I rustled through my pocket and pulled out an old shaving mirror. A pretty thing, once, with an intricate design of flowers and birds—doves, I think—decorating its iron case. The symbol of the Holy Trinity centered the piece, three ovals interconnecting in the center. Used to look silver—though it wasn't. None of us supernatural types could touch the stuff, which is why I always wear gloves. But even so, now it appeared more made of dirt than anything else. Pitted and black, in need of a good polish.

There was a time when my angelic benefactor Shargrafein would need to wait for me to find a reflective surface, be it a looking glass or still water, before she could badger me about what I was or wasn't doing. But I guess I'd pissed her off one too many times. She'd forced this little trinket upon me, and now it was always right there in my pocket to give me a metaphorical headache.

I flipped open the clasp and found myself accosted by her reflection.

"Sorry to keep you waiting, sweetheart," I said.

"Do not call me that," she replied, in a voice like velvet and sweet as white cake. It was something, hearing words coming from the mirror. There were no lips to move, only the vague form of a woman's face, though she appeared more like swirling smoke. I think I get under her skin—rather, I know I do—but she gets under mine, too. Fair is fair, in my book. Tit for proverbial tat.

"Apologies, oh, Illustrious Shar of the pearly gates," I said, bowing my head slightly. "What can your humble servant do you for today?"

"I am in no mood for games, Crowley," she snapped.

"Pretty sure you say that every time."

"Then perhaps you should adjust your attitude."

"What's the matter, Shar—Paradise ain't comfy?"

"You know nothing of Paradise."

"Never professed to, you keeping me stuck here and all."

The mirror shuddered ever so slightly. Such a frail little thing to contain the immortal being within its reflection. But the Hand of God is steady, and I kept my grip.

"You are insufferable," Shar said.

"Just a bit rattled from what I walked into back there," I replied. "How is it that you always seem to send me stumbling upon death and destruction after it's over with? Just occasionally, it'd be nice to stop some."

"If only the agents of Hell warned us before they struck."

I smirked. "Was that sarcasm, Shar?" I grabbed the cuff of my shirt between my fingers and the heel of my hand and rubbed the mirror's surface. "Seems I'm rubbing off on you."

"Enough."

The way she said it shut my trap tighter than a nun's thighs. Shargrafein is a pain in my ass, but she's my handler in the shadow war between Heaven and Hell that I was unwittingly thrust into. And an angel. There's a ton of things about what I am and who I serve that I don't reckon I'll ever understand, but she's guided me on this here mortal plane since the day I awoke in Cathedral Rock with a burn mark on my chest.

"*He giveth and taketh away,*" the Good Book says, and I know if I became too much of a hassle, she'd do just that and take this . . . gift away. Punch me straight to the icy pits of Hell.

I guess that's a lesson we all need reminding of now and again: not every gift comes with ribbons and a bow. Thing is, you survive long enough, the only thing left to fear is not surviving any longer.

"What is it you need?" I asked again, a little more pointed this time. "I saw what I saw in Lonely Hill. Confusing way to rob a bank, you ask me. If they're fixing to keep this spree going, then Elkhart's the most likely place to be, ain't it?"

"As always, you see nothing," Shar rebuked.

"I saw an evil son of a bitch, plain as day. Throwing hellish magic and leaving corpses."

"No. What you witnessed was a flagrant disregard for the lesser kingdom—that of mankind. One of Lucifer's kin empowered one of the Children within that bank. This isn't the spawn of demons misplaced in your world, as it was in Dead Acre, or a mere monster surviving off its call to the darkness. Those powers were bestowed upon that man, same as yours. This is an act of war."

"Against whom?"

"Against the Throne you serve until we deem otherwise."

I sniffed a little laugh. "What's Heaven care about cash?"

"It's not—"

"Well, I suppose I've seen more than a fair share doled out to the priests during Mass. Guess it makes sense they got banks up there."

"Crowley!" Shargrafein's voice boomed, interrupting my rant. "It's not about money." This time, the mirror whistled like the glass was right on the precipice of becoming a thousand little chips.

A raven flapped out of the nearby brush. Timp whinnied, but I gave her mane a tug to remind her I was still there.

"It's about chaos," she continued, more calmly. "I sense Abaddon or even Chekoketh behind this."

"Remind me which evil bastard that is again?" I asked.

I recognized the name Abaddon. We all did, us Hands of God. But sometimes, my memory goes a little fuzzy with all these wacky names.

The last book says Abaddon is "a king, the angel of the bottomless pit" and describes him like a plague of locusts resembling horses with crowned human faces, women's hair, lions' teeth, wings, iron breast-plates, and a tail with a scorpion's stinger. Sounded downright charming.

But Chekoketh?

"He goes by many names as he appears to Earth's many peoples," Shar explained. "Among the most notable, Loki, Prometheus, Anansi— but here, he is most commonly called Coyote."

Right. Now his name rang a bell, and it unsettled me. I thought about the raven who'd just flown the coop when Shar called my name. It was no secret that the Native American people in these parts often spoke of a trickster god who often masqueraded as a raven. Abaddon was Hell's lord of destruction, but at least he was honest about his role. This Chekoketh would just as soon bed you then kill you, and you'd never know his true intent until the knife slid between your ribs.

"The job's the job," I said, hiding my very real concern. "What's it matter to me?"

"It means, be wary Crowley. Hell grows bolder. The Fallen Ones scheme. The Throne fears it won't be long until they try to open another Hellmouth."

"Huh. Ain't like your kind to fear," I said.

According to my knowledge—limited as it might've been—a new Hellmouth hasn't been raised in centuries, back when the American frontier was no more than a few wood houses and a brothel. Before America was anything, really. There're dormant ones here and there, from old times, that occasionally leak something hellish through, but the Hands of God keep them under control . . . mostly.

We're spread out all over this fine planet, I've been told. I've only met a few, but I reckon by the things I hear, there's gotta be at least a hundred of us from here in the West to the Orient.

"You think this bank robber was what—one of the Fallen?" I asked.

"It is impossible to know yet," Shar said. "You saw very little."

Admittedly, by then I'd gone soft on Shar's warnings. Every time we talk, it's "Hell this" and "Hell that." Constantly warning me that

Lucifer's minions are after me at every turn. Eventually, you just get used to being ready for anything.

However, if this was truly the work of one of the Fallen Ones, eager to open a Hellmouth . . .

"Of course," I groaned. "Tell me again, what's the benefit of being up there in the clouds, looking down on us? You're telling me what I saw—well, it wasn't you or the White Throne who told me where they were headed next. And considering you ain't turning me around, my guess is I'm right."

"Do not presume to understand what is beyond you, Crowley."

"Oh, I wouldn't dare. But it ain't angels these bastards are killing. Sometimes, I worry you forget that."

"The White Throne takes the deaths of the Children very seriously," she said. I started to protest, but she cut me off. "Just focus on the task at hand. You do not have the luxury of worries."

"Sure, Shar. I'll take your notes to heart."

"I mean it, Crowley. No dawdling. No veering from the path. And for the final time, my name is *not* Shar."

"And what should I—"

Just like that, she was gone. No clap of thunder or beam of light, just my little mirror flickering back to reflecting my weathered face and the pale old moon behind me.

I sighed and clacked it shut. More riddles and skittles. I swear, sometimes I think I'm right and the beings above and below, they only involve humanity because they've got nothing better to do. That they created us needy creatures, and then we grew beyond needing them so much.

It's like the West is a big old chessboard, and there's demons and angels trading rooks with pawns. Was this checkmate? Doubt it. Probably just more of the same.

That raven crowed somewhere overhead, reminding me of what Shar had said of Chekoketh. All I could do was hope this current situation didn't actually involve him. When actual demons start getting involved, things get dicey. I prefer simple assignments, with simple answers.

"What do you think, Timp?" I asked. "Is it time for Kingdom Come?"

She gave a deep snort, then a whinny as she shook her tawny mane.

"Yeah, I doubt it too. Hell can't have nearly as much fun if they break this old world open."

Timperina pushed through a field, brown with summer. Hell, it's always brown around these parts, and worse the farther west you go. Green becomes as rare as decent, honorable men.

My gaze lifted toward the path, snaking through dry brush. I hadn't even realized how quiet it was. Peaceful even.

That notion went to Hell in a handbasket.

"Help!" someone shrieked.

Timp reared up on her hind legs and neighed. She might have darted if I hadn't steadied her.

A woman came stumbling out of a thicket, doing her best to run.

She wore a fine dress made of some kind of rich cotton, but its bottom was muddied and torn. If she'd been wearing shoes, they were nowhere in sight, and I could only imagine how many stickers and prickers would be digging into her bare flesh.

She saw me a second later and threw herself onto the dirt right in my path, not caring that her knees scraped against rocks and Lord knows what else in the darkness.

"P-please, you have to help me . . ." she whimpered.

I squinted at her, out in the middle of nowhere, with not even the glow of a campfire in sight. There was no blood on her that I could see. That was a good sign, at least. But tears aplenty streamed down her dirt-caked cheeks. Something put the fear of God in her; of that, there was no doubt. Enough for her to throw herself at the mercy of a traveler at night who looked, well, if I'm being honest, as dangerous as me.

Can't say I approved. What if I was anybody else?

She pled more, grasping at Timp's hooves. My girl was careful not to hurt her as she clopped away from the lady's touch. I watched the woman, then looked to the road.

"*No veering from the path,*" Shar had said, as if she knew this was coming around the bend.

Of course, I stopped. Undead Hand of God I may be. Ex-outlaw with enough blood on his hands to make a priest blanch, sure. But one thing I am that even the White Throne can't take away is a gentleman.

And so, giving Timp's reins a light tug, I did what any gentleman should.

"What's got you ruffled, miss?" I asked.

Gazing down on her from atop a horse Timp's size, I must've looked damn intimidating. Hair down to my shoulders, a big black duster, and hat to match. A shaggy beard—not that I needed to shave. Since the day the White Throne brought me back to life, I hadn't touched my beard, and it hadn't grown a hair longer nor any more flecked with gray. Who was I to know if the hairs were as dead as me? If I shaved them off, would my face remain smooth as silk for all of time?

Just the thought of it makes me shudder more than old Lucifer ever could. Not a risk I was willing to take. You expect a baby-faced demon hunter to shake the hearts of the wicked? Not likely.

All this and still, the woman came right up beside me and clutched the sole of my boot.

"My Lyle, he . . . he . . ." she sniveled. She kept going like that for a few seconds before I put an end to it.

"Slow down," I told her gently.

I clicked my tongue, warning Timp not to get all rambunctious if I strayed too far. Swinging my right leg over the saddle, I nudged a bit of distance between her and me before sliding down. The echoes of my spurs clanked like an angry rattler.

I was no fool, and I certainly wasn't a virgin to the wild. First thing I did was check from side to side. Bandits loved to prey on backwater roads like this. There's this old saying that there's honor amongst thieves, and I reckon that's as much myth as half the creatures I find myself battling. Wasn't above those types to throw a pretty lass out like a fishing lure and see what hapless traveler went to biting.

My hearing was good before the Almighty brought me back. Now, it was keen as a hawk. We were surrounded by nothing but the soft rustle of wind against the brush. No men lurking in the shadows. Nothing.

The woman clasped her chest, stuck between crying and hyperventilating.

"Take a breath, slow and easy," I said as I took her by the shoulders. "What's your name, miss?"

I couldn't see the color of her eyes in the night, but I held her gaze until she found the wherewithal to focus. Her arms lifted as her chest heaved.

"Agatha . . ."

"There you go, Agatha. Breathe. All right. Now, start slow and tell me what in God's name you're doing out here? Haven't you heard there's outlaws about?"

"My Lyle and I . . ." She inhaled sharply. "He brought me out here to show me his favorite spot down by the gorge. But something . . . something grabbed him, and . . ."

"Some*thing?*"

She blinked. "Or someone. I don't know, but I heard screaming and growling and . . . Oh, please."

She fell against me, arms around my neck. All the things I've seen and done, this caught me by surprise, my being unapproachable and all that.

Unable to feel by human definitions, I still sensed Shar's vexation with me for even stopping, like a bee zipping around in my chest. I could almost hear echoes of her shouting *"Stay on the path!"*

I told myself it was just a night dog, then told Agatha to "show me the way."

FOUR

Shargrafein's mirror rattled around in my duster pocket, so I shoved that son of a bitch into one of Timp's saddlebags before moving on.

Even as Agatha took my hand to lead me into the brush, I asked the question I often found upon my mind in those waking hours when sleep escaped me. Why not curse more people to be like me? Make an army of Black Badges. That way, it ain't no damn hitch when one of us decides to roam a bit and help someone in need.

I suppose it's a staffing issue. Imagine trying to run a railroad from across the Atlantic, let alone between worldly realms. And trust me, among ruffians like me, I'm damn pliable. Always was the type to join a crew of outlaws, not start one. Knowing when and how to take orders is just part of the game. Hell, sometimes it's harder than leading.

But occasionally, in this endless cycle of unlife, I can't help but do something for me. I'd spent my past lifetime doing wrong by a lot of people. Serving the White Throne feels good sometimes, but I couldn't just ignore a lady in peril because Shar needed me. An angel should understand my need to atone, shouldn't she? Shouldn't she give a damn about Agatha too?

"It's just this way," Agatha said, freeing the grimy hem of her flowered dress from some thicket before pushing onward. The moonlight caught her freckled cheek, glinting across sticky tears as she glanced back.

I paused and let go of her hand. Something had changed from the road. No tremor in her tone, no wobbly knees or hands itching to grab onto anything for support. She grew steady as a field surgeon, her every step composed despite bare and bloodied-up feet.

Meanwhile, dried stems snapped under my boots. Hardened dirt crunched. Each sound drew my right hand freshly to the pearl grip of my pistol. And the—this time—unmistakable howling of a wolf. Maybe a whole band? That got my left hand down too.

Wasn't a werewolf pack, I didn't think. They were usually in more mountainous regions where hiding was easy. Here, it would be all too simple to get caught feeding. However, in these times, you never know. More years I'm around, the more Americans and immigrants flock to these previously wild parts, the weirder things seemed to get.

"You sure this is the way, Agatha?" I asked, more as a way to gauge her level of self-possession.

Naturally, those words brought a swell of Shar's displeasure to me. Imagine having an itch on your bones, impossible to reach but you'd still scratch off all your skin trying.

That's basically what it feels like when Shar's angry. I'd sensed it all across the searing star burned into my chest. Problem is, I also tended to feel it when something hellish was about. Makes it damn difficult to decipher one from another. On the one hand, Shar's pretty much always pissed at me. On the other, there's often demons and the like lurking around.

Robbed of nearly all feeling, a burning on my chest was the one Heaven saw fit to leave me with. Not the touch of Agatha's hand. Or the kiss of a cool breeze. No.

So, in my humble opinion, Shar and her masters could wait a goddamn second.

Agatha reached the crest of a ridge before turning to wave me on. No words, just beckoning. I picked up my pace, but I kept my where-withal, checking the shadowy places before, finally, tugging on her back collar. She didn't stop. Didn't react. So, I moved ahead of her and stuck out my arm.

"Sorry, miss, but I'm thinking I should go first." She stared at me blankly, but she stopped this time. "And no, it ain't 'cause I think you can't handle yourself. But only one of us is armed."

I gave my holsters an audible tap. It was as much to remind her I was packing than to ease any of her fears. Something wasn't right, and I still wasn't sure she wasn't luring me right into the waiting arms of some bandits. After all, Ace Ryker and my Scuttlers were never above or afraid of using damsels to trap wannabe heroes.

Agatha simply kept staring. Finally, a fly landed on her cheek to sip the salt of her tears. I thought for sure it would stir her to action, but nothing. Didn't even swat it away. Maybe she was being sincere, after all.

Poor girl. In total shock. As if no parent or teacher had ever thought to warn her what happens when you go off adventuring into the wilderness with some boy.

No matter. No use in looking back. Too late for could-haves. So, I went forward, her following close behind.

I scampered down an incline littered with sharp rocks and brambles. My foot twisted on one, and I grabbed a thorny vine to slow my descent. It kept me from sliding off into a ravine, but those suckers filled the fingers of my glove, and, for a rare occasion, I was thankful to feel nothing.

Once steady, I turned to lend her a hand, knowing that if my boots and gloves were so susceptible, she'd be in dire straits. Except, Agatha didn't seem to have any trouble at all. I suspected she'd just been this way before and knew what to expect.

I skirted along a thin ledge, a narrow stream gurgling below. Again, the canine howled, and I searched the ridge across the way.

Then it hit me. Not a wolf or a coyote. My recent dustup with werewolves back in Dead Acre must've had me on edge, hearing things that weren't. That howl belonged to a train whistle—a couple of miles out, by the sound of it.

"There's a fall right where the tracks cross," Agatha said. She'd been silent so long, I nearly slipped from the jolt of it. "Lyle said it was 'his spot.' Loved listening to the water."

"Don't they all." I chuckled mirthlessly. All these decades later, young men were still up to the same tricks. "How far down?"

"Can't miss it."

"That ain't why I ask. You hear that?" I closed my eyes and took a whiff of the brisk evening air. The water. The wind. Dead branches rustling.

"Nothing," I answered for her, taking her lack of response as understanding my meaning. "If something got him. Well . . ."

"Oh, please, don't say that!"

Agatha started crying anew and very nearly hurled herself at me. I was lucky to catch her before we both found ourselves tumbling down the steep slope to what was sure to be her death and my inconvenience. I could still break bones, though they tended to not stay broke long. Gets tiresome, snapping the pieces inside my flesh suit back into place and waiting to heal, but all in all, it beats death.

"Careful, now, miss," I said.

"I'm sorry." She sunk back, wiping her eyes and smearing dirt. "I just . . . I don't—I can't think it. That Lyle . . . We're going to be married, him and me. He said so."

It took ample effort to hold back a grin. Oh, to be young and naive again.

"Just try and be careful," I said. "The pass narrows up along here—"

A groan echoed, soft and reeking of pain and fear. The sound of a man in trouble.

"Stay here!" I ordered.

Within a step, I had both my pistols out, hammers pulled back. When you ain't afraid of dying, moving along ledges like these is a cinch. So much error in balancing is caused by fear. Without Agatha as a concern, I barely thought about it, and I was on the other side in moments.

Another groan. I skipped an incline, leaping down and holding my Stetson atop my head with the barrel of my pistol—another thing I wouldn't suggest to those fearful of a bullet to the brain. I touched down on the landing of a small cave halfway down. The ravine ran to my left. Above, train tracks crossed a short bridge. I had trouble believing it could support the weight of a locomotive, but I've been wrong before.

And wouldn't you know, just like Agatha had said, on the other side of the pass was a thin waterfall feeding the stream.

As I gained my bearings, Shar's judgment stung at me worse yet.

"Oh, quiet, you," I told her aloud, knowing somehow, some way, she was listening.

I whipped around with my pistols raised and edged slowly into the cave's open maw. A kerosene lamp burned nearby, running low and barely casting more than a hazy orange glow.

That whimper came louder now from within the darkness.

"You Lyle?" I asked the night.

I got no immediate reply, so I asked again.

The agony he was in became evident with his next moan.

"Hold on," I said, pushing in deeper, following the sound of his voice. "Keep making noise so I can find you."

He listened, but the shape of the cavern made it hard to tell where his voice was coming from, sending echoes every which way. I carefully made my way to the lamp first and lifted it. When my pupils adjusted, the first thing I saw was blood. So much blood, fresh as a baby's breath.

Amidst it all lay a pathetic-looking man, hunched up against the wall. His flesh was sallow and his cheeks gaunt. Through the tears in his shirt, his ribs bulged like the ebony keys on a piano. He looked completely starved.

He'd clearly been here a while. Longer than a while. This man was on sitting on death's doorstep, and something was purposefully keeping him alive. His right leg was a stump above the kneecap, wrapped with rags to stem the bleeding. Was that to keep him from running?

"Christ in a manger," I whispered

I hurried to his side and knelt there. Despite his pained groans, he didn't seem panicked. Just like Agatha, he seemed to be in a state of shock. Then his head swiveled slowly, and he affected a thin smile.

Blood all around us, missing limbs, and darkness . . . that smile was more terrifying than any of it.

"You made it," he said, teeth coated in blood.

He reached out to touch my cheek, fingers so frail that the skin seemed pointless. I grasped his wrist.

"Who did this to you?"

"We're going to be married, Agatha and me," he said. "Didn't you hear?"

"Yeah, I heard."

Talking to him wouldn't get me anywhere. Starvation clearly had him hallucinating. Awful thing to say, but he'd be better off dead. Even considered delivering the blow myself.

The strangest part was that the rest of the cavern appeared to be vacant. All this blood, it couldn't have come from only him. His leg was gone. No bones. No weapons. No chest of belongings if some manner of bandit holed up here.

"Isn't it pretty here?" My gaze snapped up to spot Agatha by the mouth of the cavern, walking slowly my way.

I raised both pistols at her.

"Have you lost your ever-loving mind, missy?" I pointed one of my Peacemakers Lyle's way and said, "You said he was in danger."

If she heard me at all, she was ignoring.

"Our parents said we couldn't be together." Agatha's voice was barely above a whisper. "We were going to be married . . . here. In secret."

"Our secret," Lyle added from behind me.

I eyed her warily as she closed the distance between us. Was that menace in her eyes? Was she not what she appeared?

"They say if you listen closely to the water, it's like God's playing a song just for you." She closed her eyes and hummed a short, sweet melody.

"There ain't no God here," I said, ready to blow a couple holes through her if I needed to. Looking back at Lyle, I yelled, "What the hell did you do!"

Agatha continued humming, and that same melody grew louder from elsewhere, picked up by what sounded like a harmonica. Now, I can't feel much outside Shar's nagging, but those notes, they resonated with me, down deep into my bones. I found myself unable to move, halfway between crouching and standing. Mesmerized.

The train whistle sounded again, temporarily drawing my attention upward but just as quickly, I felt entranced again.

Behind Agatha, a shadow unfurled from within the crisscrossing beams of the railroad bridge. I witnessed the curved horns atop its head first, big as wagon wheels. Long, sharp claws scraped along the wood before the creature dropped, landing on two cloven hooves. Moonlight illuminated a face that was half man, half beast. At least what I could see of it through the tussles of my straggly hair.

Gun to my head, I'd call it a giant goat-man, but that'd be a disservice to most goats. And this thing . . . intimidating wasn't even the word. A mortal man would likely have soiled himself then and there from the horror.

Situations like this are why I keep my weapons loaded with silver bullets. They put men down fine enough, and that particular metal has a nasty effect on creatures not meant for this world.

I once heard a rumor it was because Judas Iscariot took silver in exchange for the betrayal of his Lord. Don't know if it's true, don't even really care. Like I said, I'm happy to follow the lead rather than take it. Do my job, keep my head down. Right now, that meant blowing holes in Billy Goat Gruff.

Only problem was, presently, despite my best efforts, I couldn't pull the triggers.

The ugly beast had a harmonica made of what looked like bone pressed to its lips and played music sweet as an angel's harp. Like my hands, the rest of me was seized up. All I could do was stare as it clomped closer.

With it so near, I could see now that it bore even less a likeness to a goat than I'd originally thought. In the center of its face, it had a single eye as big as my whole damn head. It shone like moonlight, bright yellow, a dark slit for a pupil.

"What are you?" Lyle asked me.

My eyes shifted enough to see Lyle still on his rump. Wasn't like he was going anywhere with only one leg. Except, now, he eyed me in a way similar to the beast. Like he wanted to eat me.

"Many humans have come here to die. To feed me their fear. Their souls. The essence of their lives."

It was evident now that he was speaking in the creature's stead. Even his voice had dropped an octave or two. The beast was using Lyle and his would-be fiancée like mouthpieces while his own played that incessant tune. If I hadn't already hated the screeching instrument, I did now.

"You are afraid, even if you tell yourself you aren't," Agatha said. Her voice, like Lyle's, had gained a cavernous quality.

I found myself unable to respond, as if my lips were sewn together by some eldritch force. In a few long strides, the creature was upon me. But then, it stopped. That big-ass eye looked me over, up and down. The creature knelt, studying me. I could feel it in my head, scratching around.

My chest itched something fierce, too, and it wasn't just Shar's ire.

This was a Nephilim—the result of the heinous act of Lucifer's Fallen sticking their vile little peckers where they don't belong. In this case, thousands of years ago, that meant the Early Children, as Shar likes to call them—human women. I can't imagine the scene at those births. Though, they don't all come out looking as bad as this goat beast.

In fact, there seems to be no rhyme or reason to what those foul fornications created, or what their creations then conjured. Everything from vampires to fairies and every wretched thing in between.

All I know is they keep me busy. Job security. As long as Nephilim remain on Earth, it keeps me out of Hell a bit longer, even if demons like Chekoketh decide to stop causing grief.

What precise kind this one was, I wasn't sure, but it one was one of the lesser Nephilim. Thankfully. The more sophisticated ones usually closer resemble humans, able to blend in. But that don't make these more monstrous, brutish types any less worthy of fear.

Fear can be like drowning in ice water. You just suck down a little bit, and it fills your lungs, ever-expanding until you can't take it anymore. Even if you're dead like me.

Before I'd kicked the bucket, I couldn't spell faith. But once you come to terms with being brought back to life, you got no choice but to have a little. I finally forced my mouth to form words, and with great effort, began reciting one of the few things I recalled from studying under Father Osgood as a kid growing up in Granger's Overlook.

"And do not fear those who kill the body but cannot kill the soul—"

"You have a body," Lyle cut me off in the voice of the lesser Nephilim, "though no life runs within." The beast cocked its head at me like a curious hound while Lyle spoke. "Where is your soul? You are empty."

With its free hand, the beast lowered my arms. It spread its fingers across my entire torso as if tracing the points of my star-shaped brand. Long, sharp nails raked across my chest. It drew gashes but no blood— just a sort of flaky dead flesh.

It circled me, and a sickly greenish hand curled over my shoulder and crawled up my neck.

"Where is your soul?" Agatha said, repeating her lover's words.

Soul is never a word you want to hear from a hellish being. They feed on souls, and this one . . . well, it seemed to have developed a liking for playing with its food. Hard to believe somewhere down the line, this thing had human ancestors. Or at least one.

Or maybe it ain't. Whatever anything from Hell is capable of, men have done just as bad or worse. Only difference is men are born weaker.

Nephilim have all sorts of twisted, unique abilities, and apparently this one's songs could send a body into a trance, hypnotized, allowing it to control another's actions with a combination of melody and thought.

Controlling others . . . Hands of God may all have differing opinions, but there was no unholy power that unsettled me more than that one.

Currently, my thoughts and my sight remained my own, likely because of Heaven's hold on me, but otherwise, I was its puppet as long as it played. Most times, monsters like this one lurk in the darkness— the stuff of legend. Sometimes, they cause too much a ruckus, and *then* the White Throne dispatches me. Why wait?

Looking at Lyle and Agatha, my heart hurt. I thought about Shar and why she'd told me to stay on the path and not veer. Why were these two not worth the trouble, yet a couple of supernatural bank robbers were? Why were the countless others this vile beast made victims any less important than some stolen money?

"You are unable to die, yet stuck here to live," Lyle began, and then Agatha joined him to simultaneously say, "Like me."

"I'm nothing . . . like you . . ." I strained to respond.

"My minions did well to lure you here," Lyle said as the beast encircled me. "But they are so feeble. Disposable." The beast extended one of its razor-sharp talons to Lyle's chin and slowly dug in. The thing tore through the soft flesh of the man's throat and peeked out through his open lips. The poor man kept talking like it didn't affect him. "Vessels for blood."

"You stop that, now!" I warned. "Let him be."

It was strange. Without true feeling in my limbs anymore, I moved mostly out of habit. Muscle memory. But without control, it was like I was floating in the ether, formless. All I could hear over the hypnotic music was the soft rattle of my guns in my shaking hands, struggling against the Nephilim's influence.

"But you. You are . . . strong. You'll make a fine prize for the Fallen Ones," Agatha said. "Perhaps then, they'll see I'm worthy of standing at their side."

One of my pistols slipped from my grip. I didn't want it to, and yet there it went, clattering to the stone with all that deadly silver in the chamber. A chord played, and I took a step, then another, and another still, toward the young woman. I couldn't fight it.

"Lyle and I, we're going to be married," Agatha said.

"You'll be together soon enough." My lips and tongue moved to speak those words even though it wasn't what I was thinking. The beast had my mouth now. Next thing I knew, the one pistol I still held dropped, and my hands extended toward Agatha. My eyes were frozen facing hers, but in my peripherals, I noticed the beast still shuffling around me.

"That's all I've ever wanted," Agatha said.

Against my will, I clutched Agatha's throat and found myself squeezing. Her aloof expression turned to horror as the goat creature seemed to release her from its mind control and let her express her true feelings as she saw the man she'd sought to save her crushing her windpipe.

She couldn't speak. Couldn't breathe.

God, do I hate it when Shar is right. What's the worst place for a Black Badge to be? Falling prey to a Nephilim that can somehow wrestle dominion away from the White Throne and use me as it pleases.

"No!" Lyle screamed, bloodcurdling and full of rage.

The melody modulated keys, and my body spun, dragging Agatha with me. Now I was facing Lyle, who crawled along the floor of his own volition, free of hypnosis now too, it seemed, digging his nails into rock, desperate to move faster. Blood poured from the wound in his throat while the Nephilim pinned him by the shirt with the tip of a hoof so he could only watch.

"I feel their fear." The beast spoke through me this time and I didn't like it. "I am their fear."

Agatha's trembling lips went purple. Veins bulged along her neck and around her temples. My full weight folded her flat onto her back. I had a fleeting reminder of the way my old boss Ace Ryker thought he could treat all women before I turned on him. I tried to use that memory as fuel to force me to relinquish the hold I had on her, but it was useless as teats on a bull. The beast's effect was too strong on me.

As Agatha went over, kicking and clawing and screaming, a necklace tumbled out from the neckline of her dress. A golden locket that I guessed Lyle had purchased for her back when he'd professed his love. Probably the most exquisite item she owned. The thing was so polished, it may as well have been a mirror.

"Snap out of it, you fool!" Shar bellowed, a shade within the reflection. Her voice struck me like a thunderclap, and her presence momentarily broke the trance. I found myself in control again.

Thank Heaven for young love and its obsessive need to prove itself with gifts and trinkets.

Agatha gasped for air as my hands unclenched, and before the beast could react, I dove into a roll and retrieved my fallen pistols.

I didn't turn to fire at it. I knew I wouldn't have long unless I somehow landed a kill shot. Instead, I shot two rounds straight at the ceiling, keeping the guns as close as I could to my ears without accidentally burning them off.

The ringing made me deaf to everything else. Dizzy too. My eardrums would heal like every part of me tends to, but without that particular sense, the Nephilim couldn't control me.

I staggered to my feet where one of its massive, clawed hands swatted me aside. Once again, I lost possession of my damn pistols as I rolled into the wall.

Pawing for the rifle on my back, I flipped to my side to find that the beast had a screaming Lyle by the waist. How that man was still living, I did not know. The beast's jaw unhinged, ready to engulf the man in a single bite and leave no trace that he'd ever existed.

I fired, clipping the beast on one of its horns and blowing half of it off in a flash of white-hot smoke. It unleashed a primal roar so shrill it shook rock from the ceiling. A second shot took it in its shoulder, causing it to drop Lyle and stumble back.

Hands free, it raised its instrument again and frantically began to play. What looked like smoldering steam rose from where the silver bullet was still lodged beneath its skin, but it didn't seem to care much. I've been shot by silver and it hurts like a son of a bitch. This thing was no weak Neph.

My third shot went wide when Agatha grabbed hold of my rifle.

"Let me go!" she shrieked, and I knew she wasn't talking to me. I would've apologized if there'd been time, but instead, I pushed back and jabbed her in the chin with the middle of the barrel.

I didn't intend to hurt her, or did I?

That's when I realized the ringing in my ears had stopped, and my aim was swaying toward her like I was about to tear her open. The injured Nephilim was regaining control. I screamed at the top of my lungs before it could, and the echoing of my voice drowned out its music. Swinging my rifle back, I put another bullet straight through the bastard's chest.

A werewolf . . . that would have put it down, but even as the silver sizzled through the beast's fur and flesh, and swirling light filtered out, it only seemed to get madder.

It charged, scooped up Lyle's body, and flung him. I tackled Agatha out of the way as his body soared over us before shattering against rock and landing in a heap.

She threw herself onto him and pawed at his chest. But I'd heard the crunch of bones. He was dead. Put out of his misery, I reckon, before having to live in this harsh world with such injuries—though Agatha wouldn't see it that way.

The only good part about it was that her wailing further reduced the beast's song to background noise. I sprinted toward the cave's exit, firing my rifle one-handed behind me, putting round after round into the Neph until it clicked empty. A thing that size, I made sure to spread the damage around, chest, arms, and legs. Anything to slow it down.

The onslaught made it attack versus trying to entrance me any further. I dipped under the swipe of a claw, tossed my rifle, and went to draw my silver-coated hunting knife from its slot in my boot.

The monster was fast. Damn fast. One of its hooves kicked back and caught me in the chest, sending me flying out of the cave. When I landed, I slid, rolling over the edge of the ravine. I managed to catch myself on a protruding root. The force of it probably jerked my shoulder out of its socket, not that I'd felt it.

Made it difficult to pull myself up, though.

Patting the back of my belt with my free hand, I unhooked my lasso just as the beast grabbed my right arm. Its strength was obscene, raising me before its monstrous face as if I were a plaything. This was the view so many poor mortals had likely called their last before it had devoured them soul and all.

Its eye wasn't just yellow up this close. It was roiling like a portal to the planes of Hell itself. Felt I could give a wave and old Lucifer would wink back. I braced for its attack. Only, the beast didn't unhinge its jaw.

No, instead, it lifted its instrument with the other hand.

"*You're mine!*" Its black, leatherlike lips didn't move, yet the words rattled around in my brain, projected within my own thoughts.

At the same time, the train whistled again, louder this time. The bridge over the crossing juddered violently.

I looked straight into that big yellow eye and said, "Sorry, friend. I'm already taken."

Then I whipped my lasso out and snagged it around its massive, intact horn. The ordinary-looking strand of onyx-black rope was blessed by the angels themselves. Given to me after I was revived—one of the perks of being a Black Badge, I reckon.

The moment it ensnares a being not meant for this realm, the weight of Heaven's judgment falls upon its victim like a hammer, should they deserve it. Wish it worked on normal men, but as Shar always says, it's never too late for the "Children to repent of their sins."

Good for them.

As expected, a shaft of searing bright light descended like a pillar of fire from the clouds. The Nephilim froze, giving it a taste of losing its functions like it'd inflicted on so many others.

Its mental grip on me loosened. I leaped onto a strut supporting the bridge. Though it shook from the rumbling of the train above, I held fast, climbed upward, pulling myself onto the tracks with the grip of my lasso still in hand. To my right, the train barreled toward me. The conductor was surely aware of me now, ringing that whistle as loud as could be. The beast roared even louder.

Now, I'm not exactly sure what would happen to me if I was pulverized by a steam engine at full speed; if my body would reform or be left a pulp of blood and mashed bones. Would I be forced to live on as sludge stuck to wheels and gears?

I had no plans to find out.

I waited until the last possible second and jumped off the other side of the bridge. The Neph was tall, so I didn't need it to go far, but the momentum of my jump hoisted it up across the bridge. I dropped to the rocky landing hard enough to tear the soles of my boots. My rope came spiraling down, followed by the thud of the monster's head at the end of it, tongue hanging out of a slack jaw.

I could hear nothing over the racket of the train zipping overhead, but I turned and saw the beast's body sliding off onto the other side of the landing, innards cascading out of it like chunky rabbit stew. I thought about all the people that might be represented by that goo and nearly spewed.

It didn't last long. Its body began to disintegrate into blackish dust, fading away to bits. Banished to Hell, whatever was left of it. Motes of light danced around my lasso, and the Nephilim's head followed until it vanished in a wisp of darkness and light.

"Back where you belong," I muttered, knowing full well that now I was talking tough at a thing no longer even in front of me. But I only mustered the will to speak just then, when all that was left of it was imprints in the ground. That, and its bone harmonica.

After I finished recoiling my lasso, I knelt to retrieve the instrument. It seemed like nothing special. I brought it to my lips and gave playing a note a try, and crushing bleakness overwhelmed me like a wave. It was like I could sense all the dead parts of me.

I jerked back, then exhaled slowly before I found resolve. The thing was clearly still tainted by the dark magic of a Nephilim. So, I stuffed it in my belt satchel for safekeeping. Better with me than in the wrong hands, plus, supernaturally enchanted items are rare in this world. I couldn't stomach getting rid of it just yet.

The sense of dread eroded fast after it was away. Out of sight, out of mind, I reckon.

A part of me wanted to play it again. Unpleasant as it was, at least it was something new to feel. But hearing Agatha's cries as the train distanced snapped me out of feeling sorry for myself. Nothing ever gets you used to the sound of pure, gut-wrenching grief. Even if I'm around for another two hundred years, which I suppose I might be, it'll still cut to my core.

"Yeah, yeah, I know, Shar," I said, knowing my guardian angel was shaking her head in disappointment. "But I can't just leave her there."

I snapped my shoulder back into its socket on a crossbeam, rolled out my neck, then strode back toward the cave.

Shar could hold her horses. Besides, I needed my guns.

FIVE

Look, I didn't want to drag Agatha all the way to her ranch. Could barely get a word out of her after everything that went down. Monsters, mind control, and first loves lost—she was distraught. But from what she said, it was basically on the way to Elkhart.

Last time she'd ever go off in the wilderness.

She'd learned a valuable lesson. Least, she'd better have. Normal folk should stick to trails and roads. Worst thing is you run into a couple of bandits looking for a score. Mortal trials. Most times, your pride ends up more bruised than your physical body. And on the rare occasion, when you don't just pony up and pay the piper, you may get shot and die.

Judging by the look in poor Agatha's eyes, that would've been better than what that goat beast did to her and young Lyle, whose body, bloated and missing parts, was now somewhere down the Pope River. Can't help but feel bad for whatever sod might find him if the wolves don't devour him fully first.

Point is, stick to the damn trails. There are plenty of things as bad— and worse—as that beast lurking. The West is wild for many reasons beyond the lack of law reaching out here. Humanity. We gather in our towns and cities, and that tends to drive off things preferring to not be surrounded. Drive them to places like this.

The sun was on the rise, painting an expanse of otherwise swarthy vegetation in a deep crimson. Life was becoming even more scarce out here. Soon, it'd only be hard dirt with tawny bushes and cacti poking up.

Just as Agatha had described, in what few words she could manage, a small ranch sat in a clearing to our left.

Shar's frustration rose through me like the tide as I brought Timperina close, and her words echoed in my mind while my badge itched unremittingly on my chest.

She could wait. Far as I can tell, she's got an eternity.

"Time to wake up," I said, then heaved my shoulder where Agatha had been sleeping. She shuddered awake, both arms squeezing tight around my chest. "This your place?"

She muttered what sounded like an affirmation to me.

"Good." I stopped Timp by a fence penning some cattle. Then, I hopped down and extended a hand up to her.

Agatha flinched out of reflex. It'd be a long time before that natural response would leave her.

"Well, you can't sit up there forever," I said. "Timp's old legs'll get too tired to handle two of us."

Timperina snorted and stomped a back hoof at the mention of her name.

That sound also made Agatha recoil. She'd heard enough cloven horrors to last a lifetime and more. I waited patiently until she blinked against the blooming sunlight and seemed to actually register that she was home. There didn't seem to be much joy, though. Considering she'd left with a lover and returned alone, I understood.

I further extended my hand, and this time, she took it. Helping her down, I held on until her wobbly legs found strength enough to allow her to stand on her own.

"Now, remember, if anyone asks what happened to Lyle, blame the wolves," I said.

"He doesn't deserve—"

I placed a finger over her lips. Shook my head. Tears welled in her eyes as she stared up at me. They were pretty eyes, despite the sorrow marking them. A light gray flecked with something like lilac. She'd make a fine wife to someone someday—just not Lyle.

"You say what you really saw, you'll be fit for a straitjacket in no time," I said. "That boy wouldn't want that for you. He'd want you to move on. To live."

Those words chewed at me as I spoke them, but I meant them all the same. Agatha still had everything in front of her. More than I had.

"Now, go on." I gave her a gentle nudge down the trail. Anyone inside the ranch would be able to see her from there. She'd be safe, even without me accompanying her the remainder of the distance.

Staggering a few steps, she turned back. "Who are you?"

"Just a passerby." I tipped the brim of my Stetson, and just as I grabbed a clump of Timp's mane to pull myself up, the door of the ranch flew open. An older man ran out wielding a rifle.

"Dammit, Agatha. Did you go runnin' off with that boy again!" Judging by his tone, I could only guess he was the disapproving father. Always was one. And then came Ma, chasing after him, shouting for him to calm down.

Timperina bolted before I was all the way saddled, and we sped off in the opposite direction, screams echoing at my back. I guess there was one person who'd be pleased with who the goat beast had claimed as a victim.

Oh, well. Least he cares enough to care. My dear old pa? Most he usually had to say involved the back of his hand across my cheek. May he rest far from peace.

* * *

I don't know why I find myself drawn to helping folks like Agatha. Was I lying to myself, thinking it was about atoning for the many sins of my former life? Maybe I just want to feel something, anything, besides the constant numbness I've felt for so long. Maybe it's rebellion. Probably a bit of both, truth be told.

I didn't make it far from the ranch before the need to answer Shar could no longer be ignored. I clutched at the marks on my chest, desperate to relieve the infernal itch. But I pushed a few miles farther on the road to Elkhart anyway, just to spite her. Until the urge to rip my own head off became too much.

"Shar, my dear," I said as I flicked open the mirror. Her faceless entity swirled to life, and all the grand vista of reddish cliffs around me seemed to grow strangely dim in light of her.

"Did you get it out of your system, Crowley?"

"That's a mighty odd way to say *thank you.*"

"Thank you? Thank you?!" A crack snaked down the center of the glass.

"You and I both know that abomination had no place in this realm," I said. "I got rid of it. Ain't that why I'm here—why our beloved benefactor saw the need to spring me to life after death?"

"You are here to do as commanded! Unless Hell would be preferential to you."

"Always threatening with that. Might be time for some new material, old girl. Getting stale."

"It is no threat," she said, her voice level and, well, threatening.

She sure knew how to tug on my leash when I pulled too hard. Was it so simple? One word and I'd go plummeting through the dirt and the rock down into the icy depths? As if angels and demons could make arrangements so easily. Could they? And if they communicated openly, why all the damn games I get caught up in?

"What's done is done," I said. "A Nephilim is banished, a girl's life is saved, and a boy's soul is left over for Heaven. Plus, I'll sleep easier."

"And that is what is most important to you, is it not? All the Children, thinking only of themselves."

"Sounds a bit like jealousy," I said. "I think that's one of your sins, ain't it?"

"Always so brash. So eager to play hero."

"I ain't playing games," I said. "Those kids needed help and I don't know why they're somehow less important to the White Throne than some string of robberies."

"The ruminations of Heaven are far above those of men."

"I don't know what that's supposed to mean, but I did what I did and that girl's alive for it."

"Life is not all about this plane, Crowley. When will you learn?" Shar cackled, and her form began to swirl away.

"Learn what?" I said to fading mist.

Her essence mended the crack in the glass before she was gone, leaving me staring at my own ugly mug. I was covered in blood. Guess that's what happens when you decapitate a monster.

SIX

Crunch!

I must've dozed a bit asleep in the saddle. The sound startled me awake and I checked my mirror, wondering if that was where the strange sound came from. Timp's whinny, however, drew my attention to the road. As we came around the bend of a rocky outcrop, a large strip of the trail was frozen like a shallow creek in January. Except it was July, and this was no creek.

It was slick and melting from the hot sun, but still, the ice was at least an inch thick. Dead of summer, there was only one way ice was forming out here, and I reckoned it had to do with my Lonely Hill bank robbers.

Shar's final words to me caromed around in my skull. Asking when I would learn. Was she about to teach me one of her lessons?

Timp whinnied again and reared back when one of her front hooves slipped.

"Calm down, girl," I whispered in her ear. "Take it slow." Her hoof slid out again. "Slower."

She got the balancing down after a few more steps, and I made sure not to shift my weight. Timp probably would've loved to go around, but the stubborn old girl needed pushing these days.

I studied the ice as we went. Tracks left grooves through it, swerving this way and that. They looked like they belonged to wagon wheels, but there was no crash in sight.

Leaning forward, I kept my ears peeled. The silhouettes of carrion birds circled overhead in the ruddy sky, but plenty of critters died in these parts, ready to be picked clean by vultures. And the wind didn't carry any fresh stink of rotting flesh. Humans smell worse than anything after we die.

The tracks took a sharp turn near the ledge. It was strange enough to cause me concern, like whoever it was had careened over the edge. I swept my legs off Timp and landed in one smooth motion, my boots sending splinters across the ice.

A few strides later, I was looking down onto a promontory at three men, naked as the day they were birthed. They sat upright, tied up back-to-back-to-back. And not civilian types like Agatha and Lyle. These were hardened men—skin creased and leathery, and not because they'd been left out in the sun for God knows how long. One, a dark-skinned man, sported a clean-shaven face, the others finely groomed mustaches. These were men who knew how to take care of themselves.

I skidded down the rut, coming to rest on the outcropping.

The sight below was unnerving—a web of ice spread across each of the men's mouths like unholy bandit masks, chapped the skin all around it. Any longer and frostbite would settle in, and that wouldn't be a pretty sight.

Beside them, the cart responsible for the wheel marks rested shattered and broken. The three men were kicking dirt, clearly desperate to stay as far away from that precarious ledge as possible.

"Quit moving, or you're gonna bring the whole shelf crashing down!" I shouted.

Somehow, that made them move more, toppling over one another, their bodies wrestling for the topmost position.

I fired a round from one of my pistols into the air to quiet them. It worked, at least for the moment. Stomping over, I grabbed the dark-skinned one and held the hot barrel against the ice covering his mouth. His eyes went wide as it slowly melted down through the middle before cracking off his face.

"Mary, the fucking mother!" The words came out like his mouth wouldn't work right. He winced and strained his arms, trying to touch his jaw where the skin around his mouth was left purple, lips drained entirely of color.

"What happened here?" I asked for what seemed like the hundredth time over the last few days. First the frosty bank, Agatha and the Nephilim, and now this? Things were always pretty hairy, but not like this. Hell was working overtime, it seemed.

"Y'ain't gonna cut us loose?" His tongue clung to the roof of his mouth with every word, still unnaturally frigid.

"I ain't in a hurry," I said. "Not 'til I know you didn't deserve . . . whatever this is."

"Fuck you," he said.

"Got a mouth on you, don't you? Maybe I should have kept it shut."

The other two yanked and made him roll to the side. I gripped him by his frostbitten cheeks and held him upright. "Who did this?"

"Some freaks."

"That don't narrow it down much." I looked to the other two and shoved the man away. "Either of you wanna talk, because your friend here is pissing me off."

Both of them nodded vigorously.

As I moved to help the others, the first seemed to grow a tongue. "We were transporting cash overnight for our employer. Next thing I know, the carriage is sliding all over the place. Toppled off, right over. Luck provided this ledge, or we'd be dead as dirt."

"Right," I said, drawing out the word. "And the bindings?"

"They were on us before we could even get a shot off."

"You Pinks?" I asked.

"You a marshal?" he retorted.

I sniffed, knowing the answer to my question just from reading his expression.

Pinkertons. They all had the same look. Hired guns only rich folk could afford. Tough as nails, and out here, they usually skirted the letter of the laws they swore to uphold.

"Sounds like the bank wasted money," I said.

"Why don't you untie me and say that, boy?"

"Boy." I scoffed. Sure, his hair was graying, but I probably had a decade or more spent on this Earth on him. Truth was, I didn't care for his tone, neither. I'm sure he was frazzled, his crew getting run up on like that, but this wasn't the best way to treat a savior.

I sighed. Graciousness was a dying virtue.

"What'd they take?" I asked.

"You fucking blind? They took it all! Everything! Can't you see that? The money, guns. They took our goddamned clothes. Our clothes! Who fucking does that? Barely got a look at them before they yanked us out of the wreckage, said they'd 'taken enough,' and knocked us out cold. Next thing, we're lying here with our mouths frozen shut. In July. It don't make any fucking sense."

"Why not kill you?" I scratched my chin, asking myself more than I was anyone else. If this was the work of the crew from Lonely Hill— which I had to assume it was—they didn't seem to be doing much killing back there either. Not the normal modus operandi.

He blinked. "That's your question?"

"It's *a* question."

"Goddammit, untie me!"

The others grunted at the demand as well, as if finally realizing I hadn't even bothered to get that ice off their faces yet.

"Fine," I said. "C'mon." I knelt, and he dragged the others toward me, their bare thighs chafing along the dirt. I pulled my knife, pushed his head toward the ground, and set the blade against the rope behind his back.

"What'd they do with the cash?" I asked.

"The fuck you think they did with it?" the Pink asked.

I'd just started cutting when I pulled away and looked him dead in the eyes, pointing the tip of my blade in his face.

"Listen up, Buttercup. I could toss the lot of you into that gorge, and folks would think it was nothing more than a few Pinks getting drunk and driving too soon. You want that?"

The other two protested emphatically but he kept his face stern.

"Now, you'd best answer me with some respect on this one," I said as I started cutting again. "You see which way they were headed?"

Despite his attempt at holding onto whatever dignity he could, the gentleman started acting like one now.

"When I came to, I saw a trail of dust across the gorge, leading toward Elkhart," he said. "Same way we were heading to make a deposit at the bank there."

I paused. Whether by chance or purpose, the outlaws stumbled upon these men on their way. That meant Dufaux's Elkhart branch was their next target for certain.

"Mr. Dufaux ain't gonna be pleased," I said, testing the waters.

At the mention of the man's name, something like fear flashed in the Pinkerton's eyes. But then, he set his jaw firm and said, "No shit."

About what I could expect.

Elkhart was a far bigger town than Lonely Hill, and there was bound to be enough guns to slow the robbers this time. But in a town that size, they could blend in, get right to the vault without a shot fired. Even if word of the last robbery had reached Elkhart's ears already, they wouldn't know what hit them.

"Next time, earn your pay." I sliced the rope and left the dark-skinned Pinkerton there to help his brothers-in-arms.

Was I jealous? Perhaps. Back in my day, I wish there'd been a lawful way to make a living using my particular set of skills. Let alone with federal backing. The West was changing, that was for damn sure.

But wallowing wouldn't stop the fiends I was after.

Without another word, I climbed back up, crunched across the ice, and mounted Timperina. Gave her a startle, I moved so fast. And I swear, I could see Shar in the glassy ice watching me with a look that said, "*I told you so.*" That if I hadn't stopped for Agatha, I could've beaten the outlaws here and put a stop to things already.

Nope. It didn't matter. What was done was done. My pursuit would end in Elkhart, where I'd take down the ice-wielding outlaw and banish whichever demon had sway over him right back to Hell.

SEVEN

Timid Timperina didn't get a chance to hesitate on the ice anymore. I drove her off-trail and got her galloping across the dry wilderness. The outlaws had at least a quarter-hour's head start, probably more. But I moved fast and Timp could still run with the best of them for a short while.

After about an hour or so, structures formed within the haze about a mile off. Gunshots *cracked*. Cows moaned in what passed for fear from such simple creatures, and a flock of birds took to the sky from a nearby tree.

I grasped the Winchester off my back, spinning it into the proper grip while checking to make sure she was loaded.

Elkhart was organized along three tiers, dotted with shops and homes made from ruddy clay. The bank stood proud at the center of the ground level, the only building as tall as the church, which was high above it all, steeple reaching for Heaven.

Figures.

The whole place had gone off like a powder keg. A tidal wave of people ran toward me and in all other directions. Women and children mostly, screaming in terror, but some men were with them. The others took cover behind porches and storefronts, armed and ready to defend their homes.

One of whom I assumed to be the outlaws was on the roof of the bank with a marksman rifle, which answered for sure the question of whether there were two or three of them. The thing was so loud it made every other shot seem like a whisper. Just as Sheriff Dale had thought, it wasn't looking like he was shooting to kill. Just sending people running for the hills and doing a damn good job of it.

Another odd thing. Where all other birds had scattered from the chaos, a hawk circled above him, screeched.

An open stagecoach was parked outside the bank, a wall of ice arcing in front of it, so I couldn't see much. Bullets chipped away at it while the vague, ice-blurred shapes of the other outlaws moved on the other side.

Dirt plumed upward a few feet from me and Timp.

The marksman was aiming at me.

I swore and fired at the roof to send him into cover. Then I jumped down and gave Timp a slap to send her off to safety. The marksman didn't relent, firing back, dust exploding by my feet and sending fragments into my eyes. My guess was, now that I was posing a threat, he would be shooting to kill.

A deputy heard me coming and swung around. By the look of me, I'm sure he figured I must've been with them.

"I'm on your side!" I shouted, firing again to keep the marksman at bay before sliding to safety behind the crates the deputy hid behind. "What the hell's going on?"

He stammered, trying to respond but ran short on breath. I saw then that he was injured in more than one place. "They showed up, and next thing we knew, they're robbing us from behind some sort of wall . . ."

I laid my hand on his shoulder to get his attention, doing my best to avoid his many wounds. But it was nearly impossible. He winced when I touched him, but it was better he not get distracted trying to wrap his mind around how a wall of ice got formed.

"Get your men to focus on the marksman," I shouted over the gunfire. "Keep him down."

"On it—"

My head snapped upright as his words got cut off . . .

* * *

I found myself looking through the deputy's eyes back at my own ragged face, speaking those same words I just had.

"On it," I said, though it was the deputy's voice.

Then, the crate to my left splintered, and a bullet sliced through my skull. It all happened so fast. Even the pain. A sharp burst like lightning, then nothing . . .

* * *

The next thing I knew, I was kneeling next to him, gasping, back in my own body and imagining what had to be the worst headache possible. I knew the pain was all in my mind, but that didn't matter. Looking down at my hand, it appeared one of the marksman's bullets had pierced right through it—and consequentially, the glove I wore there. Amongst other things—like reloading silver bullets—my gloves kept me from accidentally Divining folks.

I blinked hard to drive away the experience of the accidental Divining. The deputy's head hung to the side, body slumped next to me, skull blown open, brain matter spilling into a trough meant for horses.

"You bastards!" Another deputy shouted and ran out of the general store, firing two pistols up at the roof. The marksman didn't return fire this time. Didn't even show face. Then, out of nowhere, that hawk I'd seen above zipped across my view and slashed the deputy's throat with razor-sharp talons.

That was a new trick.

In case it isn't clear, hawks don't typically join in gunfights and hunt down the law of their own accord. It seemed the ice-wielder wasn't the only of these outlaws with abilities some wouldn't consider natural.

Some. As if anyone thought any of this was normal.

I stowed my rifle, then charged out with my pistols drawn, taking the same cue. Only, I didn't fire upward. I fired straight into the ice wall. I vaguely recognized the impact of enemy bullets riddling my chest, but only because it slowed me a fraction.

Sprinting full-bore, I threw my whole body into the ice with reckless abandon. My shoulder shattered through its center, sending shards in a wide arc.

On the other side, I rose from the dirt, staring into the eyes of the brutish ice-wielder. I'd only seen him in Sheriff Daniels's Divining back in Lonely Hill, but up close, I realized it wasn't white wolf skins he wore over his shoulders and head. His own hair was pale as snow, long and wild. Beard too.

What skin I could see over his mask was leathery, and his eyes, dark gray, on their way to black soon. He bared his teeth, mostly human but with two sharper fangs beginning to form.

This was no mere man. No Nephilim either. This entity, I recognized.

Over the years, rumors and myths had become rampant about a mysterious creature known as a Yeti. Folks say they're half man, half gorilla or something similar. Sightings of them by hunters or fishermen in the mountains became ghost stories told around campfires.

The truth is both less exciting and far more terrifying.

A Yeti is nothing more than a desperate fool willing to bargain a piece of his or her mind in exchange for a slice of Hell's power. A half possession of sorts, allowing the person to become a plaything for a demon. Over time, the demon loses interest, as they are wont to do, leaving the poor vessel to be consumed by madness. Becoming more and more monstrous, they often find themselves living in the woods, scavenging for food, growing their hair wild for lack of care.

Hence all the rumors.

This one was still in the early stages. Still mostly human-looking . . . Mostly.

The Yeti reached out and clenched his big hand around my throat, lifting me with the strength of ten men. He drew me in close.

"Dufaux's reckoning has come!" he screamed, guttural and raw, sending spittle all over me.

"I'd worry about yourself."

I shot him in the shoulder with my last round. The silver bullet sizzled and went right through. He cringed, barely. I hit him a few times with the butts of both empty handguns but the blows just bounced right off of him.

"Whatever demon you pledged to, they're using you," I said.

"Enough!"

He tossed me aside like a spent canteen. I crashed through a wood beam holding the roof of the general store's veranda up. Said roof crumbled down atop me.

After shoving aside all the shards, splinters, and boards, I found I was pinned to the ground by a sharp, broken plank skewered through my arm. I worked it back and forth in an attempt to free myself. While I did so, the Yeti's companion stalked toward me—the one I'd seen in the sheriff's memories, darting around Lonely Hill swift as a jackrabbit being chased by a cougar.

Her hair was black as night, long and silken. She wore a mask and cut a menacing figure, holding two feathered tomahawks, one in each hand.

Jumping at me, she shrieked and brought one tomahawk down. I barely managed to shift out of the way, but dammit, she shaved off a sliver of the brim of my hat.

"Hey, that wasn't cheap!" I shouted. Then I punched the post with my free arm. It budged a bit. I struck it again, and it broke off just above my flesh.

Now, any normal man would've passed out from the pain, but me? Didn't feel a thing. I rolled back, my arm slipping over the splintered edge, just as she swiped down a second time. An instant later, the other tomahawk swung at me again too.

Now free, I sprang to my feet, grabbing the post. Little bits of dried skin and flesh flaking off my arm as the wound was already beginning to close itself up. Probably gave her quite a shock, but she kept her composure enough to unleash a battle cry and charge at me with both tomahawks. They crisscrossed like a twister, and it took everything I had to avoid being chopped to bits.

I dodged two wild swings, then parried with the post. Our weapons locked, and I got a close-up view. The parts of her face that showed over her mask were covered in thick white paint, with red lines down her throat as if left by extended fingertips. The parts of her skin that showed through flaked paint bore a native coloring. And the hate there in those dark orbs? It was palpable.

"A little money worth the blood of all these men?" I growled as we struggled.

"Like your kind spared us, *Łiga Ndeeń*!?" she spat in a heavy accent.

That accusation cut harder than any axe. She kicked out and caught me in the gut. I doubled over and her tomahawk continued on its course, slashing me across the back. Blood should've come spraying out, and this time, the surprise when it didn't slowed her. I ducked and shouldered her, then rose with an uppercut swing that caught her below the jaw.

Ma always taught me never to strike a woman, but I doubt she'd fault me here and now.

Tomahawk-lady flew back against the open carriage filled with bags and bags of money. I moved to press my advantage when the Yeti came charging me. His shoulder connected with the force of a cannon. I slid across the dirt, coming to rest ten paces from the bank. I rose, ready to get back into the fight, but a stream of ice pinned my boot to the ground. I looked right and saw the Yeti, arm outstretched toward me. Where the woman had unbridled rage, his still seemed relatively controlled. Though in time, the more he drew on his unholy powers, the more command he'd lose.

He sneered at me, the gesture rife with contempt. Might as well've been a middle finger.

"Stay out of this if you value your life," the Yeti said to me.

If only he knew who he was talking to.

Then, to the others, he barked, "Time to move!"

He hefted the woman back onto the cart.

"Stop there!" shouted one of the lawmen. He rushed the wagon with courage or stupidity and grasped the Yeti by the sleeve. The Yeti turned, gripped the man's wrist, and ice formed over the whole of the lawman's arm.

The scream that tore from the deputy's throat could've woken Hell. Tomahawk-lady leaned out and brought down one of her blades and his arm exploded into a prism of shattered ice. He fell backward, grasping what remained of his arm, writhing in the wet dirt.

Without another word or action, the Yeti climbed to the bench up front and snapped the reins. There was too much money loaded on to be just from one bank, which meant they came here straight from Lonely Hill without stopping . . . unlike me. Shar was never going to let me hear the end of it.

I spotted a lockbox toward the back of the cart, bearing the name of one Mr. Dufaux—likely the one stolen from the Pinkertons.

I yanked at my frozen leg in a failed attempt to break free.

Stuck for the second time.

The horses whinnied and got startled, loose bills fluttering in their wake.

As they moved, the skinny marksman hopped from roof to roof and finally leaped off in a damn impressive feat to land beside the woman in the cart. As he crossed the air, his shirt flapped up. Something was there. A raised scar of sorts from being branded . . . except it was, well, glowing bright blue in the creases. I was far, but gun to head, I'd say it depicted some sort of giant bird I'd never seen before, with what looked like scales instead of feathers and streaks of lightning under the wings.

After he landed, what must've been the same hawk that I'd watched tear open one of Elkhart's finest promptly settled on his shoulder. The native woman leaned over, pulled down her mask, and planted a kiss on the marksman's forehead.

The other townsfolk opened fire, their rounds spattering harmlessly against the sides of the cart.

I holstered my pistols and unsheathed my rifle. Then, yelling, I slammed the butt of it against the ice pinning me to the ground. The supernatural ice held up even with my fierce strength, but that's the thing about my condition. I may not be stronger than a normal man in a physical sense, like a Yeti, but without fear of injury or exhaustion of muscle, I can throw my body and weight around in ways no man would ever dream.

Eventually, the ice shattered, and I was free.

I whistled for Timperina as I sprinted, blowing past the newly limb-less lawman.

Didn't need to see Timp coming. I listened for her hooves and then reached back, yanking myself up to her saddle on the move. I hastened to reload my rifle as we bounced down the path, buildings racing by. As I fed the last round in, a bullet zipped past my ear. I sent one back.

The outlaws rumbled up the hill out of town. Another shot from the marksman caught me in the ribs, passing clear through. I'm sure he expected me to fall, but I didn't budge in the slightest.

"Steady, Timp."

I aimed down my sights, and my next round hit the marksman right across the meat of his biceps. A half a foot to the left, he'd have been dead, but it blew him back onto his ass and forced tomahawk-lady to catch him. He accidentally kicked the money-filled lockbox, and it fell to the dirt. The hawk flew up, and as the woman laid the sharpshooter back, I noticed his eyes roll back into his head.

At first, I thought he was dead, but then I had another thought.

The hawk redirected course and zoomed straight at me. I tried to shoot it, but the bird swooped around, dodging my aim. The marksman was controlling it, similar to how that Nephilim took over Agatha and Lyle, except no music needed to be played. Purely mental.

I swore.

It went for Timperina's eyes. Too close for my rifle, especially whip-ping so close to Timp's head.

My poor horse started rearing in the traces, squealing and banking left. I damn near got tossed from her back, but I grabbed my knife with one hand and slashed, forcing the hawk to veer away.

"Yaw!" I kicked, spurring Timp along as fast as she could go. She wouldn't keep this pace long, but I closed the gap with the heavier coach and left the hawk playing catch-up to me now.

Sheathing the knife and gripping my rifle tight, I exhaled slowly. The Yeti's head fell between the sights. Just as I pulled the trigger, his wagon hit a dip, and the bullet just missed its mark. Lucky bastard. He must've seen it, because he reached back and tossed a bag of money up into the air. Only, no money flew out of this one because the thing was frozen solid upon his touch.

I steered away from the path of the projectile.

The marksman's eyes rolled back into place, and he sat up. I chanced a glance backward to spot the hawk lifting to the clouds again. My head then spun around to see the kid raising his weapon, tomahawk-lady holding his arm to help him.

I'd entirely missed the point of the frozen money bag. It wasn't meant to hit me. The marksman fired, and the thing went off like dynamite. Thousands of tiny silvery fragments exploded in every direction. I didn't think twice.

Turning Timp away just in time, I threw my body down across the length of her to act as a shield. Supernatural ice stabbed into me all over, and I couldn't feel it, but I knew something went right into my head since the impact caused whiplash out of my control.

Then, I went straight to black.

EIGHT

I don't dream. Haven't since the day I died. That's why I knew this wasn't a dream but a vision. Visions are different. They're real—a glimpse into what is or what could be. Mostly what was, like in this case, as I fell back into the past . . .

My breath swirled before me while Big Davey and I toiled with the hearth. We'd found an abandoned house in the hills north of where we'd pulled our last job, robbing a railroad magnate of some very valuable bonds.

Spirits were high. Inhibitions were low . . . a potent mixture for trouble.

All around us, the Scuttlers were celebrating a job well done. Drinking, carousing, playing games of chance, cheating at games of chance. All the things we outlaws were so damn good at.

"Fucking hell, Crowley, you need a real man over there to get that fire going?"

That was Morris "Mad Dog" Morrison, bitching about me even while he dressed a nasty-looking wound. Always figured his daddy must've hated him, giving him such piss for a name. Truth was, all the firewood was soaked to the core from sitting out in snow and sleet. I'd been at it for the better part of an hour already.

Big Davey stood at my side as he always had. For the most, we were inseparable.

I was raised in a good Catholic home back in Granger's Outlook before I went and got mixed up with the Scuttlers and left Ma and Pa for a life of thieving and outlawing. When I was real young, my weekends were spent serving Father Osgood, caring for the Lord's house, and whatnot. I shudder to think how many hours were spent scrubbing them pews.

Davey ended up there, too, only his parents died outright, and he needed taking care of. On the surface, it was Father Osgood done the caring for. But really, I like to think Davey and I kept each other afloat.

Where I was tall, dark, and handsome, Davey was light-haired and complected, freckles dotting his whole body like a disease, and well . . . I guess he was tall too. Not saying much in the way of whether or not he was handsome, but the ladies didn't mind sharing company with him.

"Hold your horses," I growled back at Mad Dog, who waved me off dismissively.

"Bet he makes love like he makes fires," Big Davey whispered to me. "One quick spark, and it's done."

I laughed as I struck the flint a final time, and the flames roared to life.

I turned and bowed low. "You're welcome, you ungrateful pricks."

"'Bout time," Morrison said.

Instantly, I felt winter's cold bite give way, and my hands thawed.

"That feels good," Davey said. We took a seat by the fire, cross-legged on a bearskin rug, and got to work polishing our guns like we always did.

"You getting tired of this?" I asked him when I was sure no one was listening.

"Tired of what?"

"This . . . all of it. Them. The job. When's the last time you got to spend any of our hard-earned greenbacks?"

"I'll spend 'em when I'm dead, I reckon," Davey said.

"Ain't that the truth? Scary thing is, that might be sooner rather than later the way Ace's been acting. Getting a bit too big for his britches, you ask me."

"I don't know," Davey said. "His britches are getting pretty big, too."

My snicker didn't last long before my stare turned distant. "That lady on the train, she didn't have to die."

"I didn't see much," Davey admitted, "but how was Ace to know her husband was connected?"

"What does that matter? We were already free and clear. Now we'll have vengeful folk after us, and he wants us to cross the border south and run? 'Conquer new lands,' he says? For what? So he can shoot whoever he pleases for a few extra bucks?"

A gruff voice called out, "What's the haul?"

Hiram Church was of medium height and build. Nothing special about him except he was missing a leg, replaced by a wooden peg. Heard it got bit off by a mountain lion, but people tell stories. Hiram got called the first mate because he looked like a damn pirate, and he was Ace Ryker's right hand. We also had the private joke that he was called his right hand because he would jerk Ace off like one. Though none of us would dare say it to their faces.

Truth was that Hiram was just a good old-fashioned suck-up. Bumsucker. Yes man. Whatever term you got for it, he was the definition.

But the two of them were the only constants in the Scuttlers. Ace could be such a hot-head that few stuck around very long. Sometimes they left for greener pastures. Other times, Ace introduced them to a three-cent friend.

Another thing we said was that Ace Ryker killed more of his own men than he did anyone else. Wasn't true, mind, but we all talked too much for our own good.

"Not enough," Mae answered. She was the only lady among us, and that word had to be taken lightly. I think in a fair fight back then, she'd have squashed me like a bug. Mae was bigger than an overfed gorilla and twice as mean as a starved one. She stood six-foot-two, and I wouldn't guess at a lady's weight, but she beat me. Took a special kind of woman to join up with a crew like us.

I don't know what brings most of us to do it. Wasn't my first choice, outlawing—I'd always wanted to be a doctor, believe it or not. I know, big gap from one to the other, but I'd always preferred saving lives to ruining them.

So why the Scuttlers? Ain't much else to do for a runaway son of a coal miner. Had no education past Madam Forester at the Granger's Outlook schoolhouse and hours spent at the church with Father Osgood. Though most of that was cleaning and running errands. No such thing as the Pinks back then, either.

But there I was. Sometimes, a man's gotta do what he's gotta to keep the taxman at bay . . .

Like any of us pay taxes. Or have skills suited for anything else.

"Never is enough," Hiram said to Mae. Then, he turned to all of us, his peg leg clacking on the wooden floor. "Live it up, fellas! Tomorrow, it's greener pastures!"

A stone settled into my belly at the mention of tomorrow. Ace had been talking about conquering new lands so long, most of us thought he was just flapping his gums. The Scuttlers had always been a small-time gang, but now, Ace decided it was time to go international.

No mention that the bounty on his head and his crew's after who he killed was enough to fund a whole town, so there was a reason to run. He just made it seem like an opportunity for everyone now that the Scuttlers legend couldn't grow much bigger.

Everything was a job to Ace. Always and forever.

Problem was, I didn't want to run. I'm sure I wasn't alone in that, but even if I was, we shouldn't have had to. Ace made a stupid mistake and we were all being punished for it under the guise of "new opportunity."

"Crowley!" Norman "Mac" Macmillan shouted, dragging me from unpleasant thoughts. He kicked under the table and slid out an empty chair across from him. "Grab a bowl and sit your ass in for a hand. I could use a win."

Mac elbowed the others beside him, Emmett Banks and Colby Harkins. They all shared a little ha-ha at my expense. It was fine. Giving each other a hard time was just what we did.

Davey and I shared our own quick glance.

"You can bring your lady friend, too, if you like," Mac said, talking about Davey. But I was already rising.

I rolled my eyes and gestured to Cook with two fingers. He ladled stew into a couple of tin bowls and offered them our way.

"Rabbit?" Big Davey asked.

"Was when I started," Cook replied.

I chuckled.

The bowl was hot, but it kind of felt good after being out in the cold for so long. We did like Mac requested and took a seat with him and the others and let them deal me in. Davey was never much for poker, so he just stood behind me, spooning what turned out to be mostly broth and some old carrots into his gullet.

"Ready for the long haul?" Mac asked, tossing cards around the table.

He was a rangy man, slender as they come. Like a stiff breeze would knock him on his ass. Wasn't the kind you'd expect to find amongst this rough-and-tumble crew. Hell, Mae might've lost him between her cheeks if she'd sat wrong. Guess you don't have to be particularly meaty to blow shit up—that was old Mac's job. Explosives master extraordinaire.

"Not sure any of us is," I said casually, taking a bite.

Mac stopped dealing, but I only counted three cards on the table in front of me. I looked up from my bowl to see him eyeballing me.

"What'chu say?"

I took another bite and shrugged. "Nothing important. Just talking."

"You scared of greasers?" he asked, a yellow smile appearing beneath his overlarge nose.

I didn't answer. I wasn't exactly afraid of dying. However, if I'd have known what awaited me, I probably would've been.

"How 'bout you, little Dave?"

"Much rather be alive and poor than dead and rich," Davey answered, following it with a slurp of his stew.

"Pussy," Colby muttered.

"You know what they say," Davey said. "You are what you eat."

Just then, Mae approached the table, wearing a scowl that would scare a ghost. Everyone abruptly stopped laughing.

"Guess that makes the rest of you boys assholes, don't it?" she said.

"Goddamn, Mae's coming in hot!" Emmett said.

Mac shook his head, smirking, and got back to dealing. "Best not let Ace hear you talking like this," he said. "He's got grand plans for us with all that money. Build ourselves a nice little kingdom south of the border."

"Kingdom," I said with a sniff. "Say, where is our Royal Highness, anyway?"

It hadn't occurred to me, but I hadn't seen him since we returned. As if taking a cue, Ace Ryker, drunk as a skunk, came traipsing down the stairs. Ace had a full head of lustrous hair and a perfectly narrowing beard, with mustache hairs that curled at the end. By his ratty jacket and clothes, you'd not think he was worth a damn, but Ace was never one to care about fineries or how he looked. He let his gun do the talking for him, and a tongue that may as well have been silver.

"Lookie, lookie," he said, stumbling. "Guess the place wasn't as empty as we thought."

From the pass, the house had appeared abandoned—in a mild state of disrepair, the stables and paddocks out front, empty. The fields in the back looked to've been untilled for ages. There was a creepy shrine in one corner of the main room with red candles melted all the way down to hardened puddles. And a skull. Human. Probably of some ancestor. Far be it from me to judge someone's beliefs.

"Found 'em hiding upstairs."

In one arm, Ace clutched a child—might've been six years old, maybe less, maybe more. I don't know. I'd never known many children for good reason. His other hand was clenched around the wrist of what I could only assume to be the girl's mother.

A beauty for damn sure.

I could tell she wanted to shove him down the stairs but refrained for fear of injuring her daughter.

"How old's the girl?" Mad Dog asked, a sick grin on his face. I hoped that wound killed him.

"*Dios mio, por favor, No. Oh, Dios!*" The mother muttered pleas in both English and Spanish, but no one was listening except me, it seemed.

"Shut up, bitch," Ace said, slapping her across the face with the back of his hand. She slammed against the wall.

The little one cried, but it was more like a whimper. Poor girl was terrified.

Ace lifted the mom. "You are something," he whispered, running his mouth along her arm and sniffing. Couldn't help but notice a small tattoo on her forearm. Couldn't make it out, but it's always odd seeing ink on a lady.

Ace reached her neck, let his tongue graze a moment, then whistled. A few of the others joined him. "We're heading down to rule your people soon. I think, maybe, you'd like to keep us company?"

She spat into his face. He wiped it away slow, then tore her shirt from neck to hem. She cried and tried to cover herself, backed up against the wall with nowhere to go. Her eyes flitted between the ragged members of my crew, most standing and circling like hungry wolves.

The young girl just watched now, stunned into silence. Terror paralyzed her.

"Now, now, girly, don't worry," Ace said then, kneeling and grasping her by the sides of the face to stare into her eyes. A place you never wanted to be. Like the Devil, he had a way of convincing you to do just about anything if you dare got caught in his trance.

"We ain't here to hurt you," he went on. He ran his hand through her dark hair and brushed it over her ear. "We help our guests. And your mama is worth helping."

"And helping ourselves, too!" one of the men chortled. I couldn't tell which, I was so incensed watching what was unfolding before me.

"Take care of her." Ace pushed the young girl to Hiram, the most revolting of all of us. A guy that I knew had absolutely no limits, which was probably what endeared him to Ace.

"Let her go!" the mother shrieked. She threw herself at him, but Ace caught her by the wrist and forced her back against the wall, knocking the air out of her. He pinned her there, placing a kiss against her collarbone, then lower.

He hadn't always been that way, Ace. I mean, he was never exactly a good guy, but when I joined up, he was more about getting the cash than any of this power-trip, god-complex bullshit.

But you ever just had enough of something? It already wasn't sitting right with me that Ace wanted to uproot our lives over his own mistake and call it generosity. You don't shit in my water and tell me it's coffee.

But with this? He just kept pushing and pushing and pushing . . .

"Let them go, Ace," I said, standing. I didn't reach for my Peacemaker since I knew that would be starting a war, but the implication carried.

"Or what, Crowley?" Ace asked, snickering like I wasn't even a threat.

"Or nothing," I said. "Just didn't think breaking into this lady's house and passing her around like salt was what we were all about."

"And you know what we're about?"

"Guess not what I thought."

"I'm getting pretty tired of your complaining. You want out, there's the door, hero," Ace said, continuing to kiss the woman's neck. He had his hand over her mouth, so her protests were muffled. Hiram held her daughter, big arms wrapped around her shoulders.

Everyone laughed except me and Davey—even Mae.

"Sure, Ace," I said, taking a small step toward him. "Gimme the girls, and I'll be on my merry way."

"Somebody shut him up already?" Ace groaned.

Mac, ever the one to please, tossed the table up, sending cards and cash soaring. It hit me in the hip. Didn't hurt, but it surprised me. I staggered, barely, bumping into Big Davey.

"You can't stomach some just rewards," Ace said, pointing at the door without looking up from the woman. "Then go sleep with the horses."

"Fine, fine," I said, giving Davey a glance. "I'm going."

I walked to the door, and Davey took a hard step my way.

"You going with him, Davey?" Hiram asked. "I always knew you two were sweet on each other."

He made smooching noises right next to the little girl's cheek. She squeezed her eyelids tight and muttered to herself in Spanish. Davey gave me a look, then he stopped where he was, leaving me walking alone.

The whole room laughed at me, calling me all kinds of names.

I grabbed the doorknob with my left hand.

"You all gonna follow him to the ends of the Earth?" I asked. "Think what happened on that train is the last mistake he'll make?"

Davey watched me but said nothing.

"He makes us rich," Mad Dog said.

"She had it coming," Hiram added. "They always do."

"You really gonna try and turn my crew against me, boy?" Ace cackled loudly. "Old no-fun James Crowley? There ain't a soul on God's green Earth that would follow you. Stop embarrassing yourself."

I gritted my teeth. "You'll all get what you deserve then, I reckon."

I gave one last look at Davey.

"Now, where were we, beautiful?" Ace asked, dropping his voice an octave to sound all sultry. All I heard in response were whimpers.

"*Por favor*, let her go . . ." the woman sniveled. "Let my Rosa go and I'll give you anything you want."

I threw open the door and drew my twin Peacemakers.

Cold hit me like an ox plow but didn't stop me from firing a round at Ace. I missed, but Big Davey surprised me by drawing his guns on the Scuttlers, too. His bullet hit Hiram right in the heart, over the little girl's head, killing him good. He always was a dead shot.

We ran out front, forgetting to account for the mounting snow. Seeking quick cover, we ducked into a barely standing stable.

Ace and his boys were shooting at us, cutting lines in our meager defenses. Splinters broke off all around, slicing at our skin. We slid along to the other side, where there was an opening for us to shoot back. The spaces between slats were so big they could easily follow our movements.

I sucked in a deep breath when a plum shot caught me in the shoulder.

"Shit," I swore. "I didn't think you were with me."

"I wasn't sure either, but screw Ace," Davey said, popping up from cover and shooting back.

By the sound of it, he landed a couple.

I waited a second and joined him. Wasn't sure where everyone was, and I was concerned we'd put a bullet in Rosa and her mother, but we shot back nonetheless. One of my shots hit Mac square in the gut, and I couldn't help but smile. I reloaded once, using the iron from a pouch on my hip, but that was all I had, so I needed to make my remaining shots count.

Squatting, back to the wall, I turned to Davey and said, "Sorry, friend. Didn't mean to get you caught up in all this. Just got tired."

"Knew I shouldn't have skipped Sunday Mass for the last hundred weeks," Davey replied.

I'd have laughed if a bullet hadn't gone straight through him the exact same time.

He collapsed, dead before he hit the ground.

I rubbed my face, telling myself I was wiping sweat, but they were tears, no doubt. Salty and hot. It was then I knew I wasn't getting out of there alive.

"Let the girl go, and we can all air our lungs and go home still breathing!" I shouted.

Ace laughed, and soon, all his lackeys joined in.

"You ain't in any good place to bargain, traitor!" Ace called back. "There's ten of us, one of you, by my count."

Not sure how they knew they'd killed Davey, but I wasn't about to let them be sure.

"I ain't alone, friend. Put down the gun."

Two shotgun blasts put holes through the stable on either side of me. Then someone fired a rifle and it pounded straight through my spine.

I slid down, back dragging against the old, splintering wood.

Darkness encroached around my vision. It's not true, what they say about your life flashing before your eyes when you die. I saw nothing. No bright light. No happy memories from when I was a lad, like there were any.

All I saw was pain manifest, lightning coursing through my whole body. Then, I saw the blurry shape of Ace Ryker come into view before me, laughing like the piece of shit he was. His ice-blue eyes stared deep into my soul, and he leaned in close to me. His breath reeked of alcohol. It was the last thing I remember smelling.

My eyes drifted over his shoulder to a lone figure running through the snow. The woman in her tattered clothes holding her daughter, Rosa, fleeing into the haze. Just as I'd have hoped, they used the scuffle to escape.

Helping that poor woman and child get away was the greatest act of my pitiful life. May never've become a doctor, but I saved two lives that night. Nothing that made up how many deaths I'd been responsible for with the Scuttlers mind you, but I'll take one little victory.

Ace followed my gaze and turned back to me, sneering.

"You don't think we'll find her?" he said.

I felt his boot stomping down on my wrist, but I was past the point of feeling pain. I didn't see it happen since everything felt like a slow waltz, but cold fingers squeezed around my throat until what little breath I could find was no longer there either.

If he was close before, he might as well be an extension of me now. His cold hands squeezed harder. Hot breath on my neck.

Like I needed help dying. Only reason I was still hanging on and fighting back the darkness was to buy the woman more time to get her daughter farther. Every second counted, and I knew Ace was too lazy and drunk to want to give chase.

"She can have her head start, you damned fool." He shook his head. "Turning on your own for some greaser bitch?"

He shoved me against the wall. My throat was dry like it had already turned back into the dust it was made from. But I was a stubborn son of a bitch. I couldn't let him have the last words. There was more time to buy.

"Seemed the right thing," I croaked out.

Ace clicked his tongue and shook his head. He knelt, knee crushing down on Davey's head, and looked right into my face. He didn't grin like he often did when he got the better of a man. He regarded me like I was some pitiable soul. Like a disappointed father of sorts.

I hadn't noticed before then, but all my former compadres were now behind him, watching my death like it was a show at the playhouse, totally ignorant of their own, injured or dying at their backs.

A tragedy, no doubt.

"Ain't no heroes in the West, Crowley," he said.

Then he leveled his Le Mat revolver at my chest. One shot from that thing would put a hole through me the size of one of Mae's beefy fists.

"That's true," I gargled, "But sometimes, shit deserves to get buried in the sand."

Like I said, I wasn't about to give him the final word.

NINE

The sound of Ace's gunshot woke me from the memories. My hands sprang up out of reflex, though my arms hit something solid. The *thump* and showering of fine powder after the strike were a good indication that they were blocked by some sort of wall, located only inches above my face.

I opened my mouth to speak, to ask anyone who might be listening what the hell was going on, but coughed as dust filled my throat. It coated my tongue like a film of grainy paint that I had to scrape off with my teeth just to get out words.

There's darkness, like midnight with a cloud-covered moon, and then there's the darkness where no matter how hard you try, there's just nothing there to see. This was that second kind.

I blinked away more dust and tried to focus.

I said it before, Black Badges could see in the night as well as a mountain lion, but in this—the total absence of any light at all—I merely strained and strained some more. It was all in vain. Couldn't see a damn thing.

"Hey!" I managed to shout. My words stopped inches away, like they were being caught in a fishnet.

Might as well have been since even as I patted around and kicked my legs, being unable to feel anything and now see anything had me floating in a senseless prison. The only sounds were deadened *thuds* made by my movements and a slight ringing in my ears that wouldn't abate. And the smell? Barely anything. Stagnant air. Dirt. Earth.

Shit.

Looked like I'd finally made it. Looked like old Lucifer had finally caught up to me in the form of a Yeti and sent me packing to Hell. That's what this was, I figured. Though, where was all the ice? The cold? The frost and little demon imps driving ice picks through skulls, and worse?

"Nah," I groaned.

That son of a bitch couldn't take me so easy. This was something else. Just didn't know what yet.

I rolled a bit, and something slipped from my pants pocket. A slight, otherworldly shimmer from something provided the scant illumination I needed for my enhanced sight to kick in.

I quickly scooped up Shar's mirror. The two pieces were loose, barely able to clasp. I find that hinges, like men unhappy with their lots in life, tend to protest when called to duty. The glass itself had a crack down the middle that Shar had apparently decided not to mend this time. A reminder? Even in this oppressive darkness managed to shine bright as the Almighty himself because you-know-who was waiting in the fractured reflection—an angry wisp, a storm cloud on the cusp of bursting into a lightning show.

"I warned you, Crowley," Shar said. Where my voice had been muffled into near silence, hers blared like thunder. "You could have reached Elkhart first. You could have stopped them."

"And you could've told me," I hissed, then gagged on some more dust. "All-knowing my ass."

"This is how it must be, Child."

I nearly scoffed at the title, as if I were anything close anymore, but she continued.

"If you knew the beginning from the end, you would take short-cuts. All you needed to do was follow the path laid before you. Now, look at what your impetuousness has caused. Like an infant throwing a tantrum."

"Hey, it's you people who labeled us all Children."

"And continually, you prove us correct."

My fingers clenched, wanting to crunch what was left of the mirror for good, but it was my only source of light. Just like always, in such desperate need of her, like an addict.

"So, what's this—Hell?" I asked.

"Your own personal one, perhaps," she responded.

I swallowed hard. She wasn't wrong. I'd lived my whole life and unlife in the West, under the big open sky and the range. Where even on the darkest nights, the moon couldn't be missed. Wide-open space was my friend, and this . . . well . . . my eyes searched my surroundings and found the answer fast.

Slats of wood formed a box around me. Above and below. Side to side.

A goddamn coffin.

And there came a subconscious fear that I hadn't even known I had until that moment. Being confined in dark, tight spaces. What did them newfangled doctors call it? Claustrophobia? It's a fear I'm sure any rational man or woman might have, but worse for me. They'd suffocate and die and get that sweet release, but Old James Crowley? Naw, I didn't even need air to breathe.

So, what would happen after an hour? Two?

Hell, it could've been that long already.

How about a day?

I could wind up trapped down here, alone with my thoughts for all of eternity.

"I'm starting to think angels and demons ain't so different," I said as I bucked and kicked, a new kind of hopelessness setting in. But I couldn't shift Heaven or Earth in my form. I wasn't a Yeti. Didn't have that kind of strength.

Maybe I should beseech a demon for an upgrade.

"If you think this is Hell," Shar said, soft and sultry, "I do so pity you. You cannot even begin to comprehend the anguish."

"I'm starting to get an idea." I kicked to break free once last time, then groaned and lay flat. "Fine. I'll bite. What happened up there?"

"You chose a beast of burden over enacting the White Throne's judgment."

I assumed she meant Timperina, which didn't help calm me.

"Timp ain't just some horse," I spat.

Which was a lie. She was, by all accounts, just a horse. That didn't mean she wasn't the one being in the world I'd call friend, but there was no arguing that. I'd chosen protecting her over my quarry, and I'd do it again every goddamned time.

How long had I been out that someone mistook me for dead; had time to give me a proper burial? My feet were bare. Duster was gone. My guns and my knife—all gone. I'd been scavenged and tossed away, and yet Shar's mirror must've looked so beaten it was mistaken for trash along with me.

I patted around the space more, my unfeeling hand scraping along the back of my head until my fingers sunk through a wound. I could only tell because they snagged on something and got stuck. I yanked, and the moment I did, that dull ringing in my ears vanished.

Bringing it around to the light of the mirror, I saw it, a cluster of wet dollar bills, still with some of that Yeti's preternatural frost on the edges. They must have speared straight through into my brain stem, paralyzing me until the last bit of magic ice melted and it dislodged.

"Not the way money usually undoes a man," I said, flicking the wad against the wall of my tomb.

"Who knows who that possessed sinner will harm next," Shar replied. "Or what the Fallen One influencing him is after."

"Yeah, yeah, I get it, Your Glorious Divinity. This is all on me. But what about his partner who can apparently control animal minds? That troubles me more."

"I'm not yet sure how the Pagans fit into the equation."

I moaned. "Of course you aren't."

"But rare is a Yeti. Only a Child so consumed by hate could commune with one of Hell's minions in such a reckless way to forsake the soul. And when the power becomes too great, and the human parts die . . . self-control goes with it. There will be casualties."

"I'm well aware of how this possession works, Shar—"

"That is not my name."

"Shar*grafein*." I spoke the second half of her name like it was a curse word. "So, why don't you help me out of here so we can end this?"

"Perhaps we should dispatch another of our Hands. Let you lie here, considering the difference between acquiescence and obedience."

"Look, I'm sorry for having a heart," I told her. I tried to keep the panic from my voice but I don't think I had much success. "I promise I'll play nice. Do just what the White Throne commands. Now let me out."

"Perhaps *they* might listen better."

"Let me out!" I banged against the sides of the coffin again, and somehow, they seemed like they were closing in more. Dust billowed, further filling my throat. "I get the lesson!"

"Do you?"

"Goddammit, you're as bad as Ace sometimes!"

I winced. No answer came, but using her Lord's name in vain straight to her was probably not my smartest of decisions, current situation considered. But you bury a man alive and tell me he won't spew some of the worst kinds of curses before his air runs out.

"I'll follow your path or whatever else you need of me like I always do," I said, grinding my teeth. I could sense her incredulity. "Sure, I stray. Ain't that just what *Children* do? But I'm loyal, dammit. Got no choice but to be. I'm loyal, you hear?"

The memory of me turning on Ace flashed through my mind. I wasn't loyal to my last boss, though he had it coming. Would she hold me to that?

"I get the job done," I said to hammer home the point. But my voice had grown soft by now. Shar didn't answer, so I kept talking. "And now that that icy bastard and his pals put me down here, it's personal. You better believe that. I'm gonna send all three of them on a freight train straight to Hell. You tell the White Throne that. Straight to Hell!"

Silence responded.

The light of the holy mirror winked away, casting me once more into what felt like unholy darkness. Maybe that was Hell, eternal separation from the light.

"Shar!" I screamed.

My legs and arms thrashed like a fish out of water, far out as could be. I knew rage wouldn't get me anywhere, but I couldn't help it. I hated getting bested. Visions of Ace Ryker and his tapered beard, cool blue eyes, and crooked grin flashed across my mind's eye over and over again. Visions of that day I died because I'd tried to save someone who couldn't save themselves. And here I was, all over again. Doing the same stuff.

Trying to be a hero in a place where there weren't any.

Minutes passed, me getting more and more pissed off. My limbs didn't tire from exertion—they couldn't—but my brain sure as hell did. Punch by punch, I lost myself to frustration until I was just lying on my back staring up into endless black.

All these years serving the White Throne, and a possessed Yeti was to be my undoing. Well, not really. I was the one at fault. Stubborn as a mule, like always. Saving that little girl and her mother from Ace, protecting Timperina, Agatha—damn that soft spot in my black, dead heart.

Then a tremor came. The entire coffin rattled me around like a stagecoach through rocky terrain. A thin sliver of light pierced through one of the coffin's fine lines, and I heard its lid groaning. So, I went back to pushing with all my considerable might.

And what do you know? The lid cracked off and flew upward.

I gasped as if I needed the air. I was staring up at bright sunshine.

I set to clawing my way upward out of what was to be my forever home and heaved my body over the ledge of a deep hole. I laid there for a moment, facedown in the dirt, and not a second later, a snort greeted me. Glancing up, Timperina's long tongue licked me chin to forehead. I grabbed her head, pulled her close, and gave her a loving tug on her mane. Then, I used the momentum it provided me to rise.

"Quite a bit of trouble you caused, girl," I said.

Then I turned Timp aside so I could get a look at her. The ice explosion had left a few little nicks here and there, but mostly, she was no worse for wear.

"C'mon. Let's get on."

We turned, me leading her by the reins, and I stopped dead.

A winding trench wove from my grave through the cemetery, some-how not disturbing any other plot or headstone. A thin funnel of wind and dust swirled in front of the nearby church, slowly vanishing into the pale, cloudless sky.

A twister. Common in these parts, only, they usually wreaked chaos. This one's path seemed almost purposeful, affecting nothing except for my own grave.

Standing by a freshly dug hole across the yard was a scrawny kid. Must've been the gravedigger. He stared, all color drained from his face. Then, he dropped the shovel and silently ran in the opposite direction of town.

Now, I'm not one to complain about miracles, especially when they benefit me, but I glared down at the cracked mirror in my palm and muttered, "Show off."

TEN

Elkhart was a sizable settlement. The cemetery was behind the church on the topmost of three tiers. From there, it had only been a short walk to the sheriff's place, also hovering over the whole town like some kind of guardian angel or judge.

Too bad they hadn't had better luck.

Put up a better fight than Lonely Hill had, but these towns are only prepared for outlaws with gunpowder, not Hell magic.

Elkhart had been ravaged by the fight. Ice had melted and mixed with the clay to create a sloshy mess—though most of it seemed dried up by now. The unnatural rime had lasted far longer back in Lonely Hill. Debris floated on the air instead of flurries. Flecks of wood and hay. Ripped flyers for that Revelation Springs Founders' Day Fair swirled about, just like the one I'd seen in Lonely Hill. Buildings were shot up and destroyed, locals hauling lumber and supplies to patch things up. The general store was missing windows. Its signage hung sideways. The second-story balcony sagged on one side with a broken column beneath it. That was where I'd been flung by the Yeti.

From up where I was, I could spot the bank and the square before it. There were no bodies littering the streets as expected. This shootout had claimed more lives than the last for sure, but where were they? And though the bank was empty, it was just that . . . empty. No snowflakes dithering about or lingering darkness caused by devilry. A big empty room with a big empty vault, which I could see through a big-ass hole where the front roof had once been.

Matter of fact, everything inside seemed all cleaned up.

How the hell long was I in that coffin?

It was a question I was hoping the town's lawmen might answer, amongst a few others. Problem was, it seemed the whole damn town was outside their station. All that was missing were pitchforks and torches.

"We want retribution!" one man shouted.

"How will you get our money back!" cried a woman, clutching a small child to her hip.

"We trusted you!"

The complaints and shouts carried on and on in this fashion. Everyone was too distracted with their displeasure to even notice me, let alone realize that a man who'd been dead and buried walked amongst them again.

A good thing.

The White Throne never specifically said we needed to hide what we are, though it seemed implied. I'd get done with this place and move on to the next quickly as I could.

I hitched Timp nearby, giving her an extra pat on her neck so she'd know I'd be right back. Got a healthy snort in return.

"Missed you, too," I whispered in her ear. Then I shoved through the crowd, hoping no one thought too hard about my presence. Approaching the sheriff's office, I tried the door, but it wouldn't budge.

"Best back away from that door!" a voice warned from inside. Sounded shaky, nervous.

I knew I might receive a hole in my chest for it, but I kicked in the door anyway, breaking the lock, splintering the frame. I'd had enough messing around for one day. Behind me, the crowd erupted in cheers like I'd just done them a favor. They tried to follow, but I slammed the door right in their faces, then dragged a chair over to bar the knob.

A couple of desks filled the single room, covered in papers, sets of handcuffs, and a ring of keys. A number of bounties were pinned on the wall. All in all, it was the typical setup, complete with a cell with bars made of iron along the back wall, currently empty.

Also in the room stood a lone man. He had his weapon raised, muzzle pointed at me. His finger was ready on the trigger, a sure sign he was planning to fire.

"Who the hell do you think you are!" he shouted. Then his brow knitted. "You?"

It looked like my old friend Dale from Lonely Hill was a deputy once again. Though his badge looked every bit as different as his eyes. Sunken. Dark. Like he hadn't known the graces of a peaceful night's sleep in some time.

I could commiserate. And then I saw what was atop his head, and my eyes narrowed. "That's my damn hat you're wearing!" I growled.

The gawking deputy steadied his weapon, but I could see his hands trembling.

"T-they said you died," he said. "Got buried. The rider in black who done chased off them outlaws. Saw your grave, I did. Y-y-you . . . was dead."

"I got better."

I stepped forward. The hammer of his gun clicked, but I ignored him. I snatched my hat. He didn't shoot. I knew he wouldn't. Not after all we'd been through.

I dusted off my Stetson and set it atop my head.

"Where's the rest of my stuff, Dale?"

He just stared dumbfounded, so I slammed my fist on his desk.

He winced and shuffled to the back of the room and returned with my duster, belt, and other things.

"Think it's all here . . . mostly," Dale said, looking down at it all as he walked. He tripped over a lip in the floor and my belt fell, satchel along with it. As it hit the floor, the Nephilim's harmonica slid out. Guess whoever buried me didn't think the thing had any value. Probably true, but I was glad it remained in my possession. In the wrong hands, something like it could be deadly.

Dale cursed and tried to pick everything up. I beat him to most of it, but his hand reached the harmonica just before mine and he lifted it.

"Odd piece, this," he said. All at once, it became the singular focus of his attention. His eyes almost crossed. "Where'd you get it?"

"Hand it over, Dale," I demanded.

"Is that bone?" He spun it around in his fingertips. "I wonder what it came from. I wonder what died . . ." He peered up at me. "Who'd want to play a part of the dead."

I watched as his lips started to droop and his eyes sagged. He didn't look scared, just, sad. A simple man like him, its dark qualities were probably amplified.

"Dale, c'mon now." He ignored me. "I said hand it over." I tore it out of his grasp and stowed it back in the satchel before a dark cloud filled my thoughts as well, being in its presence.

Dale blinked and shook out his head. "You got some strange things, Mr. Crowley."

I scoured through the rest of my belongings and found my silver-dusted knife, both pistols, belt and all, containing my lasso, satchel, and a nearly empty pouch of silver bullets—which I promptly used to reload the Peacemakers.

"My rifle?" I asked while I fitted the bullets.

"This here is all we got of yours, Mr. Crowl—"

Between Shar, him, and everything in between, I was at my wits' end. I seized him by the lapels and slammed him against the wall. And there I was, staring straight into the eyes of Ace Ryker. Not the real thing, mind, but an old bounty poster hung up right behind Dale. The paper was so weathered you could barely see the image anymore.

I returned my attention to the sheriff or deputy or whatever the hell he was now. Then I asked a question I should've already asked.

"What are you doing here?"

"Can you put me down first?"

"No." I lifted him another inch for good measure.

Dale stuttered a bit more, then found his words. "Folks in Lonely

Hill got rowdy soon after you left. Started saying things about how our beloved Sheriff Daniels died . . ."

"Like, whose bullet really killed him?"

"*Things*," Dale replied quickly. He swallowed hard. "So, I came here after you. Thought I could make things right . . . but . . ."

"You were too late." I loosened my grip on him. He landed like two noodles with boots attached. "Join the crew."

Straightening his collar, he sidled away from me, but there wasn't far to go. "Well, the sheriff here didn't know any better. Hadn't heard stories. Not yet. Just knew I was wearing a badge. Told me to look after Elkhart so he and the others could go out for revenge for what those freaks did on Saturday."

I paused, letting his words hang on the air a bit.

"Saturday? What's today?" I asked.

"Tuesday."

"Tue—" I plopped down on one of the chairs. I'd missed nearly three days thanks to Shar's games. Three days where those magic-fueled outlaws could be causing a ruckus, hitting whatever town was next or slaughtering anyone who dared come after them.

I eyed the room. Took a deep breath I didn't need.

"Just you here?" I asked.

Dale nodded.

I rose slowly. "Where's my rifle?"

"I could guess?" Dale said. When I didn't respond, he continued. "Pinks were gathering up all they could. Must've grabbed it before leaving town."

Sons of bitches can't leave well enough alone. Robbing the dead. Though dumb as they were, my pistols were worth a lot more than my rifle. The damn fools.

"Where are they all going?" I demanded.

"Like I said, after revenge. Mr. Dufaux put a bounty on them outlaws big enough to buy whoever catches 'em a homestead of their own."

He gestured to a paper not yet pinned up, featuring a drawing of a burly man with a giant beard, a native woman with the features on her half-painted face drawn so stereotypically I couldn't help but roll my eyes, and a blank head with a question mark.

FROZEN TRIO WANTED DEAD OR ALIVE FOR MULTIPLE ROBBERIES OF DUFAUX BANK AND TRUST

A reward of $5,000 cash was being offered, and they were said to be somewhere north of Elkhart. About as descriptive as bounties get in these parts. Oh, and that they were considered armed and extremely dangerous . . . though, nothing about magic.

Dale sat next to me, resting a hand on my shoulder like we were old pals. The glare I shot his way informed him otherwise.

"What am I supposed to do for these people?" he asked, reeling his hand back. "They'll rip me apart. And what if the others don't come back? Crowley, you gotta help me."

The poor guy was panting.

"You're safer here than going after those *'freaks,'* as you call them." I put venom on the word, though he couldn't have known it'd been offensive to me too. Plus, he wasn't wrong. They were about the strangest crew of outlaws I'd ever run into. I picked up their bounty to analyze it closer.

"I don't think now's the time to go bounty hunting," Dale said.

As my gaze passed across the unidentified marksman, I remembered something.

Without hesitating, I searched across the desk.

"Hey now!" Dale protested, but I ignored him.

I tore open a drawer and rummaged to find a fountain pen inside. Then, I began drawing on the back of the bounty. Dale leaned right over my shoulder, watching me like I was losing my mind. Maybe I was.

"Was it that strange ice weapon got you?" he asked. "Like antidynamite or something it was. My God, did you get buried alive, frozen? How'd you get—"

"You recognize this?" I said, shoving the drawing into his hand to shut him up. Some questions were better off left unanswered.

On the paper was my best rendition of the symbolic bird brand I'd spotted on the back of the marksman. Knowing his abilities and the fact that they were glowing, I knew there was something to the markings. Had to be.

Some shouting started from some of the townsfolk trying to shove their way inside. The chair holding the door scraped along the wood, and I stepped across the room to jam it back into place.

"Quiet!" I barked.

When I turned around, Dale was studying the drawing. "Where'd you see this?"

"Never mind that," I said. "What is it?"

"Ain't sure exactly."

"But you've seen it." I could tell by the look on his face.

He nodded. "Couple of years back." His face started to glow at the memory. "Got invited to one of Mr. Dufaux's Founders' Day galas up in Revelation Springs years back. It's that time again . . . I'm sure you've seen the signs. Didn't get invited this year. It was like a dream. Sheriff Daniels took me as I was just starting as a reward. Biggest house I'd ever seen, still to this day—"

"Can you get to the damn point?"

Dale cleared his throat. "Mr. Dufaux had this symbol—" He stabbed his finger at the paper, "—on an Injun statue or a . . . a what'chu call it—all stacked and such . . ."

"Totem?" I asked, hoping to hurry him up.

"Yeah, yeah. That. A totem. Pretty thing. Colorful and all carved up."

"Dale. Get on with it." I slapped the desk again.

"Sorry, Mr. Crowley. I'm just nervous. I . . . Dufaux had it displayed proudly in his courtyard. Right in the middle."

"That a fact?"

"Certain as Hell is hot."

I didn't bother correcting him about that. All I could wonder is why Mr. Reginald Dufaux would have the same symbol in his home that was glowing upon the back of one of the men robbing him.

Sounded to me like I had my first real clue about who these folks were.

I knew Yetis could only exist through pure hate and remembered how the Yeti had condemned Dufaux during the robbery. Spat his name with disgust.

This was personal. A feud, perhaps? Something stolen or pride wounded? Could even be something to do with the statue.

I was done trying to follow the money bank to bank. The robbers were too far ahead of me now. It was time I headed right to the source in Revelation Springs. This Mr. Dufaux. If he knew something more, I could get a leg up. If Dufaux knew nothing, I had a feeling the Frozen Trio would be coming for Revelation soon anyway. Him living there meant it'd be the biggest, richest branch of his banking institution.

"Thanks," I said to Dale, snatching the drawing out of his hands and stuffing it into my pocket.

"Wait, what?" He moved to block me from the door and pointed a thumb over his shoulder. "You can't leave me here alone with them. We gotta talk about what you saw. May-maybe we can find 'em. Together. Get the bounty for ourselves—"

"I work alone," I said, brushing by him. I kicked the chair aside and the door flung open, letting all the Elkhart rabble inside.

"Now, now, one at a time," I said. Then I looked back at Dale. "Good luck."

He smiled a nervous smile and got to it. "Hi. Can I help you? What's your name, miss? Excuse you!"

I slipped out unnoticed and loaded onto Timperina.

Keeping me buried in a box . . . Shar's message got across. It was time to slow down, focus, and bring holy justice to those who called upon the aid of demons.

And yet, it was Shar I was more concerned with at the moment. Her lesson was harsher than usual. But hey, no one ever said angels were all benevolent.

ELEVEN

I had one detour to make on the way to Revelation Springs. I know, I know, pissing Shar off for no good reason ain't smart, but this was a worthy diversion. Plus, Shar hadn't bugged me about it yet.

Dealing with a Yeti was easy, relatively speaking. Abnormally strong, but I could handle a magic-wielding brute with a solid plan, some silver, and a whole a lot of gunpowder. Though, like Shar warned, his power would only grow with time, madness with it, which would make everything tougher. Tomahawk-lady was no slouch either, and the marksman . . . I was, and always will be, wary of things that enter the minds of other things.

With the music-playing Nephilim, it'd taken time and a melody for that beast to dig into the brains of its hosts. However, that young outlaw and the hawk—that was instantaneous. One mind, flipping back and forth.

If he was a Neph, he was a kind I'd never encountered before. That means he probably wasn't, and I needed some answers.

Did his abilities extend beyond that? Could he work a man like a puppet, not just a bird?

On my way, I sewed up the hole in my glove. When I was done, I raised my mirror, checked my teeth. Where I was going, for some reason, I always liked looking my best.

"Must you do that, Crowley?" Shar complained, stealing the view of my not-so-pearly whites as she swirled about in the sheen.

"Well, good day to you too," I said.

"All days are good when Lucifer's forces are in their place."

"Pleasant."

Timp's hoof slipped on a rock, and I nearly dropped the mirror.

"You must learn to be more careful," Shar said.

I leaned over to steady Timp, then glanced sidelong at Shar. "I thought you'd be scolding me for this little sojourn."

"I have no feud with the Pagans," Shar replied.

"You'll find one. Always do."

"Continue pursuing the bird, and you may yet find the answers to what demon empowered the Yeti. Which is as important as thwarting the possessed themselves. Remember, the steps of a righteous man are ordered by the Almighty."

"Righteous?" I laughed. "Now that's a word I've never been called."

"You have found the path again, Crowley. Follow it and root out this plague of wickedness, and whichever of our endless foes lies behind it."

"Still think it's Chekoketh?" I asked.

"The rumors suggest he may be up to something."

"Rumors? I thought gossip was a sin?"

"And we were getting along so nicely, Crowley," she reprimanded.

"You're right. You're right. Let me know if those rumors flesh themselves out at all, would you?"

"You handle your affairs. I'll handle mine."

She swirled away. Of course, she had no useful information from on high. However, I'd be a liar if I said hearing from her didn't buoy my spirits. All this friction and butting of heads, at least that was behind us. My holy duty to the White Throne was to banish Hell's mischief from Earth, but if I could root out the demon behind it? That was always a bonus. Got me a longer leash for the next time a poor lass like Agatha cried out, and I couldn't help but stop to save her.

Revelation Springs wasn't too far off course. Though, in the West, it's so rare you find anything that's *on* the way. But I had friends in high places, so to speak. Only this one wasn't an angel.

I gave Timp a nudge to speed up, but I could tell she was hesitant. A thick fog rolled in as we followed the Devil's River, a few dozen miles north of Dead Acre and due east of Revelation Springs. It was a fitting name if there ever was one. Dead or dying trees spread across the flats like skeletal hands reaching up from the grave. After my experience underground, the whole thing made me shudder.

It was like all the life out here was being sucked up and repurposed within, but up ahead, I could hear life. The falls rumbled and I could practically taste their waters.

Timp whinnied. I felt bad. The incline was steep, and she was getting up there in age.

"Almost there, girl," I said, patting her neck.

Grabbing her mane tight, I leaned in so she could hear my breathing. The fog was so thick now I couldn't see anything else. But she knew the way. One hoof in front of the other, up treacherous terrain to a haven somewhere between Heaven and Hell.

A shadow darted to my right. Timp blew out her nose.

"Steady, girl," I said, catching a whiff of the visitor. Many enemies lurked in places like this, but our guest wasn't one. "Friends come in many forms."

The fog swirled, shifting, like Shar's movements within glass only at a much grander scale. I could sense Timp's nerves even though she'd been this way before. Her sinewy neck was quivering, tailing whipping hard behind me.

Then she reared and kicked her hooves.

"Whoa!" I shouted, but she wasn't listening. I nearly toppled off her, trying my best to regain composure.

More fog clouded about and Timp strafed back and forth, doing a short, tight circle. When the fog cleared, a shaggy-haired, droopy-eared dog stood before us. The kind of animal that a ranch hand might keep around to stir the sheep. A mangy hound that fits in everywhere and is tossed scraps just to keep it from yapping.

"Sorry to drop in on you, Mutt," I said. "Wasn't sure where else to go."

The dog didn't respond, just let its tongue hang out as it panted. A good sign. When he turned and walked slowly, clearing a route through the blanket of mist, I knew I was welcome to follow.

Timp took a bit of jostling to get moving, but she got on eventually. Walls of red stone closed in on either side, a narrowing ravine up a mild incline. Mutt scurried along, hopping over rocks that Timp easily crossed.

The waterfall revealed itself at the narrow end of the chasm. It was wide enough for but a single man to pass, one at a time. Mutt stopped at it, looked back, and barked once before leaping through the watery curtain. I heeled Timp forward, but when we got to the water's edge, she resisted, digging in, and refusing to carry on.

"C'mon now, we could both use a bath." I gave her mane a whiff. "You, especially. Whew, girl, that's rancid."

She shook from side to side and tapped her back hoof.

"Be open-minded," I said with a chuckle.

Another more vehement shake followed.

"All right now. Fine." I sighed. "If you insist."

I hopped down and hitched her to a broken tree trunk. She could be finicky around here. Plus, werewolves roamed these parts. Though they didn't usually care to get too close to the falls—knowing who was out here and all—their howls were often enough to send Timp running. I didn't feel like yet another chase, but she was never one to be forced.

"Wait here," I told her as I stepped forward.

Water gushed over me. I stopped for a minute, putting my head back and running my fingers through grungy hair, pulling at the knots. Scrubbed my face of many days' worth of caked-on dirt and mud too. I had no need to drink but I wouldn't say it didn't make me feel good to swish a bit. Like I was a new man.

On the other side, the fog completely lifted.

No matter how many times I visit what I've designated "the Garden"—this shelter of the Skinwalkers—I'll never get used to it. Lush, wet plants splayed out before me for what seemed like miles. Ferns with leaves the size of wagons. Prehistoric-like flora. Stuff nobody's seen around these parts for millennia, yet here it was.

I called it the Garden for obvious reasons; it reminded me of the fabled Eden—only thing missing was the snake.

Steep cliffs rose on either side like we were inside the crater of a dormant volcano—which, maybe we were. If this were my home, I'd keep it a secret, just as they had for all this time. It was absolutely stunning. Everywhere I looked was green. A verdant oasis in the middle of the dry desert. And in the center of it all was a tall tree with solid white flowers.

Huupi Sokobi, they called it. Best translation I had was the "Life Tree." They believed that with its branches reaching up and its roots digging deep into the earth, it was a link between the heavens, Earth, and the underworld. United above and below. Beautiful sentiment, I suppose.

Birds soared overhead—some breeds I don't even know the name of. Rodents skittered through twisting branches, playing like they had no care in the world. The dog, however, was gone. Instead, before me stood a young native boy with sharp features. Couldn't have been older than thirteen. Fur-covered rags hung loosely from his bony frame, and that same object which seemed like a collar before now hung from him as a necklace.

"You always going to hide around me?" I asked, knowing no answer would come.

Young Mutt—as I affectionately called him since he'd never shared his real name—and I had a history. He'd saved me from werewolves once, and I'd helped him bring a number of them down. I figured if anyone could help me, it was Mutt's people.

Skinwalkers and Werefolk have an eternal feud, you see. Not unlike Heaven and Hell. Shar won't exactly give me the specifics on where they both come from—shocker—but I do know neither are demonic spawn exactly. Probably cursed by the like long ago until, eventually, the condition became normal in their blood. They don't exactly fit the Nephilim mold, which is why I was here.

I always figure Shar knows more than she's willing to share. I think she doesn't want me to know that there's a route to gain power apart from above or below. Or, maybe—who knows—maybe she *doesn't* know herself, and in this great big Earth God made for us, some supernatural things manifest all on their own.

The Skinwalkers, like her, prefer to keep me in the dark, and I'm content to stay there when I can. All I know for sure is that Mutt's people are helpful when I'm in a pinch and that werewolves are a damn thorn in my flesh.

I never mind siding with good folk. And these people? They're as good as good gets.

I just hope Shar doesn't decide one day that Mutt and his band are scions of Hell and need to be banished.

"Why are you here?" Mutt asked.

The young Skinwalker didn't speak much even though his dog form didn't mind yapping, but his voice seemed older than he appeared. More mature. And he was always straight to the point. I liked that. No beating around the bush or spewing nonsense like outlaws tended to.

"I need you to look at something for me," I replied.

I pulled out the drawing of the lightning hawk markings. His eyes narrowed, and he took it, turning it over to see the bounty. His gaze lingered on that all-too-stereotypical image of the native woman. His lips pursed.

"Don't worry about them," I said. "Just the bird. Now, I mean no offense, but the way it was done, the patterning—it looks native. Only, I don't recognize what tribe it might belong to. I thought Comanche but, something's just a bit . . . off."

Mutt looked around. A few of his people strolled by wearing bright colors, paying us no mind. They were a peaceful people, at least to me, not yet touched by my kind's incursion onto land that belonged to their kin. Guess that's the benefit of having a hidden sanctuary like this.

Each of them, like Mutt, could turn into a dog form on a whim. It didn't take a full moon or inspire bloodlust like with the weres.

If I'm honest, I ain't too sure what the ability does except help them blend in. They're damn good with medicine, too; I'll give them that.

Maybe if Ace had dragged me here after shooting me through the chest, I'd have made it and still had a heart beating there. But I digress.

"Well?" I asked.

Mutt studied me momentarily, then pointed to a mud hut across the hidden valley.

"Mukwooru?" I asked. He nodded, and I didn't dare question him.

And so I went, crossing stairs and paths carved through stone and meager wigwam huts, ducking under unblemished branches, and brushing away spotless leaves. To either side, home after home dotted the path. None was bigger than the next. No way to determine one's wealth or worth by the size of their domicile or the exquisiteness of their clothing.

Mutt's people went about their daily lives around me, fetching water from the falls, tending livestock, and hammering tools into place. Part of me wished I were still alive and living my own way so I could beg them to let me stay. But that was a pipe dream. Mutt kept ahead of me, and once he reached the hut, he held open drapes made of bones and beads.

"Thanks," I told Mutt.

Then, stepping in, I removed my Stetson; it was a sign of respect and showed I had nothing to hide. A woman knelt in front of a burning pile of sage. The smoke and smell filled the little wigwam, and for once, I was glad I didn't need to breathe. I could only imagine how that would fill the lungs of a mortal man.

Mutt moved in to stand silently beside her. They had the same chin, nose. Her son, if I had to guess it, though nobody had ever given me that answer.

I knew her. She knew me. She went by Mukwooru. Meant something like "spirit talker" in their native tongue, but I wasn't sure if it was her name or title. Her hair was gray with some streaks of youth left in it, but it was mostly covered by a buffalo skull cap. Her beautiful leather dress was covered with beadwork unparalleled, the long frills at her arms and hems falling like blades of wheat.

She leaned back and spoke quietly to Mutt. I didn't understand most of it—partially because I didn't have a grasp on the intricacies of their speech, but also, her voice was barely a whisper. I did, however, hear how she punctuated it with "*Black Badge*" in English. I'd shared my favored title with Mutt once, and I guessed he'd passed that along.

"Good to see you again too, Mukwooru," I said, lowering my head in deference. It just came natural to me. Always just hoped I wasn't offending. Didn't know much about them at all, really. Spilling secrets to a dog and getting nothing in return—I was starting to understand the worth of their ability to blend in.

Mukwooru didn't say a word in return. Like mother like son, I guess. My stance shifted uncomfortably.

"Oh, right," I said, remembering how it worked. It'd been some time since an incident in Dead Acre with a lovestruck necromancer. After that, I'd been around the Garden a few times with Mutt. Most recently, I needed some help tracking down a witch's coven doing some kind of voodoo that looked a bit too much like Skinwalking.

Falling to one knee, I rustled through my belongings. A gift for a gift. A simple way of living, yet, one I could respect. Outlaws like I'd been—we lived much the same way amongst our own crew. Eye for an eye, tooth for a tooth, gold for gold, blood for blood, and so on.

My hand rifled through my belt satchel. I knew I'd kept the Nephilim's harmonica for a reason. I pulled it out quick and practically tossed it on the ground between us, glad for the chance to hand it over to a people that might understand its eldritch power and maybe be able to do something good with it.

"A gift," I said, my words coming out labored.

Mukwooru slowly extended her wrinkled fingers and lifted the harmonica. Nobody spoke, but her beads rattled as she spun it to observe every angle. She brought it to her nose, and her nostrils twitched. Then her lips. Before she could even play a note, a tear pooled in one of her eyes and she lowered it, clutching it to her chest.

I don't know what that cursed thing made her see, but it was enough for her to extend it back to me.

"You keep," she said, accent thick as oil. She dropped it back onto the floor, or rather, pushed it away as if it stunk of shit.

"But—"

She snapped her fingers to silence me. Then, she said something else to Mutt in their language. He handed her the drawing, and I continued staring at the little bone instrument. I should've known the accursed thing wouldn't be so easy to ditch.

Luckily, the gesture of offering it seemed to do the trick. I begrudgingly scooped it up and stuffed it back into the darkness of my satchel.

While I did, Mukwooru traced the lines of the drawing. Her forehead wrinkled into worms while murmuring in her language. I couldn't help but wonder if my handiwork was just so poor I was confusing everyone. Never claimed to be an artist.

"*Piasa*," she pronounced, finally.

"What?" I asked.

"Pi-a-sa."

Three syllables. One word. I gathered that much. Still had no idea what it meant, though.

She tapped on the drawing and said the word again. My brow furrowed, and I glanced at Mutt, who flapped his arms like wings.

"So, it's a bird?" I asked.

Mukwooru shook her head. "No. A god."

"Where I come from, there's only one of those," I jested and quickly realized it wasn't the time.

"Born of thunder." She imitated the sound of a lightning strike. "It is the storm. Long vanished. It, and its guardian tribe."

"Extinct?" I scratched my chin, then my head.

"Not extinct," Mukwooru said. "Gone."

I wasn't sure there was a difference, but I didn't argue.

"Where did you see this?" Mutt asked me.

"The man I'm after," I said, taking a small step toward them. I turned the drawing over and pointed at the question mark that represented the sharpshooter. "He had that symbol branded on his back, glowing. I got the impression he could enter the mind of his pet, a hawk. And he used it to attack me. I've never seen a power like that. So fast, back and forth. A bit like you folks, though I'm not implying it was you. He used the thing's eyes to help pick off targets from rooftops."

Mukwooru rose from the floor just a little, straightening her curved spine. She looked up to Mutt, then to me.

"Very rare ability." She raised a hand to her chest and tapped. "Skin-walker." Then she poked the question mark on the bounty. "Mind-drifter."

"Well, that's nifty, ain't it," I said, throwing a smirk at Mutt. He didn't seem amused, though. Never did. Getting the boy to crack a smile would be a bigger miracle than the one which freed me from my grave.

"Is it just hawks or . . ." I asked, letting my thoughts hang in the air.

"You are friend to our home," she said. "But that is all I can offer."

I grimaced, mouth drawing a sharp line. That wasn't enough. I didn't come all this way for riddles. I could get that from Shar. I had to know. So, I did something I was good at. I pushed my luck.

"Well, can he enter your mind? Mine?"

Her glare fixed on me, icier than the Yeti's. What is it about the women in my life, able to throw daggers like that with their eyes?

I didn't relent. "Is he from around here? Are they? The people who worshipped this god?"

She snapped her finger again, and this time, the smoke from the sage billowed in response.

"No. More." Her tone made it clear that was it. She held the bounty paper out for me to take.

I looked to Mutt. He stared back and his expression said we were done.

"Fine, fine." I snatched the paper, not daring to cause any more trouble. Allies were rare enough in these parts. "Thank you kindly, ma'am. Next time, I promise to bring something you'll hang on to."

I went to stand, and as I did, Mukwooru lunged over the sage, her face bursting through the smoke, a bit too reminiscent of my angelic handler. Grasping my wrist, she beseeched me with a question. "The Mind-drifter. Will you kill him?"

I eyed her a moment. I wasn't sure what answer she wanted. If I said yes, would she view me as a murderer? But what if she wanted this man dead? She didn't act like his kind were too desirable. I went with what I thought was a neutral response that I couldn't be held personally accountable for.

"If that's what the Almighty intends."

"And if not?" she pressed.

"He's dangerous. He and his crew have killed plenty already and he's no doubt destined for Hell, much like I am."

"Answer me."

I looked straight at her. I wished I could lie to her, but I knew she'd see right through it. She didn't get a reputation like hers, didn't reign over an enlightened people like hers for not being able to see through a man.

"I wish that were up to me," I said, sighing. "I truly, truly do."

"Your people, always fast to kill. You bring no gift worth taking. Instead, gift me this. Do not kill unless he is truly deserving."

My mouth hung open, unsure what to say. Deserving of life or death was a question reserved for beings above my pay grade. Sure, the Mind-drifter had killed those who fired back. Who worth their salt in the West hasn't? And controlling the will of other beings felt deeply wrong to me, but it was only a hawk from what I knew so far. A pet that maybe loved him. And I'll be honest, sometimes it'd be better if Timperina understood what I was thinking.

The only rules I had to go by were those doled out by the White Throne, and they were as incomprehensible and wishy-washy as ancient texts.

Deserving . . . what a loaded word.

Mukwooru released me and returned to her kneeling position. Eyes focused on the smoky plume of incense, she flicked her wrist toward the exit. Mutt hurried over to get the drapes for me even though I was already halfway out.

It wasn't the best terms on which I'd left the Garden, but it was honest. Mutt's people always seemed to appreciate that. I just knew, next time I returned, I'd better bring something more valuable to trade for information or help. Otherwise, I might find myself knee-deep between werewolves and Skinwalkers, without a side to choose.

TWELVE

Mutt led me back through the waterfall in silence. And maybe it was because I'd just handled that damned harmonica so much, or perhaps it was knowing that I was leaving the most peaceful place I'd ever encountered, but as soon as the water streamed across my face, a sense of longing came.

Living out in the West, mostly amongst various shades of brown and ugly, thorny plants—the Garden has a certain appeal. A soothing effect. Hell, if my people found out about this lush little oasis, there'd be a race for it that'd make the gold rush look like the gold crawl.

Timperina waited to greet me right where I'd left her. Only, that soothed nature didn't seem to extend to her. She faced me head-on, bobbing her head and anxiously tapping her front hoof.

"What is it, girl?" I asked.

She snorted, then whinnied and threw her head to the side. Dammit, did I wish I spoke horse.

"I wasn't gone that long."

The full moon, already hovering in the sky, told me I was lying. Back in dog form, Mutt's ears stood, flicking back and forth. I had hearing better than most men, but it was nothing compared to animals. I listened hard as well and thought I heard what grabbed his attention and got Timp all riled up.

Howling. And this wasn't a train.

Mutt took off first, and I mounted Timp to follow. Naturally, she didn't want to.

"Oh, c'mon, you big baby," I said, though I didn't blame her.

We raced down through the fog, following Mutt's path for the easiest route. I checked my ammo on the way. Didn't have many silver shots left for my pistols and my rifle remained missing-in-action. My plan was to craft some more rounds once I made it to Revelation Springs, but you know what they say about plans . . . Men make 'em. God laughs.

Howls turned to growls, then came the shriek of a man. Mutt took a leap off a ledge, which Timp couldn't manage, so I guided her around the long way. A clearing in the fog revealed three werewolves circling their prey—a man pinned down beneath his own dead horse.

"Help!" he cried out.

"Looks like someone wandered a bit too far away from home," one of the werewolves said, or more like snarled.

"Fresh meat," said another, snapping her jaws with an audible *clack*. The females are smaller but not generally weaker.

Their prey started sobbing. "Please . . . someone, help!"

I could've left them to their meal. It was natural, so to speak. Nobody would stop a wolf from feeding on a deer. But then, I saw the face of their little snack.

"Son of a bitch, Dale!" I cursed.

Considering I didn't sense the agonizing itch of Shar's presence as I pondered saving him, I reckoned he had some role to play in what was to come. Or, maybe, he was right in my way, and Shar decided to throw me a bone, let me play hero.

"Not so fresh if you ask me!" I called down.

All three werewolves stopped and looked up at me as I drove Timp down the ridge, pistols trained on them. The one in the middle had a scar across his eye and a tuft of black fur along the center of his hunched spine. Ugly things, they are, but that's what you get when you slam two beings into one in a way that isn't meant to be.

Werewolves may not be direct demon-spawn, but they are wicked in a sense, even if they don't mean to be. The affliction brings about a bloodlust they can barely control when the moon turns full, especially in the younger ones. And I'd had my share of run-ins with them. Considering we ran in the same preternatural circles, it couldn't be helped.

"You . . ." the scarred one said.

My brow knitted. "Have we met?"

"You killed my cousin, Wolf Hunter! Gave me this." He ran one of his long, jagged claws across his scarred eye.

"Did I now?" It was impossible to know. I don't go around hunting the weres like he implied, but we got into a fair share of skirmishes. I skidded Timp to a stop, setting her perpendicular to the fight so I had a clean shot to my left.

"All you inbred runts look the same to me," I said. "Now, you all back away slow, and we can all go our own ways. Don't be stupid. I've got the high ground."

"He's mine, Roscoe!"

The smallest of the three bounded toward me. Don't know what she was thinking, dashing toward an armed man one of them just called Wolf Hunter, but I put a bullet through the center of her head all the same. The price of being stupid, if you ask me. Steam and silvery sparks showered out as she tumbled down rock and landed in a messy heap of tangled limbs.

That was easy. Only spent one of my three remaining shots.

The other two split up, skittering along the rocks to get at me in a serpentine manner. I lined up a shot on one of them and took it. But what these shapeshifters lacked in brains, they made up for with dexterity and testicular fortitude. A last-second turn caused me to only catch it in the arm.

I decided to save my final bullet when Mutt jumped out of cover and crashed into the closest one's head, nails raking across the side of its face. So many sounds rose in the night, I wasn't sure which was Mutt and which was the werewolf, but I watched with bated breath as they fought.

How something so small as Mutt brought that mammoth down, I do not know, but it happened all the same. Saw it with my own eyes.

The thing bellowed and thrashed. I set a boot against Timp's saddle and shoved off. She gave me a purposeful buck to help propel me. Sometimes, Timp and I are just purely in sync.

As I fell, I lassoed the abomination around one of its big paws. Heaven's raw judgment rendered it still and kept it from doing Mutt any damage as I yanked, throwing the thing off balance and sending it careening down the incline. It yelped, bouncing against rock, and then again until it was too far down to hear. Dropping to the clearing, I rolled, caught my balance, and rose with one pistol cocked and ready to blow a hole through the scarred pack leader named Roscoe.

"Enough!" he thundered.

I held my fire. The werewolf had Mutt by the throat, all four legs kicking as he squealed to break free. Dale cried behind him, yanking futilely to free his leg from beneath his dead steed.

"Drop the dog," I warned.

"Toss the gun," Roscoe countered.

"Don't be a fool. Those shots were loud. You don't think his people will be here soon? Chop you up. Eat you. Use your bones to decorate their doorways? They don't waste a part."

"All I wanted was a tasty meal." Roscoe snarled back at Dale, who hid his face in terror.

"Don't I know the feeling," I lamented.

"You murdered my pack!"

"You don't know that other one's dead."

Roscoe growled.

"Look," I said. "You drop him, you walk away. I got no personal quarrel with your kind except you constantly getting in my damn way."

"And my meal?" Roscoe asked, turning back toward Dale.

"He stays too."

"I think I'd rather kill the Skinwalker. For my *pack*." A guttural sound rumbled deep from in the werewolf's gullet. His claw slid around the soft part of Mutt's throat, and the dog squealed. That was when I noticed that I could hear every last one of those noises. It was eerily quiet up here. Gave me an idea.

"Wait," I said. "I'll make you a deal. A trade. In exchange for his life." I nodded to the body of the werewolf to my right, head still steaming silver. "And to pay for hers."

"That was my sister," Roscoe spat.

"She attacked me first."

All I got in return was a soft growl. I stowed one pistol, then I slowly reached into the satchel I wore on my belt. Maintaining eye contact the whole way so he wouldn't get jumpy, I pulled out the cursed harmonica.

Roscoe scoffed. "That's all?"

"That's all?" I said, feigning insult. "It's made from the talon of a bear owl. Worth a small fortune. And the sound? Pure as a cut diamond."

It was a lie, but it made Roscoe perk up. I noticed his grip on Mutt loosen a hair.

"What's it gonna be?" I said. "Before his folk get here, and we all wind up dead."

"I'm thinking!" Roscoe snapped.

I may not have been able to trade the harmonica, but if it had enough power to scare Mukwooru, then I might as well put it to the test.

"Here, just listen." I brought the instrument to my mouth. I can't vomit—at least, I don't think I can—but I had the sudden urge to. My mind was flooded with images of Mutt's throat getting gashed, Mukwooru getting pissed, and me getting buried amongst the roots of the Life Tree for all eternity, where even Shar couldn't break me out.

I exhaled slowly out of habit. A calming measure, though it did nothing substantial for me. I had to focus through the gloom.

I knew a bit about harmonica playing from the old days. Hard to run with a crew large as the Scuttlers and not watch someone diddle around with a tune when we got stuck waiting around a campfire.

So, I played what I thought was a G. Now, the truth is, I couldn't blow a melody from my ass after a pot of beans, but wouldn't you know it, the note hummed out perfectly into the crisp air, and the fog itself seemed to fold around the sound. I kept eye contact with Roscoe the entire time.

His face gave off a woozy look, and as the note hung, I lowered the harmonica and whispered, "Drop him."

Mutt fell that very instant.

Roscoe's eyes opened wide the very next moment, stunned at what he'd just done. I couldn't say I blamed him. I stunned myself a little too. I was no lesser Nephilim, but some of the goat beast's powers clearly remained in its instrument. Only, that ill feeling augmented me.

Controlling something else, that was a game for beings more powerful than I. It was wrong. I knew it was wrong and I hated doing it. But it had worked.

Resisting the overwhelming bleakness, I raised my Peacemaker, using my forearm to balance the barrel, and fired. At the same time, Mutt recovered fast enough to bite the werewolf's ankle. Roscoe lurched in pain, so instead of a kill shot, I blew a hole right through his roaring mouth. Blood and smoke spewed from his torn cheek. He flew back, scrambling to a stop just before joining his brother in a tumble down the ridge.

"I'll kill you, hunter," he growled. The words were muddled and confused sounding. "I promise you that. I'll eat your damn bloody heart!" By the end of his threats, he was shouting because he'd fled out of sight and vanished into the veil of fog.

"Good luck finding it!" I called back, knowing he wouldn't hear me. I'd be damned if he was getting the last word.

I turned to Mutt. "You all right, friend?"

He whined but nodded his scruffy head. Seeing him okay made me feel a bit better about crossing a line I didn't particularly care to cross.

"Is he . . . was that . . . I . . ." Dale tripped over his words, and I'll be honest, I'd almost entirely forgotten he was there. His jaw hung slack as his mouth struggled to make sense of things. I crammed the cursed harmonica away, a cool sense of relief washing over me once it was out of sight, and strode toward him.

"Mr. Crowley, w-what were those things? I-I followed you here. Thought maybe you knew something to get the bounty, I . . ."

"Hey, Dale, you see that?" I asked, pointing to the right.

He quickly looked that way, and the moment he did, I bashed him in the back of the skull, knocking him out cold. He'd be fine . . . ish. Seeing unnatural events like he'd just witnessed does things to a man's brain. Best cure I've found is to jumble them up, tell them they banged their head and they were just seeing things.

"Sweet dreams," I said, patting him on the shoulder. Then I grabbed his fallen steed and hefted the heavy animal off his leg. Mutt joined in and gave me a little extra pull to get it done. When I stopped, I realized he was in his human form.

"Thanks," I said, falling back onto my rump for just a second's respite before Shar started bugging me to hustle. I gestured toward the dead werewolf nearby. "Guess that one makes us even, huh, kid?"

"Even," Mutt said softly.

"Even Steven."

His head tilted. "Who is Steven?"

"Nobody." I chuckled. "You'll tell Mukwooru it was me now, won't you? Get me in her good graces for the next time I come calling?"

He nodded.

"I knew I liked you. I'll take the fool with me. Keep him in the dark . . ." I paused. "I might not mention Dale to your people if I were you, considering what he saw."

"I won't lie," he said flatly.

"Leaving out certain details ain't lying, per se."

He didn't respond.

"Suit yourself." I pressed an elbow against the horse's corpse and used it to stand.

I extended my hand to Mutt. He eyed it for a few seconds, then gripped just the tips of my fingers. Shaking hands wasn't a custom his tribe was awfully familiar with, it seemed. Living in safety and seclusion here, half their time spent as dogs with paws, it made sense. But I wasn't about to lick him or sniff his ass.

"Good luck in your people's war, kid," I said.

"Good luck in yours, Black Badge."

One side of his lips lifted into the most awkward smile I'd ever seen. Another relic of spending so much time outside his human body.

What strange acquaintances I've got these days . . .

THIRTEEN

Revelation Springs was a place I occasionally stopped in my travels from one demonic bounty to another. A way station of sorts, in a dry, arid, rocky region where humans couldn't live if not for the few natural springs dotting the area. Stunning rings of color banded the warm, crystalline waters, conjuring up a sense of peace within my soul. That wouldn't last, so I just tried to enjoy it while I could.

A geyser to my left shot off, spraying water across a field of pock-marked rock and sending lizards and whatever else might've been hiding nearby skittering away.

"What the—"

Evidently, it woke up the guest slumped over behind me on Timperina's back, too. Dale sprung awake. He nearly took a tumble, but I caught him by the belt and pulled him upright.

"Morning, sunshine," I said.

Dale stammered some more and I couldn't really blame him, knowing his last memory of consciousness.

"You took a nice knock on the head, fighting off them wolves," I said. "Lucky I showed up when I did, you damned fool."

"Wolves . . . ?" It was sort of a question. Dale stretched around me, eyes wide with fright. "Them things weren't just wolves. They was standing, talking—"

"Damn, how hard did you fall?"

He opened his mouth to speak, but no words came out. Then he rubbed the back of his head, right where I'd whacked him. He winced at the touch.

"I guess pretty hard . . ." He glanced around. Then, under his breath, he added, "Wolves . . ."

I hate lying to anyone, but ignorance is more than bliss when faced with certain supernatural truths.

"Where are we?" Dale asked a moment later.

"Coming up on Revelation," I said. "Now, considering I didn't have time to ride you back to Elkhart, I suppose we should talk about how you abandoned your post to follow me without asking."

He had no rejoinder, just a pitiful, "I need that bounty, Mr. Crowley."

"You and I both know this ain't about a bounty."

I listened to him sigh, long and mournful.

"Yeah, well, I'd like to stop 'em from hurting any more people," Dale said. "Sheriff Daniels was a good man. He didn't deserve . . ." I heard his jaw grinding. "I truly don't know if I was the one who shot him or not, Mr. Crowley, but I think—"

I saw enough in Sheriff Daniels's Divining to know Dale was slinging lead in a panic, trying desperately to stay alive and maybe hit one of the Frozen Trio. I wish I could ease his mind a bit. Maybe just a vague reassurance.

"Accidents happen when bullets start flying."

"Yeah, but Sheriff Daniels should still be alive. If I'd only been—"

"What? Prepared for your first shootout?" I laughed. I was only guessing it was his first, but he didn't argue. Was easy enough for me to tell. "I got news for you, Deputy. Few ever are."

"I bet you were."

I smiled. He wasn't wrong about that.

Fourteen years old and some wisecracker took a swipe at me in the saloon after I'd said one too many words to his girl. I wasn't even being fresh, just thought she looked interesting enough to hold my attention. Well, he dragged me outside for a duel. I didn't even have a gun, but he was so confident, he loaned me his extra. I put a bullet through his kneecap before he even had his barrel clear. Never walked right again.

That was when I got a taste for the rougher side of life on the frontier. What can I say? Ain't every day in a boy's life he finds out what he's good at.

"Nah," I lied, sparing Dale unnecessary heartbreak. "My legs wobbled like a newborn calf. My palms were so sweaty, I barely kept a grip on my piece."

"He deserved better than he got," Dale said, referring to the sheriff again.

"Well, if retribution's your goal, I'll choose to forgive you following me without asking," I responded tersely. "The truth is, come Hell or high water, I'm gonna take this Frozen Trio down. You plan on helping, you'll get your cut, and maybe, just maybe, you'll find whatever else you need."

I knew he was after forgiveness, and I've read all the balderdash about forgiving being divine and how it ain't my job to seek vengeance, but it's a whole lot easier to forgive others than to forgive yourself. No God or higher being can help with it. You either find that path on your own, or it eats away at you until you die, old and crotchety.

Revenge wouldn't help neither; I knew that. Dale could put a bullet into the whole Trio, and he'd wake up with that same pit in his gut. But dammit, if it didn't feel good nonetheless, watching as the bastards who made you feel like shit—like less than shit—suffer and breathe their last.

"I'll do whatever I can to help you," Dale promised. I knew he meant it. Not the smartest fella; however, he'd been honest enough since we met.

"Good. I can't seem to get rid of you anyway."

I gave Timp's sides a light kick as we rounded a large spring nestled into rainbow-painted rock like a fancy bowl. Then, Revelation Springs came into view in all her glory—a haven in the middle of nowhere much like Mutt's, only this one bore no green and wasn't trying to hide.

A crisscrossing of buildings popped up, some three or four stories tall. The stone and rocks were so red you wouldn't know how much blood had been spilled on them.

It'd been a while since I'd been here, and the town had grown. Probably call it a city now, at least for the West. All things are relative. A train puffed up smoke as it pulled out of the station just on the outskirts. A legitimate station, too. Good for them. A couple hundred people were milling around, carrying umbrellas and luggage. Coming or going, I don't know, but it was something.

When I spotted red-and-white-striped tents being set up along the western side in a clearing extending from the church, I remembered they were probably coming. Little stands and what looked from here to be goats and cattle and little midget ponies. A proper carnival was happening soon, based on fliers I'd seen throughout the region recently, with all the fixings and plenty of visitors milling about to take part in the coming festivities.

What perfect timing.

"You'd think Dufaux would call all this off?" I said. "What with all the violence in the region."

"*The Founders' Day Fair*? No way," Dale said. "People train in from far away for this. My daddy used to take me. Had to ride up on our carriage. Which wasn't much. Lost more than a few wheels, them days. But he was good at fixing. Oh, and there's a stand that sells the best—"

"I didn't ask."

He *harrumphed* a response.

If there was one good thing about a festival coming to town, it was the crowds. Nobody looked at me funny, worrying I was the law or something worse. In fact, no one cared at all.

Though, of course, that was a double-edged sword. It meant the outlaws could slip into this place just as easy. The Trio had made a habit of rolling into towns, going straight to the bank, and hitting it. Though that wouldn't be possible in a place this size. Crowds also meant more innocent people who could get caught in the crossfire.

"Pooey," Dale whisper-shouted. He ducked down and tucked his head to my left. "That's Sheriff Culpepper and his crew from Elkhart. He sees me, I'm dead."

Just as he said, a crew of armed men loitered outside the stables. Their leader, this Sheriff Culpepper, looked more like an outlaw than I ever had—wearing black, head to toe, Stetson to stirrups. His posse, likewise, was the typical bunch of farmers and ranch hands in need of a few bucks and some excitement. Rarely did they consider that going off on a dandy like this one might leave their ladies without husbands and their children daddyless.

I wouldn't have been laughing after my hometown got sacked, but there they were, sharing jokes and spitting up wads of tobacco.

"I'm sure they've completely forgotten about you," I said.

"Am I that forgettable?"

I couldn't tell if Dale was kidding or not.

"They got a hard-on for a bounty is all," I said.

Dale laughed nervously. "Right . . ."

We passed them down Revelation's main avenue, and after we were clear of their eyes, Dale sat back at attention.

Busy was an understatement. Hell, if I told someone Revelation Springs was just busy, it could've almost been considered a lie.

As you can imagine, there was a saloon right at the start of the main avenue, and it was packed as saddlebags. Out front, patrons chatted up corset-wearing courtesans while they sipped on drinks that would've cost a buck less last week. The Gold Mine Hotel had a line from the front desk, out the door, and then some. Seemed to me, this *Founders' Day Fair* was a big deal even if I'd never heard of it. Such revelry was never really my scene.

"Picklefinger's it is," I said to Timperina, patting her side. A town this big had more than one saloon, and Picklefinger's was the cheapest around.

My guess is even they wouldn't have room enough for both me and Dale, but we'd try that before resolving to slumming it in the wild. As much of a dump as Picklefinger's might've been, it also had a clear view of the bank across the square.

"What?" Dale asked.

I ignored him and kept pushing deeper into town. All roads converged on the big central square set around a bubbling spring with mineral bands inside that had the appearance of gold strips. A small geyser in its center shot off every hour or so. Tourists loved the thing, sometimes getting too close to the hot water and scalding themselves. It was no accident the city's physician had his clinic around the corner.

Carts filled the square, farmers selling produce and meat to take advantage of visitors. I saw some things I once enjoyed and wished my having been revived from death hadn't stolen most of my senses. I always loved those crisp, red apples in all their glory, candied and sweet. No utensils needed, no cooking. Just scoop it up and take a bite of joy. Nowadays, it wouldn't be the same.

Simple things got a simple appeal.

A big cloth banner that read *Founders' Day Fair* was strung across the street from the top of the Town Hall on one side to the Miner's Guild on the other. Local deputies stood at every nearby corner.

Picklefinger's Saloon was right next to the guild. It was quaint. That's a word people use when they don't wanna say it's a grimy, dilapidated shithole. I was sure it wouldn't be around much longer before Revelation Springs's new blood decided to make improvements.

"All right, Dale," I said, stopping Timp. "This is where I leave you."

"I thought you wanted my help?" he answered, sounding awful whiny.

"I want you to hang around here and keep a lookout for anything suspicious. You've seen our outlaws—"

"Barely."

"More than most. So, keep an eye out, and if you see anything dubious, anyone walking into that bank who looks like they're after more than their own savings, you fire that pistol of yours three times into the sky."

"Three."

"Yep. One after the other."

"Don't you think that might draw attention?" he said.

"That's the point. My attention, the law's attention . . . Plus, it'll clear the square of innocents."

"Right. And how about you?"

"I'm gonna go pay our friend Mr. Dufaux a visit and see what he knows about that bird symbol and if he's lost his mind not canceling this fest."

Dale tittered. "Are you insane? You think you can just waltz right into Mr. Dufaux's house? He'll have guards everywhere."

"I'll knock."

Dale swung his leg and hopped down from Timperina to the square. He smiled. "You've already been buried once, Mr. Crowley. I sure would hate to see this one take."

"Ain't a grave I've seen that can hold me for long." I moved to trot ahead when Dale's features darkened. He grabbed onto Timp's saddle. She threw her head. He was more than a little lucky he didn't get kicked considering how temperamental she could be.

"Thank you. Seriously," he said, withdrawing his hand. "For everything."

I tipped my hat.

Timp turned her head and snorted, giving him another fright.

"Oh, Mr. Crowley?" Dale said, grabbing my leg this time.

I stopped and peered down in way of a response. He removed his hat and shuffled dirt with his boot.

"Spit it out," I said.

"It's just . . . I ain't got much money."

"That all?" I laughed. "Go inside. Talk to the barman. Goes by Picklefinger. Can't miss him. Tell him you're with me. He knows I'm good for it."

He nodded. "Picklefinger . . . right." He stood there for another moment.

"Can I go now?"

He smiled. "Right. Thank you again, Mr. Crowley. I won't let you regret it."

With that, he scampered off toward the saloon muttering

"Picklefinger" over and over like it wasn't plastered all over the damn building.

"We'll see about that," I said as I continued on around the square. From all directions, farmers constantly hollered about their produce. A couple of . . . actors, I reckon you'd call them . . . were putting on a show, using the gallows as a stage. Judging by the performers' costumes, from frontier garb to native feather-crests, I guessed they were reenacting the events of the founding of Revelation Springs. The gathered crowd was small, but occasionally, someone tossed a penny in their tin can.

The festival wouldn't start in earnest until tomorrow if the dates painted on the aforementioned banner could be believed—but these sorts of events tended to linger on for a week or more in some cases. Whatever it took to drive interest, get more bodies into shops and buying things for more than they ought to be sold for. And people called my Scuttlers criminals.

There were rich folk amidst the throng, women in puffy dresses and men sporting monocles and gold time-tellers. They all fanned themselves from the hot sun, and who do you think sold them said fans?

What a damn hoax.

I eyed Revelation's bank, standing on the far west side of the square. It was a big old building with fluted columns outside and a massive arched doorway large enough to fit that goat-Neph and more. Dufaux Bank and Trust was carved into the stone cornice. Thing looked like a Grecian temple, all pristine white. Dufaux spared no expense. Why would he?

Two Pinkertons were stationed right outside. Deputies carried bags of what I assumed to be money inside from a stagecoach parked out front. Seemed odd to me, moving cash at a time like this. You'd think Dufaux would keep everything locked up tighter than Heaven's gates.

One of the Pinkertons giving orders noticed me and stared. He was one of the three I'd found tied up, though not the leader. I didn't spot my rifle on any of them, though you better believe I looked. He'd been chatting with the local sheriff before I distracted him.

I lowered my Stetson in salute and continued by, surveying what I could of the square. Even the Yeti and his crew would have a bitch of a time hitting this bank and getting away with it. Surrounded by other buildings on the sides and back, the only way in was through the front doors—two big wooden monstrosities, twice the height of the guards out front and ornately carved. Each one of those must've cost more than most men make in a year. The vault inside was sure to be absolutely top-of-the-line.

Smart outlaws would hit their main target first, as not to alarm anyone. If robbing Dufaux's monetary sanctuary in Revelation Springs and getting the score of a lifetime was indeed their goal, starting small made no sense. Then again, these were no ordinary outlaws.

Leaving the main square and crossing through the rest of the city, there wasn't a single damn shop not overflowing with people tossing money around like cards. Finally, I found myself in what might've been considered the outskirts. It'd only been a few years since I'd been back, but damn, had they built this place up since. Out here was more like I'd remembered it, shanties dotting the ridge of a large quarry, some even with tattered cloth strung up for shelter. A poor place filled with poor people.

I'd guess Mr. Dufaux and whichever other men the plural word "founders" referred to wouldn't mind if this area got tossed up in the next twister. Grime and red dust coated the faces of men, women, and children, so it was hard to tell where most of them were from—though many had distinctively native features. And they watched me go by with cold glares, likely envious that I got to sit so high on the rump of a horse, shaded by a big old hat.

Beyond their homes was a vast quarry, and farther past that, miles in the distance, a warren of sharp, striated rock formations painted all variations of red, with one that almost looked like a falcon's wing, feathers and all, sticking up sideways.

The quarry itself was dug deep and filled with various switchbacks and terraces carved around colorful hot springs, as well as tightly constructed wooden scaffolding. Must've cost a fortune to get so much wood out here where there were no trees, but when a mine is filled with gold . . . well, you get the picture.

Out here in the West, a settlement doesn't pop up for no reason. Either it's got water, or riches, or in the case of Revelation Springs, both. Made for quite a little hub of activity out in the middle of nowhere. And all these impoverished people had the luxury of digging and sloshing to harvest gold.

I'm no man of science or learning, but I had to hypothesize that the heat of the water had quite the effect on the minerals. Made for some dangerous conditions as well. And I doubt a baron like this Mr. Dufaux made up for it with high pay. Men like him gave the bare minimum and hoarded the rest.

As I continued northwest up the road, I spotted his villa, proud on a mesa with views over both his mines and Revelation Springs itself, and I could practically see him standing by his window like a lord, lording like lords do.

There was well-to-do, then there was rich, then there was something else entirely. Dufaux fell into the lattermost category. I'd seen the estate before, though only from afar. Never had much reason to meet with Revelation Springs's de facto leader until now.

The road skirted the fairgrounds. It was roped off to the public, but from there, I could see all the many things one would expect from a traveling carnival. A tent marked Freak Show was prominent, as well as a shooting range, games of chance, and a big old stage. I passed the church and started up a long incline right to Dufaux's front gate.

The mansion was two tall stories, with a double portico at the front bearing columns similar to the bank. Only difference was that these were wrapped in a band of scintillating gold at the bottoms. Two buildings born from the same mind. One that liked to say, "Look at me. Look at me."

I've visited manors and plantations of countless types, but this was close to a fortress. Mid-height walls surrounded the place except on the backside, where there was a steep drop into the deepest portion of the quarry. The more cynical side of me imagined the master of the house tossing people through a back window when they forgot to add cream to his tea.

It didn't take an eagle eye to spot the gunmen on the homestead's balcony, with more behind some of the windows. And as I got closer, I counted even more patrolling the property. Perfectly manicured bushes formed patterns within, pinpricked with flowering trees. All florae not meant to grow in this region, organized around two shallow, diamond-shaped pools.

In a place filled with natural springs, Reginald Dufaux had built his own.

I stopped at the gate, noticing that the spikes on top were gilded—as if anyone who decided to try and climb over would prefer being impaled by gold over iron.

No sooner than I stopped, a gun cocked and aimed through the bars. "State your business."

I peeked through at a clean-shaved dark-skinned man.

God Almighty, if I could just catch a break. You'd think working for Heaven would help, but no . . .

FOURTEEN

I knew the man holding the gun—the very same leader of the Pinkerton crew from outside Elkhart.

He wore a bowler hat this time, casting shadows over the hard features of his face and making the light play funny over the jagged scar running up his left cheek. And now that he was all dressed in fine leathers, half hiding a bandolier and at least four six-shooters, he cut a more intimidating figure than when his business was flapping in the wind for all to see.

"You," he said. "They told me you died."

"Who's they?" I replied.

He took a puff of a cigarette and blew a large cloud. "Wrong, apparently. You here after the bounty like everybody else?"

"Just traveling through. Heard there was a party."

The Pink rolled his eyes.

"Saw your crew down by the bank," I said. "Is this really the time to be transferring more money here?"

"Boss's orders. Had us empty every vault he's got left in the region and bring it all to Revelation. Those bastards try to hit another sorry town, they'll find only dust. Even left notes for 'em."

"Fine strategy," I said. "Now they only gotta hit here. Wanna set a table for them, too?"

The Pink snorted. "Let 'em. Between the bounty dogs, Dufaux's men, and mine, there's enough gunpowder in Revelation to blow the whole place sky-high."

His eye flitted toward a wagon inside the property. It was mostly filled with tables and chairs, but the parts of a shiny new Gatling gun sat underneath it all, just itching to be mounted up.

"Let's hope it don't come to that," I said. I hopped down from Timp's back, watching close as the man trained his weapon on me. "If we're gonna keep on meeting like this, you got a name, or should I keep thinking of you as the Naked-Pink-Who-Ain't-Pink?"

"Why not?" he said. "I've been thinking about you as Asshole-Who-Left-Us-Naked-on-a-Cliff."

I laughed and extended my hand through the bars.

"James Crowley," I told him.

"Cecil, Cecil Jackson." He spun his pistol left, right, up, down, made a big show of it as he lowered it into his holster. I could tell, now that he was all dressed up, that Cecil Jackson was a man who'd killed before. Now, I wondered if he took joy in it. Must be a certain kind of man attracted to the life of a hired gun.

He merely stared at my hand. I hated that kind of bravado, like shaking my hand was some exhausting task. I reeled it in, realizing he was just that guy.

"Now, I'll ask again, what do you want?" he asked. "This here's private property."

"I need to speak with Mr. Dufaux."

"You and everybody else. He ain't taking uninvited guests right now. He's busy preparing the house. So why don't you head back down, enjoy the festivities and spend a little green."

He turned to walk away. Another part of his little show.

"You know, I wish I could. But I ain't in the mood for games."

He stopped like I knew he would, turned back, and said, "Do whatever you like. Just not here."

"You wanna be the one to tell your boss you turned away a man who knows secrets about the outlaws who've been hitting his banks?" I reached into my satchel and Cecil's fingers wrapped the grip of his gun.

"Relax, friend," I said, pulling out the Frozen Trio bounty. I pressed the drawn-on side against the bars so he'd see the symbol.

"Nice doodle," he said. "Don't quit your job. Now, get."

He started to turn again.

"That bird symbol was branded on one of their backs," I said. "It's called a 'Piasa' or . . . something."

"You got a fucking point?"

"A friend told me Mr. Dufaux might know more about it."

Cecil huffed, then snagged the drawing. While taking a long pull on his cigarette, he studied it closer. Then, without a word, he started off across the yard toward the mansion, drawing in hand.

"Awful polite, huh, girl?" I said to Timp.

She snorted.

"Ain't a wise man who turns away salvation!" I called out to Cecil, but he was nearly inside by then.

I waited a short while longer, unsure if he'd return. A cloud drifted over the hot sun and made all the mansion's gilded parts a whole lot less sparkly.

Then came a whistle. A couple of goons emerged from somewhere behind the wall, unlocked the gate, and dragged it open. These, for sure, weren't Pinks. Locals hired to defend Dufaux's little fiefdom. Ruffians and inbred swine.

One, face the color of Timp's hide, held a rifle not quite pointed at me. He waved it, and I walked Timp inside by the reins. We were escorted down a white stone path, joined on the other side by another gunman. We passed between the garden pools, fountains in their centers. Each one was carved like a bird, wings outstretched. I thought about that drawing and figured it mustn't be coincidental.

Other guards in the main house, or the stables and outhouses to the side, watched me too. Workers, all looking like they came from that poor part of town, were busy unloading party supplies.

A tanned boy with so much dark hair I couldn't see his face jogged up and took Timperina's reins. Bad idea.

"I got her," I said, but it was too late. She pitched a fit until I stepped between her and him and eased her with a hush.

"You should know better than that," I said to the kid.

The boy looked concerned, but when I stepped aside and gave her a hearty pat, Timp let him lead her away.

"She likes apples and could use a good brush," I advised.

The goons then walked me up the front porch, right to a pair of doors that seemed more fitting for a president than a glorified prospector on the frontier, but I digress.

Cecil waited for me inside, tapping his foot, cigarette hanging from his lips.

"Mr. Dufaux wants to see you," he said, a little dab of spit flipping out over his lip.

"Gathered as much," I said.

"And we'll *gather* from you."

He clutched the grips of both of my pistols and gave them a tug. I grimaced but let him and the others take all my armaments. This, he certainly seemed to take joy in. Stripping me of my effects, just like I'd found him.

Nothing draws ire from a proud man more than shame. I wasn't happy about losing my guns—never was—but what could these mortal thugs do against me anyway? I wasn't looking for a fight.

"You won't find a rifle on me," I said. "*Apparently*, someone took it off me in Elkhart. Know anything about that?"

"You think I keep track of every bit of iron I see?" Cecil asked. "Guns are guns."

"You strike me as a man who knows that ain't true."

"Yeah, well, if you lost yours, that's on you. Buy another."

I bit back the words I wanted to say. He missed the knife in my boot. Fool.

As soon as he figured I was suitably deprived of deadly force, Cecil led me inside Dufaux's grand entry hall. And grand it was.

If you were to think of the stereotypical rich man's home, you wouldn't be too far off. A gold and diamond chandelier hung in the lofty foyer with a split, curved staircase wide enough for two horses to climb side by side. And wouldn't you guess it, an oil painting of Dufaux presided over all of it. No wife, children, or anything like you'd often see in paintings like it. Just him, hands folded over a walking stick.

No smile. No warmth. No family. A hard man for a hard environment.

Only a few steps in, a native housekeeper took my coat to hang up. I didn't even have a chance to ask.

"I . . . Thank you—"

She said nothing in return, but her eyes spoke volumes, like no one ever spoke to her.

"Let's go," Cecil said, guiding me around the staircase to a corridor on the left.

We passed a body-length mirror and all I saw in it was me. I don't know if I was hoping to see Shar or not, but her absence told me I was moving in the right direction. I think. I felt a shove—hadn't noticed I'd stopped—and just like that, we were alongside a beautiful courtyard.

Pillars had vines hugging them like spiderwebs, weaving up through crisscrossed trellises. Workers milled about here too, setting up tables amidst yet more plant life that had no business thriving in these parts. All of it was perfectly organized along crossing newly mulched paths. And there, right in the center, was the same symbol I'd been chasing.

It was a small totem of sorts sitting upon a pedestal, the open-winged bird proudly positioned at the top. But now, seeing it from this vantage, it wasn't just a bird. Its wings looked sinewy, like some mythical dragon, two little spikes on the tip of each. It had what appeared to be horns or antlers, and, unlike any bird I've ever seen, had long, sharp teeth. The pedestal itself was adorned with zigzagging lines of gold, giving the impression of lightning striking the tier beneath it. The style seemed authentic, nothing like Dufaux's ostentatious mansion. Nothing he'd designed.

Dale wasn't lying. The Piasa was here in Dufaux's garden for any visitor to see.

We stopped at a pair of closed doors on the western side of the courtyard.

"Sit," Cecil ordered, pointing to a suede-upholstered bench.

"I'll stand," I replied. They'd already taken my guns, but I'd hold on to my dignity.

"You'll do what you're damn told—"

The doors swung open, and out stormed a chubby little man in a single-breasted suit. His golden mustache curled neatly at the ends like little pigtails.

He stopped, face cherry red, looked back into the room, and pointed. "You've got some nerve, Reginald!" He barked. "These outlaws are a scourge. You jeopardize the town! They could be anywhere. We should be postponing the festival until they're brought to justice."

Smart man, whoever this was.

"Founders' Day will go on, as it always has," came an answer, rich in timbre. That authoritative, convincing voice could only belong to Dufaux. You don't get a house like this one without some of those qualities.

"You went behind my back!" Chubby shouted back.

"I own your back, Mr. Mayor. Now, put on a smile, dance, and show this town that there is nothing to fret about. Just a slight hiccup."

"You . . ." The mayor clenched his jaw and fists, then pointed again. This time, no words came. Instead, he tore his hat off his balding head, smacked it against the wall in frustration, and stormed across the courtyard. Didn't even notice I was there.

Well, that about settled who was really in charge around here. As if anyone was confused.

"Well, come in already," Dufaux called. "I don't have all day."

I beat my escort to the punch and stepped through the threshold first. I'd expected an office of some kind. Instead, I was looking at a dining room. A mahogany table with the look of old-world Italy, carvings of grapes down the legs—fine craftsmanship—stretched the length of it. China that looked so fine it might've actually been from the Orient was set like he was expecting guests.

Dufaux sat at the far end, enjoying a plump, juicy steak. A wine glass was half-full of red, with another native-looking domestic standing behind him holding a carafe, ready to refill.

Come to think of it, the stable hand was probably native, too. And nearly all the houseworkers I'd seen roaming by. Important? I don't know, but Mr. Dufaux clearly had a type and I wasn't keen on thinking he was being generous.

He was a surprisingly large man, though he wasn't obese per se. Just big. Looked like he could've been a wrestler if he'd wanted, and he certainly could crush the skull of the scrawny helper behind him. I'd place him around sixty years old.

There were many odd traits about him, but the first thing I noticed was how he chewed. It wasn't dignified, which meant he didn't come from noble stock. He chomped down like a rat, like this was his last meal, savoring every morsel rather than making a show of it. Juice streamed through the stubble on his chin, and he was in no rush to wipe it up.

Was that important too? Again, I wasn't sure. Though, men who come from little and make a lot treat losing their riches a bit different from those who've never known what it is to have nothing.

"Expecting guests?" I asked.

Dufaux wrinkled his brow in what I thought could've been a smile but his eyes remained on his dish. He swallowed his bite, then snapped his fingers.

"You awake, boy? Get our guest a glass."

The boyservant at his back shook his head as if waking from a daydream. Probably of owning a house like this for himself.

I lifted my hand. "Thank you kindly, Mr. Dufaux, but I'll pass. The stuff goes right through me." I wasn't exaggerating. Liquor of all kinds is a waste on me. Sure, I could taste it somewhat, like food, but it had none of the effects men desire from such a vice.

"Suit yourself." He snatched his own glass and downed the rest. The moment it *clacked* back down on the table, his boyservant started refilling it. The young man's hand trembled as he focused intently upon not spilling a drop.

Dufaux smacked his lips. Then, with an asparagus stalk in hand, he pointed and said, "Take a seat."

I obliged, finding a chair opposite him with a sea of space between us. I had to lean to the side just to see him around a centerpiece of vibrant, fresh flowers. And they weren't the local variety either.

Cecil waited against the wall by the exit. He made sure his vest was stretched open and flaunting a whole lot of iron. He blew smoke from his cigar.

"Cecil here says you saw something peculiar on one of the outlaws," Dufaux began.

"I did."

"Well?" Dufaux went back for another piece of steak, and I felt like reminding him that not making eye contact while talking was rude. Even Ace Ryker made a man meet him eye to eye. But Dufaux, not once yet. He might as well have been talking to a fly.

"Well, first, I heard the leader talk about you by name," I started. "Has me thinking this ain't purely a spree. That they're specifically interested in what *you* own."

"Them and everyone else from here to south of the border."

"I reckon you should be more concerned."

His fork screeched across the bottom of his plate. That finally got him to glare at me. "You've been through town, haven't you?" he asked. "If they come for *my* bank, it'll be their funeral."

"Not like you aren't sending out invitations, consolidating all your wealth in one place. It's a taunt."

Dufaux bent forward, looking ready to scold me. Then he squinted, licked his lips, and sat back.

"He's the roughrider who showed up in Elkhart, isn't he?" he asked Cecil.

"Sure is," Cecil said. "Showed up just as it got hit. Put on quite an act. Now he's here, ready for the festival. A man who looks like a marshal but swears he ain't. Might make another man suspect he's in on the robberies."

I laughed. "Maybe you missed the part where I shot a couple of them while you and your boys were stripped like soft newborn babes."

"You son of a—" He lunged at me.

"Cecil," Dufaux said sternly.

Cecil grunted but backed off immediately.

"Got your dogs trained good," I said. "I'll give you that much."

Dufaux ignored the comment, though I could hear Cecil fuming behind me.

"Are you an outlaw, Mr.—"

"Crowley," I finished for him. "And not for a long while."

"And not a marshal either . . . right. Well, I heard you gave this Frozen Trio hell in Elkhart. Even managed to wrestle back the lockbox full of cash that's funding the bounty on them. One Cecil here *lost*." He spat the last word with venom.

Cecil approached the table now, cheeks losing their color. "We got ambushed—"

"Shut your damn mouth!" Dufaux slammed his fist on the table hard enough to knock his glass over. Wine oozed across the table and onto the polished wood floor. The native boyservant immediately knelt to clean it. Dufaux waved him away like a biting fly.

"Leave it! And you." He pointed at Cecil, shirt-cuff stained red. "Don't I pay you enough *not* to get ambushed? So why is this stranger getting your job done for you?"

"Like I said, I think he's working with them," Cecil argued.

So this was Cecil's plan? Scapegoat me to get back in his employer's good graces.

"Now hold on a minute," I said.

"You here scouting?" Cecil said to me. "Those outlaws pay you off? Get you to fake your death in Elkhart so you could sneak in here?"

"Right. That's why I cut you free then?"

I noticed Dufaux snicker just a bit while we argued.

"You tell me," Cecil growled.

Dufaux pushed out his chair with a screech loud enough to shut us both up. Then he stood and paced around the table. I'd underestimated just how large he was earlier. Maybe he wasn't Yeti-sized, but the floor rumbled with his every thunderous step. His exquisite outfit—a

mustard yellow waistcoat embellished with some kind of arrow pat-
tern—stretched tight across his midsection as if no tailor could quite
custom an outfit to fit.

"That it?" he said to me. "Did you come here wanting payment for
chasing them out of Elkhart? Trying to steal the money directly out of
my pockets, too?" He dug out some coins and let them trickle through
his fingers onto the floor.

"I'm just here to claim that bounty," I half lied. I didn't care about
it, but if I got my work done, I'd certainly earn it and put it to good use.

Dufaux stopped, placed his two giant hands on the table, and
stooped over. For the first time since we'd met, he looked me straight
in the eyes. His were hazel, mostly brown with flecks of gold. Fitting.

I couldn't itch outside my angel's nagging or a Nephilim getting
too close, but sitting there silently while he sized me up . . . it made me
want to. For once, I think I'd rather have been conversing with Shar.

Finally, Dufaux sucked in through his teeth. "You aren't with them,"
he decided, just like that. "But if all you came here to tell me is that
they might be after me, then I'm afraid Cecil here just wasted my valuable time."

Cecil shrunk back. For all his bluster and guns—and I could tell—
he was afraid of Dufaux. Or maybe just afraid of losing a well-paying
gig. Either way, fear is fear.

"You didn't show him the drawing?" I asked Cecil.

"What drawing?" Dufaux said.

Cecil stuttered. "I didn't think—"

"Goddammit, I don't pay you to think either! Show me."

Cecil's dark eyes shot bullets my way as he pulled the crumpled
drawing from one of his back pockets and tried to smooth it. Dufaux
practically broke Cecil's fingers when he grabbed it and spread it flat
against the table.

His brow furrowed. "What is this?"

"A mark, branded onto the back of one of the outlaws," I said.

Dufaux scrutinized the drawing for a few long seconds. It was hard
to place the emotions crossing his features. And, now that'd I'd seen

the totem in the courtyard, I realized just how poor my sketching skills were. However, Dufaux recognized it, that was for certain. And there was something else. Something I'd just seen on Cecil's face and awfully mortal. Was that fear, too?

"On his back, you say?" Dufaux asked.

"Shoulder blade to shoulder blade," I said. "I showed some folks and heard you had something like it displayed here. Figured you might know what it means, and maybe I could get a leg up on these bastards."

"Well, I don't know how it'll help you, but those were the markings of the Piasa Tribe," he said, sighing.

Try as he might, the boyservant couldn't help himself. A sense of wonder stole over him at the mention of his apparent people, and he leaned forward to see the drawing, breathing down Dufaux's neck.

"That was on his back?" he said, addressing me, I think.

"This doesn't concern you, boy," Dufaux snapped. "Out! Now!"

He quickly pocketed the drawing. To someone else, that action might have seemed mundane, but I was sure he kept it on purpose.

The boyservant stumbled but obeyed, practically running from the room.

I hesitated a minute, trying to understand Dufaux's emotions. He sat back down and continued eating.

"Tribe?" I asked, finally.

"You aren't from around here, are you?"

I shook my head.

"They were small. Used to inhabit this region. A strong, proud people. These, here, around me." He pointed where the boy had been standing as if he'd already forgotten he'd dismissed him. "They are what's left. When I found this wondrous place of water and gold, I traded them the riches of our people: medicines, fine wine, faith, the luxuries . . ."

"And in exchange?" I barely had to ask.

"Their land, of course. To mine. To build my home. Don't look at me like that. Their chief, Apenimon, was a dear friend." Dufaux let his head hang. "Then, a plague wreaked havoc on these parts, you see.

Sickness like Hell itself had risen to punish them for worshipping their heathen bird god." He clenched his jaw and blinked slowly.

Was he acting, or genuinely sad?

"I was too late," he continued. "Apenimon. He was among the first to die, followed by many more before we discovered a cure. Mostly the young, healthy enough to fight infection, were spared. And as you see, I try to give them a life here."

"That's awful kind of you," I remarked, knowing it was smarter to butter him up at this point than say how I really felt. I thought about the boyservant. Some life for the kid, waiting on rich men and digging their gold. Though I will say, out here in the West, there are worse ways to live.

"It's the least I can do," he said.

I smiled and nodded.

"That totem in my garden; it belonged to them," Dufaux went on. "I keep it here in their honor. You see, it wasn't just I who brought salvation upon them. When I stumbled upon the springs, half-dead after getting lost in the hot sun, Apenimon rescued me. Fed me. Nursed me back to the man I am today . . . using my medicines, of course."

"Of course."

"I've long considered him the cofounder of this here town. And helping what's left of them is the least I can do, isn't it?"

He took a bite of steak. It seemed like he was being completely honest about everything until that last part. He certainly wasn't keeping the totem around to honor anybody. His house was full of trinkets and keepsakes, and that was just another one of them. It just happened to come with a sad story, give people something to talk about at his little soirees.

"You sure you saw that symbol on one of the Frozen Trio?" Cecil asked, bringing things back to the purpose of my visit.

"Silly name," Dufaux said under his breath.

I nodded. "I am."

Dufaux sighed and sat back. Just thinking about it all seemed to exhaust him.

"Perhaps someone blames you for what happened to the Piasa Tribe?" I said.

Cecil seemed like he was going to say something, but Dufaux raised a hand to silence him.

"It could be," Dufaux said. "I just wish I knew why. We broke bread together, worked together, made honest trades of medicines for land and food. Thanks to me, these lands of theirs thrive, and tomorrow's festival is as much for Apenimon as it is anyone."

"Time has a way of corrupting memory," I said. "Or maybe one of your workers felt wronged? Ran off and . . ."

"Are you accusing me of mistreating my employees?" Dufaux asked, pointedly.

"Now, now," I said. "Just sounds like you're playing a little loose on the details. We all get mad from time to time."

His glare settled me. I could tell I'd crossed a line, and men like him, who own enough land to start states of their own—they only allow themselves to be pushed so far.

Dufaux snapped his fingers, and I heard motion behind me.

"I do apologize I couldn't be more helpful, but I appreciate your resolve," he said. "You're the only man after this bounty who came by to speak with the man footing the bill. For that, you have my respect. Bring these outlaws to justice, and you'll have full enough pockets to settle down, buy a nice ranch, and take a pretty wife."

"I don't reckon I'm suited for family life," I said.

"And on that note, we agree. Life is too short to stress about other mouths to feed." He pulled his chair back in and flicked a napkin so he could finish eating. "Now, I bid you farewell. I must hurry. I have plans to attend to."

"Right, the fair." I stood and donned my hat. "I suppose me getting an invitation to your special dinner is out of the question? Seems anyone who's anyone will be there." Couldn't hurt to ask. The more access to Revelation I had, the better.

"You ain't anyone," Cecil said. I ignored him.

Dufaux smiled placatingly. "It's nothing a man of your . . . nature . . . would enjoy. Cecil will lead you out. Enjoy the festival, if you can."

"Oh, I plan to." I stood, tipped my hat, and started off. Cecil tried to grab my arm to lead me, but I shook free.

On the way out, Dufaux shouted, "And send the boy back. Is he just going to let that wine soak?"

I couldn't help but chuckle. There's a fine line between running a strict house and berating. Dufaux might've not even realize he'd pushed one of his former employees far enough to rebel. To want to hit him where it hurts.

That potentially explained the Mind-drifter's motive. But what about tomahawk-lady and the Yeti? Were they all people Dufaux had wronged over the years? One trip through his house, and I knew he was the type who made plenty of enemies on his way to the top. Even the town's mayor was no more than a patsy to him.

"What's so funny?" Cecil asked.

"Nothing at all," I said.

He nudged me hard in the back. I didn't feel it, only knew because I was propelled through the doorway, looking out upon the courtyard. And there was that totem again. Didn't seem like anything special, just an effigy.

"Mind if I get a closer look at the totem?" I asked.

"You've been here long enough."

"I'm sure your boss wouldn't mind. You heard him. He respects me."

"Respect and a bag of feed is worth a bag of feed." Cecil yanked me back into the corridor and kept me moving briskly toward the exit. The native maid handed me my coat on the way out. As she did, I noticed a decorative silver dish on a nearby table, not yet filled. I scooped it up fast, folding it within my duster so nobody would notice.

Dufaux had enough. He wouldn't miss it. But I needed more silver ammunition for my next meeting with the Yeti, and stuff like that couldn't be found in most shops. Even during a carnival.

"Horse!" Cecil shouted, giving me one last jostle out onto the porch. The mop-headed stable boy came running, Timp's reins in hand.

"Happy hunting, Mr. Crowley," Cecil said, giving me a wave.

"If I do catch them, you want me to strip them and tie them up for you or . . ." I turned back to face him as I said it, but by the time I got around, he was slamming the door shut. I guess I could've been kinder. His pride was wounded, same as mine would've been. Hell, same as it was. The Yeti had slowed me down worse than anyone had in a long time.

But it was good to light a fire under Cecil. I didn't know much, but I was certain that at some point soon, the Frozen Trio was gonna hit Revelation Springs with everything they had. All Dufaux's magnificent wealth was in one vault for them now.

A wily gambit for both sides. A lot can happen when you're asleep in a coffin for half a week.

Revelation Springs was a tinderbox.

FIFTEEN

Picklefinger's Saloon had been a part of Revelation Springs since the town was settled. It always looked run-down and disreputable. To most, it was a last resort. Where you went when you weren't in a hurry—for a drink or to grab a bite to eat, to wager more money than you should on parlor games, maybe pick a fight.

Apparently, however, it hadn't just been the Gold Mine Hotel that benefited from the *Founders' Day Fair*. Even from the outside, I could tell that it'd done wonders for old Picklefinger's patronage as well. Both the front porch and the balcony were nearly overflowing with sojourners from all over. Behind them, the whole facade was windows. A hand with one thick, green finger was painted on each, but I could still see inside through the glass fogged by sweaty men. Looked like standing room only.

Climbing the steps, I heard my name called from behind me.

"Dale," I said, turning.

"Might as well call me Jesus," he said.

"Excuse me?"

He laughed uncomfortably. "No room at this inn. You know, like . . . with Mary and Joseph and—"

"You ought to work on your jokes, friend."

He frowned. "Been running all over town, looking to get us a room or two since I've been told there's none here neither. Nothing at all unless you wanna sleep in a stable with your horse."

"Her *name* is Timperina, and it wouldn't be the first time," I said. "But c'mon, I'll talk to Picklefinger myself."

"Don't think it'll do no good. He said they're 'packed to the rafters.'"

"We'll see." I waved him on, and we entered.

Inside, it was like a zoo. Actually, it looked like a side show—of the carnival variety. Seemed the fine people at the other venues wanted to keep some of the riffraff clientele out. But hey, what better place for the Bearded Lady, the World's Strongest Man, and a half-pint dwarf than a place called Picklefinger's?

"Some place," Dale said. "But like I said—"

I didn't hear what he was reminding me of. Something felt . . . off. An itch in my chest, and it wasn't Shar. Instinctively, my hand moved a bit closer to my Peacemaker. It didn't take long for me to spot what had me on edge.

Turned out, anyone unlucky enough to be forced to spend the night here would be getting a private show. Leaping from the balcony to the chandelier and back again was the carnival's Beast Boy. I'd heard about him, but never seen him. Described as half-man, half-ape, though I knew better. Always suspected he might be a Nephilim, and now that I was seeing him in the flesh the first time? I knew I had to be right.

Call it a hunch. A sixth sense.

The strange, short guy had long body hair, coarse and matted, an unnatural shade of dark yellow.

It's rare, but not all Nephilim are inherently evil or desperate for power like that goat beast. At least not in my eyes, though I suspect the White Throne feels differently. Wicked by association and all that.

But some seem to forget their allegiances to Hell and just want to get along. This little guy is proof enough of that. He wasn't eating anyone or cutting deals for souls. Just did his thing, performing while his compadre—a colorful jester type—took up tips in a metal tin.

Chances are if I gave Shar the opportunity, she'd tell me to send him packing, so I wouldn't. But I'd keep one eye on him. If Lucifer did call upon the creature for a favor, somehow I doubted he'd refuse it. Call me a cynic.

I made my way to the bar and said, "The usual," to the barman who wasn't looking.

"Going to have to wait your turn," he said, eyes still focused elsewhere.

"You're gonna make an old friend wait?"

"Look, buddy—" he started, turning to face me. When he saw me, a giant, gap-toothed grin split his face.

"James Crowley!" He slapped the bar hard, his already wet hands splashing in something questionable. His pointer finger was totally black with frostbite, and in the dim lights—and it was always dim in here— almost looked a grungy sort of green. Hence his nickname. Joshua "Picklefinger" Hayes, the one and only.

He'd gotten frostbit while climbing some this or that mountain in the north. It was a whole heroic tale about saving a damsel, which I'd heard him tell every time I passed through town. My best guess was it was all hogwash, but he sure knew how to spin a fine story.

Joshua had run Picklefinger's ever since. These past years hadn't been overly kind to him. His now bald head was surrounded by a ring of bright red hair that fell to his shoulder blades, and I wasn't sure he could turn around back there without his belly clearing the shelves.

The man was built to eclipse the sun, and I told him as much.

"Not all of us can be immortal," he replied. "Seems like you haven't aged a day since we met."

He didn't know the truth of his words. This was one of the first places I'd stopped in after coming back from the dead. Woke up not too far away, actually. It's all thanks to Shar—giver of gifts and blessings. And yeah, minus some extra wear and tear from serving the White Throne, I looked exactly the same.

Not a new gray hair. Not a new wrinkle.

I puffed out my chest. "Amazing what whiskey and eating right can do for a man."

"I'd better fill you up then," Picklefinger said.

A sign of a good barman is when he can remember your drink. Pick-lefinger's the best of the best. Three years since the last time I'd darkened his doorway, stopping through town on my way out to the West Coast to deal with a gaggle of sprites, or was it fae? Truth is, they're both the bad sorts of Nephilim, and hard to tell the difference. Anyway, all those years passed, and he poured me three fingers of the high-shelf bourbon.

Funny thing, with his bulbous finger, that means he poured a little more than most.

"Here ya go, friend." Picklefinger offered it to me with the compli-mentary mini pickled cucumber everyone had come to expect. "What brings you to town? Don't tell me you're here for Founders' Day. You hate smiling and enjoying yourself if I recall."

I laughed, took a sip. "Look at this place! Why shouldn't I?"

"Nuh-uh. I don't believe it. Not you."

"Believe whatever you'd like." I reached back and patted Dale's shoul-der, dragging him just a step closer. "I think you met my friend, Dale?"

Picklefinger noticed him for the first time. "This ninny?" He laughed. "You really are full of surprises. Said he was with you. I asked him where the cuffs were."

"Now hold it there—" Dale started.

I squeezed his shoulder to shut him up.

"He says you couldn't spare us a room," I said.

Picklefinger's gaze narrowed. "This is for real? You're running with a deputy? *You?*"

"Thought it time to make an honest man of myself. Now, how about that room? I'm sure you've got something."

He leaned in. "I'm sorry, Crowley. Look around." He could barely hide his excitement at such a full house even while delivering the bad news. "There's just nothing left. Tell you what? I can telegraph the Rarebreed—it's just a few miles north of here in Yantsville. Quaint place. You'll love it. Don't even got a bank yet. Easy ride back in the morn."

"I've gotta stay here," I told him.

"Any other time, you know I'd help you out." A few patrons at the

other end of the bar were getting rowdy waiting for Picklefinger's attention. "Look, make yourself at home in the bar. But like I said, there're
just no beds."

He turned to tend to the folks, but I stopped him, kept my voice
low. A place like Picklefinger's would be crawling with travelers. Likely
many other bounty hunters who'd be happy to kill off competition if
they got a whiff that I, too, was after the Frozen Trio. Not to mention
any of these folks could be helping the outlaws. Could be them in here
even, all dressed up to hide. Maybe that's what's burning my chest, and
it wasn't Beast Boy after all.

"Say, Picklefinger. You get a lot of folks through here," I whispered.
"Any ideas who might want to get back at Mr. Dufaux for . . . something? Who might hold a grudge?"

"This about those robberies?" Unlike mine, his voice was normal
volume. So much for not blabbing.

"Just a curiosity."

He eyed me sidelong, but he didn't turn away. People in positions
like Picklefinger know that most times, it's best to say too little than
too much.

"Well, I'm not sure there's a man or woman within a hundred miles
who hasn't been rubbed wrong by the old baron here and there," he said.
"But you didn't hear that from me. This here is his land I rent. And his
city has built me a fine life."

"Hey! Ginger!" called one of the drunken, angry patrons.

"Names like that'll just get spit in your gin," Picklefinger barked
back over his shoulder. "All right, I—"

"Need to get back to work," I finished for him. "I'll leave you to it."

"Good to see you again, Crowley. And there's plenty of floor space
to pass out on if you drink too much."

At that, he left me to do his job. I lifted my cup of bourbon. My
chest hit the bar. Half my drink spilled out just before I could take a
sip. Someone had bumped me.

"Ten bucks, and I'll give you my room," slurred the culprit. I turned
to see a fella that was more beard than man. Judging by his hat and

his gun, he'd picked up a few bounties over the years. Had that look. He leaned on my back, one of his smoky blue eyes twitching slightly. "Sound like a deal?"

"Sounds like ten times the going rate," I told him, turning back to my drink.

Dale leaned in and whispered. "I got a few bucks I could chip in."

I glared at him. "Thought you said you were broke?"

His face went red. "Come on, Crowley. I don't—I don't wanna sleep in the dirt."

"Listen to your little friend," the Beard said. "Ten greenbacks, and the room is yours."

I heard an uproar from the other side of the saloon and watched as a man stood shouting and running from the room with a cloth sopped in red over his hand. Gave me an idea.

"Tell you what," I said to my new friend. "I'll play you for it. I win, I get your room."

"And if I win?" he said, skeptical.

"Twenty bucks."

"Stranger, you don't look like you've owned twenty bucks in your life. You're gonna have to show me the money first."

I leaned over to Dale. "Got that cash?" I usually had some, but another result of my burial in Elkhart—my pockets had been picked clean.

Dale stuttered a response. "I . . . that was when I was buying a room. Not . . . gambling."

"Don't be a baby. It ain't gambling if I can't lose."

"This is all I got in the world," Dale complained.

"And you'll still have it. C'mon. Piper's calling."

Dale rummaged around in his bag and retrieved a handful of crumpled-up banknotes.

"Ten bucks?" I whispered to him.

He looked sheepishly at me.

"This is only ten," the Beard said. "You said twenty."

I dug around in my satchel, looking for something worth enough to wager. I heard a clatter and looked down to find Dufaux's silver dish had fallen from my bag. Damn my feelingless hands. I bent, snatched it up, and shoved it away.

Beardy pointed to my bag. "Toss in the silver, and you've got a bet."

"That's worth a whole lot more than twenty bucks," I said.

"You want the room or what?"

"Mr. Crowley," Dale said, tugging on my arm. "Why don't we just give him the ten for the room?"

"Price went up," Beard said.

"We could find someplace else?" Dale whispered.

The bounty hunter leaned in close. I could smell the liquor on his breath. "You both too pansy?"

I looked around the room. A couple nosy patrons were watching us now that things were getting interesting. And I'll be honest, watching the bank from a room or sitting by the front window, it didn't really matter to me. But when you've been around as long as I have, sometimes, interesting tips the scales.

"Five-finger," I told him. "Last one to bleed wins it all. The room, cash, silver, and pride. What do you say, pal?"

A wicked grin racked his features, and I say racked because it looked like it hurt him to smile. And that smile told me his answer. While Dale whispered protests, I followed the bounty hunter to the spot from which the previous loser had just run. His blood covered a tree stump set between two wooden chairs that looked like they'd break if anyone bigger than Dale sat in one.

But we sat, and they didn't.

A small crowd gathered as it always does. One thing I've learned in my time, men out here live to gamble. And why wouldn't they? Surviving these parts is a gamble enough. What's one more?

Beard stood again for a second and raised his hands as if conducting an orchestra. Christ, he started singing.

> *I hear the drink calling, but I ain't got a dime*
> *The boys say a knife will help passin' the time*
> *So I sat down to play, taking bets on my aim*
> *What's started with five, I pray winds up the same*

I knew the song. There were five more verses, and I was glad he didn't sing them all, though he wasn't a terrible singer. When he was done, the man guffawed and sat back down, pulling a knife from wherever he was keeping it. The blade had hundreds of nicks. He spun it along his finger and handed me the hilt.

"Ladies first," he said, which stirred up some more laughter.

"You're gonna bleed, stranger," said one from somewhere behind me.

"Anton don't never lose!" shouted another.

"Mr. Crowley, I really don't think this is a good idea," Dale said.

I ignored him and grabbed the knife. "First blood?"

Anton nodded once. I know, it wasn't exactly fair considering only dust runs through my veins, but what's a guy to do?

I placed my hand palm-down on the stump.

The rules of the game were simple. Some called it the knife game, others five-finger fillet, and others still stabscotch. I called it dumb, even when I was living. You can have any number of players, really. Though, it's best mano a mano. The first player does like I did, places his hand facedown, and spreads his digits. Then, with the other hand, he grasps a knife. It can be any blade, as long as it'll cut when it hits.

I've seen kids playing with sticks, but they'll reach a certain age where that just won't fly anymore. The game is about having nerve.

I took a deep breath, faking anxiousness. I wanted Anton to think I was nervous. But I'd been doing this undead thing for a while now. Took me a bit, but I discovered all the things I'm good at. And it turns out, without fear of losing a finger, I was *really* good at this game.

I started off nice and slow, setting the pace. I cleared all eleven gaps—from thumb to pinky back to thumb—without a problem, then handed Anton the knife.

He did the same, never breaking eye contact with me. Show off.

I was tempted to try the same trick when I got the knife back, but instead, I just accelerated my stabbing and slammed the blade into the stump when I was done. Dale squealed from the *thud*, like his heart was getting ready to give out.

Leaning back, I watched Anton match my speed.

"Faster!" the crowd jeered.

Then a fella—teeth as yellow as the sun—hovering over Anton's left shoulder picked up the song again.

> *Won the first round of drinks when I finished intact*
> *Went straight to my head, my aim started to crack*
> *See, I started with five, but now I'm down to four*
> *We're all reckless and stupid but, hey! Pour me one more*

The crowd had gathered in by the end, their fervor seeming to energize Anton. He did as they asked, speeding up. I'll hand it to him, the guy was decent. When he was done, he flipped the blade with a flourish and stabbed it down right back in front of me.

"Let's go, moneybags," Anton taunted.

I spotted Picklefinger standing at the back of the gathered crowd. It seemed our little game had become more important than tending the bar. As a matter of fact, Beast Boy had stopped swinging, staring down at us from his perch on the light fixture above. The others from the carnival were watching, too.

> *What's one little finger when I've still got his friends*
> *The whiskey is strong, and my wounds they will mend*
> *I started with five, but now I'm down to three*
> *It's reckless and stupid but, hey! The drinks are all free*

Anton stood and joined them, sweeping his arms side to side like a maestro.

> *The barmaid was dancing and gave me a start*
> *The knife struck my hand, and it wasn't too sharp*
> *So I bit off the rest, and I gave the salute*
> *Yes, I started with five but hey! Now I'm down to two*

I raised the knife, and as I did, I caught a glimpse of a familiar smoky swirl in the blade's reflection.

"Stop this foolish game of the Children," Shar said. "You're drawing attention."

I disregarded her warning—a thing I'd become quite the pro at these days. With Beast Boy in the room, the itch in my chest was dull and constant anyway. Plus, Shar was wrong. Attention might be good at this point. Draw the Trio or any allies they might have out of hiding if they were amidst.

They knew my face after Elkhart. So let them come to *me* if they so pleased. I'm sturdy enough, and better I take their focus than all the innocent people of Revelation Springs.

"You're not bad," I said to Anton over the din. "But you're all flash."

With that, I placed my hand down, memorized where it was, and closed my eyes. Now Shar couldn't distract me.

> *The tale will be told from the slaves to the masters*
> *Like Arthur and all of his round-table bastards*
> *I'm getting faster and faster and drinking a ton*
> *Yeah, it's reckless and stupid, but hey! It's bloody good fun!*

I began stabbing, the crowd so inspired by my risk they *ooh*'d and *aah*'d with my every motion. Dale made sounds I wasn't even sure could come from a grown man. When I finished and stabbed the blade down, I opened my eyes again. The knife was swaying, metal humming.

No blood.

Though, I realized I'd messed up. There was a line across my left middle finger where, apparently, I'd sliced clean through it. Looked like a knuckle at first glance, but it wasn't. I quickly covered it with my other hand, hiding the lost fingertip within a fist.

"I'll be taking that room," I boasted.

"Think I didn't catch you peeking through eyelashes?" Anton said. "My turn." He grabbed a dishrag off the tray off a passing barmaid, then tied it over his eyes in a blindfold. He sang the first line, and the rest picked it up.

A man in the corner with a hook for a hand
Bet a hundred against me and struck up the band
The game will keep going cause I ain't no chump
I started with five, but hey! Now it's a stump!

Anton's fans cheered for him while he flawlessly went through the motions without being able to see, same as I had. I honestly wasn't sure how to up the ante next.

The whole bar practically joined in on the final refrain, singing it slow.

I started with five, but now I've got none
It's reckless and stupid, but hey! It's bloody good fun

Anton was moving now, but on his way back, he stabbed hard, and I spotted a dab of blood on his ring finger.

The whole place went quiet except for Dale whose "Ha!" echoed.

Anton had nicked himself. And while, technically, that meant he'd done better than me, I had no choice but to cheat. I had the White Throne's work to do here in Revelation.

Hearing the silence, he tore off the blindfold and gawked at the wound.

"Good match." I started to rise when one of his compadres pushed me back down.

"Not quite," Anton said. "I like to play a fair game."

"You agreed to first blood. That there's blood."

Anton sucked at his finger. "You gotta cover your eyes like me. I know you peeked."

I spun to see men gathered around me. Some cracked their knuckles. Others, their necks. What was certain was these men were hankering for a fight. Win or lose, I was pretty sure this was always gonna be the outcome. I always forget . . . maybe Shar knows some things.

See, I couldn't play another round. As soon as I uncovered my cloven finger, I'd be outed as a cheater. Which was maybe true, but "first blood" is an awfully specific set of rules.

"You calling me a cheater?" I asked.

"Or just a big scaredy-cat," he said.

"You got some nerve."

"Uh, Anton, sir," Dale interjected, meek as a kitten. "Mr. Crowley won, fair and square. We really do need a room."

I'm not sure he meant to, but leaning in caused him to flaunt the badge on his chest. I probably should've warned him to take it off.

"You think that means anything here?" Anton said, flicking the badge.

"Please, in the name of the law—"

A fist pistoned from Anton's buddy with the yellow teeth and cracked Dale across the jaw. Something about being in a busy saloon with a partner, surrounded by drunkards and loons, had me feeling like the old days before God saw to making me a tool. I couldn't help but throw down.

Shoving the tip of my finger in my pocket first, I lunged at Anton and repaid the debt by giving his jaw a wallop. I put so much force behind it, he flipped ass over tea kettle. He toppled over the back of his chair and cracked a floor plank where he landed. Sometimes, I don't know my own strength.

Dale sprung up quick, hopping on one of Anton's pal's backs and punching his ribs. Not the best technique, but the young, hapless deputy-turned-sheriff-turned-deputy-again was scrappy, that's for sure.

More fists came at me. I blocked with my forearms and swung back. Probably got hit from behind a few times without knowing it too. One thing led to another, and our little fight swelled across the whole saloon as more and more men got jostled.

Picklefinger was all "here, here," and "now, now," but nobody listened. There was a code of honor when it came to brawls like this. Nobody drew their guns. We weren't out to kill each other, just to prove a point. If a gun went off, it would be the barkeep shooting the floor to tell us enough was enough.

But old Picklefinger didn't do that. Complain as he might, a bar like his had a reputation to uphold. That was just the way of things.

Dale got caught in a throat lock. I picked up a chair and bashed his attacker across the spine. Then, I found myself being yanked backward. Anton had grabbed me and thrown me, but my elbow caught his ribs and cracked a bone.

Rising, I spotted Beast Boy, who'd now joined into the fray, howling as he swung down and kicked a man in the side of the head. So, he wasn't totally averse to some violent fun. His victim staggered, grabbing the Bearded Lady's whiskers to try and stay upright. That earned him an open-handed slap that knocked him right out.

"You damn cheater!" Anton growled. He speared me with his shoulder, and together, we slammed into the bar. Then he clawed at my throat. I managed to reverse the roles, him with his back against the bar, but he got a boot up and shoved me rearward.

All hell broke loose when I bumped into the World's Strongest Man.

The enormous, rippling heap of muscle spilled his drink all over. He slammed a fist the size of a cow head down on the corner of the bar, breaking off a chunk. Then he grabbed me by the collar and hefted me into the air.

"Let him down!" Dale hollered, running over and batting at the man's chest. Might as well have been a hug. Beast Boy noticed, hurrying to defend his performance partner. He drop-kicked Dale in the chest just as the Strong Man flung me. Seconds later, we were both hurled bodily through the side window, landing in the alley between the bar and the Miner's Guild.

Glass shattered, and we rolled out onto wet earth. A man and his lady who'd been doing God knows what in the alley screamed as they dodged us. The horses hitched up on the side whinnied and reared, pulling the hitching post loose. Together, all tied up, they took off. I took a hoof to the gut and one to the shoulder. Dale was luckier, in a sense. He'd landed right in the water trough where Timp remained the only horse still calmly drinking. Poor girl was used to this kind of activity.

He rose a little, but he didn't look like he had enough strength left to fling a pebble at a house rat. Beast Boy was clearly stronger than his stature implied.

I heard footsteps, and Anton strolled outside with his buddies. He blew out his nose, a clump of blood shooting to the dirt.

"These boys troubling you?" said another voice.

Just what I needed. Another newcomer to get in on the fight. Turning my head, the first thing I saw was a familiar hawk perched on the top of the Miner's Guild rooftop, facing the bank. Well, I saw two of it since I was so dizzy from the fall.

I blinked in disbelief, and when I opened my eyes again, it was gone. Either it had flown off or never had been there to begin with. A figment of my imagination.

Then spurs jingled. A pair of fine boots slapped down next to me, and I found myself staring at the sheriff of Revelation Springs, with a mustache so wide it crossed both cheeks. And not alone either. He was with a couple of deputies as well as Sheriff Culpepper of Elkhart, probably doing their rounds to ward off the outlaws.

"If cheating is a trouble, then yeah," Anton said, eyes wide and nodding.

Before I knew it, a bunch of men grabbed hold of me and pulled me to my feet. The world was spinning. Doesn't matter how immortal you are; getting your brain rattled and scrambled like eggs will confuse the best of us. A few more men got Dale, dragging his sopping wet self out of the trough since he could barely stand on his own.

"Seems like you fellas had too much to drink," the Revelation sheriff said, leaning in to get a better look at me. "You need a place to sleep it off."

"Not even a sip," I said.

Just then, Picklefinger arrived at the mouth of the alley, glowering down at me with his arms crossed over his belly.

"Tell them, Pickles," I said.

All he did was shake his head and head back inside. Guess I couldn't blame him. Shattered windows would cost a pretty penny.

"Don't know these men at all," Anton said, acting all flustered. "And one of them just clean swung at my friend for no reason, when all we're here to do is try and help end that damn Frozen Trio."

"That's a goddamn lie!" I argued.

I reached into my pocket.

"Hands where I can seem 'em!" the sheriff growled, but I wasn't looking for a weapon.

"Wait, I know him," Sheriff Culpepper said, pointing at Dale. Then he chuckled. "This is that squirrelly fella who rolled into Elkhart after the robbery, wanting to be deputized. You're supposed to be back there."

Dale's response was unintelligible, whether from shame or a swollen tongue.

"Deserting your post." Culpepper clicked his tongue. "That ain't right."

"Neither is vandalizing this fine establishment," the Revelation sheriff said. "I saw this one riding in."

"Just another crooked bounty hunter chasing riches," Anton added. "Gives us decent ones a bad name."

"Couple of Mr. Dufaux's Pinks said he was trouble," the Revelation sheriff said. "Clearly, they were right."

"Pinks get paid enough to be right about something," Culpepper chimed in, earning a laugh from everybody.

"Got a nice empty cell these two will be mighty comfortable in until they sober up." The Revelation sheriff bent down directly in my face and sneered. "Welcome to Revelation."

SIXTEEN

The rusty barred door of our cell shut with a tinny *clang*. The tittering of deputies echoed after they disappeared around the corner.

This was a substantially larger building than the one-room jail in Elkhart. The cells had their own wing. One of the others contained a snoring wayfarer, and I reckoned as the festival heated up, a few more would earn a stay.

My guns were taken, yet again. Belongings too. Including Shar's mirror. Always a silver lining if you look for it.

At least they didn't strip me down. I did get quite the kick out of watching one fool of a deputy rummaging through my stuff and getting all self-murdering when he handled the cursed harmonica. But just like in Elkhart, he mistook it for being gross and worthless and left it where it was.

Dale slumped against the stone wall. He'd regained his wits but seemed completely dejected over what had happened.

"I told you we'd get a room," I said. Didn't even get a smirk out of him. "What? It smells better than a stable. Jesus, Mary, and Joseph would've wished for something so pleasant."

"Why couldn't we just find another way?" he groaned. "Now they know I'm here. Culpepper's right. I deserted my post. I could be hanged."

"Oh, relax. Nobody's gonna hang you." I moved to sit next to him.
"You don't know that."

It's true. I didn't. The intricacies of the law are beyond me—which
they are to most, considering every godforsaken town out here has their
own made-up rules. Maybe it wouldn't be so bad for more feds to make
things consistent this far west.

Dale's chin dipped to his chest. Whether out of exhaustion or disappointment, I'm unsure. I'd wager both.

"Either way," he said, "now we ain't never gonna get that bounty."

I considered telling him about the hawk I'd seen, but decided against
it. He was agitated enough. Plus, I suppose it could've been a coincidence. The world has plenty of hawks in it after all. Still, a bird like that
out at night, making no noise, just staring at the bank as if it were the eyes
of the Mind-drifter. If the Frozen Trio wasn't here yet, they were close.

See Shar? If I hadn't caused a ruckus I never would've been thrown
outside and, maybe, seen the hawk.

"You think some flimsy metal bars are gonna keep us from divine
retribution?" I asked. "Not a chance."

"Divine." Dale scoffed. It was the first time I sensed cynicism in the
man. Getting the crap beat out of you can do that. "First you 'rise' from
the dead—then you play five-finger with your eyes closed like a maniac.
Get us locked up. I'm more thinking you're a devil, Mr. Crowley."

I nearly laughed. Matter of fact, I might've.

"Naw. I ain't no devil." I placed my hand upon his shoulder, only
remembering then that a chunk of my middle finger was missing. I
searched my pocket, finding it there and glad it hadn't rolled out into
the mud.

"All I know is something ain't right, and you ain't telling me,"
Dale said.

"I'm on your side, Dale. You're either gonna have to trust me or part
ways. Wasn't me who invited you, after all."

He didn't look up, just fixed a thousand-mile gaze on the floor. I'm
guessing this was his first time ever being on this side of the bars. Ador-
able. I was there to witness his right of passage into manhood.

"Sheriff Daniels always warned me I was too trusting," he whined.

"Be that as it may, it's better to trust wrongly than never to trust at all."

"I think that's love you're thinking of."

"Regardless . . ." I tapped the wall above us. "Look out there."

He didn't move. I gave him a slap.

"C'mon. Look."

He groaned and glanced up.

I nodded to the window.

Reluctantly, he stood and followed my urging to look out the barred slit of a window at the top of the cell. The room was half underground, but through that narrow opening was a street-level view of the town square and *Dufaux's Bank and Trust*. I could hear the geyser shoot off and splatter water onto stone.

"Well, I'll be," he said.

I smirked. "See, we ain't missing a thing. Plus, we get a roof over our heads. Timp's gonna be jealous when we get out."

"What if they hit the bank while we're locked in here?"

I swallowed. I hadn't quite thought of that yet. The key was on the on-duty deputy, completely out of sight in another room. Even if I dislocated my shoulder, I couldn't reach through bars that far.

One idea. I could tell the next important person I saw that I'd spotted the same hawk that was flying around with the Frozen Trio.

Sure . . . *Hey, mister, I saw a bird on the rooftop while you were arresting me. Pretty sure he's magic.*

I sighed.

It was the best idea I had, and it was a shit one. It would need to be good enough for the moment. Being honest, sitting there on what I imagined was a cold, stone floor—it was nice. I needed that brief respite. A quiet night. Maybe I'd even catch a snooze.

Worst case, the outlaws hit, and I could throw my body at the cell door with such reckless force I'd break it off its hinges. Might snap my neck doing it, but I'd just crack it right back into place.

"Don't worry about that," I said. "Let's just try and get some shut-eye."

Dale slid back down, closed his eyes, and leaned his head on the wall. Then he opened one eye. "How do you do that?"

"What?"

"Sleep. You know, after you . . ."

"Shoot a man?"

He winced. I breathed out through my teeth. Sheriff Daniels's fate was still eating away at him.

"Easy," I said. "You just do it, knowing that when your eyelids peel back, nothing can change what's come before."

"Right . . . Okay."

I nodded encouragingly, and he gave it a try. Maybe I really was going soft, caring about Dale's well-being. But wasn't that what God's hand was supposed to be about? Helping others?

"You laughing at me up there?" I whispered to the ceiling, hoping Shar heard me, wherever she was. "Yeah, I'm sure you are."

A light whistle in Dale's breathing told me he'd found his way to sand-land. With him asleep, I removed my finger from my pocket and pressed it back into position. It wasn't an immediate process, but this wasn't my first time losing an appendage. If I held it there firmly for some time, the skin would eventually mesh and heal itself.

If that worked for something bigger like a leg or my head—I wasn't yet sure.

While holding it in place, I did like I'd told Dale and shut my eyes. I may not get physically tired, but any man, living or dead, gets weary and worn down. Luckily, my benefactors left me with the ability to sleep to pass time. Never a deep, wholesome slumber, mind you. More like an afternoon siesta, always somewhat aware of my surroundings.

Presently, it was the fracas of a busy Revelation Springs night. All the fun I was missing out on. Drunken arguments and fights, dogs barking at stray cats. Dares to take a dip in the town square spring.

No gunshots, though . . . yet.

I didn't have visions of the day Ace killed me this time either. That was a relief. More often than not, that's what I'd get. Not sure why it couldn't ever be a nice romp with some pretty lady or a night of merriment with Big Davey after a score—God rest his soul. The thought of how he'd died dropped a fifty-pound weight in my gut . . .

"Hola. Hello. Is there anybody here I can speak with?" A Latina woman's voice cut through the darkness of slumber after who knows how long. At first, I thought it was a vision of some sort. But no. It was real life. "Excuse me?"

She was far off, probably poking her head through the station's front door. A loud knock got the deputy on guard duty to startle awake. He started to yell about being closed to the public, then his voice got soft and gentlemanly. I couldn't make out everything they were saying, but it sounded flirtatious.

Probably some lady of the night looking for an easy bit of cash from a bored man. I could only imagine how dull it got, sitting around guarding. Despite my last few days, bank robberies and jailbreaks were a pretty rare occurrence in a town like this.

I tried to listen closer just for some entertainment of my own. It seemed the harder I tried to hear, the louder the vagabond in the cell next to me snored. However, after a few minutes, the voices got quiet anyway. Did the lady take the deputy out back for some fun? God Almighty . . . I couldn't even recall what that sort of fun felt like. Lucky bastard.

Then I heard footsteps. Loud. From within the station.

By now, Dale was snoring like a freight train, too. I crawled along the floor to look out. My finger was back in place, mostly. Just a tad crooked.

I clasped the bars and peered through. Probably looked like a mad man. If I had a beating heart, it would have skipped when I saw who came walking around the corner.

A gorgeous Latina woman with dark hair, eyes as green as the Garden, and sparkling the same. Rosa Massey. She wore frontier clothes—a great departure from the last time I'd laid eyes on her in Dead Acre when she'd been dressed in funeral blacks. Rolled-up sleeves showed the snake-and-dagger tattoo on her left forearm. She even had a pistol holstered at her hip—a fine one at that. Looked like a regular outlaw queen.

And spinning on her slender finger was a key ring. Saints and elders, that smile. If in the Garden of Eden, Adam and Eve's weakness was a shiny red apple? Her smile was my apple. All at once beautiful, impish, and seductive.

I'd done Earth a service saving her back when she was a child. And then again, as an adult, last time we met a few months back in Dead Acre. And like the Almighty with that first man and woman, I was certain Shar wasn't happy about this turn of events. Or had she led us together again on purpose. To tempt me? Test me?

"Why, Mrs. Massey," I said. "As I live and breathe." I was too stunned to immediately recognize the irony of that particular phrase escaping my lips. "How?"

"Back at that saloon. I knew I recognized you," she said. "I was just entering when you started that fight."

Yet another benefit of me drawing attention to myself, apparently.

"Started it!" I protested playfully. "Lies."

"Well, you sure didn't finish it." She laughed at my expense. Anyone else did that, they might've earned a curse. With her? I just chuckled right along.

"Wait a . . . I—" I shook my head. "What are you doing here?"

"Saving you, it seems." She leaned against the bars and started testing keys. Taking her time, too. Like she was completely unconcerned about any lawmen stopping her.

The sound of scraping and clanking metal seemed to rouse Dale. I heard him yawn. "Who is . . ." He paused. I glanced back and saw his mouth agape at the sight of her. "That?"

"Our way out," I responded.

Wasn't what I planned, but Shar's always talking about following the path laid out before me. Somehow, someway that I won't question, Rosa Massey was right where I needed her. That probably said something more than I was willing to admit at the time.

Rosa found the right key and slid it deeper into the lock. I awaited the audible *click,* but she stopped.

With that heart-halting smile on her face, she said, "I let you out, it makes us even for Dead Acre."

"That's fine," I said. "But that doesn't make us even-even. I'm still up by one on my count. Or did you forget when I saved you and your momma way back when? Got myself shot to dea—" I caught myself. That Rosa. She untied my tongue and confused every part of me. I had to watch losing my wits around her. "Well, I got shot a lot."

"*Si. Eres mi salvador.*" Again with that smile. "So now I'll only owe you one."

"That's a deal." I stuck my hand out through the bars, and she shook it. If only I could've felt it.

"Wait, wait, wait. Who are you?" Dale said.

"This here is Rosa Massey," I answered.

"An old friend," she said at the same time.

"Oh, are we friends now?" I asked. "Do friends make friends cancel out favors before breaking them out of jail?"

"Good ones do." She smirked. "Do you want out or not?"

"By all means."

The lock clicked a couple times more, and then the rusty door swung open. The moment I stepped out, Rosa threw her arms around me. I didn't expect it, so I froze. Barely got my arms up to hug her back before she'd pulled away.

Sure, we had a history. Almost like we were fated to keep running into each other or something beyond my understanding. But there've been very few people in my life who would hug me. A man can only take so many years of loneliness before it wears on him. And I was growing weary.

"You coming?" she said to Dale.

He blinked, then looked at me, then blinked again.

"Well?" I said.

"If we break out early, we'll only get in more trouble," he said softly.

"What's more?" I said with a laugh. "We're already in jail."

"A better chance at hanging?"

I blew a raspberry and waved him off. "They only threw us in for the fun of it, Dale. Otherwise, they'd have left more than one guard. Shit, you're a deputy. You know how this works. Tomorrow morning they'll forget why we were even here and let us out anyway."

"Then why don't we just wait until morning?"

"He's a deputy?" Rosa asked.

"Not here." I ground my teeth. "Okay, fine, Dale. Maybe it wouldn't be that simple. But still."

"We damaged that saloon pretty good," he said.

"They don't give two shits about Picklefinger's windows or you ditching Elkhart. Hell, they probably put you at the post knowing that was the safest place in the damn region now that it'd already been hit."

As soon as I said it, I wished I could grab the words before they reached his ears.

"Oh," he muttered.

"Now, Dale. You know I didn't mean it like that."

"No, it's true. I . . ." His head and shoulders sagged. "Even still, failure that I am, I'm meant to uphold the law, not break it."

I felt bad for saying what I'd said, but I didn't have time to watch a grown man sulk. I liked Dale fine enough, but a crisis of identity was the last thing I needed to be dealing with.

"You want to stay? Stay," I said. "You can stare out that window at the bank as long as you want. But here." I tossed him the keys. "Anything happens, you use those, get your gun, and shoot three times like we talked about. Then you go get your revenge for what happened. Got it?"

He stared at the keys for a few seconds. Nodded. I didn't give him a chance to second guess things before I turned and headed away with Rosa. I won't lie, deep down, part of it may've been that I wanted some time alone with her to reconnect.

"How'd you get past him anyway?" I asked as we rounded the corner.

She didn't need to answer, because there, in the station's main room, I saw how. The deputy was collapsed forward onto his desk, fast asleep.

"Slipped something into his mouth," Rosa said.

I gazed at her. I was surprised, but also not. I honestly didn't really know that much about her besides that I enjoyed her company.

"Should I ask what?" I said. "Or how?"

"Do you want to?"

"Not really."

She smiled and leaned on what looked like the sheriff's desk. I'm pretty sure I got caught staring at the way the muscles on her forearm stretched, making her snake tattoo seem to wriggle.

"Your guns are over there," she said, snapping her fingers then pointing to a storage rack in the corner. "I recognized them."

"Got a good eye." I walked over to retrieve my armaments and supplies from the second law building in however many days. Things weren't going very smoothly for me lately. But all my effects seemed to be in order, even the silver plate. I took extra care to avoid staring into its reflection. Now wasn't a time I wanted to deal with Shar's . . . however she'd react.

And I didn't feel one bit bad about grabbing a spare rifle to replace mine.

Maybe these weren't the lawmen who took it, but fair was fair. And she was newer than mine had been too, though a Winchester all the same. No reason to change when you're already using the best.

When I turned around, Rosa was already holding the front door open and waiting for me. You know what they say, an open door is as good as an invitation. I was beginning to think there was more to this than just settling scores.

"You coming?" she goaded, her finger wagging me over like a serpent.

SEVENTEEN

The sky was reddening, one of those moments where the sun and moon were dancing a brilliant duet amongst the clouds. Rosa strode down the main avenue as if she hadn't just sprung me from jail, and I followed, leading Timp by the reins.

Couldn't just keep her tied up at Picklefinger's all night, could I?

"Good to see you again too, girl," Rosa said as Timperina nuzzled against her neck. Even *she* seemed to like Rosa. A rare feat, indeed.

Though, this clearly wasn't the same Rosa I'd seen months ago back in Dead Acre. At least I didn't think so. She displayed no fear of anyone punishing her for this wrongdoing. Then again, maybe having just lost her husband the way she had unlocked something in her. Or perhaps without a home life to care about, it revealed the woman's true colors.

I didn't know much about her, after all. Not really. Between saving her and her mom when she was a girl and seeing her again, many years had passed. Her mom had died of sickness, and Rosa was forced into adulthood far too early. Who knows what she was before she'd met her late husband, Willy Massey, and tried to settle down in Dead Acre. There might've been bounties posted for her all over south of the border for all I knew.

Could be that she had some evocative nickname like the outlaws

I was after. *Lady Serpent* or *Medusa* or something meant to keep children up at night.

My thoughts had me so enraptured that I'd barely realized how far we'd walked. Night fell in full. A small campfire blazed a short distance outside Revelation—nestled between two rocky hillocks west of town past the fairgrounds. It was a pinprick of light, growing evermore as we silently walked.

I tried not to think too much deeper about Rosa and what'd led her to carry iron like she was.

"We should be safe here," she said when we were close.

I snapped out of it and glanced up.

It was quiet, but in the wild, you can't mistake silence for safety. Still, so near to town and all the folk finishing setting up the festival, I had to guess this place was as safe as any other.

A stagecoach sat on one side, white tarp reflecting moonlight in an ethereal blur. It was in good shape, likely new or a rental from one of the bigger cities—the kind rich folks chartered when they wanted to make sure everyone knew how rich they were. However, even at such a distance, I could tell no one currently rooted by the flames appeared overly wealthy.

"Me and the others decided we'd rather stay outside of town," Rosa said. "When I spotted you, I was heading in to get a drink since my company abhors fun, and . . . Well, you know the rest."

I sniffed. "Smart. Smells less like shit out here—pardon my language, Mrs. Massey."

"I can handle it."

"Doesn't mean you should."

"Well, if nothing else, just call me Rosa. There is no Mrs. Massey anymore."

I frowned. "I know it hurts, but the bond of marriage lasts for life."

She stopped and glared at me, cross. "Have you ever been married, James?"

"No, ma'am. I can't say I have."

"Right. Then you can't know such things."

She wasn't wrong. I'd courted a lady or two back in the day, sure, but never anything serious. I was always too on the move. The nature of an outlaw's life. Though, as we neared the fire and that itchy sensation on my chest struck up, I couldn't help but feel that I sort of understood married life. Old Shar and I had the bickering part down at least, and it wasn't like she'd be any help milking the cows.

I took Rosa's arm, then let go almost as quickly. "I'm sorry, Rosa. I meant no offense."

"I know you didn't." She affected her best smile, circumstances not-withstanding. "Now, come. I'm sure you can stay in our camp unless you'd rather be any elsewhere."

Nowhere else in the world I'd rather be, was what I wanted to say. Instead, I remained quiet, bobbed my head all timid-like, and followed her into the campsite.

At once, three things happened that changed the whole mood.

Our feet snapped over dried-out twigs and leaves.

Timperina whinnied.

A gun cocked behind us. I didn't dare turn.

"It's me," Rosa warned.

"Not alone, it's not. Who's your friend?" questioned a man with messy hair the color of dirt. I couldn't quite place his accent, but it sounded like he was used to sipping tea and eating biscuits. He sat alone, sketching something in a journal with charcoal. A tobacco pipe hung from his lips, barely smoldering like he'd forgotten to keep it lit.

"James Crowley," I said and stuck out my hand. "A pleasure to make your acquaintance."

"Harker," the man answered. No first name. No smile. He didn't even stop drawing, his utensil quickly slashing a few harsh lines.

"He couldn't find anywhere to stay in town," Rosa said. "Do you mind if he stays here with us?"

"Long as he stays quiet," Harker said with all the charm of a bleeding blister. "He's working." The man gestured over his shoulder with the stub of his charcoal. Within the stagecoach, behind a pale pink curtain—or at least that's what it looked like in the moonlight—shadows cast by a lantern danced. Whoever was inside, his voice carried on the air, muttering under his breath, sounding frustrated.

"Of course," Rosa said. "I'm your guest."

"They're okay, Irish," Harker said calmly.

A woman appeared from the darkness only a few feet away from me. Didn't even hear her move. Her short hair, red as the burning fire itself, trickled down from beneath a black derby hat. She wore a long denim jacket down to her thighs that, in silhouette, might've been mistaken for a dress. Iron-buckled straps on the outside held a series of knives, varying in length from bottom to top. And as she holstered her pistol, I saw more knives strung to her coveralls.

"Christ's coming!" I blurted. "You move like a church mouse wearing slippers."

"What's the craic? Know how feck near I was to t'rowin knives? Who's the culchie?"

I stared at her, dumbfounded by her accent, as she strolled past us and grabbed a chunk of bread from a satchel I hadn't previously noticed.

"Irish, this is Mr. James Crowley," Rosa said.

"Crowley's fine," I said.

Irish took a big bite and spun a spit over the fire where a chicken roasted. "Welcome ta stay. Just don't act the feckin maggot, right?"

"Sure . . ." I nodded. Then I whispered, "Interesting friends," to Rosa.

"I wouldn't call us that just yet, would you, Harker?" Rosa asked.

The man grunted. Not really an answer one way or another, but whatever he was drawing seemed to be sucking all his attention. Rosa took a seat across the fire, as far from Harker as she could get, and patted the spot on the log beside her. I hitched up Timp with the other horses first.

Shar's tingle for my attention grew as I moved to join Rosa, but I didn't let it bother me. It made no sense. This wasn't like Agatha, drawing me off course. Not at all. From up where we were, I had clear sight of Revelation, bank and everything. I could even see the lanterns outside, illuminating it as brightly as the church steeple.

The grounds were all set for the *Founders' Day Fair*. Seeing it all empty, knowing there'd be hundreds milling around there tomorrow in search of escape from everyday life . . . That was something.

"What in the world are you doing here, Rosa?" I asked.

She shrugged. "It beats cramming in with everyone in overstuffed hotels."

"Not here, here. I mean Revelation."

"Same as everyone else. Heard about the festival. Needed a distraction."

I knew it was a fib because it was the same one I'd used on Cecil. Which begged the question, why lie to me?

"The way people talk about this little fiesta, it better be the greatest event ever held," I said.

"I doubt it," she replied. "I'm sure it'll be just like any other."

Harker groaned loud enough to make sure we heard it. Then he slapped his journal shut, picked up his chair, and carried it away. Rosa held her hand over her mouth to keep from laughing. He went as far as he could before losing sight of us, up the crest of one of the low hills where he could draw on his own in the light of the nearly full moon.

"He gets pretty serious with his art," Rosa said.

"Yeah? What's he working on?" I asked.

She shook her head. "Pretty private about it too."

Irish watched us from the fire like she was attending a play. She tore a chunk of flesh from the chicken, licked her fingers, then got to work on it, all without taking her eyes off us.

"So, are you planning to tell me why you're really here, Rosa?" I asked after a short silence.

"Why are you?" she retorted.

"I asked first."

She nudged me with her shoulder. "And a gentleman should answer first."

"You're trouble, you know that?" I chuckled. She didn't argue. "All right. Fine. I'm after a bounty. Some outlaws hitting up banks in the region."

"Well, if you're after them they won't last much longer."

"I hope that's true." I didn't add that if I didn't stop them, all of Revelation Springs might wind up frozen in an ice cube. Pesky details.

"Your turn. Why are you really here?" I asked.

Rosa lifted her chin. "Because I can be."

Most men might've thought she was withholding, but not me. I caught her meaning right away. That there was a harsh truth. No husband anymore, no expectations, she could go wherever she pleased. Do whatever she desired. Wherever the wind took her . . . so they say.

"What about the Massey ranch?" I asked.

"Not my ranch," she said. "Willy's father didn't need my help. Even if he never said so."

"I'm sure that ain't true. It's hard work, losing a son."

Rosa exhaled slowly as she nodded in agreement. She may've looked beautiful here under the moonlight, but it's the scars you can't see that hurt the most.

Moments passed. Irish still stared.

"Strange company you're keeping, though," I said again, getting the hint that a change in subject was necessary. "Where does a girl living in Dead Acre meet a crew from across the Atlantic."

"They found me, actually." She poked the fire with a stick, sending cinders dancing. Irish didn't even flinch, just kept eating and watching.

"Oh?"

"Their leader—" She pointed to the wagon. "—he claims he studies supernatural happenings. Said he was in Crescent City when he heard about the strange things that occurred in Dead Acre. He had questions."

My body tensed.

"Life would be unbearably dull if we had all the answers to all our questions," I said. "What'd you tell him?"

I didn't want her to know how concerned I was. I knew what happened when people who saw the kinds of things I dealt with started raving about it. They were thrown in padded cells. Ostracized from society as lunatics or even witches.

Others became like this companion of Rosa's: obsessed with proving what they'd seen was real—making it their life goal to reveal the supernatural for the whole world to see. As if that would help? Sometimes, it's better not to prod the hornets' nest lest you chase them all outside.

"What I understood," Rosa said.

Irish took another noisy bite.

"This entertaining you?" I snapped at the woman.

"Oi! Ain't gotta eat me head off."

"Just wouldn't mind a minute or two of privacy."

"Well, just feckin say so en." Irish tossed a chicken bone aside and grabbed another portion without a care in the world that she'd just knocked half the remaining carcass into the flames. Then, she made a rude gesture toward us and went and sat beside the horses. Timp nipped at her until she fed her a bite. Irish let her chew right off the bone before eating more herself.

"Just be careful," I told Rosa. "Like you said, there's a lot nobody will ever understand about what happened that night."

"I always am," Rosa said. "*Mi mamá* raised me that way."

"So that's it, huh? You really are just here for a bit of fun?"

"They were heading this way after Dead Acre, and they still had more questions. So I hopped along. Seemed like the right time to see the world—or at least more of it. I missed out on so much with Willy . . . not that I'd trade our time for anything," she quickly added.

"Don't worry, I understand."

I did. Didn't take me long in Dead Acre to realize that she and her late husband truly were close. Rosa had her own issues, no doubt caused by what happened with Ace as a child and then years on the run with just her mother until she passed.

Rosa drank. A lot. Desperate to drown out her many inner demons from what I could gather.

Of course, the man who'd killed her husband didn't think that. A necromancer, able to raise the dead to serve his will. He'd been hiding out as her bartender, and I guess after years of chatting, thought Rosa drank because she hated her husband and that she fancied him. So he took it upon himself to remove the obstacle keeping them apart. In this case, that obstacle was Mr. Willy Massey.

I did my part, stabbed him in the heart with a silver-dusted knife and banished the necromancer's soul to Hell for what he did. But that wouldn't strip her of the memory of those ugly skeletons literally rising from graves or of losing the man who'd tied her down, metaphorically speaking.

"The last time Willy and I were together—" she started before getting choked up. Tears welling in her eyes caught a shimmer of moonlight.

"You don't have to say," I said.

"No, I do." She took a few rapid breaths. "The last time we were together, we were fighting over him spending so much time at work. Don't mistake, I appreciated what Willy did, trying to make a better home for us, but we had a fine home already. All we needed and more. I just wish I'd had the chance to say goodbye, you know?"

"Better than most. But I'm sure that wherever he is, he's looking over you, Rosa. He'd be stupid to ever stop looking. And if he got you to marry him, I'm sure he ain't *that* stupid."

She smirked through the sheen of her tears. "He wasn't."

A few crickets serenaded us as another bout of silence passed. I didn't think it'd be this awkward, but I rarely spent time with people—especially not those I'd saved. It was better that way. They couldn't ask questions I couldn't answer, and I couldn't get attached. Still, fate kept throwing this woman at me, and goddamn it, I couldn't help but play catch.

"So, you carry a six-shooter now?" I asked, again desperate for a lighter note since our conversation somehow kept finding its way back to sorrows.

"Five-shooter," she corrected, drawing her Colt Paterson revolver from her holster.

I whistled, and the crickets stopped momentarily. Timp looked up, but I clicked my tongue, and she went back to begging for scraps.

"And a knife." She went to reach for her boot, but I grabbed her hand and shook my head.

"Never show anyone where you keep it," I said.

"Even you?"

"Even me."

I found myself staring directly into her eyes, transfixed. I knew I shouldn't, but she held my gaze there, and I could recognize the look on her face. Like she was small again. Like I was her hero.

"It's strange seeing you again without needing your help," she said.

"I prefer this way," I replied. "You seem to attract rotten men."

On cue, a man cried out, "Rosa, dear!"

Not saying whoever it was happened to be rotten, but the timing was almost comical. We both turned and saw her other companion— their leader as she'd called him—leaning out of the carriage. He didn't get out, just knocked on the wood.

"Rosa! I have a few more inquiries for you." He had an Irish brogue as well, though far more refined than his loony bodyguard, if that's what she was.

Rosa placed a hand on my knee, using the leverage to help her rise. "I'll be back."

I moved to follow her.

"Relax," she told me as she sauntered off toward the stagecoach. "He's harmless."

"Just a reflex."

Even in the face of a necromancer's black magic, Rosa had handled herself well. I just hoped she'd spare some details with whoever this stranger was. Not that it affected me. She hadn't seen what I could do. Not really. As far as Rosa knew, I was a man like any other. I merely happened to age gracefully.

She disappeared into the stagecoach, leaving me alone by the fire.

With time to myself, I set down my belongings. It seemed everybody had already eaten their fill of the chicken, and if they hadn't, Irish made sure they wouldn't have much of a chance. So, I moved the spit with my gloved hands. I snatched up one of their empty iron skillets and shoved it over the flame.

Pulling out the decorative silver dish I'd stolen from Dufaux's villa, I placed it inside the skillet. It would take a while and wasn't a perfect fit, but it would melt from the inside and fold itself into place.

Of course, I knew that until it was moldable and ready to be cast into bullets, that shiny, reflective surface would expose me to the wife I'd never chosen. I braced myself, knowing what was coming.

"What are you doing, Crowley?" Shar said, as expected. She appeared like an aura, swirling inside the silver.

"Oh, would you relax, Shar?" I said, quiet. "I know what I'm doing."

"Past experience proves otherwise."

She evinced within me a fury like no one else was capable of. I bet I did the same to her.

"I needed fire and a place to wait. So, what does it matter if it happens to belong to an old friend?"

"Friend?" Shar's cackle was like a knife against pewter. "Friend, you say? Rosa Massey is a lost soul, a child clinging to the familiar in hopes to revisit the past. She's not your friend, Crowley, any more than I am."

"Ouch."

"She's merely an adoring fan."

I harrumphed. "Can't I have one? The Almighty gets millions."

The fire went dark, and embers floated up in a puff of air.

"How dare you." It roared back to life with Shar's words.

"Oh, you know what I mean. Don't get your feathers in a bunch. You do have those, right? On your big old white wings?"

"You would blanch at the sight of me."

The fire crackled as a foot sprayed dirt over some of it. I glanced up, startled to find Irish had returned. She squinted, staring down at the silver, tilting her head from side to side.

"The feck's that?" she asked.

"Silver," I said.

"You hearin' that, though, oi?"

When I looked back, Shar's presence was gone. The silver was starting to bubble.

"All I hear is crickets and you," I said. "If you'll excuse me, I've got bullets to make."

Irish shook her head, cleaned out her ear by sticking a finger in, and walked away muttering unpleasantries. Pretty sure I saw her suck on that very same finger, too.

Weird lass.

I got to work setting up my mold. All Black Badges should have them, as well as a supply of gunpowder. It's a skill any gunman worth his salt has, making bullets.

A three-pound platter like this, melted down, could make enough bullets for me to turn that Yeti into a hunk of swiss cheese. And Shar was right about one thing. Taking down the possessed beast had to be priority numero uno. I had to be ready.

I'd only spent a few minutes working before I heard footsteps coming from the stagecoach.

"Excuse me," the leader of Rosa's entourage said.

I nearly dropped my tongs.

He stepped down from the coach and crossed the camp toward me. I was disappointed it wasn't Rosa.

The man wasn't much older than I'd been when I died, but little bits of gray peppered hair the color of wet hay. He was well-dressed, too, like he came from money or made a lot of it. Or hell, maybe he'd just saved up his whole life savings for a nice suit and that stagecoach.

"Was I too loud?" I asked.

"Not at all. Not at all," he said. "The lady just needed a few moments to herself."

"What'd you say to her?" My tone was more defensive than intended.

"Relax, friend. I only listened. But the truth can be . . . exhausting, can it not?"

"I find some truth can be relieving."

"I suppose that's a way to see it," he said. "Depends on the truths."

I leveled a glare his way. "She's fragile still. I know she may not look it, but what happened to her shouldn't happen to anybody."

His eyes glinted with wonder. He wasn't intimidated by me in the slightest. Nodding, he said, "And what *did* happen, exactly?"

"Now, now. I ain't your subject."

"Very well." He strode closer, examining my work, inquisitive gaze flitting this way and that. "Though, now that I'm out here, curiosity demands I inquire what it is you're doing."

"Just casting bullets."

The man scratched his chin. "Normally done out of lead, no? And that's, what, silver?"

Truth is, silver doesn't make the best bullets. It gets too hard. Shar had taught me some tricks—one of the few things she's ever been truly good for.

"Keen eye you've got, Mr. . . . What do I call you?"

"Oh, my humblest apologies. Abraham Stoker, but most just call me Bram." He stuck out his hand, and I removed my glove to give it a shake.

"James," I said. "But most call me Crowley."

"Not related to the Crowleys of Warwickshire, are you?"

"Not that I'm aware."

"Peculiar folks, them."

"I wouldn't know."

He joined me, cross-legged on the dirt. Sitting so close, the smoke from the fire gushed into his face. He didn't seem to care.

"So," he said, scooting closer, "why silver?"

Looking him dead in the eye, I cocked an eyebrow and whispered, "Kills monsters better."

I was just trying to have a bit of fun. His vacuous expression was unreadable, but something happened in me that I was very unused to . . . I grew uncomfortable.

Made me laugh nervously. "Just a bit of humor."

"Are you certain?" Bram asked, his own eyebrows knitting.

"Of?"

He held up a finger, then reached into his coat. When his hand returned, he held a small pocket-sized notebook. He turned away from the fire to look through his monocle and flipped through some pages.

"Can you read?" he asked.

I wasn't sure if I should be offended by the question, so I just nodded.

"Read this, then." He handed me the journal, marking a specific page with his thumb until he was certain I had it.

These creatures, Vampir, despise sunlight—no, they detest it to the point of death. Additionally, I have come to discover their vulnerability, a sort of allergic reaction to garlic and, most odd—silver.

There was a lot more, but I'd read enough.

"Fine story you're working on," I said, slipping my glove back on. "Never met a novelist before."

Bram's eyes squinted, serious as death. If he had to smile to put out a fire, the whole of Revelation would burn to the ground.

"That's just it, Mr. Crowley. I'm not writing fiction. I've traveled a long way, having spent many years researching and studying all across Europe. Now, the New World has been calling my name in the darkest hours of night."

"That so?" I asked.

"I've seen things . . . things most wouldn't believe. But I bet you would, wouldn't you? Just like our mutual acquaintance, Rosa."

"I suppose that depends on what kinds of *things* you're talking about." I plunked a fresh bullet into a water-filled container. As it sizzled, I leaned back a bit to ensure no silver bits steamed up into my face.

Bram prodded at the paper three times with a stubby finger.

"You're a hunter, aren't you?" he asked.

"Aren't we all when we're on the range and need to eat?" I replied.

"You know that's not what I mean." He plucked the bullet from the water. I knew it was still hot, but he handled it anyway and spun it around. "Silver isn't as effective against men or animals as iron. I'm not a fool, Mr. Crowley."

"Fine." I snatched the bullet back and leaned in close to him. "You want the truth?"

He nodded eagerly.

"It ain't that exciting," I said.

"Come on, then. Let's hear it."

"I'm with the festival."

Bram rolled his eyes, but I continued.

"I've heard the rumors, too. Same as you. Figured I could spin a tale about blood-sucking monsters down south, charge some rubes a pretty penny for some silver bullets, and be on my way a few bucks richer."

Bram rose without a word. He brushed off his pants and took one step toward the stagecoach. Then, he turned and looked back at me. "I don't know what you are, James Crowley, except one thing."

He paused, waiting for my response. I threw him a bone.

"And what's that?"

"A liar."

He was trying to be clever, but I could tell by his expression that it was feckless braggadocio. The man was disappointed. Probably spent every waking hour hunting for clues about the supernatural only to be shut down when he was sitting right beside the God's-honest real thing. I may not've been a vampire, but I'd taken on a brood of the vein-drainers before. More than once. I could fill a dozen of his little journals with tales.

"It's not only effective against vampires," I said to him. What can I say? Rosa had me feeling generous.

He turned only his head. "Excuse me."

"Silver. It's good against all sorts of wicked things."

Now his body turned too. "And practitioners of necromancy?"

"Don't get greedy."

Bram smirked. "You're the . . ." He opened his journal and flipped a few pages. After a moment, he said, ". . . 'black rider' who came to Rosa's aid, aren't you?" He then started writing as he spoke. "The one who faced down the Devil incarnate himself?"

"She didn't give you a name?" I asked.

I don't know why I was surprised. Rosa told me her mama raised her to be careful. I'd made the right move all those years ago choosing them over Ace. I was more sure of it now than ever.

"Never." He punctuated writing another sentence. "If you're ever willing, I'd be thrilled to discuss the experience with you. And any others. I can pay—"

I wagged a finger. "I said, don't get greedy."

He chuckled softly before turning about.

"Goodnight, Mr. Stoker," I said.

"Bram. And goodnight to you." Walking back to the coach, he called out to the hills. "Harker! Come down here. I have something I need you to sketch for me!"

When I looked down from Harker's perch, there was Rosa, emerging from the stagecoach. Her eyes looked puffy, but she tightened her jaw and tried to look strong. I waved her over.

"You okay?" I asked.

"Just tired," she lied, taking a seat. "Can we talk?"

"About?"

"Anything but dying husbands." She blotted her eyes with her sleeves. "Anything at all."

I finished another bullet then pushed myself back onto the log beside her. I looked around, making sure Bram, Harker, and most of all, Irish, weren't eavesdropping.

"You ever heard stories about Nephilim?" I asked, knowing, of course, she hadn't.

Then, I told her the tale of the goat beast and the two lovers. The true one, with all the gore and horrors. Though, the way I told it, she probably thought it was just a scary yarn men spin by campfires, but I guess I wanted her to know without saying that her husband's death could've been worse. Or, maybe, it was just nice to talk to someone about what I'd been up to since coming back to life without being constantly scolded like with Shar.

Rosa had already seen plenty and I feared she was about to see even more.

EIGHTEEN

Night passed. Eventually, Rosa conked out midconversation. Her head lulled against my shoulder, and I might've never moved if I hadn't needed to finish molding bullets. As such, I'd gently guided her into a more comfortable position, got her a blanket from one of Bram's horses' saddlebags, and proceeded to finish my work.

No rest came for me. That brief respite in the prison cell was all I seemed destined to get. Day crept up fast, and it was time to return to my duties. I told Timperina to stay in the camp where she'd be safe, and she whinnied her disapproval but didn't fight much more. She was always eager to seem adventurous, but I knew, deep down in that horsey heart of hers, she was happier moseying around, finding stray strands of grass to gnaw on.

Sun rose and we headed out. Bram and the others went on ahead, faster. He was keen on buying some artifact said to be on sale from some traveler or other. Something that would further his research into the supernatural. I didn't have the heart to tell him that when it came to American festivals . . . everything was a show. Trinkets and bibelots with grand stories were more likely to be items rummaged from someone's work shed than the real thing. Unlike that cursed harmonica in my belt pouch.

Rosa and I kept a more leisurely pace. Doing something so mortal as approaching the fairgrounds by her side almost had me forgetting about the Yeti, the Piasa, and Dufaux.

A grave error, perhaps.

One that I was sure to get an earful about from Shar the next chance she got. But it wasn't even high noon and surely not a wise time for folks to be robbing banks. Be that as it may, I had a job to do.

My eyes were peeled for three things. First, anyone who looked like they were up to no good. Just because I'd only seen three of the so-called Frozen Trio didn't mean it couldn't be a quartet.

Second, the Revelation sheriff and his men, who might not be too thrilled to see a man they'd thrown in the drunk tank out and about without them having turned the key. If they even remembered or cared, way they were acting, I had no doubt a few whiskeys or more were passed around last night. They should've all been posted around the bank anyhow, so it wasn't too large a concern yet.

Third, my eyes searched skyward. I swore I'd seen the Mind-drifter's hawk last night and fast motion in the sky confirmed it for me . . . momentarily. But alas, it was only a falcon entertaining some children at the command of a falconer. Considering its master was old as time itself, he wasn't the outlaw.

In my field, there was always the concern that a Black Badge would become so obsessed by the supernatural that he or she would start looking for devils behind every bush. I wasn't there yet, but closer than I probably would've liked to admit.

Another racket drew my attention. A train pulled into the Revelation Springs station, bringing even more travelers just in time for the commencement of the week's activities.

"Looks like fun," Rosa said.

The idea of fun had long since passed from my mind, but I had to agree. If I'd lived a different life, I might've found myself looking for a recreational diversion today instead of trying to save the world from demons—or at the very least Mr. Reginald Dufaux and this region's money.

We entered the fairgrounds proper to the smells of cooked meat, burnt sugar, and other scents. Those were the pleasant ones. Thing about festivals is the animals—and dare I say, the workers—involved bring their own stink. Strangely, smell's something I kept in my unlife. Guess they figured it didn't bring with it any true joy so why not throw the Black Badge a bone. Even still, just like my sense of taste, it's just a bit duller than it used to be.

Tall red-and-white-striped tents rose on each side of the avenue, leaving space between for cut-throughs. Colorful triangular flags made of cloth hung from freshly braided ropes as if suspended in midair, flapping with the light breeze. People were everywhere. I never was comfortable around a crowd. Maybe even less so now.

"Look at the size of him," Rosa marveled.

The scar on my chest tingled. The World's Strongest Man, Beast Boy, the Bearded Lady, and others I'd already encounter at Picklefinger's strode by. Beast Boy avoided my gaze in a way that seemed purposeful. The Strong Man gave me a distinct look that told me he hadn't forgotten our little kerfuffle last evening. I nodded, and so did he. No hard feelings.

They kept on by and entered one of the largest tents, the one labeled with a big sign that said FREAK SHOW. I couldn't believe anyone would subject themselves to that, no matter how odd they looked. Though I suppose making an honest living makes a fool of most, and better the Beast Boy drain wallets than souls. Still, I had half a mind to step up onto that stage, rip my own head off, and smile at all the mortals who took pleasure in watching such spectacles.

"Ladies and gentlemen, those from far and wide, on behalf of Revelation Springs and the founders, we welcome you to the twenty-third annual *Founders' Day Fair!*"

I heard the voice, evidently being amplified by means of a bullhorn, but couldn't see where it was coming from yet. As the speech continued, the speaker making jokes about this and that, Rosa and I picked up the pace. And by that, I mean her grabbing hold of my sleeve and pulling until I had no choice but to break into a light jog. We tried our best to follow the sound but didn't need to. The gathered crowd told us where to look.

The chubby little mayor I'd run into at Dufaux's came into view. He stood upon the church steps adjacent to a raised platform occupied by well-dressed musicians, the local sheriff, Cecil, and who appeared to be the town reverend. The mayor wore some of the choicest duds I'd seen on a man—a bloodred three-piece suit embroidered with gilded filigree, topped with a tall felt hat decorated the same. A timepiece hung by a gold chain from his pocket, and he wore a matching cravat or ascot. I honestly don't know the difference.

"It's been quite a year," he said. "Those of us who call Revelation our home are very proud of all we've managed to accomplish."

There was a polite clapping, scattered mostly.

"As the festivities commence, our very own founder would like to share a few of his own sentiments."

At those words, I thought I saw disgust cross the mayor's face. Based on how he'd been treated at Dufaux's villa, I figured I was probably right.

He stuck a hand out to his right. "My friend, Mr. Reginald Dufaux!"

Seldom has the word "friend" ever sounded so bereft of its meaning.

Still, the crowd cheered honestly. Even Rosa clapped mildly beside me.

As Reginald Dufaux climbed the steps, I swore I could see the steeple swaying from the heft of his staggering frame. Taking the bullhorn from the mayor with one hand, he retrieved a handkerchief with the other. Making no attempt to hide it, he wiped the mouth of the horn, then cleared his throat.

"Can we all keep this round of applause going for Mayor Stinson for how hard he's worked to keep our little town running so smoothly?" Dufaux said. "A better public servant, no man could ask for."

"Coming from a man who'd know a thing or two about servants," I murmured.

Rosa shushed me.

As the applause died, Dufaux made a show of looking around, standing on the tips of his toes to get a view of the city beyond the fairgrounds.

"No little town anymore, I suppose," Dufaux said. "No, Sirree. I defy any northerner to come down here and not be impressed."

Several in the congregation nodded and vocalized their agreement.

"When I founded Revelation Springs along with my dear friend, Chief Apenimon, the true father of these lands—may God forever rest his soul—I never dreamed she would become the thriving city she is today."

He lowered the bullhorn and raised a hand to his mouth as if stifling emotion.

"Good grief," I whispered.

"I say, look around you, folks," Dufaux went on. "Beyond the beauty of the springs themselves, gaze upon the city. Some of the finest craftsmanship and construction this side of the Atlantic. I echo Mr. Mayor's words: We are proud. Very damn proud."

Mayor Stinson now stood off to the side of the church steps, watching like the rest of us. There was no mistaking it, now; his face looked like he'd sucked a lemon dry.

"When I first discovered the land already occupied by Apenimon and his people," Dufaux said, "it was like God Himself shone the sun upon this very spot. As if I could hear His voice, much like I imagine Him to have sounded on the day John the Baptist baptized His One and Only."

"Better back up before the lightning strikes," I said.

"He seems sincere enough to me," Rosa said.

"The best liars always do."

"It was a grand epiphany," Dufaux said, "like the Lord revealed to me the very purpose of my existence. Hence the name, Revelation Springs."

He paused like he expected us all to praise his wit. No one did.

He cleared his throat.

"Little did I know that buried deep under these sacred grounds would be riches unknown. Veins of gold big as rivers, just waiting to be hauled up and used for God's glory and your gain."

Sure, he didn't. I was sure that bastard was every bit the crook I figured him to be. But that wasn't why I was here. The precise opposite, actually. My goals, like it or not, would lead to the preservation of his vast wealth.

Lucky me. Saints and elders, I hated the idea of keeping that man's coffers full. Or maybe it was just envy . . .

"Apenimon would have been proud, too," Dufaux said. He crossed himself and looked skyward for the briefest moment. "As I do each and every year, I hereby dedicate this *Founders' Day Fair* to his memory. And to all of you. Enjoy yourselves and God bless!"

At that imploration, he spread his arms wide and bowed. The crowd applauded. I felt like cheering that he'd finally shut up. The reverend crossed himself and stepped forward as if to speak, but was quickly blocked as the band struck up, playing a lively tune to which some danced. On the far side of the stage, a rail-thin man, shirtless and wearing what appeared to be a diaper, juggled torches with one hand while blowing fire into the air. Another, dressed in the same garb, shoved a sword down his throat. Excited children fled from parents who shouted for them to "stay together" while lovebirds walked hand in hand.

Rosa and I did no such thing. Instead, we continued along the main festival throughway toward town where I would leave Rosa behind to try and enjoy herself if she could, while I did what I had to do.

Being set up on the outskirts of Revelation, the grounds were mostly dirt and pebbles. No grass grew in these parts apart from the occasional sprig or six that clumped together, practically begging for water or shade.

The carnival crew had done a fine job clearing the field of cacti and boulders, but some were left behind and were being used as seats—the rocks, not the cacti.

As we strolled, we were accosted by a group of performers. They all wore garish costumes, the men with masks like demons or the Devil; the women, painted faces the likes of which I'd only heard of in the Orient. I'd never been there myself to know.

"Come, dance with us!" One of the ladies grabbed me by the lapel of my duster and pulled.

"No thanks," I said, but the woman didn't listen. She coiled around me like a snake, one hand moving up and down my body. The tips of her fingers on her other hand coaxed my chin, maintaining eye contact with me the whole time, save for when she was directly behind me.

For a moment, Rosa wore a wry smile, likely thinking there could be fun to be had at my expense. Then, her hand lashed out. When it did, the dancers stopped their gyrations, and I looked down to see Rosa gripping the wrist of one of the demon-faced men, hand halfway into my satchel.

Apparently, being numb to touch left me particularly susceptible to pickpockets. Not an issue I'd yet encountered since I rarely carry anything of value besides my guns. It was a lesson I'd have to remember.

"Try your thieving on another," Rosa said, shoving the man's hand aside.

The others, three of them, kicked backward in a choreographed move that put plenty of distance between us.

"We are no thieves!" proclaimed the woman who'd been dancing with me. She appraised her caught companion and affected an expression wrought with odium.

"Good dancer you might be, miss," I said. "But your acting skills could use some shoring up. Now, get on before we turn you in."

"That won't be necessary," said one of the other men.

They twirled and twisted away, weaving in and out from one another in the most hypnotizing of fashions. To my mind, they'd have plenty of luck picking pockets with all the visitors marveling at sights and trying whatever the snake oil salesmen threw at them. And there was one, legitimately, a short distance away, claiming his oil cured death.

"Some nerve," I said, starting to walk again.

"You have to eat to live," Rosa replied, as if that explained everything. It was, however, helpful insight into how she might've lived before she'd found Willy.

For the next few minutes, we passed everything one would expect from a traveling festival. Though it seemed Dufaux's influence had at least kept away some of the most blatant scammers and mountebanks. Not all of them, however. As it happened, we found ourselves passing a parked wagon at the end of the row, painted entirely purple but for the silver-flaked swirls and embellishments.

A sign out front read: MADAM ETHELINDA'S ETHEREAL EMPORIUM.

The broadside of the stagecoach, facing us, had a large window with silver curtains tied back. Couldn't see inside from our current angle. The front, where the horses would find themselves hitched, had a three-step staircase. It was lowered, if not inviting, leading to a half door like you'd see at a stable, also bearing silver curtains at the top with sparkling frills dangling along the bottom hem.

Each step had two wax candles burning—you guessed it, silver in color. They seemed to just be waiting to be knocked over by some rambunctious kid or drunkard. Paper lanterns were strung from the caravan's roof to a post cemented into a planter surrounded by some wooden folding chairs. Probably looked real pretty at night.

Rosa stopped to read the list of services posted. "Readings and Channelings. That sounds fun."

"Sounds like something," I said.

I was dead sure this Madam Ethelinda was no more than a keenly attentive charmer. Her sign had a red eye in one corner, a yellow hand in another. The bottom left bore the likeness of a crescent moon with a small star at its zenith, both blue, and across from that, a green feather or leaf. It was difficult to make out with the chipped and faded paint.

I glanced at Rosa, and she quickly adjusted her sleeve to conceal her tattoo. Wasn't sure why, but the woman had her right to privacy. She clearly didn't want to discuss it, and I was fine with that for the time being.

"Mind if we go in?" she asked.

"I really do need to get to town," I argued.

Her eyes rolled clear around her sockets. "It'll take a quarter-hour, if that. Are you truly that eager to get away from me?"

I smirked. "Desperate."

"It's settled then." She tugged me by the hand. I resisted. "Oh, c'mon. Just a bit of fun," she said, pulling again.

Then, a thought struck me.

"Wait . . . This is about Willy, ain't it?" My investigative tactics were crude, but even a dull blade would cut if applied firmly. "You ain't gonna get what you need from some hack at a traveling carnival."

Rosa let me go and stepped back. "And how would you know what I need?"

It was a fair question.

"Maybe I don't," I said, "but I'm confident this Madam Ethelinda won't be the one to provide it."

Rosa tapped her foot impatiently. "For your information, Madam Ethelinda is a world-renown clairvoyant."

Now it all clicked.

"So, *that's* why you're here, huh?" I said. "You think this woman can help you commune with Willy."

Her face reddened slightly and her nose crinkled. "Would that be so bad?"

I sighed. An answer didn't come to me. Sure, I understood. Closure and whatnot. A chance to say "I love you" one last time. To say "goodbye," perhaps even to apologize. And while there were legitimate clairvoyants out there who could communicate beyond our worldly plane, they were quite rare, and often dangerous Nephilim to boot.

I highly doubted this Ethelinda was the genuine thing. More likely, she was a peddler no different from the snake oil salesmen, preying on grieving widows like Rosa, using smoke and mirrors, games, and other baubles to evoke a sense of wonderment.

"James, when you've been through what I've been through, let me know if there's a better way," Rosa said, a harsh edge to her tone.

I bit my lip, then nodded. "You really think this is gonna ease your suffering?"

"I can hope."

"Me too."

"I'm just—"

"Scared to do it alone," I finished for her.

She smiled at me. It was somber and frail-looking, but it was a thank-you she wouldn't need to verbalize. Without another word, she started toward the steps.

I followed her a bit, then thought twice and softly grasped her arm, stopping her.

"You sure?" I asked. "I mean, really sure?"

"Yes."

"There's no going back if you crack open a gate to the other side."

"I said, I'm sure. Besides, you don't even believe in her."

I didn't respond. Truth was, whether or not Ethelinda was the real thing, even the grifters leave their clients viewing the world a little bit differently after a session. Oftentimes, belief itself is enough to do the job. If there's one thing I've learned being surrounded by angels it's that faith is a powerful thing.

"Now, you can either support me or go on into town," Rosa said. "Either way, I'm going in."

Now that was the Rosa I'd come to know. She stuck to her guns, and this was no different. I might not agree, but she had a right to pursue her passions as much as anybody.

I followed her again. In for a penny, in for a pound, I think the saying goes. For the first time since Elkhart when Shar and I came to a truce, I could sense my guardian angel's true indignation again. This wasn't merely a tingle, her trying to prod me back on the path. The mirror in my pocket seemed to buzz like angry hornets and the need to dig my fingernails into my scarred chest flared.

I ignored her for Rosa. How could I allow this grieving woman to delve into the den of a possible charlatan alone? To be taken advantage of. Exploited.

Dale was watching the bank for me. It was why I'd brought him along—well, it was why I suffered his having followed me without even so much as a warning. Fifteen minutes spared to help one of my few friends or acquaintances that wasn't a horse. That's all I needed. I'd face Shar's castigations afterward, same as I had so many times before.

Unlike the rest of the carnival, the fortune-teller had no long lines yet—no one waiting their turn to be told how grave the danger they're in or how the love of their life has golden locks. It was just me, Rosa, and the pungent smell of burning incense.

A head poked from the window, and I wondered how long the woman had been eavesdropping. Typical way for fakes to acquire tidbits about prospective clients before actually meeting them. I couldn't make out many of her features, shrouded in shadow as she was, but a ring, like a bull's, hung gleaming between nostrils on her bulbous nose.

"I've been expecting you," the woman I assumed to be Ethelinda said with an accent that might've been French, but a bit off. Like she was from the untamed isles south of the mainland.

"Sure," I answered.

Rosa gave me a hard look. "If you're going to make fun . . ."

"No. I'm sorry. I promise I'll be on my very best behavior."

We stood at the bottom of the stairs, looking up.

"After you," I told Rosa.

She took a tentative step up, and I wasn't far behind. We were careful to avoid knocking over a candle and starting a fire. When we reached the top, Ethelinda awaited us at the threshold. The lower portion of the door was open now, and the curtains were drawn.

"Now," Ethelinda said. "Which of you has come to seek my wisdom?"

I considered reminding her that she should know such things, but I kept quiet for Rosa's sake.

"I am," Rosa said.

"Please, please," Ethelinda said, waving us forward. "Come inside. Come, come. Don't be shy."

We did as she beckoned, and when we were fully indoors, I got my first proper look at the madam. If you told me this woman knew old Chris Columbus, I wouldn't argue. She wore so many wrinkles on her brown-toned skin, she'd give an elephant a run for its money. She was verily covered in tattoos, including several on her face and neck. However, the oddest one was the eyeball in the center of her forehead.

She must've seen me staring.

"It's the third eye," Ethelinda said. "Allows me to see clearly what others cannot."

"Huh. So, I get one of those, and I'll start predicting the future?" I knew I shouldn't have said it. Rosa became visibly irritated, but Ethelinda placed an ancient hand on her forearm.

"So, I take it you are not a believer, Mr. Crowley?" she asked.

Rosa gasped. "How did you know his name?"

Ethelinda tapped the eye on her forehead with her middle finger.

"Please," I said. "My name must've been shouted a dozen times at Picklefinger's last night. Those entertainers were staying there. I'm sure she was too."

Ethelinda kept quiet.

"I'm sorry about him. He doesn't believe," Rosa said.

"On the contrary," I said. "I believe a great number of things." *But this ain't one of them.*

Ethelinda stared at me with eyes so pale they bordered on pure white.

"May I?" she asked, raising two many-ringed hands, palm up in front of her. "On the house."

I returned her stare and smiled. "I'll pass."

She smiled faintly too but didn't lower her hands.

"*James,*" Rosa whispered in a sing-song way. "What are you so afraid of?"

"I ain't afraid."

But I was.

Ethelinda didn't stay at Picklefinger's last night. I spotted a bedroll at the rear end of her coach, and it looked freshly slept in. She hadn't heard my name there. I suppose she might've heard it another time. Maybe Rosa had just said it outside, but who could remember? Only someone who makes a living off remembering the tiniest details.

"Then let her do her thing," Rosa said. "She said it's free."

Ethelinda nodded, all kinds of jewelry jingling and clattering. *Free.* I nearly scoffed. Nothing's free in life or death. A sample meant to get folks hooked, traveling festival to festival to meet with Ethelinda as much as possible.

My gaze met Rosa's. This was happening regardless of what I wanted, and I got the impression me going first might ease her mind a bit. And I'll be honest, the part of me that was apprehensive was for good reason. I wasn't sure a man who should be dead could take part in these sorts of affairs. What if a portal to Hell opened wide and Lucifer's own icy fingers wrapped tight around my throat? Or worse for everyone, it all backfired and a Hellmouth split the realm.

But for Rosa, I could bite my tongue and my pride and be her guinea pig.

"Fine, fine." I held my palms out.

A pruny left hand loosely gripped my right. Then, Ethelinda began tracing the lines on my palm with the other.

Her head cocked sharply and her hunched back straightened just a bit. Then, she leaned in, squinting. With a gasp, she took a staggering step rearward and bumped into a table covered in a silvery velvet drape where a crystal ball threatened to roll off its stand.

Ah, here's where old Ethelinda tells me to avoid riding horses for a week or to beware powdered women or men in stovepipe hats.

"What is it?" Rosa asked, eyes wide as saucers.

"I see . . . nothing . . ." Ethelinda whispered. "Just darkness. Mr. Crowley, you have no lifeline."

I laughed, though I didn't feel like it. Those words were eerily similar to the ones uttered by the goat-beast Nephilim a few days earlier.

"*You have a body,*" it had said with Lyle's tongue. "*Though no life runs within.*"

Did this woman truly have the sight, or was this just one of the many things she told visitors to elicit emotion and lead them to spend money on some other kind of reading?

"Reading palms can often be unreliable," she remarked. There it was. Now she's gonna suggest—"But this time, I am certain of what I see. Nothing."

Rosa regarded me, and I hoped my face betrayed none of what I felt inside.

"Well, I assure you, madam, I am very much alive," I said.

Out of the corner of my eye, I could've sworn I saw Shar roiling within the crystal ball. I could almost hear her voice warning me that "*All liars shall have their part in the lake which burneth with fire and brimstone.*"

Sure, Hell's more ice than fire, but translations be damned, the notion remained true.

Ethelinda spent a few more seconds eyeing me up. Then she turned from me as if the news about my lack of existence was suddenly irrelevant.

"Miss Rosa," Ethelinda said, somehow knowing her name, too. "I believe you had some questions?"

Rosa stuttered over a response while Ethelinda adjusted her headpiece and took a single step to the right. With the table, two chairs, and all her many items and artifacts all over, there wasn't much room. She sat at the far end of the table.

"Rosa, darling, please, have a seat," she said though she never took her eyes off me.

I stepped aside and let Rosa through to take a seat across from Ethelinda.

"I suppose this one won't be pro bono," I said. It wasn't a question.

Without acknowledging me, Ethelinda carefully lifted the crystal ball from the table. I knew how these tricks worked. The ball would be attached to a foot pedal of some sort under the table, and that would blow smoke into the glass, swirling around, giving the sucker on the other end a false sense that something mystical was going on.

However, like many other things about this encounter, I was left nonplussed. There was no hole in the table. Not even a slit in the cloth. If there was, Ethelinda had done a damn good job hiding it.

With the ball gone, she pulled out a set of tarot cards, giving them a good shuffle.

Rosa spoke up. "Madam Ethelinda, I'm here hoping to com—"

"Shhh."

I'm pretty sure that if I'd ever been the one to shush Rosa, I'd be suffering for it. But when the fortune-teller did it, Rosa obeyed.

Ethelinda flipped a card and placed it faceup on the table, directed toward Rosa.

"Hmmm. This one is simple. The Lovers." She then glanced up at me.

Here we were, seeking this charlatan's guidance to commune with Rosa's lost love, and she was about to make the mistake of thinking that card meant something about the two of us being one.

"Though it is not him," Ethelinda said. She shook her head slowly. "No, not him at all."

"Ouch," I remarked. Nobody heard me.

Then Ethelinda flipped a second card.

"Ah, yes. The Death card. You have lost someone close. Very close, and the previous card tells me of the nature of your relationship. I am so sorry, my dear." She reached forward and placed a hand on Rosa's arm—right where that snake-and-dagger tattoo rested beneath Rosa's shirt, I might add.

I couldn't see Rosa's face, but I could imagine it. Her hand lifted, one lithe finger pressing into the corner of her eye. Reminded me too much of when I'd reconnected with her in Dead Acre, sad and lonely in the Sweet Water Saloon.

Flipping a third, Ethelinda said, "Temperance." Then the final card. "Strength."

"What do those mean?" Rosa asked, all verklempt.

Ethelinda was quiet as she surveyed the cards. Then, nearly at a whisper, she said, "It is dangerous to go looking for the dead."

Rosa said not a word.

Ethelinda glanced up. "You are here in hopes that I can help you to visit with your late husband, yes?"

Rosa nodded slowly. I was flabbergasted, honest. I still assumed there might've been some sort of trick to what she was doing, but what it was, I had no idea.

My chest wasn't itching much apart from what I knew to be Shar vying for my attention, so I didn't think there was anything hellish going on here. It seemed, whether I wanted to admit it or not, this woman possessed some manner of connection to the supernatural.

"You have much strength," Ethelinda said. "More than I have seen in a woman for many years. However, you will not rest until you've used that strength to your own ends, and the results will be cata-strophic. Your energy . . . it is . . . chaos. There is no constraint. No understanding of what you have been endowed with. If you continue down this path, it will only lead to more heartache. You will be responsible for much death."

Rosa stared blankly.

I tapped her shoulder. "C'mon. I've heard enough."

Ethelinda's tricks might've been convincing, but even a blind horse finds a paddock every now and again. She was playing games with a broken heart.

"Please, let me talk to him," Rosa whimpered. "Let me talk to my William."

Ethelinda closed her eyes and shook her head. "If I open those doors for someone like you, they may never close."

"Someone like her?" I said, offended for her. But, again, nobody acknowledged my existence.

"I need to talk to him!" Rosa yelled so loud it gave me a shudder. She slammed an open hand down on the table, cards snapping up. Ethelinda remained calm, as if this sort of behavior was commonplace. Rosa grabbed for her. "I need to. Please. Please."

My hand gripped Rosa's upper arm. "Let's go, Rosa. You don't need this hoodwinker telling you any more lies."

As if taunting me, Ethelinda flipped one more card, this one facing me. There was no denying this one. A red man with a goatee depicted in a Victorian style, two horns, and a pitchfork.

Ethelinda's gaze met mine and, now, the itch in my chest became more than just that. Like hands were clawing at my ribs from the inside out. It burned like fire . . . worse even than the cave; worse than anything evoked by the goat-Nephilim.

The fortune-teller's eyes narrowed. "Follow the path at your own peril, James Crowley." Her words hung on the air and it was like it wasn't even her voice anymore. "He's coming for you."

I stared at the fortune-teller. Her formerly near-white eyes were now pitch black. It wasn't just her words that were icy, either. Frost seemed to creep around the edges of Ethelinda's table and I saw steam rising from Rosa's lips as she breathed heavily. In July.

We stared at each other, the fortune-teller and me, for what felt like it could've been hours. Then, everything around me went dark, even Rosa. That damnable itch in my chest suddenly went numb.

I was cold.

I don't get cold.

Then, the sounds of screams and gunfire broke through it all.

NINETEEN

Three shots.

Bang!

Bang!

Bang!

Dale's signal.

I snapped out of the trance the strange fortune-teller had me in and focused on the task at hand. Ethelinda's eyes returned to normal, and for a moment she looked woozy and out of sorts.

"Stay here," I told Rosa. "And don't listen to another word this witch has to say."

"Like hell I will." She reached for the pistol in her holster.

I shook my head. "No."

I didn't give her a chance to argue before I took off down the steps and rushed outside. Rosa wasn't gonna be happy, but there was no way I'd be responsible for getting her mixed up in another battle with the supernatural.

Madam Ethelinda, however, needed no persuading. As I left, she'd rushed to the rear end of the wagon and squatted in the corner, shaking.

Smart woman. It was a shame the swindler hadn't seen this coming. Whatever games she'd played on me, I was done with them. She was meddling with things that no mortal ought to.

The sight now laid before me outside was a vast departure from the fun and frolicking it'd just been. The band no longer played happy tunes, and I heard no shouts from hawkers or carnies or invitations to step right up. Just screams, pounding feet, and a whole mess of confusion.

It's never tough to find the source of gunshots. You just run in the direction opposite everyone else. In this case, people were fleeing from the center of town and through the carnival.

Deputies all around waved for folks to evacuate while making their way toward the town square. One shouted at me, but I ignored him. He wouldn't give chase, having much more important business to take care of than one rebellious cowboy looking for a thrill.

To my left, I spotted Cecil and his men escorting Dufaux and some other rich-looking guests to his estate behind those big safe walls. I bet the Pinkerton had been biting his teeth, waiting for this.

Once again, I searched the sky, expecting to see the hawk above but didn't. I tried my best not to bowl people over as I sprinted. Finally, I came to a skidding halt with a good view of Picklefinger's, just across the square from the bank. A passel of the local sheriff's men had taken up posts on all sides. They were prepared, if not trained, for something like this.

"Crowley!" Dale ran full-bore toward me from the direction of the jail, nearly tripping over his own feet. "Did like you told me . . ." he huffed. "Three shots."

"Good job," I said. "Did you see them?"

"They dragged that cart right in front of the bank . . . Guards started shouting 'move along,' and they got they throats cut. Thought they was being sneaky, but I saw them go down quiet. But the bank's chained shut for the holiday. They got nowhere to go."

I pushed him out of the way so I could take a gander. A wagon was indeed parked right outside the bank's entry, filled with oranges and covered by a tarpaulin to look like it was meant for trading. A good disguise with the entire square being cleaned up from the market the day before. Lingering and terrified vendors were huddled up, hiding all over, but luckily most of the town and its visitors were at the festival grounds.

Two dead bodies lay outside the doors, like Dale said. Regular lawmen by the looks of it. A few outlaws dressed like tradesmen found cover behind the cart, though they wore masks now as they fired back at other lawmen and bounty hunters. Didn't spot Anton, who probably drank himself under a table in sadness for losing to me in five-finger.

No ice shield up yet either. No hawk. And, this time, there were more than three perpetrators. I'd counted four already using the cart for cover.

Had the Frozen Trio recruited more? They had taken more time before this hit.

I didn't have time to worry about *who* was robbing *Dufaux's Bank and Trust*. Obviously, this wasn't coincidental. People who clearly hated Dufaux, hitting on the day of the celebration of his self-proclaimed kingdom?

"The hell is this?" A man I recognized came riding up on a white stallion. Would've been pretty heroic-looking if it weren't the Revelation sheriff who'd locked Dale and me up the night before.

He slid off his horse and got in our faces. "Nobody said you two could leave!"

I ignored him, watching the bank where one of the masked outlaws rose from hiding and risked being shot. All the others wore red masks, but his was black as midnight. He glared, right across the square, seemed like at me. He then tore the tarp off the false orange cart. With my un- naturally sharp vision, I spotted something red beneath them. Bright red.

Dynamite. By all the saints and elders, the cart was loaded with it.

I pulled Dale and the sheriff to cover behind a grocer's stand. The sheriff fought me, but I got strength he could only dream of. All the outlaws and lawmen on the other side of the square were oblivious to what was about to happen.

"Everyone dow—"

An explosion shook the earth and cut me off. Like Dale said, the bank had wisely been closed for the holiday. The big, fancy front doors all chained up. But all that dynamite blew the whole thing wide open and clouded the entire square in smoke and dust and burning shreds of canvas.

The sheriff's horse took off running, but he, himself, I seized by the shoulders. "We're on the same side here, Sheriff! We learned our lesson."

Bullets chipped wood all around us as the outlaws slung lead from cover inside the bank and behind the columns at its entry.

The sheriff stared at me. By the look of him, his ears were ringing. I gave him a shake.

"Yeah. All right," he said finally. "But this ain't over."

"Fine by me."

The geyser in the center of the square suddenly sprayed water up, providing some semblance of cover. Shar flowed in the reflection, clear as day. My ever-present benefactor watching, judging, and I suppose helping if it was her who sent up the water.

Either way, I yanked Dale and the sheriff upright posthaste, pointed to Picklefinger's, and we continued on foot around the square. The saloon had a perfectly angled vantage of the bank. I kept myself on the inside position where I'd be most likely to get shot, just in case. This region didn't need to lose all its lawmen in one week.

Then I saw a boy, around the same age as Mutt, standing alone in the square. He must've gotten left behind in the chaos or maybe was around the markets causing trouble, but either way, he was one stray bullet from an early grave.

"Go!" I gave Dale a nudge to hasten him toward the saloon and used the momentum to push off toward the boy. Bullets hissed and snapped as I weaved my way through the market. Sliding, I whipped my body around and scooped up the boy in one smooth motion.

"You hurt?" I asked while I ran back toward Picklefinger's with him cradled in front of me.

A bullet must've hit me in the back because some force I couldn't feel sent me careening through the saloon doors. I stumbled a few last feet, crunching through a table and chairs, but I got him inside.

Placing him down, I brushed the hair out of his eyes and patted him all over, checking for wounds. He was scared silent, but okay it seemed.

"Get to the back room and stay low," I said. "Go. Now!"

He did as told and disappeared through a back door I knew led to Picklefinger's storage area.

The saloon was empty this early on except for some ladies in corsets cowering in a back booth, and a man slumped over in another, still passed out from last night's revelry.

"Everyone get down!" the sheriff ordered. He placed his back to the front wall beside one of the windows.

Dale climbed over the bar and had his pistol aimed out through the door's opening. I could see it in his eyes; he was terrified. And I had to admit, I wasn't too keen on him being behind everyone, knowing what happened to Sheriff Daniels last time Dale was in such a position.

Everyone left outside in the square, good or bad, risked getting shot. The smog from the dynamite made it hard to say who was who. Horses neighed as a few more men wearing red masks rumbled in on a stagecoach, mowing down several deputies or bounty hunters who'd wrongly thought they had good cover.

I recognized the coach from the festival. The goddamn snake oil salesman. Dufaux really was a fool not calling the whole event off and making blending in so easy.

They stopped the coach by the bank, no doubt to load stolen money into it.

That added three more outlaws to the fray as they took cover and started shooting outward. A lot more than just a trio and damn organized too. A green, inexperienced crew hits all at once, throwing all their might around like an angry bull. A smart crew comes in waves, eroding their enemy, putting fear in them, always making them wonder if there are more coming in just behind them.

And oddly enough, still no sign of the Frozen Trio. What was this, another gang looking to take advantage? But what advantage? Who hits the most secure bank around like this? Much as I wanted to ponder the implications of such a heist, there just wasn't time. Whoever it was, they needed to be stopped. Now.

"We need a plan," I said, joining the sheriff by the front window. The simple one was me charging the bank doors myself and taking hundreds of shots, unharmed. But here's the thing: a shotgun blast through my belly might heal, but it'd certainly slow me down, and should my legs be shot to hell, I still needed muscles to run. What would happen if a salvo of bullets tore through me until I was rendered temporarily useless?

Besides that, I brought silver bullets, and I didn't want to waste ammo before I spotted the Yeti.

"My men are prepared for this," the sheriff said. "It'll be a good old-fashioned standoff until it's not. The fools got themselves surrounded in there."

"Until they blow a hole in the back wall!" Dale squealed from his cover.

"They'll need a bigger cart of dynamite," the sheriff said. "Dufaux spared no expenses. That thing is solid stone."

Picklefinger emerged from the back room, wearing a scowl. "You gotta go and make my place a target?"

"Sorry, old friend," I said. "About that too." I pointed to the window I'd been thrown through the night before.

"The kid all right?" I asked.

Picklefinger nodded.

"Get to the back, Mr. Hayes," the sheriff demanded.

In response, Picklefinger grunted and retrieved his shotgun from behind the bar, giving it a *chock*.

"I'll be defending my property if it's all the same to you," he said.

The sheriff didn't press the issue. His attention moved toward someone running low from the direction of the festival. The sheriff started waving for whoever it was to speed up, and the newcomer ducked inside, panting.

"Oh, now it's a goddamned party," Picklefinger groaned.

I turned to see one of the deputies who'd arrested me and Dale. He had large black tufts of hair surrounding his ears. The deputy spotted me then too.

"You son of a bitch," he said. "I should've known you was a part of this!"

"Part of this?" I asked. "Don't be an idiot."

"Was that woman who got sweet on me working with you, too? I don't know what you're all up to, but no one breaks out—"

"Not my fault it was so damn easy."

The deputy lunged at me.

"Chops, we got more important things right now," the sheriff said, making a barricade of his arm. "Besides, if he escaped and you didn't tell me, then it's you who's in trouble."

That shut Chops up fast.

I peered around the doorframe. By now, I could see Elkhart's Sheriff Culpepper and his posse setting up on the south side of the square. One thing was certain, with all these folks around, whoever was robbing that bank wasn't getting out. Not breathing, at least. And Cecil and his Pinkertons weren't even here yet.

A shot fired and clipped my hat. I pulled back and took it off, giving it a look. There was a big hole in the brim right next to the spot where the tomahawk-lady had carved off a strip.

I swore. "I got this from John B. Stetson himself, dammit!"

"A shame," Chops said, looking back outside.

A bullet zipped nearby, shattering one of the whiskey bottles behind Picklefinger's bar. Dale yelped and ducked.

A tiny spot appeared on Chops's throat. Black at first, then a stream of red started to dribble down, soaking his collar. The bullet had gone straight through him before striking the bar. The deputy opened his mouth to speak, and blood gurgled out like a fountain.

I heard Dale retch.

The sheriff grabbed his deputy by the vest and pulled him down as if he'd save him from further damage.

"Those bastards," he whispered.

Chops was mostly inside cover, so he shouldn't have been able to be hit from where the enemies were by the bank. Which meant a marksman had arrived with an angle on us—the Frozen Trio was finally here.

I went to look again, and a bullet snapped against the wood frame right beside me. By instinct, I returned to cover.

Having dealt with the sharpshooting Mind-drifter before, a plan for how to get the jump on him popped into my head. I pulled off a glove and pressed my fingers against Chops's skin, my back to everybody else in the saloon so they wouldn't see my eyes glowing bright and blue.

My head snapped back . . .

* * *

I could feel Chops's fear as my own, him making jokes to cover for it.

"A shame," I—he—said and smirked.

Then, he turned and saw the glint of muzzle fire from across the street in the bell tower of the Town Hall building. The panic was worse than the wound. He wanted to scream, but when he did, only warm blood poured out. Then it got cold. All cold.

His sheriff clutched him as he thought about how he didn't even want this job but he and his wife needed money after she got pregnant. They had to settle down somewhere, and the sheriff had made that possible.

It was unclear if he suffocated in his own blood first or lost too much of it or simply couldn't breathe. But as it all faded to black, the man's last thought was, "Why am I even here?"

* * *

Focus returned to my own eyes. I grabbed at my neck, echoes of that painful experience confusing me momentarily.

"Why am I even here?"

That thought threw me a bit. It's the eternal question. The one the White Throne is meant to be an answer for. And there it was, like most, at this man's end. And the worst part about it, is that unlike the living, I knew my purpose: to serve, dutifully, Heaven and its scions without question. No hope of finding love or retirement. That was it. Forever. Or until they were through with me.

I blinked and forced myself to focus as I put the glove back on.

What did I see through Chops's eyes that mattered? I'd feared the shooter was the Mind-drifter, but this one was a white man in a straw hat. Pale as could be, with freckles even, which I could see because, unlike his compadres, he didn't bother with a mask.

Now, I could just stand up, take some bullets, and shoot him, but I'd have an awful lot of explaining to do if these men watched a plum go through my brain and I just kept on talking and walking. Getting myself tied up by them as if I were some sort of witch wouldn't help me exorcise the Yeti's demon.

"On top of the Town Hall," I said to everyone in the saloon. "Don't look."

I had a door on my left and a shattered window on my right with a three-foot span of wood and concrete blocks at my back. The bar behind which Dale stood was directly in front of me, about twenty feet away or so—maybe thirty.

"Get down," I told him, shocked I had to do so.

He obeyed and not only kept himself alive a spell longer but gave me a clear sight to the mirror behind the bar he'd been blocking. I begged for a moment that Shar wouldn't show up, and she didn't. Perhaps I was doing all right on my own for once.

I slunk down until I could see the top of the Town Hall in the reflection. With my right hand, I held my damaged hat. My left pulled back the hammer on my Peacemaker.

"What'chu doing?" the Revelation sheriff asked.

I ignored him, then slowly raised my hat into the hole where the window had been.

The shooter popped up and shot, hitting the hat and sending it spinning across the room. At the same time, I fired my gun over my left shoulder and out the door. I watched in the mirror as the bullet found its mark, striking the outlaw dead.

"My word," the sheriff said.

I sniffed. "Lucky shot."

With cover restored, I hurdled out the window and along to the railing. The standoff outside the bank was still hot and heavy. Men on both sides dropped. The black-masked outlaw who'd blown up the cart had a spot right inside the bank doors, defending while others inside worked on the vault. He was a hell of a shot. Every time he popped out of cover, he put a bullet in someone or came close enough to scare them into retreat.

I was tired of waiting. If the Yeti wouldn't come out, I'd go find him.

A voice rose, clear and distinct over the constant racket of gunshots.

Cecil and his Pinks rode out into the square like the cavalry at Gettysburg. He had a pair on him for sure. From that spot, any outlaw could put him down with hardly an effort, but they seemed to be shocked by such a brazen arrival into a bullet storm.

"Come out with your hands raised!" Cecil yelled; the geyser punctuated it with a low burst of water at the same time.

The gunfire stopped, mostly. The lawmen and bounty hunters in the square took better cover in the brief respite so they could reload. Outlaws did the same.

"It's over," Cecil went on. "The place is surrounded. We got you outnumbered five to one."

"Not once you're all dead!" the robber in the black mask shouted back. Most noticeable thing about him was that he sounded human, not monstrous like a demon-possessed Yeti. Even though he was clearly the one running this particular band of outlaws, he wasn't big enough, hairy enough, wild enough to be the Yeti. Then there was the whole distinct lack of ice thing. I just couldn't stop pondering where the Frozen Trio was.

"Your funeral," Cecil responded before he started barking out orders, pointing this way and that. It wasn't just Pinks with him, but local guards from Dufaux's estate and the Elkhart men too. Enough reinforcements to turn the tide with ease.

The Revelation sheriff moved to the porch and waved at Cecil. "Took your damn time!"

Cecil looked down his nose. "Mr. Gutierrez, I've got this under control."

"It's *Sheriff*, and last I checked, this is my damn town!"

Cecil sniffed and smirked. "Last I checked, this town belongs to Mr. Dufaux. Now, tell your boys to stay out of our way."

Leaping down, he unhitched a wagon drawn by one of his men and gave the horses a slap. They took off running. That's when I remembered what I'd seen back at Dufaux's place. The Gatling gun.

"Three thousand rounds a minute," Cecil admired, patting the weapon. "And we've got enough rounds to fire for half an hour."

"You're gonna take that whole building down!" Gutierrez warned.

"That's a sacrifice Mr. Dufaux is willing to make."

Cecil climbed up onto the wagon, placed a foot on the sidewall like he was the conquering hero of some faraway kingdom, and shouted, "Light it up, boys!"

The whole square filled with gun smoke, and the bank facade started taking holes in a coordinated attack. Cecil, however, did not fire up the spin-gun. All the outlaws were forced into cover from the barrage. I stood, watching. Things had started out hairy, but this was about to become a massacre.

Cecil raised his hand, and the outpour of gunshots slowed to a trickle. "Last chance before we cut the place down!" he yelled.

A few beats passed before one outlaw came running out from the cover of their stagecoach, his feet crunching over the singed earth from where their cart had exploded.

"Don't shoot!" he shouted. "I give up! Please!"

A single shot rang out, but it wasn't us. He fell forward. The turncoat took a bullet to the back of the head and dropped in a heap, killed by the outlaw leader in the black mask.

"Traitor bastard!" the boss man shouted.

It was hard to feel sorry. Good or bad men, you don't abandon your crew in the middle of a job. After, in the quiet times, like I had—fine. Thought maybe I was a bit biased. However, at no time when the bullets start flying and you've already made your choice who to throw in with do you change your damn mind.

"Damn fools . . ." Cecil sighed. He clicked his tongue like he was beckoning a horse, and one of his men hopped up onto the wagon with him.

He spun the crank, and the Gatling gun unleashed hell upon the outlaws. Wood from the stagecoach splintered everywhere. His ammo man kept the gun fed so it wouldn't stop, and it was . . . wow.

Wanton destruction from a machine like that—it was a work of beauty. And by the look of how that Gatling gun was taking care of business, there'd be nothing left within the minute. The snake oil coach was basically sawn in half, the outlaws left alive behind it earning the same fate.

I watched, stunned. A weapon like this didn't exist back when I was a Scuttler. If it had, I would've sought another profession. And to think, a doctor invented the damn thing.

And the sound? Deafening. Like thunder cracking over and over without a second in between. It wasn't a supernatural thing, but it may as well have been. I don't think God or His angels ever meant for His Children to wield such destructive power.

Cecil grunted, and the line of fire trailed upward, ripping across the bank's facade and then devastating the shop beside it. I looked back. At first, I thought it was a tactic I didn't understand. But then I saw that he'd been hit by a bullet from behind.

I whipped my head around to see the door of the Miner's Guild swing open. A crew of ruffians poured out, opening fire at the backs of Cecil's men. An ambush. One of the Pinks had his brains splattered against the Gatling gun cart.

At the bank, the outlaws still inside pressed the advantage, shooting at the deputies and bounty hunters.

"Keep on them!" I yelled at Cecil, who had recovered and was pulling himself back up to keep up the salvo. Seemed like it was only a surface wound, or he was even tougher than I'd thought.

I charged headlong at the ambushers, trying to make myself a target. I wasted a single silver bullet on one of them, right through the chest. As the man fell, I caught him and used his body as a shield and then a battering ram as I pushed him into another.

A rifle swung at my head. I ducked, spinning around and splitting open a gut. As I rose, I saw Gutierrez and another deputy charging with me. Dale brought up the rear, though by the time he reached me, the ambush would be thwarted.

A bullet hit my arm and made it recoil back. Didn't hurt, but it made me growl as I glared up. The man tried to fire again, but I beat him and hip-fired straight through his face. A waste of silver, but I was tired of playing nice.

I stepped over to the fallen outlaw. His mask had been pulled down by sliding against dirt. Seeing what was left of his face—no more than a smattering of disgusting yellow teeth, I realized I knew him. It took me a few moments to remember, but he was one of Anton's singing buddies. The one stooping over his left shoulder while we played.

Was that Anton in the black mask leading this thing? Posing as a bounty hunter while working for the Frozen Trio? It's what the Scuttlers would've done. Get someone familiar with the area to blend in to get the lay of the land—cozy up to the locals, throw people off the scent.

But . . . why have Anton do that if the Mind-drifter could just see everything through the hawk's eyes? This all felt different, like an army recruited to hit the bank. Only, the army was way too small. They'd barely even gotten the chance to start trying to crack open the vault.

"How the hell did they think this would work?" I said to nobody in particular.

Dale answered. "Maybe they just wanted to kill people?"

I shook my head. "Nah. Most outlaws ain't heartless."

Gutierrez looked down at one of his fallen deputies. "I strongly disagree with that sentiment."

"You came to the wrong town!" Cecil yelled, ending our conversation. The Gatling gun started up again. We'd thwarted the ambush—the last gasp of these outlaws to turn the tables.

I approached Cecil, back into the volume of that relentless spinning gun. Anger had him tearing into the sides and columns of the bank, stone crumbling off in chunks.

"Cecil, enough!" I got closer and grabbed his ankle. He kicked me, but I knew he was just lost in the moment. Seeing red. "Enough!" I shouted once more.

Cecil looked down, and reason suddenly flooded his features. He stopped cranking, dropped to one knee, and clutched his side. Surface wound or not, the recoil from holding onto that thing must've had him aching.

"Something ain't right," I said. "This ain't the same crew."

"Like hell it ain't," Cecil grunted.

"I saw them, and it ain't the same damn crew," I said more force-fully. "We got to take one alive."

Cecil grimaced. He looked between me and Gutierrez, then nodded to the latter. Gutierrez whistled across the square, getting Sheriff Cul-pepper's attention and that of his men on the opposite side. Hearing that whistle echo after all that shooting was off, the silence now was almost oppressive.

Gutierrez gave a hand motion, got the affirmative. Then Culpep-per started his advance.

I did the same from my position.

"What's the plan?" Dale whispered in my ear.

"Last chance!" Sheriff Gutierrez called out from behind us. "Lay down your arms and come out."

Culpepper and his men got in position around the bank, behind whatever was left for cover, and aimed. They were close to it now. Would be hard to miss anyone who came walking out.

"This is over!" Gutierrez went on. "Come out now, and maybe you'll be spared the rope."

"All right, all right, fine!" The outlaw in the black mask appeared in the entry, hands to the sky and empty. Guns around the square cocked all at once.

I squinted. Dust was everywhere, but he was roughly the same height as Anton. Similar build. Damn it all to Hell. How did I miss this?

"We'll come out since you asked so nicely," Maybe Anton said.

"Screw this. That bounty's mine." One of the gunmen on our side who had the look of a bounty hunter squeezed his trigger. Lucky, I got there just in time and batted his arm aside. The bullet *thunked* off the stone a few feet away from the outlaw.

"Hot damn, I said we'll come out!" Black Mask hollered.

The bounty hunter turned on me with a glower. "What the hell, man? You're after the same thing as me. These lawmen don't need it."

"This ain't the right bounty," I said.

Then the bastard made a fate-altering decision. He started raising his weapon like he was gonna try to unload on me. I punched him across the jaw so hard it sent him sprawling. Then I returned my attention to the bank.

"What are you waiting for?" Sheriff Culpepper asked.

"What?" Black Mask said.

"You coming out?"

The outlaw cupped his hand around his ear. He made a big show of it too, leaning in, other arm stretched back like a wing. "Sorry, my ears are ringing from all the . . . you know."

"Let's go!" Sheriff Culpepper moved toward him, pistol raised. The others pressed forward at his back.

I saw red and a flicker of orange. Someone inside the dark bank had placed a stick of dynamite in Black Mask's rear, outstretched hand.

I cried out, but it was too late. The outlaw heaved it underhanded.

The thing went off right beside Sheriff Culpepper and his men and blew them to pieces. I don't have the stomach to describe it. Others in the broader arc were scorched and blown backward. Anyone who wasn't within the radius of the blast opened fire as four outlaws flooded out of the bank to join with their leader before splitting up.

In all the chaos and the smoke, it was hard to see who went what way, but I got my eyes set on the one in the black mask built like Anton. He shouldered into a deputy and stabbed him in the stomach before fleeing down an alley.

"Come back here, coward!" I shouted.

I took off at a sprint down between two other buildings, knowing the routes converged on the next street. Dale cried out behind me that he was coming.

Was Anton working with the Frozen Trio or not? If he was, where the hell were they? I considered shooting him just to stop the chase, but I couldn't kill the man—I needed answers. However, I did consider hobbling him as I reached the next street and spotted him running a short ways up. But with us both moving like this, I had just as good a chance of shooting him somewhere vital and making him bleed out before I could get what I needed.

Truth is, I don't have a damn clue what these outlaws were thinking.

If they had the Yeti and his friends fighting with them, they might've stood a chance. Turned Cecil's Gatling gun to ice right out the gate. But this was suicide, and they had to have known it.

"I ain't going down because of them!" Black Mask shouted back, and I must say, that voice was familiar.

He shot wildly over his shoulder. I didn't even bother to try to dodge it any more than if someone threw a stone at a rhino. He pulled another pistol and shot once more. I pushed myself and picked up speed. I may have supernatural abilities, but speed isn't one of them. Put me in a foot race, though, and I'd just keep going and never slow down.

I was starting to gain on him and considered taking out the Nephilim's harmonica, playing a chord and making him stop like I had with Roscoe the werewolf. But it was loud outside, and he was far off.

He slipped between a barn and homestead before I could rethink it. When I reached the spot, a bullet whizzed by and clanged off something metal. He shot twice more, and one might've hit me. Hard to be sure.

He kept running, disappearing through the other side. A few more steps took me to the mouth of the alley and a vast paddock before the start of the fairgrounds. Poor folks had fled this way, probably thinking they were safe.

"He went that way!" one woman shouted from the upper window of her barn. As if I had any question.

Cries from lawmen and everyone rang out from every direction in town as they chased after all the others. I stayed focused, cleared a paddock, hopping the low horse fence, and came to a stop at the fairgrounds. They were mostly empty on this side now, an eerie feeling. People crowded over by the church across the way, many inside of it. I saw the reverend kneeling outside the door, praying.

I'd lost my quarry within the many tents and stands.

"Come out, come out wherever you are!" I teased.

My taunt was met by a gunshot that went wide and missed me.

That was stupid. He fell for the oldest trick, like a kid's game of blindman's bluff.

I followed the sound and trajectory of the shot, and I spotted Black

Mask slipping into the Freak Show tent. Large paintings of those who I'd encountered in Picklefinger's lined the front entrance. The World's Strongest Man—who'd tossed me through the window—Beast Boy, the Bearded Lady, and more. I shoved the flap aside and snuck in. It was dark but not terribly so. Besides, I saw pretty well in the dark.

The nature of these canvas setups was that there were thin slits in between sections, tied together with nylon. As a result, dust motes danced in the air like fireflies in the sun rays.

I had a fleeting thought that it would've been nice if the Strong Man had been present to stop the robber from running. Even Beast Boy. Though my chest wasn't burning so I knew he was nowhere in sight. I was alone in here with who I thought might be Anton.

Then I spotted him behind a seating stand.

"Stop running!" I shouted. "You're just pissing me off!"

My arm kicked back at the same time I'd heard his gun go off. I was gonna have a bear of a time getting these slugs out of me when all was said and done. But at the moment, I ignored it and looked up in time to watch him pass behind a glass enclosure with some kind of supposedly unearthly being floating in liquid within. Pretty sure it was just a squid or a jellyfish. He threw open a flap, light pouring in, and dashed out.

I had two choices, run through to the other side, which had to be a good few hundred feet, or return from whence I came. I chose the latter, thinking it would save some time.

He really only had two choices also: run west, back toward town, or continue east toward innocent people. I figured he wasn't gonna chance returning to where all those gunmen waited to shoot or arrest him.

I was right. Wasn't long before I had eyes on him.

"Stop running!" I shouted again and fired a bullet wide on purpose. It forced him to veer off course so he wouldn't get to any potential hostages.

Black Mask took a hard turn at Madam Ethelinda's Ethereal Emporium, and I decided to cut through a side avenue. As I'd hoped, I was now running directly at him.

"I gotchu," I said, planting my foot on one of the many rocks that had been left for sitting. I shoved off and collided with him. He grunted and went down under my weight. We rolled on the ground, me on top, then him, then finally, me again. He kicked and squirmed.

"Hold still, you dumb bastard," I said, getting my lasso ready to tie him up.

By the time I saw him pull out his .38, it was too late. He blasted me in the shoulder. The force of the attack sent me flying off him, allowing him just the wriggle room he needed to shove me away and rise again. I grabbed his boot, but he just slipped out of my grip and kept running.

The chase ensued once more, though he had to be tiring.

He went up a wooden ramp that led into some shanty building I didn't recognize—something impermanent they'd set up for the week's event. I followed him inside. I'd like to say cautiously, but not at all. I rushed right in and was immediately stunned to a stop. Before me were twenty other mes staring back at me.

Mirrors everywhere, dozens—hell, hundreds even. Every step I took was jarring, all those Crowleys mimicking my motions. But it was more than that. They were all set at odd angles, creating the illusion that there was even more than just the one reflection in each mirror.

"Fun's over," I said, my voice hanging like smoke in the air.

I walked forward, and my boot clipped a mirror, making it shiver. I heard my prey shuffling somewhere beyond the prism of reflections, and followed.

"This ain't gonna end well," I warned him.

Black Mask didn't respond.

The next row was made up of more mirrors, but these were twisted, making my visage contort into horrific shapes. Whatever sort of carnival game this was, I didn't like it.

Slowly, I turned, looking for the path. Something sparkled in one of the mirrors, and I nearly pulled the trigger before I realized what— or who—it was.

"Follow," Shar said, and her swirly veneer shot off like a deer under fire. I did my best to keep up.

She brought me to another aisle of mirrors and another, her form leading me along like an actual dog on a leash. I couldn't exactly be upset she was directly and obviously helping for once.

She flashed to another position. A gun fired, and so many mirrors I couldn't count shattered, tiny glinting fragments exploding all around. The distraction was good, but Black Mask failed. I saw my target's coat flap. I shot back and repaid the favor, sending shards of glass toward him. He reached up to guard his face, and in doing so, slipped or tripped, smashing through a wall and tumbling outside.

Rushing to the opening, I aimed down in the dirt where he was trying to recover. He looked up at me, me down at him. And the moment he went to scramble off again, a knife slid up under his throat. It continued along his cheek, slitting his mask a bit, and stopped at his eye.

"Uh, uh, uh. A sharp knife ain't nothin' without a sharp eye."

Rosa's friend Irish held the knife and beamed like a maniac. Rosa, Harker, and Bram stood a short distance behind, watching. Good old Rosa. She must've ditched Ethelinda and found her party after the festival had been interrupted. A few other confused civilians roamed around near them. Harker had his art book out and was, presumably, sketching the scene.

"Are you okay?" Rosa called to me.

"I will be soon." I hopped down and approached the bastard who turned the town square into a shooting gallery. Ironic considering that right behind Rosa was, indeed, the carnival's shooting gallery game. The owner crouched next to it in hiding.

"Ye made bags of a good time, mister," Irish said.

Black Mask tried to elbow her in the gut and take advantage of his superior size, but she was quick. Her knee forced his to buckle before she wrenched his arm back. She was a breath from plunging the knife through his eyeball when I used my lasso to yank the blade out of her hand.

She looked furious. "Are ye langers?" she shouted.

"We need him alive," I said, soft, in an attempt to diffuse her anger.

"Don't ye ever get between me and my prey!" She squeezed his throat with her forearm and reached for one of her many other blades when Bram stopped her.

"Irish, please," he said. "This is not our war."

She scowled but eventually backed down and shoved Black Mask toward me. I sensed in him the desire to run, but I had my gun on him, letting the fear build in him something fierce. Best way to start an interrogation.

I bent down, staring him straight in his cool, blue eyes.

"Let's see who this bastard is."

TWENTY

The mask came off, and I froze. I'd been expecting to see Anton, but the truth was almost more than I could bear. I knew the culprit. Better than I knew anybody still alive in the world.

And I didn't even have to view his whole face. All I needed to see was the grin he wore, like all the world was his plaything. My mind immediately brought me back to the last time I saw it. The moment that changed everything . . .

* * *

"Ace, it's time to go," I said, grabbing him by the sleeve of his old coat.

He clicked his tongue. Then he clicked the hammer on his revolver. "Not until he hands over his money roll."

I checked left, then right. Grass and dirt raced by as the train we were on rumbled across the earth. Its whistle echoed through the vast emptiness, interrupted only by gunshots pinging against steel. Ms. Mae was up front, making sure the conductor kept the wheels rolling.

"More rangers coming!" Big Davey shouted over to us. He aimed out the shattered window of the passenger cart, firing back through dust at the men on horses galloping alongside the locomotive. Train guards in the car ahead were locked in a stalemate with a couple of Scuttlers at the door: Hiram, Emmett, and Mac.

We were behind them in the passenger car. Mothers hugged their children close; husbands held their wives. One railroad employee stood in the corner, the front of his pants wet.

I didn't blame him.

We'd got what we came for, though: bonds belonging to a railroad magnate worth enough to get all us Scuttlers through the next year or more, clear and free. We'd gotten intel a big score would be on this particularly unassuming train, and it checked out. A massive win for us.

But as usual, Ace couldn't help himself. Just couldn't pass up a car filled with the rich. He was like a goddamned raccoon, attracted to anything shiny. And there'd been a lot of that ripe for the plucking. Pearls, silver, watches, diamonds. Fat wallets. It was a great take until one stubborn man.

"Leave them, Ace. We gotta go!" I raised my voice.

Ace acted like I wasn't even there, nudging me aside to lean in and shove the hot barrel of his pistol right under the man's chin.

He winced, the man, tried to stay strong, brave. His wife was behind him, after all, clinging to his arm.

"Just give it to him," she sobbed.

But the man was mulish. Stupid, probably. He puffed out his chest and lifted his head, a bushy mustache donning his lip as proud as the redwoods out by the coast.

"No," he proclaimed. "Men like this can't be allowed to get their way. The West will be tamed. You, sir, are a fossil. A relic of days pa—"

Ace cracked him across the jaw with his gun. "That feel like a fossil to you!"

"Just take it, and let's go," I said.

But Ace didn't listen to me. Rarely listened to anyone anymore. He wouldn't take the man's wallet himself. No. That wasn't his style. He wanted this proud, plump, pomp fellow to surrender his own money. He wanted it tied with a bow.

Pure intimidation. When Ace left a crime scene, he liked to leave the victim's brains mottled too. Scared to go outside, to rat us out. It usually worked, but these days, he'd gotten even more headstrong about it.

Behind us, another man grunted—one of our crew taking a bullet. Big Davey helped him up into a seat, still firing blindly at the rangers.

"Crowley, we can't take much more!" Davey yelled.

"Don't tell me," I said.

I tugged on Ace harder, cursing up a storm I shouldn't ever repeat. It got him off balance, and that's when that silver-spoon-fed fool decided to fight against injustice, doing something to prove his stupidity. He lunged at Ace, grabbing for the gun.

They wrestled for a few seconds. The firearm went off, causing my ears to ring. When the struggling stopped by way of Ace clobbering the guy, the fella staggered upright. Then, he saw the error of his actions. His wife lay against the window, blood spreading across the glass and down the front of her yellow-and-pink flowered dress, a gaping hole in her chest.

Even Ace was momentarily stunned enough to let the man jump to his wife and cradle her limp head.

Innocents died in our line of work, of course. But usually, it was collateral damage. Distant, easy to shrug off, wrong as that may sound. But this . . . this was up close and personal, and completely unnecessary.

"Dumb bastard," Ace spat.

He could've put the man out of his misery. However, he holstered the gun instead. And this time, he reached into the man's back pocket all on his own, with no interference. Pulled out a wallet with a bit of cash in it. Maybe thirty bucks. Enough to buy a decent suit in exchange for an innocent life.

No need to intimidate anymore when the target's broken.

Of course, when the word got out about the murder later, we found out she was the cousin of "the Commodore" himself—the very same rich-ass magnate whose bonds we'd just robbed. A Vanderbilt. The whole ordeal was what had pushed Ace to decide it was time for all of us to lay low south of the border after hiding out in the mountains where, you know, he put me down for not playing by his rules.

"That's it?" Ace said, pocketing it. "What a fucking waste."

He flung the wallet aside before ripping the bloody gold necklace off the dead woman's neck for good measure. Her sobbing husband could do not a thing about it.

"That's a bit better," Ace said.

"You kidding?" I asked him, not even hiding my disdain.

He just shoved by me and said, "What are you waiting for?" while I was busy gawking. Then he shouted to the rest, "Let's go! We got what we came for!"

There were eight of us on the job, and we all converged by the doors where Big Davey already stood with Morrison cradled under the armpit.

"That's a lot of blood," Ace said, looking at Morrison's wound as if he hadn't just watched an innocent woman lose most of hers.

Me and Davey exchanged a look that said everything. Then we all jumped off the side of the train where the rangers weren't, tucking and rolling through the brush.

I won't lie and say jumping off a train feels good, but there're worse pains in the world. Besides, now that Mae was off-board, the conductor had already started the slow-down process in hopes of giving the rangers a leg up.

We all came to a stop, staying low while the mounted rangers kept chasing the screeching train. The delay with the Vanderbilt in the passenger cart left us a short distance off course.

Delay . . . That's how disconnected from reality we were. Here I was, calling a woman's life a delay.

Everyone was panicked, eager to get on the move and disappear into the mountains to the west. Mountains where, at that time, I had no clue I'd die saving Rosa and her mama.

But not Ace. Flipping over, that was when I saw it. He held the woman's necklace to his eyes, marveling as the sun made it sparkle, and he grinned. Ear to filthy ear.

* * *

"Ace?" I said softly.

I was stunned. He was two decades older and his face covered in blood, but I'd recognize that shit-eating grin anywhere.

"Needed a woman to do your job, Marshal?" he asked like he had no clue who I was. Then, I watched as that grin disappeared and terror filled his ice-blue eyes.

"Wait. I shot you," Ace said. Out of surprise, it seemed, he dropped to the ground. Or maybe I was just that damn frightening. Either way, he tried to crab-walk backward until Irish stopped him with a boot. "I watched you bleed out."

"Well, you didn't wait long enough," I said. "You never were a patient man."

Even all these years later, I found familiarity in despising him. The words just came to me as if no time had passed. It didn't matter how utterly dumbstruck I was that he was here.

Though, that did make me wonder . . .

What *had* happened to my dead body after I'd died? Had it rotted in the dirt for the flies and maggots? Or had I just up and disappeared until Shar chose me for rebirth? My next memory after Ace pulled that trigger had been waking up roughly three years later, inside a cavern I called Steeple Rock due to its unique shape.

"There's no room for patience in the West," Ace said. "But you know that." There it was. That grin again, only this time with blood smeared across his teeth, I guess from smashing through that wall. "Twenty years, you've still been alive, and you never even came after me? I'm insulted."

"Your legend vanished. Haven't heard your name since," I lied. "Haven't thought of you once neither," I lied again. "Figured your sins caught up with you." That one was wishful thinking.

"I found a nice living down in Mexico City, just like I'd promised. The lawmen there, you just hand them some scratch, they look the other way. Fucking paradise."

"Sounds like Hell."

"Ay, don't wanna break up the gas yer havin'," Irish chimed in, waving at me like I was far away. "But who's this gobshite, huh?"

"Guy I used to know," I said. "Nobody anymore, it seems."

Ace spat a wad of bloody mucus at me, but it was so thick it just flipped back around onto his face. He didn't even bother to wipe it.

"What brought you back, Ace?" I asked. "No more foreign lands to conquer?"

"I outgrew them, just like I outgrew you."

"Right," I said.

We all looked over when we heard hooves way off in the distance. The Pinkertons were just a puff of dust on the horizon, but it was clear it was them.

"You're with them, huh?" Ace asked. "When did you find their side of the law?"

"I serve a higher power than that."

"'Pride cometh before the—'" I kicked him in the ribs before he could finish the verse. Seemed wrong to let him. I'd lived a rotten life, but a man like Ace? Just stepping into a church should've set him ablaze.

"Why are you here?" I demanded.

"Thought that was obvious."

"Well, it ain't." I grabbed him and hauled him to his feet. "So, why? Start talking."

He smiled. Didn't speak. So I punched him in the gut.

"I said, start talking."

Ace huffed and puffed a bit and that turned into a laugh. "You always were a—"

I never found out what I always was because I clobbered him again and knocked the wind out of him.

"I'm gonna let you catch your breath, and if the next thing you say ain't an answer, it's gonna be lights out for a while," I said.

"Fine, fine," he said, voice not quite as strong or proud as it had just been. "It's easy living south of the border, but I missed the challenge. The big scores. Vengeful sheriffs. Pinkertons galore."

"Those other banks . . . they weren't you. I would've recognized the stink of the Scuttlers."

"What the hell is a Scuttler?"

I blinked.

"Oh, right." He chuckled. "What a shit name for a bunch of shit people. Been through a lot of crews since you and Davey killed Hiram and I had to rebuild. You'll have to excuse me."

I bet he thought bringing up Hiram would make me flinch, but I had no love for that man. Just because we were a crew didn't mean we were all friends. I drew my gun and shoved it right under Ace's chin. Just like he did to that Vanderbilt lady all those years ago. He didn't even flinch.

"You with the Frozen Trio?" I asked.

"I'm with myself," he said. "Same as always."

I shot off a round right by his ear. He squeezed his eyes tight and reeled. I knew that hurt him, and it took all my effort not to have pulled the trigger where my aim would've killed him. My mind couldn't resolve how absolutely insane this was, but here he was. After two long decades' worth of seeing his ugly mug every time I shut my eyes. The man who'd handed my soul off to Shar and the White Throne.

"I ain't gonna ask again, Ace!" I snarled. "How are you here? How did you know to hit Revelation today, of all days?"

One eye twitched, but he managed another smirk. My fist finally did the job of wiping it off his face. He went down again.

"How!"

He spat up another gob of blood. "You still hit like a girl, Crowley."

"Why don't ye say that to me," Irish said, stepping forward and twirling her knife.

I dropped to a knee beside him, grabbed his shirt with one hand, and shot off another round by his other ear with the other.

"Okay, okay!" Ace covered his ears. "Jesus, Crowley. I can't answer you if I can't hear."

I ignored him. My shot kicked up dirt nearby, and my heart would have skipped a beat if it still pumped when I realized who I'd almost hit. So blinded by rage, I hadn't even seen Rosa creeping nearer. The dirt from the bullet even sprayed up and hit the bottom of her pants.

She didn't notice, just quietly crept forward until she was nearby me, staring down at Ace's face. Eyes narrow, brow furrowed. Teeth clenched.

How could I be so stupid? This was the man of her nightmares too. The one who tried to rape her mother right in front of her when she was just a girl. Who taught her that the world was a cruel, unforgiving place when she was far too young.

"James, is that . . ." she murmured, barely audible.

"Irish, do me a favor and get Rosa and the others away from here and safe at camp," I said, low and level.

"Aww, but I wanna see the show," she said.

"Irish, this might get ugly. It's no sight for her eyes."

Irish hung her head, muttering, "I'm always missin' the fun." She took Rosa's hand and tried to get her to follow, but Rosa's feet were fixed. Frozen as if the Yeti had taken a run at her.

Bram arrived next to convince her. "Let's get away from here, dear."

Eventually, Rosa moved, but only when he pulled her along. Still, the entire time she kept staring at Ace, the gears in her head turning and piecing it together. She'd been young, but you'll always recognize your demons.

Irish hissed like a cat at some onlookers on their way by, scaring them off.

"That your girlfriend?" Ace asked with a chuckle. Then he whistled. "Whoo-wee, she is one fine cut of meat. Met a few like her down south if you know what I mean."

My hand shot out and clutched his jaw, squeezing until I could feel the bones ready to snap.

"You don't dare look at anyone but me, you hear?" I growled.

His eyes flitted her way on purpose, just to taunt me. So, I slammed his head against the packed dirt with almost enough force to knock him out cold.

He squeezed his eyelids as he recovered. "You used to be a lot more fun."

"Oh, trust me, I'm just getting started." That wasn't a lie. I was pissed. I was dealing with feelings and emotions that I'd thought were long gone but for the visions. But it was clear, they weren't. I could've killed him right then, right there. I even shoved the barrel of my gun into his mouth until he was gagging, just to get my point across. The dirt would look a lot better plastered with his brains. And with everything screaming through my mind, I almost did it until I felt Shar's presence, a resolute shudder splintering across my chest.

That redirected my anger enough, at least to take a beat. How had Shar allowed me to wind up here, in a reunion between all these ghosts of my past? Without even a warning, either. Nothing. My path led me here, same as theirs; all of us brought together once again by God or fate.

What sort of twisted game was I a pawn in?

"I'm gonna remove my gun from your mouth, and when I do, you're gonna start talking," I said. I could barely get my voice to project above a whisper, I was so focused on Ace. "Know in your heart that I would kill you and sleep like a fucking baby tonight."

I dragged the gun out, making sure the sight cut the roof of his mouth and banged against the back of his teeth. He exhaled and pulled himself up to a sitting position.

"I like you, Crowley," he said, calm as ever. "Always did. Makes me glad to think I'm where you got this edge, but either way, it suits you."

"Wasn't from you." I lied, and he knew I lied. I could tell by his smirk. The details of how I got to where I am today and what I am are irrelevant, but he was the instrument of my demise. He knew it.

"Talk," I told him.

"They came to me a few weeks back," he said. "Guess everyone's calling them the Frozen Trio. Stupid name. Then again, I named you idiots the Scuttlers, and no one batted an eye."

I glared at him.

"The big one, Otaktay—stupid name too—together, we had a whole plan to rob Dufaux and his town for all its worth," he went on.

"Lies."

"Why would I lie? Them three feather-heads were supposed to hit the bank with us today. A score for the ages, thwarting rich men and Pinkertons alike, showing the world that money's meant to be in people's hands, not locked up in a vault. We had it all planned. But look around. Red cowards left me high and dry. I hope you find them and scalp 'em."

"All three are native?" I asked, translating his crude, offensive language.

"Yeah, so?"

"Hey!" Cecil shouted as he, Dale, Sheriff Gutierrez, and some other men in badges arrived, late to the party as usual.

I watched Ace flinch, ready to bolt like a scared rabbit. It was his nature to avoid lawmen. I got my gun on him first so he couldn't go anywhere until he was completely surrounded.

Deputies spread out to keep civilians away—who, now that the shooting stopped, were getting closer and closer. Some vendors and entertainers even started to clean up their stalls so the festival could continue.

A couple bounty hunter–looking types who'd been at the shootout arrived too, including the one I'd punched, sporting a fresh bruise. They eyed me, disappointed since they thought they'd missed out on a bounty. Though I'm sure there were countless towns around still willing to collect on Ace's many bounties. People from families like the Vanderbilts aren't ever forgotten.

Cecil hopped down from his ride and Sheriff Gutierrez from his white stallion. They practically fought to get to us first. Cecil won. He grabbed Ace by the arm and pulled his wrists back to cuff them.

"Nice job, Mr. Crowley," Dale said. "The others got away from us, but I knew you'd catch him."

I gave him a nod of approval as I ran my hands through my hair, noticing for the first time that my hat was missing.

The Yeti, transformed as he was now, was native too. Huh. What had Ace called him—Otaktay? So, all three of the Frozen Trio were natives. I wasn't sure why it mattered, but it did. It bolstered my belief that these were folks Dufaux had wronged. Now, maybe they found each other all from different tribes done dirty by Dufaux's expansion. But in my heart, I could feel it . . . this was some sort of family affair, about more than money or hurt feelings. I was reminded of that gentle kiss on the forehead the woman gave the Mind-drifter back in Elkhart.

I tried to recall Dufaux's words about Revelation's other founder and their kinship, but there was just too much going on around me to think straight.

"You're under arrest," Gutierrez said to Ace.

"Yeah, no shit," Ace replied, chuckling.

"He say anything?" Cecil addressed me, holding his injured side.

I ignored him and kept thinking.

Whenever Otaktay had approached Ace, he was either still human or so early on he didn't look like a beast yet. Otherwise Ace wouldn't have mentioned his rough appearance with some manner of insult. Assuming Ace wasn't lying, which was a tall order. Fibs spewed from the man's mouth like milk from a cow. It's how he got men to follow him so easily. Probably how he built a whole new crew for this job, most of which now lay dead in the square.

"Cat got your tongue, Crowley?" Ace said.

I rushed back to him, ignoring Cecil's protests.

"Where are the outlaws?" I asked, grabbing him by his collar.

"How should I know?" Ace said. "I told you they didn't show. Left us high and dry. You can't never trust an Injun, 'specially not a squaw."

"Where are they!?" I brought my arm back to swing, but it never came forward. I turned to find Dale holding me back from walloping Ace once more.

"Let the law be the law, Mr. Crowley," he said.

I grimaced but brought my arm down.

"That's right," Ace said. "Listen to the little pussy."

Dale looked me sidelong in the eye, then he offered a slight nod before turning his back to me. I took it as a sign.

I pushed Gutierrez aside, kicked Ace over, and pressed my boot to his throat. And there was that stupid grin again.

The bastard was enjoying this more than ever. And even if he didn't actually know anything, all I wanted from him in that moment was to be afraid. He deserved it. I deserved to see it.

But Ace would eat a bullet just to spite me and win a standoff. He'd smile all the way down to the depths of Hell and give Lucifer himself the middle finger.

"Get off him before I put you down," Gutierrez said, weapon out and aimed at me. "You caught him, so I'll forgive last night's transgression. But make no mistake, I'm the law here."

I considered pulling my gun on Gutierrez in return, but he'd probably shoot me and open a new can of worms.

"Oh, drop the act, Gutierrez," Cecil groaned. "You've got about as much power here as a mouse. And you." He stepped to get a clear view of me. "We've come this far. He's no use to us dead."

I growled but removed my boot.

Ace chuckled. "Always the good little soldier."

My boot returned, quick as a whip to his chin. Struck him so hard it knocked him out cold this time, leaving his eyes fluttering around behind his eyelids.

"Feel better?" Cecil asked.

I wish I could say I did, but it still felt like we'd lost.

All I had were more questions.

TWENTY-ONE

"What a damn mess," Gutierrez said.

I stared down at Ace, honestly wondering what to do next. My hand slid toward my pocket, toward the mirror where I could talk to Shar. *Wanting* to go to her . . . That's how desperate I was for direction. How thrown my game was.

Explosions caught my attention, coming from the direction of Dufaux's place. Actually, they were more like *pops*.

Blue and red and gold, lighting the sky in brilliant, bright light.

Fireworks. At least, that's what it looked like.

My gaze—and everyone else's—was drawn upward. Bursts of brilliant blue shimmered and sparkled, interspersed with soaring trails of red, almost like flames. It was a truly stunning sight. Only, it was still light out—not a time for fireworks unless Dufaux truly enjoyed wasting money.

And in that light, I saw it. Darting in and out of the lines of flame was the tiny silhouette of a bird.

"Keep an eye on him," I said to the group. "And never trust a word he says."

I went to move, but Dale stopped me. "You can't leave. We got one."

"He isn't a part of the Trio. Never was."

"What are you talking about?" Gutierrez said. "You saw him back there!"

"It wasn't him."

Cecil scratched his chin, wincing as he forgot his injury. "No weird ice bombs. No axe woman."

"Right. So just watch him!"

I took off at a sprint. There wasn't even time to whistle for Timp since she was way back at Rosa's camp. Checking my ammo along the way, I made sure I was loaded up with silver. I tore through a canvas tent and blew by a dozen other stands that were slowly being reoccupied. Then I scurried up some rocks until Dufaux's mansion was in view.

As I cleared the old part of town where the shanty homes were and his walled-in estate grew closer, Cecil called out from behind me.

"Get on!" he shouted. I turned, and he stretched a hand out to me. Grabbing mine, he yanked me up onto the back of his horse. Couldn't remember the last time I rode one that wasn't Timperina.

"Fireworks weren't scheduled until the gala tonight," Cecil told me.

"What the hell's going on?" I asked.

"I don't know, but you're right. That crew was new."

The light show was still going on when we reached the estate. We slid off the horse and made for the gate, which was wide open. Dufaux's yard was teeming with guests who'd either arrived recently or fled the festival grounds earlier. Women wearing prim dresses and carrying ornamental umbrellas, men in fine suits and tuxedos.

"He's still having his party?" I said, incredulous.

Dufaux's native employees were everywhere, quickly setting up the tables and drinks for a party meant to be in the evening, but forced to start sooner thanks to the chaos in town. There were a few guards, sure, but with everyone down dealing with Ace and the botched bank robbery, it was just a ragtag bunch.

"For the more . . . distinguished guests, yeah," Cecil said. "He always does, while the rabble carouses down below."

"The whole town is being torn asunder."

Cecil turned to me and shrugged. "We got people up here as soon as the robbery started. Then Dufaux convinced them it was a show for the lowly folks and invited more in early. What do you want me to say?"

"I don't know. That this is a dream? A nightmare even."

"Mr. Dufaux trusted me to handle things in town. He's got a reputation to uphold, and he pays me to listen." The words left his mouth, but he didn't seem overly convinced by them himself.

I shook my head. "Is the money really enough?"

Cecil didn't answer. And right or wrong, it wasn't wrong. These walls were the safest place in the town, probably in the whole region. Dufaux couldn't just turn frightened guests with fat wallets away. But he shouldn't have been entertaining in the first place with the whole damn region on alert. Shouldn't have been having any of this.

Everyone stared up at the light show. Fiery embers wafted down over them and flitted across the yard to the gold mine in the back. Not embers. Saints and elders, it was burning shreds of green paper. The flames made it difficult to tell, but now that it was closer, I saw the hawk clinging onto a burning bag of cash, tracing fiery lines across the sky. Greenbacks fluttered in a long stream behind it.

Another bit of blue went off to a chorus of "oohs" and "aahs."

"He's really outdone himself this year," said some prig in a bowler hat.

"A bit early though," said a woman.

Brilliant sparkles rained down, and I felt like I was in one of those novelty globes that you shake, and bits of snow swirls around like some winter wonderland. That was when I noticed a woman in a sleeveless dress rub her arms like she was chilly even though it was daytime. How could these people think this was planned?

"Hey, you can't just run in!" one of the guards barked as I pushed by an old couple, through the gate and into the yard. He stopped chasing me when he saw Cecil with me.

A few guests yelped in fright at our haste. Then, skidding to a stop by the middle of the yard, I saw frost crackling around the edges of Dufaux's diamond-shaped pools. The bird fountain seemed to be slogging to a halt as well.

The outlaws were already here. This was it. This was their plan. Ace would distract the town's defenses while the Frozen Trio enacted their true crime.

From across the yard, a confused Dufaux—clearly trying to look in control—lumbered through the crowd toward us. Everyone got out of his way, or they may as well have been trampled by a bull. His dark, double-breasted suit was exquisite. As was the top hat sitting on his head.

One look at Dufaux's big smug face, and I handled things on my own. I pulled one of my Peacemakers and aimed up at the sky, firing off three succinct shots, waste of silver or not. Dale was far off, but I hoped he'd recognize the strategy.

Dufaux hollered something while I reloaded, but he was instantly drowned out by his guests panicking. People were ducking and screaming and shoving and tossing others aside with reckless abandon. It was a fine showing of how self-absorbed these types were. To their credit, some husbands covered their wives or mistresses, but most were cowards, stuck on their own. Someone even dove into the pool.

Must've been a shock when he felt its temperature.

I spun around.

One native woman didn't act like the others at all. She wore the garb of Dufaux's housemaids, with her long black hair tied in a bun. Only she wasn't looking at me.

I followed her sightline to a young man standing on Dufaux's Spanish-tiled roof. The Mind-drifter. He, too, was dressed like the help. Only, he had bags of money piled all around him. The hawk circled above him, still carrying a burning sack of cash.

"Dufaux!" he called out, his voice thick with accent. "A gift, from Revelation's true founder!"

The young man spread his arms and threw back his head. He moved the arm I'd shot him in back in Elkhart and winced. I could imagine the fetid wound festering under his clothing. Things like that didn't heal well around here without the proper care.

Almost as if in response to some unspoken request, the hawk dropped its payload all over the rest of that flammable money. Then the Mind-drifter kicked the pile in front of him, sending it rolling and careening all over the place. Fire caught on the trellis. One bag bounced down onto the front balcony. Tiles slipped from the roof, shattering against the ground.

The thing about homes out here in the West, in this dry, dry heat . . . they go up fast.

One of Dufaux's leftover guards opened fire. I did a quick glance behind me, and Cecil was gone. Scanning the area, I found him trying to usher Dufaux to safety.

The Mind-drifter's eyes rolled back as he leaped from the roof. The hawk's talons dug into his healthy arm, eliciting thin streams of blood that were visible even from this distance. His body was too heavy for them to rise together, but once airborne its wings allowed them to soar harmlessly out to safety over the walls of Dufaux's compound.

The guard started to give chase but a tomahawk split through his neck. Blood spurted. The man staggered, futilely holding his wound. He'd be dead before the realization hit him.

But that bit of brutality really got the panic started. Everyone surged toward the gate, an unruly mob upturning tables and spilling alcohol. Which, of course, only fed the cinders of cash raining down. The court-yard blazed, which meant more fire blowing at the house and catching on curtains, wood, and whatever priceless things lay inside.

It was hard for me to not cheer it on. However, much as I disliked Dufaux, these three were my targets.

The smoke had everyone but me coughing, waving their hands in front of their faces, covering their noses with handkerchiefs. I didn't even feel the sting against my eyes, which gave me the slightest upper hand as I charged the lady outlaw.

"Where is everyone going?" a deep, cavernous voice echoed, one that almost made Dufaux's sound childlike by comparison. Otaktay. The Yeti. "You will miss the show."

The front gates slammed closed with a deafening clang.

"Monster!" a woman shrieked.

"Demon!" a man cried out. He wasn't far off.

From the outside, two grisly hands wrapped around the bars,

covered in white fur with thick, ugly nails. More than the last time I'd seen him, for sure. Then the metal, the hinges, the lock—everything started to freeze.

The party guests reached and grabbed it, but that hellish ice must've been even colder than I realized. They howled in pain like they were burning. Others stopped short. Then they saw the Yeti. Some froze in (understandable) fear. Others ran in terror. Also understandable. One thing nobody did was try to get out of the gate again.

Pushing someone out of the way, I reached the spot where tomahawk-lady had been. "Had been" being the operative phrase. Through the smoke, it was hard to locate her, but I followed the agonized cries. Across the grounds, by the stables, she was gashing another of Dufaux's guards in the back. And with him down, that was it. No more security left up here except Cecil, escorting Dufaux somewhere in the bedlam.

I could only hope my three shots had clued Dale into something horrible happening. If not, the giant flames should've. Only be a matter of time before Sheriff Gutierrez and more men came to the rescue.

I pulled my new rifle, the one "borrowed" from the jailhouse, and aimed at the woman, but there were too many frenzied guests still. I couldn't risk the shot.

To my left, Otaktay stood atop Dufaux's outer wall. The crowd ran in the opposite direction. He leaped and landed hard, cracking earth beneath his feet. The tremor knocked me onto my hind. He bellowed a deep roar and rushed Dufaux just before Cecil could get him inside. Cecil was cast aside like a rag doll, and with seemingly no effort, the monster grabbed Dufaux by the throat and hoisted him high into the air. And a monster he was—while he'd looked mostly human the first time I saw him in Lonely Hill, Otaktay was now further along in his inevitable descent into madness.

As always, the demon was winning the struggle for this man's soul. Which demon was left to be discovered? Shar might've cared, but honestly, at this point, did it really matter? Evil is evil.

Otaktay's hair—which was all over—was ashen and wiry. Face as wrinkled as boiled leather left in the sun, discolored and gray. All his teeth were sharp, and his eyes might as well've been molten lava. His clothes were torn, barely fitting anymore as his muscles had grown unnaturally large. And the frost . . . It clung to him like an aura now, swirling about his body, sloughing off like dandruff every time he moved.

"W-w-what are y-you . . ." Dufaux stammered.

It wasn't fear that hindered his speech, though I'm sure it played a small part. No. It was cold. Just being that close to Otaktay made his lips purple and his face turn colorless.

Without regard for exceptionally fragile and human parts, Otaktay turned Dufaux to face his house. A tendril of fire burst through the now-broken window as it caught on something else.

"Watch it all burn," Otaktay growled. "Everything you stole. Your home. Your wealth. Consumed."

"Let me go, you wicked, vile beast! Unhand me!"

As much as the sizable Dufaux kicked and bucked, it didn't affect the Yeti in the slightest.

I brought my rifle up as I got to a knee and aimed. At my angle and distance, it was as likely I'd hit Dufaux as the one holding him.

"Let him go," I said. "Let all of them go. You've got me to answer to."

"No!" Otaktay thundered. "He has to watch. They all need to watch."

"Mr. Crowley, don't you dare shoot at me!" Dufaux yelled through quivering lips.

Here's the thing about silver bullets. One's just gotta graze something touched by Hell, and you're a step ahead. So, lowering my sights enough to avoid Dufaux altogether, I plugged Otaktay right in the ankle.

Silvery steam poured out. His roar was like nothing I've ever heard. Freezing breath extinguished the fire on a nearby tablecloth. Dufaux was lucky enough to be tossed aside during the entire ordeal. However, he now lay in a literal pile of shit beside the stables. I spotted Cecil back outside and rushing to his employer's aid when I heard a woman's cry from behind me.

"Stay out of this, *Łiga Ndeeń*!" I wasn't sure what those last words translated to, but it was the second time tomahawk-lady had said it to me. I was sure it was something foul. All her face paint was washed clean in order for her to blend in, showing me more than just crow's feet in the corners of her eyes. She was older than I'd expected for such a spry woman. In her fifties at least, yet still able to move how she did. Color me impressed.

I ducked just before a tomahawk slashed through my forehead. Then again, as her second one came around. Even still, I'm reasonably sure that one shaved off a couple strands of hair. She swung again, and I parried with my rifle. Our weapons slid off each other, sparking as I spun around.

"Nice to see you again, too," I said as I swung left, forcing her to favor one side. I guided her again and again until I had her backed up against a wall. Suddenly, I was ten feet in the air, swinging at nothing.

"This doesn't concern you!" Otaktay grabbed me from behind and flung me so high and hard I lost track of where I'd landed. Next thing I knew, I was upside down against a wall, covered in shards of glass and splinters I was lucky I couldn't feel.

Somehow, I'd wound up inside the mansion. Fire licked at my boots, spreading fast through the foyer and across the first floor. Mr. Dufaux's giant portrait was now just black char.

I rolled over so I could get to my knees and found myself facing an ornate mirror. Couldn't you guess who was staring back at me?

"Stop fooling around, Crowley," Shar warned.

"Oh, now you show up? You owe me an explanation when I'm through." I cracked my neck. It popped a few times.

"I owe you nothing. End this."

Just as I retrieved my rifle to return to the fray, Otaktay burst through the grand front doors, ripping one of them off its hinges entirely. The mahogany iced over, the edges growing slick and sharp.

"You're all the same!" Otaktay flung the door sideways like he was playing a casual game of horseshoes. It slashed through the wall of Dufaux's front parlor on its way to cleave me in two, but I dove out of its path. It cracked the grand stair's railing, breaking through to hit a load-bearing post. Some of the second floor caved, bringing more hungry fire down.

I shot from the hip, getting one round off through the beast's ribs. He groaned and vaulted into an adjacent room, leaving a silvery wake behind. The two bullets he'd absorbed would've had other monsters down for the count. But Hell had a true hold of this one.

I followed him into what looked like Dufaux's sitting room, only now it was covered in ash and soot.

"You kill and you steal!" the Yeti shouted, throwing a sofa at me. I ducked and rolled, firing every cartridge until the Winchester clicked empty and I stowed it. I landed a few shots, but Otaktay was something else. Werewolves tended to go down under one or two carefully placed silver bullets. He'd taken at least five and still stood.

"Thieves!" Otaktay's rage was a living thing beneath his skin, trying to break free. He rushed me, grabbed me by my duster, and flung me upward. A loose spindle split my side as I crashed through the sitting room's ceiling and into the second floor. I landed, half hanging through the hole, and quickly pulled myself up before he reached up and tore me in two.

Fire ravaged this story. Hot, acrid smoke filled the air. As I got my bearings, I heard whimpering. Clamoring to my feet, each movement threatening to collapse the floor beneath me, I called out, "Who's there?"

She coughed. The sound drew me to a closet where one of Dufaux's maids was hiding—that very same native woman who'd taken my coat a day earlier.

"Get outside," I said to her. No answer; just more sobs. "They aren't here for you. You've gotta go, now!"

When she stayed put, I did what I did best and interfered. Taking her around the waist, I ran through the French doors leading to the second-story balcony, pulling my lasso from my belt loop.

Before I jumped, I saw silhouettes of lawmen approaching the compound's walls from all directions. After I jumped, I lassoed the railing post, swung around, and dropped the lady into one of the garden pools. It was shallow but cold. She'd make it even if she couldn't swim.

I kept swinging, coming around for the first floor with my Peacemaker pulled. But before I could use my surprise move to shoot Otaktay in the back of the head, the Mind-drifter's hawk slashed down and clawed at my eyes. I managed to fend it off, but not before I lost my grip and slammed into a wall. An instant later, I landed awkwardly back in the sitting room, opening my eyes just in time to see the Yeti materialize a shield of ice between me and him.

"What demon is it that has its hold on you, friend?" I said, rising and recovering my lasso.

"The only demon is here, in this home," he retorted.

My left knee bent inward. The tomahawk-lady slid by, having slashed me there. A death sentence for a normal man to be hemmed like that in a fight, but I regained my balance quickly.

She spun in one smooth motion to face me. I noticed she only had one axe now. Smoke and flame swirled all around her, making me wonder if she, too, had some demon in her. Spattered blood painted her body from the jaw down as if replacing her war paint.

"Get it!" she called back to the Yeti. Beyond the ice, I saw Otaktay's silhouette turn and stomp toward the courtyard.

I returned my attention to the woman, having made the mistake of moving it from her in the first place. Fighting means making mistakes and just trying not to make the last one.

Tomahawk-lady sneered. "No bounty for you." Her words were stunted, like she struggled with English.

She rushed me.

I fired once.

Twice.

She ducked and weaved as she came, swift as a mountain lion and twice as fierce. Iron hummed as she swung, sending me into a dance of my own. But I was done playing games. Instead of blocking with a weapon this time, I raised my forearm and let the blade sink in through to the bone. Then, I grabbed her swinging arm at the same time so it didn't slice clean through.

She gawked at the wound and my lack of reaction.

"*Chiihdii*," she whispered.

I head-butted her hard enough to knock her off her feet, then kicked the tomahawk out of her grasp and toward the fire. My sliced leg buckled a little, but I pressed on.

"I'm not here for you," I said.

I spat just to wash the taste of smoke from my mouth, pungent enough that it bothered even my muted senses. Then I took off after the Yeti. His ice wall was melting fast from the blaze, allowing me to climb and slide right over it. More of the stairs broke off and fell all around me. I dodged what I could and shouldered through the rest until I stood at the edge of the courtyard.

Otaktay stood before the totem, glowing red from the fires raging above. Tables for when the party made its way inside were all knocked over. Plants were drowning in ash.

Otaktay reached for the totem like it was gold. I'm damn certain his hands shook with anticipation because it sure as hell wasn't fear.

Since he was out of range of my lasso, I reached for my second pistol and accidentally brushed my belt satchel, flipping it open so I spotted the goat-Nephilim's harmonica inside. I'd almost forgotten about the thing. Digging the instrument out, I ignored the melancholic beckoning it brought as I lifted it to my lips. Voices telling me I'd fail, that Heaven would cast me out to face eternal damnation. That I was hopeless. Irredeemable. Damned . . .

Fighting back a dry heave, I played, and as the note hung, I yelled "Stop!" just like I had with the werewolves.

It got Otaktay to stop all right, but only to eye me quizzically. Where they'd been affected by it, Otaktay snarled. He was still in control. Apparently, the hellish instrument didn't work so well on truly hellish things. Or maybe it was my limited musical skills.

Either way, the Yeti returned his focus to the totem instead of attacking me. Who needed a harmonica when that thing had him mesmerized like a dog with a bone?

"These things never work when needed," I complained and stowed it. Drawing the second Peacemaker fast I shot him three times in the back. He growled and collapsed onto an elbow, huffing hard enough to freeze the fountain in the middle of the yard.

"You three are starting to get on my nerves," I said as I approached. I had one silver bullet left, then I'd have to reload. I had to make it count. But the entire courtyard started to glow. At first, I thought maybe it was the moon, but it was him. It was Otaktay. Frost formed from nowhere, whirling around him in a twister. His eyes shone bright.

"We will take what is ours!" he bellowed.

A shock wave shot through the yard like a cannon as his roar carried. Ice spiked along the path, breaking everything it encountered. Walls and columns ruptured. Swathes of the roof collapsed, all of it speeding up the fire's wanton destruction.

The totem was blown back, too, flying out through the mansion and plunging into the quarry at its rear. At least, that was my estimation without being able to fully watch its descent.

Otaktay glared at me, bore his fangs, then took off through the opening like a wild beast running on all fours.

What else could I do but go hunting?

TWENTY-TWO

I didn't always make the best choices in life, and I fear that attribute followed me into the unlife I now had. I've tried to be a better man now, sure. Not to rob people who didn't deserve it or hurt people who didn't have it coming. But good choices don't always mean doing right or wrong things. Especially when it comes to serving a master like I do.

Most folks who see a demon beast like the Yeti tuck tail and run. They count their blessings and find a safe place, hoping someone else will deal with it.

Problem is, I'm that someone.

I followed Otaktay, reloading my pistols as I went, keeping one tucked in my belt. I hopped from rocky ledge to rocky ledge down into the quarry, using scaffolding when I could. I could've jumped all the way down like the Yeti had but snapping my ankles would waste even more time in the long run.

Beneath my boots, the scaffolding turned slick. A thin veneer of ice formed, sending me caroming down the rest of the way. I rolled, bounced, and just about any other thing that would've killed a normal man. When I landed, it was with a splash. I may not have felt the scalding water, but layers of my skin bubbled all the same.

I quickly crawled out of the hot spring before it turned me skeletal and took in my surroundings. Caverns and workstations filled the impressive mine, all snaking around so Dufaux could siphon these lands for all they were worth. White steam from a dozen or more similar springs swirled all about, making it difficult to traverse with confidence.

However, I had no trouble locating Otaktay a few dozen yards ahead of me, standing in front of the totem, wheezing.

Black ichor leaked from wounds all over his bulky, gorilla-like frame. The silver was doing its damage, working through him like a poison, weakening the demon's hold. But it wasn't enough. Not yet.

"You're not yourself!" I called to him. "Push out the demon that has you. Reject him, and I won't need to kill you, too."

"Why?" His laugh quickly turned to a hacking, expelling more black, bloody discharge.

"Because you've hurt enough people."

"Only who we had to. And you . . . bounty hunter . . . you're next." He let loose a primal roar that I'm sure could've woken Lucifer from slumber. Already, rocks and small boulders were cascading down the chasm from all the activity, but when he raised both fists and slammed them down, it was like a small earthquake.

A wave of ice radiated away from the impact crater, coruscating out and up the quarry. Rock shattered. Scaffolding and structures crumbled. And every spring the ice touched exploded like dynamite the moment ice touched them.

The damage to the mines was extensive. It was like the sound of low, rumbling thunder as the tunnels caved in all around us. Entire portions of the cliffs came down in sheets, pulling those poor shanty homes with it.

I'd never seen anything like it. And then I saw nothing. The spring I'd just escaped went off, a flash of white enveloping me. I couldn't even open my eyes. Hell, I wasn't even sure I was on the ground still.

Before I could prepare myself, the Yeti's grisly nails dug into my chest. That last expulsion of power had him somehow looking even more beastly. Gone was nearly any semblance of humanity in his facial features, and along with it, any hope I had of him reverting to whoever the Otaktay was who'd once roamed this Earth. The man beneath the monster was reaching the point of no return.

He pinned me against rock, ready to pound my face in. I flicked my pistol's aim and put a bullet through his belly. He swatted it out of my hands before I could get off another shot.

We were so close, I could see the back of his throat as he roared. All his teeth were razor-sharp now. Then, with speed and agility that belied his size, he pulled me forward and slammed me back again with a full, massive palm. I was sure bones crunched under the impact, but it might've been the rock face.

Ice snaked across my chest, working to hold me against the stone so I couldn't move. But as much as I might've expected it, he never started pounding on my skull. He just kept holding me there, like he didn't actually want to kill me. Like, maybe, there was a shred of humanity left . . .

Gunshots crackled across the unnaturally chilly air.

My gaze moved to the ridge of the quarry where muzzles flashed. All of Dufaux's army had come to bear. Deputies and sheriffs, Pinkertons, bounty hunters still wanting a fight—everyone. Shots peppered the Yeti's back and the frozen dirt all around us.

"Hold him down, Crowley!" Dale's voice echoed.

None of them knew I couldn't be hurt by mere bullets. Yet there they were, all firing in my direction with reckless abandon.

Otaktay dropped me and swung his hand, sending a surge of ice that carved a line in the foundation beneath where many of the shooters stood. Dale and others slid down deeper in the quarry with us while all the rest kept shooting. Those who lived, at least. The tomahawk-lady was up there too, cutting through them, so quick none could hit her.

I'll hand it to Dale. Holding the Yeti down was good advice and exactly what I planned to do. Only, I wouldn't do it alone.

Recovering quickly, I strung my lasso around the Yeti's neck. Light engulfed us as it went taut, and in an instant, unseen forces commanded him to his knees. He couldn't thrash or kick, the weight of the White Throne's judgment all too heavy.

His whole body vacillated, both him and the unholy entity

controlling him. Two parts of the same whole, split apart. I muttered in Latin, words that came to me almost on a whim as if I were speaking the Almighty's vengeance into being. I guess technically I was.

Both man and demon resisted, each making sounds godless and inhuman. The bond was strong. Otaktay's face screwed up in a look that was one part fury and one part agony. My own boots sunk through ground that should've been solid as I held tight and kept chanting what amounted to a prayer or supplication of some kind.

Bang!

A gunshot echoed like a hammer-struck bell, reverberating through the quarry and demanding attention. A hole punctured my jacket, then body, and pockmarked the dirt behind me. The Mind-drifter skipped down into the quarry from the opposite direction of town, away from my reinforcements.

He couldn't wield his rifle quite right with his injured arm, but he was still a dead-shot marksman. He fired again, hitting my neck. The force of it made my stance swing wider, but I gripped the lasso with two hands and kept devout to it.

"Ignore him, Ahusaka!" the Yeti shouted, eyes closed in pain. "Get the Piasa!"

A sinister, demonic voice filled the space around me. Almost like a snake hissing, but there were words beneath the trill. The demon possessing Otaktay was desperate not to lose its plaything. Trying to turn me too.

"Give in . . . Relinquish . . . You can be powerful too . . ."

It spoke and gave me chills. Hellish, awful chills. Now that I'd heard it, I couldn't help but wonder who it was.

A hawk screeched. I spotted it just before talons slashed at my hands, desperate to pry them free of the rope. Losing purchase, I released with one hand to swipe at the bird. I got lucky and my fingers closed around its neck. Wings flapped wildly. It cried out, snapping with its beak but unable to make a connection. My grip on the Yeti loosened, and my feet began to drag.

Bird bones cracked as I had no choice but to squeeze. Its pained sounds transitioned to the distant cry of a man as the one Mukwooru had called Mind-drifter, and Otaktay had just called Ahusaka, returned to his body. The suffering in his tone . . . the pain . . . I had no idea what to expect. Was it like when I Divined and experienced all those foul, awful moments right at the brink of another man's death?

"Why . . . are you . . . protecting him?" Otaktay rasped, his eyes granite. I could barely see his form, it withered so quickly within a whirlwind of frost and dust, between flesh and pure darkness.

"Nothing I do is for him!" I yelled back at the Yeti as the demon's tempting persisted, a whisper that was somehow also loud enough to drown out everything around me.

"Don't you wish to be more than just a tool?"

I ground my teeth, trying to shut my ears, desperate to ignore the ethereal voice. The source of all this chaos.

"Show yourself, coward!" I barked.

"The White Throne has lost. The White Throne is lost."

With how intertwined Otaktay's soul was, breaking the possession was gonna kill him. There was no escaping that fact now. Rage had doomed him, as it dooms us all.

So, I went back to my chanting, losing myself in it. All the gunfire around me sounded like meek little *ticks*. There was only me, the taunts of whatever demon possessed Otaktay, and his host. I had him. I could almost taste Shar's satisfaction.

Then my lasso snapped. The shock of it sent me staggering back and the Yeti rolling in the opposite direction. The tomahawk-lady landed between us, weapon in hand. Her tan skin glistened with sweat and blood. She glared at me, eager for another fight.

"Now it ends, *Łiga Ndeeń*. The Piasa rises!"

She went to charge at me before stopping suddenly. A pinpoint of red spread across her chest like spilled ink. She slowly grasped at the wound, looking confused more than anything, before tipping over with a lifeless *thud*.

Dale aimed from a low ledge, his pistol smoking.

"Kill him!" Dale said, running toward me. "Kill him now, Crowley!"

Losing grip while so close to banishing the demon had me stunned, but I drew my silver-dusted knife from my boot. If bullets hadn't done the job by now, they weren't likely to. I'd exorcise this demon the old-fashioned way. A blade through the heart of his host first. The Yeti—Otaktay—was as weakened as I was, flailing about to find which way was up or down. This was the time.

Dale reached me and I used him to stand. He staggered but managed to hold me.

"We actually got them, Crowley," he said. "We got—" Half his head blew off, spraying the rock behind him with red mist. He didn't fall over. Was just stuck like that, grasping me.

Ahusaka aimed his marksmen rifle from the lowest part of the valley by the Piasa totem.

"You killed her!" he shrieked. He fired again, this one hitting Dale in the side and sending his corpse to the ground. A life traded for a life in this sick circle of death we call living. Pawn for pawn.

All the men shooting down from the ridge turned their attention to Ahusaka and forced him to quickly find cover. Bullets snapped and hissed. He must've been hard to see from up there with all the particulates swirling.

Otaktay and I caught each other's gazes as we came to—him from the power of the now inert lasso and me from watching a good man die. He growled. I think I growled too.

His bloodred eyes flitted between me, Dale, and the dying woman.

Like a volcano, he was about to erupt. But then, tomahawk-lady whispered something to him with her fading breath. I couldn't hear what it was in the chaos, but his monstrous features suddenly softened. He dropped to his knees and touched her forehead with his own.

Having no time for sentiment, I charged the exposed Yeti, knife ready to do my dirty work.

He acted like I wasn't even there, scooping up the woman's limp, dead body and bounding away, just like that. Landing beside Ahusaka, he conjured a dome of ice so even the young native couldn't shoot outward.

Ice *chinked* as bullets pounded into the shield, one after another, with no more ice reforming. The Yeti, it seemed, was too injured to summon any more.

I kept charging.

Otaktay regarded me with sad, lonesome eyes before he wrapped his arm around Ahusaka. After some protest, the Mind-drifter dropped his marksman rifle to grab the totem instead.

Otaktay took him, the totem, and their partner's corpse before he burst through the icy dome and cleared the quarry in a few bounding leaps. Together, they fled away from Revelation and into the badlands to the north.

And the Frozen Trio was down to two.

TWENTY-THREE

The quarry was a war zone. I'd been to fields that suffered through the Civil War and grand military skirmishes between frontiersmen and natives. I'd walked the grounds of Little Bighorn hunting a wendigo. This had that same feel.

I stood and took a spin. The entire quarry was split open and buried in on itself in most places. It'd take an army to get it ready for mining again.

When enough bullets hit the dirt, and enough rocks slide, there's a sort of fog that doesn't lift for hours. It hangs and seeps into everything. Scratches your throat, makes you cough, even gag if the stink of bodies isn't enough. There could've been more bodies, sure, but a couple dozen between here and in the square was bad enough.

They were strewn about, bloody, broken. Some died falling into the quarry or shattered their legs and now cried out for death. Others had been gutted by the lady outlaw's tomahawk, entrails spilled out over the rock. She sure made a show of brutality. A worthy strategy to put fear in foes, I suspect.

None of those lost lives wounded me like the one only a few paces away. Lying on his back, arms and legs spread out, there was Dale. He didn't have a face to speak of, but it was him. And funny enough,

Ahusaka's hawk had landed right next to him, wings spread open in a similar fashion. Almost poetic.

I barely knew the man, but I was pissed. At him. At the damn Mind-drifter who shot him. At myself. "You should've stayed in Elkhart," I said to him, sighing and shaking my head. Then I looked up to the sky, the falling sun barely visible through the haze. "You'd better look after him."

At that, Shar's presence itched across my Black Badge scar in a manner I couldn't deny. Nor did I want to now that things had quieted. I pulled out my cracked shaving mirror and glared straight at that ethereal swirl, wishing I could wring her by the throat.

Most of all, I was mad at her and that bloody White Throne.

"You let them escape again," she said first.

"You can go to Hell," I said.

"No, I cannot."

That smug response just pissed me off further. My hands clenched. My grip was so tight I almost crushed the mirror. "Where did you send me? Rosa? Ace? Them? It's the goddamn Holy Trinity in Revelation!"

"Watch yourself, Crowley."

"Oh, I'm watching. Did you know about this? About all of them converging here?"

"I knew only what I needed to. Same as you."

"Enough!" I barked. "That ain't an answer. You set me up to fail."

I fought every urge to throw that mirror down into that pit and spit on it on the way.

"Where were you when the foundation of the Earth was laid?" she asked. "Were you the one who determined its measurements? Were you there when the stars were hung in their place?"

She was quoting Job to me, and I wasn't interested in her sermons. "No, were you?"

"You, like I, are where you were always meant to be!" she scorned. Her shade darkened and as it did, I felt something familiar in my arm. I *felt*, in general. Oh, God, did it hurt, ironic as it is to bring His name into this.

I lost control of my fingers, unable to drop the mirror or turn it away. Shar's ghastly eyes just fixed on mine as the flesh all up my arm to my elbow shriveled and flaked away. Muscle and sinew were revealed, then bone.

"What is this?" I asked, hardly able to speak. But I knew. This. This was true pain she was allowing me to feel again. The thing I always talked about craving, reminding me what it was like to be mortal. That was what was happening to my arm. It was becoming mortal again, how it should look, decomposed and underground for decades.

"Is it too much for you?" Shar questioned. "Do you surrender to damnation?" That tone of hers. Was she toying with me? Pulling my strings like I was in a puppet show for children.

"I surrender to nothing," I said through clenched teeth. My knees buckled. The pain was overwhelming, traveling up my arm and exploding across my entire body.

"If I would've told you what you wish you knew, would you have come?"

"To kill the bastard who killed me and left me with you? With fucking bells on."

"Yet, you are not here for him."

"Don't tell me what I am or ain't here for. I'll tell you this, Shar." The pain intensified. "*Grafaein*," I added with a deep groan. "Those outlaws, up close, they don't seem too much like the villains here."

"That is irrelevant."

The pain vanished, as if it were never there, leaving only numbness in its wake except for a slight itch on my chest. I blinked, and my arm returned to normal.

"Some powers mustn't be called upon," Shar said. "You must catch the Yeti and his follower, and unveil the demon behind the possession, or I fear the terror his rage will unleash next upon our kingdom."

I stared down at my arms and hands. "Your kingdom," I scoffed, standing. This wasn't church, and Shar didn't deserve me on my knees before her after that stunt. "I've got no home there."

"Catch them, Crowley."

"I plan to. And next time, I don't want your fucking help!"

Enough was enough. I finally gave into my fury and flung the mirror against the fallen rocks. I bared my teeth and watched it shatter into a million pieces. I let myself imagine it snuffing her out forever, but it wouldn't.

I couldn't escape her. I knew I couldn't.

She was anywhere and everywhere, and I was nothing and no one.

But it brought me momentary joy in the midst of shit.

An all-seeing angel—she had to know the sort of reunion I'd been walking into. Just more tests and games when the truth might've helped.

I knew how Ace operated, for instance. I could've stopped him. Saved lives.

And if Shar didn't know? Someone did. Someone up there in the clouds, taking a piss on humanity . . . They knew. If not? That's pretty damn weak.

"Crowley, who you talking to down there!" I heard Cecil shout. He coughed on the rampant dust.

"Just cursing myself!" I grunted.

"Anyone make it?"

"Just me," I said, barely loud enough for him to have heard.

I searched for the best way to climb out and found a rockslide at an incline I could handle. A part of me considered hauling Dale with me, but I decided against it. I didn't want to risk Divining him and experiencing his last moments, brief as they were.

I've found that when I know the victim—when it's personal—I feel their agony all the worse. And as unexpected and unwelcome as it was, I'd come to care for Dale these past days. I'd make sure he was laid to rest right when the time came.

As it was, Cecil gripped my hand and helped me up onto the ridge. The very hand I'd just watched be reduced to bone and ash. It gave me a moment's pause before I shook the vision.

We were by the poor section of town. A hundred or so natives gathered, looking down at their homes at the bottom of the pit, at the destruction, each more confused than the next. Why wouldn't they be? Power like what'd just been witnessed wasn't supposed to exist.

Cecil? He had the fear of God put in him. Eyes wide, exhausted, his following words matched his expression. "Crowley . . . What was that down there?"

"Damned if I know," I said.

"You were there. What'd you see!" He had me by the shoulders by then, shaking.

I brushed him away. "I saw people so filled with hate for a man, they broke the world. Hate like you and I have never known. So where is he?"

"Who?"

"Who do you think?" I asked. "The one they hate. Reginald Dufaux."

"He's safe, back at the mansion . . . What's left of it."

I started heading that way. It was a longer walk there than it had been down. When I finally made it back up the hill, people were all over—workers, deputies, bounty hunters, opulent moneybaggers who'd been guests at the world's worst soiree. They were all covered in dirt and some with blood. A lady even had her dress half-burned from the fire, and her husband was working to cover her with his coat like modesty mattered one bit right now.

A native woman sat with her head cradled in her arms. She looked up, wiped tears. When she spotted me, she rose and ran, pushing anyone aside who stood in her way. I worried for a moment she was gonna strike me, or at least try to. Then I recognized her. Last I'd seen her, I was dropping her into the garden pool after having freed her from the burning estate.

"You," she said. "My son, did you see him inside? I haven't seen him. Please."

"Get back!" Cecil ordered, catching up fast. He shoved her so hard she tripped and fell onto her behind. A few other locals rushed to help her. "I said back, all of you!" Cecil flaunted his firearm, then pulled me along.

I grabbed his wrist and jerked the weapon down. Then I turned to help the woman to her feet. "I'm sorry, ma'am. I'll keep an eye open for your son."

"Thank you," she said before being pulled away by her fellows.

"The hell's wrong with you?" I asked Cecil. "Can't you see these people have been through enough? And for what? Money? Nah. That's too simple. There's something more that piece of shit boss of yours isn't saying."

"Why are you worried about Dufaux right now? We gotta go after them," Cecil said.

"Did *you* see where they went?"

He shook his head.

"Exactly."

Cecil took a few steps ahead of me. "Well, let's go talk to that bank robber. He knows something to hit at a time like this. I'm sure of it. I'll beat it out of him if I've gotta. That little stunt of his got Billy killed."

I assumed that was one of his Pinkerton crew.

"His stunts always get people killed," I said.

"You know him?"

"Knew."

"Who is he? Let's go—"

"Later," I said. "Your boss. Now."

As much as I wanted to dole out justice to my murderer, I had to know the answer to what happened here. The "why" behind the wreckage that stole so many lives and homes.

One thing I abhorred more than anything was being lied to, and Dufaux wasn't sharing something. That look on Otaktay's face, Ahusaka's Piasa markings, and a seemingly worthless totem. Everything about what happened seemed targeted. In the West, if you aren't after money or riches, it's revenge that's left. And the Frozen Trio burned all the money they'd taken already.

Ace, on the other hand . . . he might've been many things, but a liar ain't really one of them. Sure, he fibbed and jested and loved to spin you around with his words, but he was too arrogant to lie outright. The truth's a weapon to men like him. A way to instill fear. I saw it in his eyes. His pride was wounded. He'd been duped by the Frozen Trio when he thought they were a team after a score that would secure his legacy.

Dufaux's front gates had been snapped open. Parts of it were still frozen, but judging by the mud and worn surfaces around it, the panicked crowd had eventually broken through.

Snowflakes mixed with ash drifted in the murky skies around it—reminded me of the day this chase started in Lonely Hill. The yard was a catastrophe. Horses from the stables roamed free, picking at toppled food. Things were burnt, frozen, covered in blood—a pigsty of the highest order. Wounded men and women cried out. Half had probably been stampeded by their own. A few had lost their lives in the chaos. Probably more that would be discovered later on.

Embers smoldered all over what was left of the manor itself, the flames dying out slow in the warming air. You could barely tell the mansion had ever even had a second floor, and most of the first was just a maze of stubborn, singed walls that refused to fall. The stairs had crumbled, allowing a straight-shot view to the courtyard and the empty podium where the Piasa totem once resided.

"Crowley, I've never seen anything like this in my life," Cecil said. He knelt by one of the shallow pools. One of Dufaux's guards hung face-first over the ledge, the water completely frozen up to his waist.

"Where's Dufaux?" I asked plainly.

"I . . ." He stood and sucked through his teeth. "This way."

He led me around the side of the mansion to a storm door. A beam had snapped and fell over it, and it took both of us to lift it off—though that was mainly for show on my part. Cecil was left huffing for air, so I gasped a bit too.

We went down by some lamplight. Interesting thing about basements, rich as a man might be, they always remind me of crypts. Low ceilings, stone walls, and a musty smell that nothing can chase off.

Most everything looked like storage. Foodstuffs, furniture, and all sorts of other things a property this size requires to maintain. The other rooms were bedrooms, small, without much more than lumpy-looking beds too narrow for proper adults. Quarters for the live-in help, I gathered. The ceiling sagged in places from damage to the first floor. Didn't look safe.

We had to step around a spot where a post had given out, and the damage caused a bedroom door to have broken off one hinge and hang sideways. I spotted a bare foot through the opening as I passed.

"He's down this way in the wine cellar," Cecil said.

He kept going, but I turned. One tug and the door broke all the way off, falling with a *clack* that made even the hardened Pinkerton jump.

The room was a mess, but not because of the attack. Clothes and trinkets were everywhere. Worst of all, the young native man I'd watched serve wine to Dufaux sat slumped against the wall. He looked like a bundle of kindling wrapped in dirty cloth, head sagging down against his chest. A nasty-looking gash on the back of his skull had smeared blood along the stone walls.

Dead as a doornail.

"Chariots of fire," Cecil groaned, arriving at my back. "He was a good kid. Helpful. Something must have fallen on him."

I couldn't be sure, but I had to wonder if this wasn't that lady's son she'd been worried about.

I glanced up. A portion of the ceiling had ruptured, but only on the opposite side of the room. There was no debris anywhere near the body. Not even a stone unturned. Something could've knocked him on the noggin and sent him stumbling away, but I'd have answers soon enough.

Kneeling by his side, I whispered, "*A tenebris ad lucem.*" Then, I took off my glove and took his bare hand to Divine him . . .

* * *

I staggered back, a blow to the side of his head making me all sorts of dizzy. But two pairs of arms held me up. Some of Dufaux's goons I didn't recognize.

"I will not ask you again, boy," Dufaux said, not even bothering to use a name. "That dish was a gift from General Lee himself. Where'd you hide it?"

Dufaux kicked over a meager chest at the end of the bed. Clothes and other belongings spilled out. Probably everything the kid owned. Dufaux swiped his foot through it, finding no dish.

"I took nothing," my host sniveled. "I swear it. I would never."

"First, you dare open your filthy mouth in my dining room—while

I'm trying to eat nonetheless—then you steal from me? Have I not given you a life?"

"I didn't—"

"Who else then, huh? Your mama?" one of the goons said, then guffawed.

"We saw you sniffing around," the other added.

"Only because it was missing!" the young man protested with my lips.

"Lies!" Dufaux wound up and backhanded me across the face. It hurt. A lot. Big as he was, the strike sent everyone off balance, and my young host's head whipped back against the stone. I'm not sure which one did it, really. I think I felt my neck snap from the force of the blow just before I heard my skull crunch against the wall, and my legs become suddenly useless.

Vision faded. There was some unclear arguing between Dufaux and the others. By the time the body dropped, all I saw was black . . .

* * *

I gasped back into my own consciousness. My hand moved from the spot on my head where the young man's had been gashed to my neck and back again. As usual, it took a few moments for me to resolve who I currently was and that the pain wasn't my own. I focused while pulling on my glove.

I should've known simply by the way Dufaux treated this boy when he dared to speak in his dining room that he'd have no problem being abusive. But this? Dufaux had walloped his servant so hard he'd killed him. Over a silver plate the kid hadn't even stolen.

I had.

Maybe it was guilt that sent me fuming, or perhaps it was everything that'd happened, but I swept out of that room so fast I knocked Cecil against the door frame. Around a corner, Dufaux waited by a row of wine barrels. He had one guard with him, one of Cecil's Pinks.

"Mr. Crowley, you're alive!" Dufaux exclaimed. His skin glistened with a sweat he hadn't worked hard enough to build up. "What happened out there? Did you get them?"

I bull-rushed him, forearm across his throat, and forced him back against one of the wine casks so hard the plug broke off and dark purple liquid *glugged* out. For all his size and bluster, in the wake of my wrath, Dufaux folded like a bad poker hand.

"What are you doing?" Cecil yelled.

"Is he insane?" the other Pink said. I heard them both shuffle for their weapons. I didn't care.

"Have you lost your mind?" Dufaux shrieked.

I ignored them all, knowing they couldn't do anything to me anyway. Grabbing him by his back collar, I dragged him across the room, found a chair, then forced him down into it.

The look on Reginald Dufaux's face told me everything I needed to know. That this oversized shit stain was a coward.

"You were right, Cecil," Dufaux said, panicked. "He is with them. Shoot him. Shoot him now!"

I turned to Cecil and the other and fixed them with a glower so icy they both froze. Then I whipped around. Dufaux tried to stand, but I pressed a palm against his chest. He started leaning, so I got in his face.

"You wanna know where that precious silver plate went?" I drew one of my revolvers. I didn't aim it, just held it upright, clicked the cylinder open, and emptied a silver round into my gloved palm. "Right here."

Dufaux stared at the bullet, baffled.

"I stole it," I clarified for him since it seemed fear had his brain twisted. "Melted it down so I could try and save your pathetic little kingdom. You killed a boy over a goddamned dish."

"Him?" he said. He didn't point or even look toward where the kid was.

"Say his name."

His mouth opened, but no words came out. He tried again to the same end before he just shook his head. The bastard didn't even know who was keeping his goblet full all day.

"Figures," I spat. And I really did. Right in his face. If he wasn't incensed before . . .

Dufaux edged forward, but his shoe dipped in red wine, and he regarded it in disgust before shifting his position.

"You're going to need more than bullets and bravado if you plan to come at me," he hissed. "Cecil, cuff this man and toss him in a cell."

"Your sheriff already tried," I said.

"Cecil!"

The Pinkerton's partner moved, but Cecil gave him a look. I struggled to get a read on him until he spoke.

"The boy back there? That was Tosahwi," Cecil said.

I nodded.

"You killed him?" Cecil asked his boss.

"Oh please, it was an accident," Dufaux scoffed.

"Accident?" I spoke, soft. "His skull was split open like a sack of melons, neck snapped."

"These people are mine to—"

"What happened—did the kid recognize that tattoo? Did he know too much? I can't imagine this was all about some dinnerware. And if you *did* do that to him over a fancy dish, I can only imagine what you've done to those outlaws to set them after you."

"Cecil, I demand you remove this man at once!" Dufaux bellowed.

"What did you do, Dufaux?" I asked. "Why does that tattooed marksman hate you so damn much."

"I don't know! Cecil, you damn fool. Do something!"

"You know, the marksman has a name too," I said. "They all do. Otaktay, Ahusaka . . . I didn't catch the lady's name, but I bet you know."

I looked over at the Pinkertons. The stranger looked confused about what to do, but Cecil didn't. He watched, wanting the answer as much as I think I did. Without the promise of a healthy gold mine outside to stuff his pockets, I guess he decided to stop being a patsy. Or maybe I'd read the hard-nosed gunman wrong from the start.

"Come on, Dufaux. What was her name?" I pressed.

Dufaux snarled. "Dyani."

"Dyani. Pretty. Well, she's dead now, and her blood is on your hands. How much was it worth, Reggie?"

"Don't you dare disrespect me."

I backhanded him just like he did to Tosahwi, only I held back. A little.

"You—"

I raised my hand to strike again, and he shut up. I caught Cecil's gaze in my peripherals and looked back.

"What happened in that mine," he said. "I've never seen anything like it." He waved to his partner. "We'll be outside, Mr. Crowley. Take your time."

It took a few nudges to get his partner moving, but eventually, they both retreated upstairs.

"Cecil, get your ass back here!" Dufaux yelled. "I won't pay you. Cecil, you damn nigger!"

Probably best not to insult a man whose service you still needed. Dufaux's cries rightfully went unanswered, leaving him alone and face-to-face with me. He broke into laughter, trying to act tough, but, to me, it was pitiable.

"Impossible to find decent help."

"Money can't buy everything," I said.

He groaned. "That's the damn truth."

I paced across the room, gun in hand, dragging the muzzle along wine barrels just to hear the *thunks*.

"So, are you going to kill me?" he asked.

"I'll admit, shooting you would feel good." I turned to him. "I already spared one man's life who deserved to die today. But that ain't why I'm here. Your town's a damn shooting gallery, Dufaux. Your house, your money is burned. Your mine is collapsed."

Dufaux went pale. "My mine is what?"

"Caved in, all over, as if a thousand sticks of dynamite were tossed in. It'll be a year before you can dig it out. It's over, this dream of yours."

He looked like he was gonna be sick as he clenched his chest. I worried he might have a heart attack and get the easy way out.

"All of that happened because those three natives hate you enough to call the Devil's fury down upon you," I said. He probably thought I was speaking allegorically. "Now, judging by what you did to Tosahwi back there over nothing, I'm guessing you're every bit as hateable as I figured. So, tell me, what was it? What'd you do?"

"Am I supposed to remember every quarrel the dregs of this town have with me?" Dufaux said.

"This ain't a quarrel. It's a blood feud."

"Civilizations rise and fall like the grass in summer. Every one of them wants what they can't have. Is that my fault?"

I rolled my eyes. Faced with his mortality and the man was still playing games.

"You should've been a poet, you know that?" I said. "Now you gonna talk or what?"

Dufaux went to speak again, and I sensed it was gonna be more of the same, so I slung what was left of my lasso around his throat. Whether its powers still worked or not while broken, God's judgment through it didn't affect a normal man like him. That didn't mean I couldn't exact my own brand of judgment.

Before he knew what hit him, I tossed the other end over a ceiling beam and pulled. His body stretched out so just the tips of his toes were touching the wine-soaked ground. He clawed at his throat.

"I can keep asking nicely, or this can go another way," I said. "You've lost enough today. You want your life to follow?"

I pulled tighter so not even his toes touched the ground. As he gagged, he shook his head furiously.

"You sure?" I asked.

He nodded, just as fervently.

I let go. He hit the chair, but it slid out from under him, and he crumpled to his knees.

"How do they know you?" I asked.

Dufaux took a few seconds to catch his breath. Then he spat at me. I gave another tug for good measure until he was left hacking.

"Okay, dammit! Ahusaka is the chief's son."

"Apenimon? That was his name, right?" I asked.

He nodded. "For generations, the chiefs were given that marking you saw on Ahusaka's back. Brutal, sick, and twisted, tattooing mere infants. Vile heathens, scarring babes."

My eyes drifted to the room where that boy lay slumped

against the wall, dead by Dufaux's hand. I think he saw. His face blanched.

"I . . . I thought he was dead," Dufaux said. He was talking about Ahusaka, though.

"You thought wrong," I replied.

"Clearly."

"So, what? He blames you for his father dying? I heard you at the fair, like a crooked priest, standing on the steps of the church, revering those who once had this land. You told me Apenimon got sick. So, what was that, a lie?"

"Greatness is built upon such tales," he said. "When it comes to the past, everyone writes fiction. But no. I didn't lie."

"Bullshit." I tightened my grip.

He stuck out a hand in protest. "I didn't."

I sighed and lifted, heaving his body up and choking him again.

"I can do this all day," I said.

The cursed harmonica hadn't worked on Otaktay, though I was pretty sure I'd have no problem using it on Dufaux. But hoisting the sack of shit and then watching his body crash down was too much fun.

"Who are the others in the Trio? Why do they hate you?" I asked. "Tell me, and I won't kill you."

He coughed between every word. "I . . . don't . . . know . . ."

"C'mon, Dufaux. What'd you do? Beat them all too? Huh? Was it fun? Tell me!"

As I went to choke him again and leave him dangling, he finally blurted it out. A truth as awful as I suspected but hoped wasn't true.

"Yes! I did! I killed them!"

I let him all the way down until he was lying on the floor, sloshing through the spilled wine. Tears ran down his big, flushed cheeks. I strode over quietly to gather the broken lasso. I slowly recoiled it and looped it through my belt. Looking down at him, I felt pity for about two seconds. After that, I just wanted to see him pay.

I knelt, gun dangling over my knee, not aimed at him, just the subtle threat that it could be.

"Killed who?" I asked.

"All of them. Anyone I needed to," he said. "Anyone who couldn't see the wealth of this land for what it was."

"The chief. Your so-called friend. You killed Ahusaka's father."

His strength gave out. His chest deflated, and his head dipped. That was all I needed to see, then it all came together.

"He wouldn't see reason," Dufaux said quietly.

"There was no sickness, was there?" I asked.

"I left everything behind to come out here in search of gold. Would have died flat on my back under the beating sun if one of their springs didn't splash me. It wasn't the red men who found me, you see. It was water. As if Moses struck the stone. The Almighty, tickling my cheek. Water, out here amongst the cacti and the crusted dirt, and even more, something shiny beneath it. A golden miracle. Only then did they show up and help."

"Some way to repay the debt," I said.

"Oh, I did. Told them about our cities and our technology. Showed them what they could be. And they offered to share their lands in exchange for whatever I could ship east from my familial estate. I sacrificed all of it to start Revelation. I would die for this city."

"It's a whole lot easier to die for something than to live for it."

"You don't understand," he said. "They had no idea what they were sitting on. Gold, Crowley. You've seen it. But Apenimon claimed this was some breeding ground for a big mythical bird."

"And of course, you couldn't just respect them and their beliefs, huh?"

Dufaux stuck one of his big, fat fingers out at me. "I wasn't about to let some fairy tale rob me of my fortune. Rob all his people too, for that matter. Stubborn as oxen, those redskins can be. They see nothing, like their eyes are attached to their scrotums instead of their brains! This is a new world, that needs new sensibilities, and I tried to show them that, Crowley, I truly did. But it was my God-given destiny in this frontier. I was born to create this paradise."

I'd met all sorts of men in my lifetimes. I'm not sure I'd ever seen anyone spew so much nonsense with such zeal. By the end of his speech, I'm pretty sure Dufaux thought I was convinced he was the hero he envisioned himself as.

"How'd you do it?" I asked bluntly. "How'd you wipe out a whole tribe?"

"Not all of them. I give the rest of those former savages up there a good life," he proclaimed. "I give them purpose. Work. A reason for being."

"You're still killing them today!" I pointed at the room where Tosahwi's corpse lay cold.

"I thought he stole from me. But no, that was only you. Hypocrites. You are the bane of this world." It really took everything in me not to beat this man's face into a pulp. However, I knew that would just make me no better than him. My actions, stealing that plate, led to a bad thing. Add it to a long list of regrets in my unnaturally long life. But it wasn't my fist that did the *bad* thing. Over a trinket.

"How did you kill them?" My voice was trembling.

"My family had made a small wealth in Crescent City in rat poison, thallium by name," Dufaux explained. "A trade I had no desire to partake in. I put some in the wine they purchased from me. I wasn't trying to kill anyone. Just a pinch here and there, enough to get that damn chief sick and delirious enough to sign this land over to me in full when I offered some real, western medicine instead of their mumbo jumbo."

"Snake oil," I accused.

"No. The real thing. I had every intention of healing him. Believe it or not, Apenimon really was a friend. Just a misguided one."

"Well, hell, Mr. Dufaux, I can't begin to think what happens to your enemies. So, where'd it go wrong?"

"Their witch doctor thought something was off and laid the finger of guilt upon me. So, I shot him." He said it without emotion, like he was commenting on how hot it was in July. "He didn't die, though, as you could see."

It took me a second, but then dawn's light shone bright.

"Otaktay." The ferocious Yeti had been a healer before turning to the Devil.

"Yes," Dufaux confirmed. "And he took the chief's infant son and boy's guardian, Dyani, and they ran. A woman, the boy's protector. Can you believe that? The savages let their women fight," he added with a snicker. "I tried to find them for a while. Spent a pretty penny on bounty hunters like yourself until it was no longer worth the coin."

"Poison," I said under my breath, still pacing. The coward's weapon.

I'm not sure why I was surprised, but a man Dufaux's size, you expect something more . . . brutal, more hands-on. My heart broke for that tribe. Plied with gifts and fineries, then done in by them all because their leader decided to trust a stranger in a world where you can't trust anyone.

"When he lost his son, Apenimon blew his top," Dufaux went on, without even needing me to prod him. "Who would've thought the savages would love drinking so much? I couldn't swap out the tainted wine in time. My word, it feels good to finally let this out."

He let out a long, exasperated sigh.

"By his last hours, he was no longer himself. But he signed those damn papers before he and all those close to him died. In his last, he gave me Revelation Springs, from the water to the gold. So, you see, I'm within my legal rights here. This town is mine by his own hand!"

By then, Dufaux was on his feet again. He was no threat. I watched him like a man watches a dog eating its own vomit. I was disgusted by him but intrigued. How had this man lived all this time without taking a bullet to the head?

"And no run-of-the-mill, rinky-dink bounty hunter is going to come here and steal what's mine," he said. "Do you hear that? You got the truth you came for, and you'll die with it. You won't ever see a dime from me."

I saw something drop from within his sleeve into his grip. He thought he was being sneaky, but I let him have his fun. He must've palmed the pocketknife from somewhere on his person while he was on the floor writhing. A trickster in true form.

He lunged and stabbed me right in the side. The blade sank through my flesh, between two ribs, and punctured my lung. I'm sure he thought his little surprise attack would kill me. And it damn well should've—but I stood tall and proud and stared him right in the eyes as he pushed that little knife deep as it could go.

He gawked down at the weapon, then back at me.

"How?" he gasped.

Removing the blade, he stabbed in again, then a third time.

"W-w-what are you?" he stuttered.

"The Hand of God. How do you do?"

I ripped the knife out of my side with no blood of my own and let it clatter to the floor. He stumbled back in abject horror and tripped onto his rump.

"You devil!" he howled. "You monster. What curse is upon you?"

"In this case, it's a gift," I taunted, stomping toward him, ready to wring his neck.

"You wouldn't dare kill me. You can't. You need that bounty. You . . . you crave it, I can see. You're no man of God. You're a man like any other. Weak. Pitiful. Corrupt."

I drew my revolver and watched him flinch. Watched him believe with all his soul that this was the moment he would die. Fear coursed through his every feature. Paralyzed him. He clenched his eyes shut.

When I pulled the trigger, he yelped and I'm pretty sure he pissed himself. But the shot wasn't meant for him. I turned and put round after round into all those barrels of expensive wine, spilling yet more of that precious liquid he'd used to cripple an entire population.

He sobbed, hunched over by my boot.

"Just end it . . ." he whimpered. "Everything's ruined. Just end it . . ."

I shook my head and lifted his chin with the warm barrel of my gun, forcing him to look me in the eye. "No, Dufaux. Live with it."

Then I left him there in a pool of red liquid as it ran through the cracks of the stone and over his hands. It wasn't blood, but the metaphor would have to suffice.

I knew the truth now. I would still save the world from the threat of a possessed Yeti gaining uncontrollable power, even though I now knew Otaktay's rage was justified. I would finish what I'd started for the White Throne. But I wasn't gonna do it for Dufaux or all his gold. No way.

This was personal in more ways than one.

With Dufaux out of the equation, it was high time to visit with another murderous bastard on the other side of town who might know more about where Otaktay and Ahusaka were fleeing to. And I'll be honest, while I'd been looking forward to another run at Ace, my meeting with Dufaux left a bad taste in my mouth.

None of this was right. The whole town was built on lies and deceit. Its very name, an insult to the people whose blood stained its dirt.

Cecil was waiting for me right outside.

"Don't worry," I said. "He's still alive. Mostly."

"Good," Cecil said, kicking a chunk of wood that crumbled to ash. "He owes me my last dues. And backpay for Billy's family. Then, I think it's time we scoot on out of here."

"What about the outlaws?"

He puffed a cigarette, smoke escaping with his words. "Whatever they are, it ain't worth it for me. We can find work. May not pay as well as Dufaux, but—"

"Do you know?" I cut him off.

"What?"

"About what really happened to the Piasa Tribe."

"No. And I don't want to. But I've always had suspicions. That's the job, though, ain't it? You serve who pays you, and you don't question them lest you find yourself in a shallow grave."

I nodded. He wasn't wrong. Doing that had been what led Ace to kill me in the first place.

"Maybe we should," I said.

"What?" he replied.

"Ask questions."

Cecil exhaled. "Maybe. I was wrong about you, Mr. Crowley." He stuck out his hand. "It was good fighting with you, at least."

I shook it. "You sure you don't want to finish this? I could use a man like you by my side."

"That big fella stomped his feet and caused an earthquake. He froze iron with a touch. Whatever he is, this ain't my battle. And whatever you are . . ."

His words hung.

"Right," I said.

How could I argue with that? I was fighting a war Cecil couldn't understand—that I barely understood—and I wasn't some powder-wigged president who could draft him into my army. I was just a lowly Black Badge who'd already got one accomplice killed in Dale.

"Fair enough," I said. "Good luck to you."

Cecil tipped his hat to me in response and started to walk away, then stopped.

"Oh, by the way . . . If Sheriff Gutierrez gives you any trouble, you tell him you know about him and his cousin." He smirked. "Works every time."

TWENTY-FOUR

"Reginald!" Mayor Stinson shouted, right outside Dufaux's broken gate. "Reginald Dufaux, I know you're in there!"

I tried to slip by unnoticed, but luck favored another and the mayor headed right for me.

"You! I saw you here yesterday. You two pals? Did you see him in there?" he asked, poking a finger into my chest.

What was it with leaders in this town that made them so disrespectful? I'm sure he felt big in his top hat, though without it, I had half a foot on him.

Grabbing his hand and calmly moving it aside, I answered, "Yeah, he's in his cellar, crying."

"Crying? Crying! He lost a house. People have lost their lives because he refused to postpone this . . . this . . . self-worshipping festival of his."

"A lot of people have been dead by his hand for a long time."

Stinson's brow furrowed. "What?"

"It ain't my place to say. But ask Dufaux about thallium. Don't stop pressing until you get him to spill. And, Mr. Mayor . . ." I reached out and straightened his—I'm just going to call it an ascot. He looked at me like I'd just called his mama a whore. "Won't be long before you're actually the one in charge here."

"I *am* in charge."

I patted him on the cheek. "Good. Act like it."

I brushed by him, nudging his shoulder on purpose, and started back toward town.

Revelation's fate splayed out before me from my vantage on the hill. Black smoke billowed in pillars behind me and smaller ones from the bank below, but it also looked like the sky was threatening a storm blowing in from the south.

When it rains . . . as they say.

Anyone with eyes and ears could tell there was no fast recovering from this. There wouldn't be a *Founders' Day Fair* this year beyond those precious few minutes earlier. And whether the knowledge of Dufaux's deceit became widely known or not, his leverage was gone. He caused this.

I could only hope Mayor Stinson would find restitution for the poor people who'd been lied to and stolen from, that Apenimon's legacy would be rightly restored, and Revelation Springs would be able to scrub away the stains left behind by Dufaux's gross avarice. At the very least, find a place in the world where it could profit again.

A large chasm ran from the quarry through the outskirts of town. Several homes and shops were either gone or teetering on the edge, ready to cascade into the pit below. They'd have a hell of a time figuring out how to keep people from falling to their deaths once this was all over with.

Sheriff Gutierrez's men were doing their damnedest to convince everyone that things were under control, but those who'd been hiding out at Dufaux's estate had already ruined any chances of that. I saw men and women dressed to the hilt, running around, telling anyone who would listen about monsters and vicious Indians. Nothing helpful.

The long lines at the train station told me that a large number of visitors indeed had brains in their noggins and weren't willing to stick around for round three. The workers were holding some back, finding room for others. Already, the train cars were full to capacity, with people standing on every gangway. I'd never seen so many packed in at once.

It wouldn't be a comfortable trip to wherever they were heading, but desperate times called for desperate measures.

Besides, I was sure the railroad wouldn't mind charging all these folks a hefty sum to get them to safety in a hurry. Someone was gonna be eating well for a long while after this.

The church remained pristine as could be at the northern edge of the fairgrounds, looking to have not even suffered from the occasional stray bullet like nearly every other place in Revelation Springs. I didn't have trouble imagining a whole army of angels like Shar protecting it while letting the rest of town go to hell.

"Jesus is knocking at the door of your hearts today!" cried the town reverend. He stood on the front steps where Dufaux had recently force-fed the town a bucket of shit. Ringing a bell, making sure everyone paid attention to him, he repeated, "Jesus is knocking on the door of your hearts today!"

Spotting me passing by, he took the steps two at a time. "The end is nigh, friend. Armageddon is upon us. Do you know where your eternal soul will rest?"

I gave him a once over. I guess we served the same side. "There's no rest for the wicked, Padre." I gave him a nod and walked on.

"Never grow weary in doing good!" he shouted behind me, then returned to his previous declarations.

I checked around the mad mirror house, but Gutierrez, Ace, and all the others were gone. A cleaning crew swept up broken glass while a handful of parents and children were still trying to have a good time with what remained of the stands in the back lot. The Freak Show tent played host to a dozen or so patrons. I could see the World's Strongest Man hefting an anvil one-handed through the flap while Beast Boy did trapeze above. The jester character, whatever he was supposed to be, did cartwheels and somersaults and all kinds of ground acrobatics.

Would've been a fun show to see.

Guess some people had nothing else to do if they couldn't leave. Better to be distracted than terrified.

I slipped into the ravaged town square just as the geyser went off. I didn't see Shar in the waters this time. If she had any thoughts on the subject at hand after our little spat, she was keeping quiet. There'd be a time and place for her input, but thankfully, now wasn't it.

Chunks of wood and splinters were everywhere. Ripped canvases, broken carts . . . barely anything was left intact. Enough produce to feed a town the size of Lonely Hill for a week was spilled everywhere, half of it split open and already festering with flies.

Residents milled around the front of the Gold Mine Hotel, and even Picklefinger's looked busier than a termite mound despite the bullet holes and missing windows. In times like these, people felt safer surrounded by others than alone.

As expected, the bank was a wreck. Deputies kept the rabble away, but through the open doors, I saw that the vault remained sealed. Ace didn't get the chance to carry out his robbery without Otaktay and the others. And while it was a pity that a lot of what was locked inside was Dufaux's money, much also belonged to the fine people of this region who didn't deserve to lose a thing.

All of it was an overwhelming sight, and whatever heart I had bled for these folks. But alas, I had my own business to take care of. I needed to have a word with Ace, and I had a good mind I'd find him in a cell.

However, when I arrived at the jail, I found nothing and no one except the snoring vagabond that had been locked up with me and Dale the night before.

My thoughts drifted to Dale's shot-up corpse. Goddammit, what did he have to go and get killed for?

I piddled around in the sheriff's office a moment, making sure I hadn't missed anyone. Ace's ugly mug still hung on the wall of wanted posters for the murder of that Vanderbilt. Terrible drawing of him that was so faded nobody would ever recognize him, by the way. It was half-buried under a few others, nearby newer ones for the Frozen Trio and some woman called the Grizzly Queen of the West. For a passing moment, I found myself worried I'd see Rosa's face drawn there. Pretty as she might've been, she was no Rosa.

Satisfied the building was as empty as I believed it to be, I went out the back door into an alley. Maybe I'd missed him at the fairgrounds.

I heard the strained groans before I saw anything. Wasn't long before I discovered Sheriff Gutierrez and another deputy behind the feed store a block up. The latter laid in the dirt, out cold with a bleeding forehead.

"Sheriff?" I said, nudging Gutierrez with a boot. He was just coming to and clearly confused, reaching for things that weren't there and such. "What happened?"

He didn't answer—probably couldn't think well enough to form words.

"Sheriff, I asked what the hell happened?"

I shook him, and he flinched like he'd been shot. I scanned his body for blood or bullet holes, but all I found was a big bump on the back of his head where he'd likely been blackjacked.

"I—what? Who?" He blinked heavy eyelids and struggled to focus.

"Sheriff, who did this? Where's the outlaw? His men spring him?"

Don't know why I did it, but I chose not to reveal Ace's name. Not yet. Something still wasn't right, and I wanted to get some answers before the feds got involved.

"No. No men." Gutierrez shook his head. He tried to stand but stumbled. "A woman. Came riding in on horseback and the blasted thing hoofed me and one of my deputies." He nodded toward the totally unconscious deputy, then winced.

"What'd she look like?" I snapped my fingers. "Hey!"

His attention drifted back to me. "She was pretty. Real pretty. Long hair, black as ravens, and creamy brown skin. Just my type, she was."

"Keep it in your pants, Sheriff. Details."

"She flew by quick, Crowley," he said. "Don't know what else you wanna know. She wore gold bracelets, uh . . ."

"Rosa," I whispered to myself.

He rubbed the back of his head again. "I'm sorry. Even the best of us gets duped by a pretty face every now and then."

Even as Gutierrez spoke the words, I knew he was wrong. He thought Rosa was on Ace's side, and he couldn't've been farther from the truth. I'd seen her face when she saw Ace. Rosa hadn't saved Ace's life. She'd probably already taken it as payback for what he did to her and her mama all those years ago.

I thought about Rosa and how she might now be viewed as every bit the outlaw I was for her actions. Looks like today ruined a few lives for those I cared about.

There's an old saying: "*The man who seeks vengeance should start by digging two graves.*"

Well, it's true. Though, in this case, it was a woman who needed to dig.

I whistled through two fingers for Timp, hoping she was close enough to hear. Then, without a word more, I took off at a sprint.

"Where are you going?" Gutierrez called. He tried to stand but fell back against the wall. I didn't need him trying to follow me to Rosa or Ace. I had to stop her from doing something stupid . . . if it wasn't too late.

Crossing the fairgrounds was a pain, but I made my way around the mess as fast as I could. Didn't care much who I bumped into either. I gave another whistle, but Timperina never showed. Maybe she couldn't hear over all the racket, but usually, she came zipping to me like a banshee at the sound.

So, I ran on my own. My leg had fully healed now, apart from ruined dungarees, there wasn't even a sign I'd been struck by that tomahawk. Not the arm either. Don't think I'd ever run so fast, and wasn't it ironic that I was doing so to save Ace Ryker's filthy life?

"Thanks for this, Shar," I complained as I chugged along, knowing she could somehow hear me. Lame angel if she couldn't. "Letting us all come together really was wise. Real heavenly."

I reached the campsite about a half a mile outside town, and to my relief, Ace was still alive and spitting venom. His hands were tied behind his back, affixed to one of the wagon wheels. Another rope was strung around his neck, also secure to the stagecoach. It was probably the only thing keeping him still and relatively quiet.

If those horses got spooked, though, it would spell the end for my blue-eyed murderer. The dastardly part of me felt like shooting off a round just to ensure that precise thing would occur.

Instead, I approached cautiously.

"This is barbaric!" Harker shouted, for the first time not carrying his sketching book. I spotted it, tossed in the dirt a few yards off. "We are not animals!"

Bram pressed a hand against the air. "It's not for you to decide, Mr. Harker."

"That is untrue, and you know it. Should we be accosted by the law with that man in our possession, I would wear the same noose as her."

"He's right, you know," Ace said, smiling wide.

"I will not be responsible for another man's death," Harker continued.

"Then feckin' leave, ya whiny bastard," Irish told him. "You ain't doin' us no favors fosterin' about and jabberin' your gob."

"Irish, please," Bram said. Then back to Harker, "He wounded one of our own, deeply."

"She is not one of ours," Harker said.

"Yet."

I tried to ignore their bickering and focus on the source of their discussion. Rosa sat with her revolver in her grasp, atop Timperina if you could believe that. My Timp, who never let another soul but me onto her saddle . . . until now.

"Rosa," I said. My voice was much softer than Harker's protestations of inhumanity. But I knew it would cut through.

Timp's head whipped around to face me. I swear, her eyes looked like she was nervous I'd be mad at her betrayal or something.

"Ah, the savior hath come!" Ace pronounced. "Howdy, Crowley."

At the same time, Rosa raised her pistol my way. I put both hands up, and she lowered it when she recognized me. "You don't need to be here, James." I'd never heard her voice like that. I'd heard her heartbroken and angry, but this was . . . bloodlust.

"I think I do," I said. "Timp, bring her over here."

My horse tapped her hoof. I gave her a stern look, and she turned to approach me, but Rosa quickly slid off her back to stand in front of Ace herself.

"What were you thinking?" I asked Timp as she shyly hobbled over. I rubbed her muzzle. She snorted and gave a sad whinny. I couldn't be mad at her. She'd watched us together, Rosa and me, and probably thought she was doing what I'd want.

"All right, stay clear." I led Timp aside and approached Rosa on my own. She had her Colt raised at Ace's head, her snake tattoo beneath those many bracelets plain as day with her sleeve rolled up. She was ready to get her hands dirty.

"You don't wanna do this," I told her.

"Other than getting my William back, there's nothing I want more," she replied.

"It won't change anything." Which was funny. It was those same words Rosa's father-in-law had used with me back in Dead Acre when I was trying to avenge her husband's murder. "*It won't change anything,*" he'd said a few times as I left his ranch. Funny how you never realized how true something can be until you're speaking it yourself.

"Thank you," Harker said. "Finally, a voice of reason."

"Shut it," Irish said again, stepping toward him and making him jump. He scurried away like a frightened rodent.

Bram rushed toward me. "Mr. Crowley—"

"You were just gonna stand by for this?" I interrupted. "And I thought you were a gentleman."

"This is my choice, James," Rosa said. "Mine alone."

"Like hell it is," I said.

"C'mon, tough guy. Put an end to this nonsense," Ace said. "This pretty lady might break a nail pulling that trigger, and you and I had a conversation to finish before you ran off playing hero as always."

"*Mierda!*" Rosa cursed and kicked dirt in his face.

"Just wait, Rosa! Hold on!" I demanded. My hands ran up through my hair in frustration. This was quite the predicament.

Bram pulled me aside. "Rosa told me all about him," he said, low. "How he struck her mother. Surely, you of all people can understand the need one has to face down their monsters? It's all any of us can do."

I pointed at Ace. "That bastard has done more to earn my ire than any other man alive. But this ain't the way. We need him."

"Need me? Why, I'm touched." Ace pretended to sniffle.

"He should die for everything he's done!" Rosa yelled, spit flying out.

I pushed past Bram until I was standing just an arm's length from her. "I know. I know. He should die for a lot, but it shouldn't be at your hand."

"Listen to him, sweetheart," Ace said.

"You shut the fuck up, or I'll walk away and let her gut you," I told him. It was a bluff. We all knew it, but it did the trick for now.

Rosa moved forward with the gun, now only inches from his head. Her hand wasn't even shaking. Grief over Willy, plus what must have been childhood memories dredged up by what Ace did back in that mountain cabin had her truly able to pull the trigger. I could tell. Unable to help her husband, now she could right a wrong against her and her mom long left unpunished.

"Why shouldn't it be me?" she said. "Because I'm a woman?"

"Because you're not a killer," I said. "Not like this. Not in cold blood with a man tied up, no matter what awful things he's done. Rosa. This ain't you."

"Yet," Irish chimed in.

I glared back and saw her and the others all watching with rapt attention.

"Would all of you just back away!" I hollered. "This don't concern you one frail bit."

They waited for a few seconds until Bram decided to do the right thing and lead them away.

"Again! Always yanked before things get lively," Irish grumbled.

"You possess a strange sense of fun," Harker said.

When they were far enough, I turned back to Rosa, who remained still as a statue with the gun in hand. At this point, Ace was deadly quiet. I couldn't get a read on him. He wasn't one to fear death, but none of us was sure Rosa wouldn't apply those few pounds of pressure and send Ace to meet Jesus or God, or the Devil. Maybe all three.

"There's no coming back from this," I whispered to her. "There's a big difference between fighting for your life and killing cold."

"You're right," she said. "I'll be able to enjoy this one."

"Now wait a second," Ace said. Now it was clear he was more angry than scared. "I know I've deserved this from many women in my life, but just who the hell are you? I don't even know you. So, pull the damn trigger or shut your trap." He leaned in as far as he could so that the barrel of her revolver touched his forehead.

I watched the anguish ripple across Rosa's face. Her lip twitched. Bram's words came back to me. Ace was her monster. The nightmare she likely saw in her sleep and who made her mother live a life in fear.

And he had no idea who she was.

"You don't even remember, do you?" she whispered.

"Ain't that what I just said?" Ace answered. "Or do you not *spic* English too well, honey?"

She shoved his head back and pushed with the gun, no doubt making a circular imprint on his forehead.

I stepped closer. "You remember that day you shot me, Ace?" I asked.

"Foggy, but sure."

"Well, that woman and her daughter you tried to rape . . ."

Ace's eyes went wide, and then he grinned impishly. "No shit? That's you, little girl, ain't it? You're the daughter of that whore Crowley tried to give his life for."

Rosa pulled the hammer back on her gun. The thing was rattling, she was shaking so much now. But still, it wasn't nerves. It was unbridled rage.

"Well, ain't this a touching reunion!" Ace laughed. "God works in mysterious ways, don't He? Where is your mama . . . Rosa, is it? I never did get to finish with her."

"Dead." Rosa said the word softly, but there was malice there too. Plenty of it.

"She die of longing for me, or—"

"Enough, Ace!" I barked. "You're lucky I care about her enough not to cheer her on while she puts you down like the dog you are."

I moved to Rosa's side and whispered in her ear. "Rosa, you know I can't let you do this. You're talking about killing a man and putting yourself on the wrong side of the law. He ain't worth it."

"There is no right side of any law that would allow this man to walk free," she said without looking away from him.

"And what makes you think that would happen?"

"I can still hear you," Ace said, taunting.

Rosa gritted her teeth, but we ignored him. I tugged on her arm, and this time she backed away slightly with me, though she refused to lower her firearm. That arm was locked in place.

"I've lived long enough to know what injustice is, James. I'm no fool. He . . ." She lowered her voice. "All he needs to do is wave around the right number of greenbacks to the right person, and he walks free."

"I won't let that happen."

"And who are you—God?" she snapped. I knew she was just upset, so I didn't hold any of it against her.

"Please, Rosa," I said. "He might know where to find the outlaws behind all of what just tore this town apart."

"Ah, so the truth comes out." Ace chuckled. "He don't care about you, girly. Or saving your soul. He's only after that bounty on their head."

"I don't give two shits in a barrel about that."

"Liar."

Rosa shook her head. "No. I'm done talking. I have to do this. My whole childhood, I saw his face. I saw it when Mr. Phelps took me in Dead Acre. I see it every time a man looks at me with anything more than a passing glance. I always see it. My mother double-locked every door, the rest of her life. You have no idea how long I've waited for this."

She started back toward Ace, gun steady as a surgeon again.

I slowly backed away and stuck my hand inside my satchel. I wasn't proud of what I was about to do, but I had no choice. I *had* to stop her. For her sake, and for mine. Otaktay and Ahusaka had just lost one

of their own and were bound to be after blood. More people could—
would—die, and fast.

I felt sorrow and pain flood my every fiber as I laid eyes upon that
infernal harmonica. It worked on the werewolves and not the Yeti, but
Rosa was more human than any of them. At least in a biblical sense.
She was what Shar called a Child.

But the fact that Rosa hadn't shot yet meant she might not've been
able to do it. It's one thing to talk about executing a man. Quite another
thing to get your muscles to comply.

"Rosa, please put the gun down." I tried one last time. I had to.
When she didn't listen. When she pressed the pistol back against Ace's
forehead. I did that all-too-human thing and sighed.

Ace laughed. "She ain't got the backbone. C'mon, girl. Do it. I'll go
and conquer Hell too. Do it!"

But he was wrong. She had the backbone. That look in her eyes.
If I had to place a wager, I'd put every dollar on Ace's brains painting
that stagecoach.

Rosa wasn't looking when I played a note on the bone harmonica,
low and personal. This was just about us.

"Don't shoot him," I said, trying to match the same key with my
voice. Not sure that mattered but it felt natural. Plus it helped me force
words out through sudden sense like I was going to vomit. "You can't
shoot him. You're better than that."

My mind told me she would never forgive. That I'd fail her, Shar,
everyone.

I fought through the sullenness and played another note, trying to
string together a soothing melody if I could. Rosa swayed in a hypnotic
dance, her gun hand quaking intensely now. Ace got a faraway look in
his eye too, but I didn't care about him.

I played and played. It wasn't good, but it worked. "Put the gun
down, Rosa."

She lowered the weapon and shook her head out.

"Take him," she said under her breath. She threw the gun away and
stormed off.

I wanted to go after her, but I just stared. Ace was saying something I couldn't be bothered with. My ears were burning, ringing, tingling. I'd taken her choice away without her even knowing it. And she didn't even seem to realize the instrument had played a part in it.

Just like that, I was as bad as the goat-Nephilim or the Mind-drifter. As bad as Shar, who never asked me if I *wanted* to take on this role as a Black Badge after dying. Stealing my free will. Yet, are any of us ever truly free?

The harmonica slipped through my fingers to the dirt. I couldn't bear to keep holding it. But the dark feelings it brought out of me didn't lift this time as I let it go. So, I kicked it into some brush out of frustration, where I'd hope nobody would ever find the awful thing. I'd had enough bearing the responsibility of owning it. The White Throne or its angels could handle it.

Rosa stopped at the edge of a hill and screamed toward the sky.

What had I done?

I'd like to say betraying her like that hurt me more than it hurt her, though I'm not sure that would be true. All I knew is I couldn't let her become the monster she so despised.

"What the hell was that?" Ace said. "When'd you start playing?"

"Shut up," I bristled.

"That some lullaby from when she was a child? Cut to her core or something? 'Cuz I hate to tell you, you ain't good at it."

"I said, shut up." I dropped to one knee in front of him, but in my peripherals could only focus on Rosa.

"Well, whatever it was, good on you. I'll be honest, I was really starting to think she might shoot me." Ace snickered.

"She may not've." I tore my focus away from her as much as it pained my soul. "But I will. Unless you help me."

"James Crowley. The man who won't die. Are you formally asking for my help?"

"This ain't a date, Ace. I see two ways. I can drag you kicking and screaming back to that sheriff and all those people you hurt, probably get you hanged. Or you can help me stop the outlaws who betrayed you. Maybe I say you escaped, and I never saw where to."

He clicked his tongue and leaned forward until the ropes stopped him. His brow lifted. "Now, I'm listening."

"You know where they might've gone?" I asked.

Sure, he could've been lying about the whole thing. Maybe he'd never even met the Frozen Trio—just heard their names spoken somewhere—but this was the only move I could think of. Asking Shar wasn't in the cards. Right now, I'd trust her less than Ace.

"Only place I can think of is where we met when we planned all this," Ace said. "Seemed special to them reds."

"Take me."

He took a few seconds. Enough time that I was beginning to doubt this entire gambit. Before he finally said, "What's in it for you if it ain't about the bounty?"

Avenging Dale. Getting back at them for getting me stuffed in a hole for days. Protecting lives. Serving the White Throne. Making what I just did to Rosa worthwhile. All of those were good reasons enough, but Ace, helpful as he could be now, didn't deserve to know.

"You gonna take me or not?" I asked sternly.

"Scared to share your feelings with old Daddy Ace?" he said.

"Help me or get the rope."

He grinned. "All right, I'll run another job with you, Crowley. But I need you to promise. I know you, and your word always was your bond. I get you to the Frozen Trio, you spring me, and may our paths cross again one day."

"I sure as hell hope not." I stuck out my hand. He wiggled his arm, reminding me that it was bound. So, I cut just the one wrist free, spit on my palm to make the deal clean, and we shook.

"Just like old times, huh?" Ace said. "This'll be fun. And who knows, if you won't take the bounty on them, maybe I will."

"That ain't part of the deal."

"Deals change like the seasons, old friend. Now, you gonna cut me fully free so we can get going before daylight or what? They might be halfway to Tijuana by now."

"Doubt it." I looked over my shoulder at Rosa. She sat by a lone cactus, staring off into the distance. Harker tried to approach her, but she didn't even acknowledge his existence. "Wait here."

Ace shrugged his bound shoulders. "Very funny. Don't go sweet on her, Crowley," Ace called after me. "She'll make you soft as wet clay. They always do."

I ignored him. Rosa didn't look back as I approached, but Harker fled like a cat caught snooping. I sat right beside her, just like I had the night before. So much seemed different now. So much *was* different.

I started to give her a nudge but decided against it. "You okay?" I asked instead.

She nodded. "I will be."

"Rosa."

"I would have killed him if you hadn't shown up."

I wanted to tell her she might've killed him anyway. That I'd stolen that opportunity from her, the chance to do right by her mama. I didn't.

"You wouldn't have," I said. What else could I say?

"*Mi Madre* always told me, *la ira no es más que una justificación para el mal comportamiento.* 'Anger is nothing more than justification for poor behavior.'"

"Smart woman."

"I'm just so angry all of the time . . . I thought it might get rid of that."

"Nothing ever will," I said, my heart heavy with the knowledge that I've tried. "That's all growing up is. Finding more and more things to get pissed off about."

Rosa half sniveled, half laughed, which I'll count as a win in my book. "You're a strange man, James Crowley."

"Ain't that the gospel."

She turned to me, her dark eyes boring right through my soul. It only made me feel even worse.

"So, you need something more from him?" she asked.

"Unfortunately," I said.

"Then I'm glad you stopped me. But . . . maybe I can neuter him like a bull first?"

Now it was my turn to laugh. "Perhaps afterward."

A flicker of a smile touched the corner of her lips and then vanished just as quick. "Can I come with you?"

"Rosa."

"Please? You saw I can handle myself getting him here."

"Oh, I have no doubts about that. Trust me. This just ain't your fight, okay? These people are dangerous. Way more dangerous than Ace Ryker. And if you're out there, I'm not sure I'll be able to focus on my duties."

She batted her eyelashes. "You trying to charm me to get your way?"

I scooted back. "No. I swear."

"Relax, James, I'm only kidding." She laid her hand over mine—the same one Shar had turned into a walking corpse. For the briefest second, it seemed like I could feel again. Her warmth. Her soft skin. But I knew it was just my imagination playing cruel tricks.

"I just want you safe," I said.

"I know, and I'm thankful for it. Even though I wish I could come." She removed her hand, and I felt more sorrow at that moment than anything the cursed harmonica could elicit. Then she surprised me by pressing that hand against the side of my face. "You go do what you came out here to do, you hear me, James? Don't make me have spared him for nothing."

"I plan on it."

Then, she went back to staring off at the sky, longing for a life she couldn't have anymore.

And, oh, how I wished I could stay there with her.

TWENTY-FIVE

"This really necessary?" Ace asked. I had him hog-tied behind me on the saddle. Necessary? Maybe not. But if I'm honest, hearing his tone falling and rising with Timperina's rump had me smirking.

"You tell me," I said.

"Hey, far as I'm concerned, bygones are bygones. We had our spat all those years ago. It's over and finished now."

"Maybe for you."

He blew a raspberry. "Oh, please. You act like that Rosa's mama was the first girl we all took a liking to. You just didn't care enough to pull your guns before then."

I didn't have an answer right away, and I hated him for that. He was right. Of course he was. That's how Ace Ryker lived. He didn't talk unless he knew he was right because only the truth cuts to the core of men.

"I care now," I said.

"It don't work that way. We do what we do, but the Lord never forgets."

"You'd be surprised." I chuckled, then elbowed him in the side. "Now shut up, unless you'd rather a ride back to Revelation."

He listened, at least for a little while. Timp took the long route, all the way around the ruptured quarry and through a patch of springs kicking up steam like locomotives. A geyser went off, the piping hot water sprinkling across Ace's cheek and luckily missing Timp.

"Would you mind!" he groaned.

"Sorry, friend," I said without a hint of repentance in my tone.

We made it out to the other side, into the vast badlands stretching south of Revelation Springs. The terrain was flat, dry, rocky, and full of cacti—the expected. But we had some miles to go until the flatness gave way to a series of red-colored rock formations that could be seen from far, far away in any direction. I'd always thought they were what gave Revelation Springs its appeal. Sculptures of nature spread far and wide apart like an art gallery for giants.

"What happened to you, Crowley?" Ace asked.

"I grew up," I said.

"That ain't an answer. We all grow up, that don't mean we change. You were a force of nature back then. You always knew when it was time to bail on a job, and I liked that about you, but if someone got on your bad side? Woo-wee, poor them."

I always knew when to bail on a job . . .

I gritted my teeth, thinking about that poor Vanderbilt woman and her husband.

"The more things change—"

"The more they stay the same," Ace finished for me. "I know. But you're different now. You're working with the law even. What the hell's wrong with you?"

"Guess I just finally saw their side of things," I said. "Found God and all that."

He laughed. "We were meant to meet again here. No question about it. But God? I don't know. Though I guess he taught me one lesson."

"And what's that?"

"When you got the chance, shoot your enemies in the head."

I grunted. It wasn't a bad lesson to learn, even though the head he was referring to belonged to me. But Ace never liked the quick kill. He wanted to enjoy it, revel in the fear of the schmuck under his gun.

"So, this is it for you?" Ace said. "A bounty hunter? From glory to glory, huh?"

I sighed. "Can't you stay quiet?"

"You have me staring down at dirt and a horse's ass. What else do you want me to do?"

"I'm no bounty hunter."

"You're going after a couple of outlaws with a hell of a price on their head. Am I missing the math here?"

"It doesn't concern you."

"Lincoln's hairy balls, it doesn't," he said. "One of my protégé's out on his own. C'mon, Crowley. It's just you, me, and the air out here. Who cares?"

"All right." I cleared my throat. He wanted the truth? Fine. "I'm a Black Badge."

I knew how that sounded. Mysterious and powerful. All the things Ace wished he could be.

"That some sort of fed?" he asked. I could tell he was intrigued. No better way to get under his skin than to spark his jealous nature.

"That's all you get."

"Oh, you're a cruel, cruel man."

"Now it's my turn," I went on. "Twenty years south of the border. What the hell did you get up to there?"

"What if you told you that I found love?" Ace said with mock romanticism in his tone.

"I always thought you and Hiram were sweet on each other."

He ignored me and continued. "That I popped out a couple of little ones. Got myself a farm and some fertile land."

"I'd say there's better odds of Timperina here growing wings and flying," I said. "And then I'd ask why you're back here if you found that?"

"Wouldn't you like to know?"

I wished I was facing the other way so I could laugh in his face. That was Ace's way of getting back at me? I didn't care. I truly didn't. The world was a lesser place with him in it. And if he found love, it wouldn't have been honest. He would've been using her for something. To get inside on a score. Or maybe just to have power over someone smaller than him any time he wanted.

"Nobody down there like your girl, though," Ace remarked, after I stayed quiet. He whistled, and a metaphorical razor blade drew up my spine at the sound. Maybe it wasn't the sound as much as the thought of him thinking about her like that.

"She's not *my* girl," I said.

"Naw. I got a sense of those things. If you asked, she'd be whatever you want." He clicked his tongue. Saints and elders, did I loathe when he did that. "It is strange, though."

I didn't respond, but that didn't stop him from continuing.

"Rosa was a child when you turned on your own for her. You a cradle robber, Crowley? A bit young if you ask me."

"Nobody asked you," I growled. I didn't notice how hard my knees were squeezing Timp.

She took a bouncy stride that made Ace land hard on his gut and knocked the wind out of him. It seemed purposeful to me, at least I like to think so. I tousled her mane and thanked her for helping me maintain a cool head.

Ace wanted me to snap. If not to try and escape, then to protect these outlaws who maybe he was closer to than he was letting on and I'd been duped. And if not that, then simply because he could.

We continued along across the badlands. The rain that had been threatening for hours finally started up. Timp's ears twitched.

Those clouds above had an ominous look. Angry, if clouds could be described as living beings were. And as much as this dry land could probably do with a little precipitation, it was the last thing Revelation needed in its current state.

* * *

Time passed far slower than I'd hoped, but Timp had to be careful in the dark. She didn't have sight like me, and one false step might've sent us all swimming in a hot spring. Would've been fine for me, but Ace—and more importantly, Timperina— wouldn't enjoy a dip like that.

The rain was coming down in buckets now, and judging by the way Ace was shaking, it was a few degrees shy of sleet. Which had me thinking we were on the right path to finding Otaktay.

Distant thunder rolled like a war drum.

"Crooowwwley," Ace said in a sing-song manner that reminded me of Shar's beckoning. He hadn't shut up for a minute either. "C'mon, lift me up. Let me get a drink at least."

"Just shut up and tell me which way," I said.

"Gonna be hard to remember anything with my throat so parched," Ace said.

I groaned but gave in. Pulling on Timp's reins, I got her to stop. She snorted. The old girl hated the rain. I hopped down and undid the straps keeping Ace on his belly. Then, I yanked him upright so both of his bound ankles hung off one side of Timp's rump.

"You got five minutes," I told him.

He cracked his neck once in each direction, then opened his mouth to the sky.

"Damn, that's cold," he said. "Mother Earth provides. Am I right, Crowley?"

"Where are they?" I asked after a minute or two.

"You said I had five. Got anything to eat? I'm so damn hungry I'd eat the Lamb of God without conscience."

"I don't eat. Time's up."

He bitched, but I straightened him out, got back up in front of him, and spurred Timperina along. We skirted along the side of a rock face banded with myriad shades of red. In the light, there were few sights like it. A sunset, eternally painted into the stone. But now it was getting dark fast and our world was quickly becoming muted shades of blues and grays.

"How am I supposed to hold on with my hands bound like this?" Ace said.

"Not my problem," I replied.

"You're a real asshole, you know that?"

"Rich, coming from you. Now, tell me which way."

"Keep along this path. We got a bit to go, then it's a climb. Them Injuns are like damn mountain goats, aren't they?"

"Don't make me regret this, Ace."

"Never regret anything, Crowley. It's the only way to live free."

"None of us are free."

He sucked in through his teeth. "Old age sure made you depressing."

"When you've seen what I've seen," I said, "you'd agree."

"Right. Tell me. I almost killed you, and you—what—stood at the gates of Hell and saw all the machinations of the Great Beyond strewn before you, or some bullshit like that, right? Same garbage I've heard from all them greasers high on peyote."

I rolled my eyes. It's why it never really matters if I tell people what I do. Most just assume the hot sun baked my brains and made me lose my mind. People want to believe the world is simple. It's better off that way.

"Stop," Ace said as we passed through a valley. He pointed left at a cactus growing sideways from an outcrop. Looked like an overturned crucifix. "That way."

"You sure?" I asked.

"The bastards stabbed me in the back. I got no reason to lie."

I led Timperina up a narrow, natural path through an arched rock and along a ridge.

"So, why'd they really come to you?" I asked.

"Oh, now you want to talk?" he said.

"Answer or not. Doesn't change what I gotta do."

He waited a few seconds before starting. "The boy with them was a hell of a tracker. The woman, a hell of a killer. The man smart as a whip, for an Injun. We worked together on a few jobs down south, that's it. Last one, we robbed some Mexican general blind. That was a goddamn blast." He exhaled slowly as if basking in that memory. "Either way, they were good at what they did, and I'm . . . well . . . me. Give me a plan for a big old bank to hit and a cheery festival of sheep to ruin, I'm there."

"I'm sure that plan included them being at your side."

"No shit," he spat. "We rendezvoused where I'm taking you, got a plan together. I brought some of my crew. Bought the loyalty of others. Nobody told us there was a damn spin-gun in some shithole town in the middle of nowhere. Then, you know the rest. Here we are."

"Here we are."

Timp stopped again, and I stared at two diverging paths. To the right, a narrow and treacherous way up an incline into the peak of the rock formations. The other, continuing along the valley and dropping elevation.

"Which way?" I asked.

"Give me a second," he bristled.

"We may not have that."

"Well, I'd had a few drinks the first time. So spare me."

It was dark, and the rain made visibility difficult even for me. While a man unpracticed in the supernatural as Ace might not've noticed, I did. Something about the storm was off. All those dark clouds above weren't just passing across the plains. They were converging on a point. Slowly spiraling around each other.

A boom of thunder made Timp shuffle her hooves. I calmed her, but the rock was getting slippery.

"To the right," he said. "Yup. I remember. I almost took a tumble."

"Too bad." I swung my leg off and dismounted.

First, I went to Timp and held her face, staring right into her big, dark eyes. "You stay here, all right, girl?" She blew out her nose, then shook her head as I led her under an outcrop that would protect her from the rain. "If I need you, I'll whistle like always."

"Christ's sake, Crowley, it's just a horse," Ace complained.

I moved forward, but just then, something caught my eye in one of the shiny, iron buckles on Timp's saddle. I always said that no matter what, Shar would find me. Her presence swirled like the clouds above.

"Root out the demon plaguing these lands." Her voice split my mind. "Then all will be forgiven, Crowley. Never forget. You're one of the White Throne's champions, not an outlaw."

All I could muster in response was a harrumph, though she twisted into a wisp anyway after nothing more than that lame pep talk. As usual, *I* would be forgiven, but not her. Never her for leading me into a mess of confusion like she had.

"Crowley, what—"

Before Ace could finish, I grabbed him by his boot with one hand and his shirt with the other, yanking him off the saddle as hard as I could. Half out of frustration with Shar, half because what he said about Timp plain pissed me off.

He slammed onto his side with a pained moan.

"Timperina's more human than you'll ever be," I said. "Up."

I squeezed the rope binding Ace's wrists and hoisted him to his feet.

"Well, then damn. Let me stay with her," he said.

I bent and cut the rope around his ankles so he'd be able to walk. Then I gave him a push toward the path.

"I can't climb that without my hands," he said.

"Learn."

Another push, and he had no choice but to try. I was behind him anyway, keeping an eye out and one hand on a Peacemaker. I couldn't shake the feeling that he was leading me into a trap.

But why? All this just to take me out. Plus, for all he knew until a few hours ago, I was a dead man. For the first time, I suspected Lucifer might've put him up to it. A chance to get rid of a Hand of God.

Damn . . . Being around Ace again had me questioning everything. Even myself.

A few paces up, he slipped just like he'd feared and almost took a spill onto some sharp rocks. Probably would've split his skull open . . .

A man could dream.

But I caught him, yanked him plum, and nudged him along farther up the pass.

Reaching a landing, he cursed and fell to a knee.

I cleared the rest of the way in a single bound, joining him with both guns drawn and ready. But there was nothing to shoot. He rubbed a sore spot on his cheek against his shoulder and looked to the sky. Then he flinched.

"What in the world?" Ace said.

Hailstones started falling, big as bullets. They peppered the rock face all around us, clattering like a train over tracks. The swirling clouds were black and green above us like a twister was brewing. Lightning coruscated horizontally between them in wide arcs, contained up there instead of striking the ground.

"Crowley, that's it. You've gotta untie me," Ace said. For the first time, a bit of panic entered his tone. "This ain't safe."

"Not a chance." I clutched the rope and forced him to walk.

"I can't lead you if one of those knocks me out!" One *clacked* off the rock inches away. He kicked back at my shin. My legs slid apart, and I lost grip enough for him to rip free and run.

I watched the fool high-step in a serpentine route, hailstones falling all around him. They were bigger now, some even as large as my fist.

I gave chase. He clambered up a pile of rocks from a slide long past, then jumped to the ledge above. Every move he made was desperate and clumsy. He moaned with effort as he dragged his body up using his bound hands and torso, looking like a fish out of water.

I caught him by the leg, but he shook to get free and rolled to safety. Seconds later, I was up there and found him hunched over facing a bit of sharp rock, sawing away to get free.

"You done?" I asked. I had a Peacemaker out, but I didn't even bother aiming. Ace didn't bother to stop sawing either.

"Are you?" He nodded left, and I followed his vision.

We were atop a tall rock formation, coming to a point a short way to the east at a vista that overlooked the badlands and Revelation off on the horizon. The wind howled up here, and rain slashed sideways alongside the hail.

Silhouettes—human figures—stood at the other end, sheltered under an outcropping, seated by what looked like a small camp. Just a couple of tents and supplies by a firepit that was already extinguished. One of the shadowy figures, however, was massive. And unless the World's Strongest Man had decided to take a stroll, I knew who it was.

"That's them," Ace said. "I led you here, just like I said. Now you let me go."

"Not until the job is done."

I moved to him, unbound his hands, and held him down as I tied him around the chest and arms to that very rock. Hail kept pattering all around him.

"You get off on torturing a man?" He pulled and twisted to get free, but I was damn good at tying knots.

"Learned from the best," I said.

"You made a deal!" A particularly large and sharp piece of hail hit him in the face, cutting a line from his temple to jawline. He winced and snarled. "Goddammit, Crowley!"

"A deal with the Devil . . ." I leaned in, right in his face, " . . . ain't worth the paper it's written on."

He chuckled like a maniac. "My men will come for me. They'll kill you dead this time."

"No one's coming for you, Ace. You forget: I was one of your men, and there's no way in hell any of us would've come."

Standing, I gave him one last look and walked away. I'll be honest, I wasn't sure what I was gonna do with him yet. It felt wrong not to honor our arrangement, even if it was *Ace Ryker*. But it also felt equally wrong not to shoot him and roll him into a ditch.

Didn't matter yet. His barking was lost to the whipping winds as I approached my targets. Lightning flashed, striking a nearby formation and blowing chunks of rock apart. Thunder went off like a cannon at sea.

Here I was. Here they were. Maybe that reverend back in town was right and Armageddon had come at last.

TWENTY-SIX

I readied both my Peacemakers. Now that I was close, the rain was no longer a hindrance, and I could see Dyani—the dead female member of the Frozen Trio—was laid out, naked in front of the Mind-drifter, Ahusaka.

A bloody hawk looked to be carved across Dyani's chest and stomach, and the young native's hands were covered in her blood.

I don't know what kind of ritual I'd just disrupted, but Ahusaka squeezed a fist of blood over the Piasa totem while chanting in his language. Where my own words were stifled when I shouted, his carried in the storm as if he was all around me.

"End of the line!" I called out to the deformed man beside them. I could have shot him in the back, but that wasn't my style. The Yeti once known as Otaktay turned slowly, hunched over and barely able to keep his spine straight from his injuries. Or maybe it was a result of his demon being so fully integrated now.

"I knew you'd come," he said. His voice had changed. It sounded like gravel on a grindstone. His every breath was ragged. Blood so black I hesitated to give it such a title covered his leathery skin and tangled the stark white hairs all over his gargantuan body.

"It isn't too late to turn away from all this," I said.

"It is." Otaktay limped toward me, showing almost no aggression. It was as if the silver pumping through his system was defusing his uncontrollable rage. "This place. This is sacred ground. It is where chiefs are made. Behold, the perch of the Piasa, overlooking its breeding lands . . . our lands."

I stepped closer too. "I know what Dufaux did. How he stole all this from you and lied. He's already paid dearly for it, and he'll pay plenty more, I promise you."

"He will answer to our god."

"Mine too," I promised.

"Dyani . . . she did not die for nothing." He glanced back at the dead woman's body. Only then did I realize that she was decorated head to toe with white and red paint. It wasn't blood on her chest that her charge had on his hands. No, the blood came solely from the hole Dale put through her.

"I'm sorry. I truly am." Even though I meant that with all my heart, I raised my guns and lined them up on Otaktay's head.

"Then you will join them all in death!" he roared.

I pulled the triggers as fast as I could. One bullet snuck through and blasted him in the collarbone before a spiky wall of ice erupted from the ground to shield them. I kept firing, breaking off chunks as I charged. Try as I might, I couldn't get a clear shot.

Otaktay screamed something unintelligible to my ears, and all the pieces of hail falling from the sky turned course to rush at me in a straight line. They bounced off my chest and face with enough force to keep me grounded in place. I shielded my eyes purely out of reflex.

Then I heard a groan. The wall of ice crumbled into steamy dust in front of Otaktay, too damaged and exhausted to maintain it for long. I opened up and shot twice with the one silver bullet I still had in each cylinder. They corkscrewed through his chest, blowing him back.

He nearly stumbled onto the totem but somehow managed to avoid it before sliding to a stop.

Shoving the pistols in their holsters I brought the rifle into my shoulder and fired. Otaktay roared upon impact. A small, glacial shield appeared between his palms, only large enough for his own personal protection.

"It's over!" I yelled. "Cast out the demon in you! Be free of it!"

"It won't end!" Maintaining the shield with one hand, Otaktay punched the rock, and ice splintered toward me. It never made it, piddling out into harmless frost just at my feet.

I fired again, and the bullet ricocheted off the ice shield.

Otaktay was going to hold out as long as he could, make me work for it and expend all my ammo so I'd have to reload or take things up close and personal. Or was he wasting my time on purpose? Buying time.

I realized then that I'd been focusing on the wrong foe.

Ahusaka's chanting echoed louder. His eyes had rolled into the back of his head. And all at once, more lightning began to crackle and arc overhead as the clouds sped up. Golden markings on the totem that I hadn't previously noticed started glowing the same bright blue color as the markings on the young native's back.

This wasn't just the burial ritual of a woman he cared for.

Hopping to the side, I shifted my aim toward Ahusaka.

"No!" Otaktay bellowed.

Footsteps boomed as Otaktay sprang up and charged toward me. I recovered quickly, plugging him with two more silver rounds before he struck me with the force of Hell's wrath. The rifle flew from my hand, and we tumbled toward a ledge.

His claws dug into the red stone and spared us the fall. I freed myself and lunged for my rifle, but a thin stream of ice froze my hand to the trigger housing. However, weak as Otaktay was, the element lost its supernatural power. I made a fist and it crunched. Spinning back to him, I fired.

The shot missed Ahusaka, but put a hole through the totem's wing. Lightning struck it at the same time, sending out a shockwave that blew everything around us back, myself included. Rock fractured, wind screamed, and more lightning followed, all striking right at the totem.

Coincidence or not, I cannot say.

It might've been night, but the peak burned bright as noon. In fact, it was as if the gates of Heaven burst open. The white light shone so brilliantly, I was rendered sightless. I tried to get to my feet, but some unseen force held me back. My gut roiled.

The ground shook and a screech like a hawk resounded so loud it must've been heard for miles all around. The pillar of lightning faded away, and in its place rose a massive beast like I'd never seen before. Except I had seen it before, tattooed in glowing lines on Ahusaka's back. It was the Piasa that was immortalized in that totem, just a train car's length in front of me.

Ten times the size of even the Yeti, with a wingspan that might've stretched the length of some small towns, it soared straight up toward the eye of the storm. Its body was like solid rock instead of feathers. Lightning crackled under its reptilian wings and around deep-set, yellow, jewel-like eyes.

Ahusaka lay flat on his back, eyes white. He was mind-drifting, apparently in control of the thing.

Another screech rang out as it twirled in the sky, transitioning to a dive and coming right down at me. I found my feet and whistled loud as I could before darting toward the ledge. Two spikes at the ends of its wings cut the air like knives and released a buffering hum that made focusing difficult.

I leaped as its talons—shiny black like obsidian—raked across the entire mesa, from where I was to where I'd left Ace. I may not feel, but I couldn't help but panic when bolts of lightning lashed out in every direction and through me. My bones rattled. My flesh began to sear like a thick steak. I screamed out of pure instinct and spun, firing at the beast.

I can't say my attack did much in the way of damaging the Piasa, but the lightning stopped at least. I tried to shoot again but my rifle clicked empty.

Timperina appeared from below, finding her path right under me. I turned to land safely on her saddle. My faithful girl. Always in the right place at the right time.

"Keep your head down, girl!" I yelled as she galloped around the rise, racing out of the way of falling boulders. We skirted the whole mesa, and as we came around the other side, Otaktay stood above, huffing and wheezing. He hopped down, landing before us, crushing stone with a knee as he landed off balance.

Since we were at such close range, I whipped my broken lasso around one of his wrists and had two things confirmed for me. One, its holy properties were ruined. Two, Yetis, even injured as he was, are really strong.

Otaktay flailed, and I held on, letting the momentum fling me back up onto the flats above. Timp ran off. I landed in the devastation of the Piasa's talons, a deep gash through solid rock. Grains of dirt hung all around, the static shock causing them to float.

With all my ammo depleted, I released the rifle and drew my knife as I sprinted up toward Ahusaka, the Mind-drifter. Nothing but char remained where the totem had been, and Dyani's body looked drained of color. Knowing what I did about black magic, rituals, and sacrifice, I could only surmise her essence had helped summon the Piasa from an object that was anything but common.

"Stay away from him!" Otaktay shouted.

I looked back to see him straining to pull himself over the ledge. He made it and began to crawl, scampering with what little energy he had left to try and catch me.

I kept going, scanning the horizon for any sign of the giant bird. And then I saw it, sweeping down through the clouds. The Piasa soared south over the badlands, heading straight for Revelation Springs. Straight to where Rosa and so many other innocents were.

Grinding to a stop at the foot of the Mind-drifter, I flipped the knife, ready to plunge it through his poor, deluded heart. Then I stopped. When I killed his hawk, Ahusaka had felt it. What would happen if I killed his body first? Would he become the powerful Piasa for good, still in control? Still able to kill all those innocent people.

Before I could make the decision to end Ahusaka's misguided life, my hesitation allowed Otaktay to catch up.

I slashed at him, but he grabbed my wrist and squeezed until the knife fell free. Then he wrenched my arm outward and held me up like

I was the crucified Christ. His bulky arms and legs were quaking. Injuries would allow me to overpower him soon.

"We have to stop him," I said. Otaktay growled and stretched my limbs, close to tearing them off. "Stop him from becoming a monster, like you."

"Too little. Too late."

We stood feet from Ahusaka, but I could do nothing to stop the misguided young man. If only I'd kept the cursed harmonica with me, I could've robbed everyone here of their choice. Instead, it was up to me and my words.

For once, I understood Shar. And even Ace for that matter. There are no heroes in the West. Only choices that get people killed, good or bad.

No . . . Something had to give.

"Don't let him do it," I said, looking the Yeti straight into his cold, now gray eyes. "He's got his whole life. Those people, none of them did anything except for one."

"They made him rich," Otaktay snarled. "Fat. Allowed my people to vanish."

"They survived! Just as you did. I can't ever know your pain or what got you here, but there is a man underneath your ugly mug. Save that kid."

He squeezed my neck. I didn't need to breathe, but it was becoming more difficult to talk as my throat constricted and hellish ice spread over my neck and face.

"Otaktay." I used his real name. "You protected him all his life. Do it now. Reject the demon in you."

Hearing his name did something in Otaktay. I watched his features soften like they had back in the quarry. Then, all at once, his neck stretched back as he howled in pain, dropping me and collapsing beside Ahusaka.

I looked up. Ace rose behind him, having stabbed my silver-dusted knife right into his back.

"Man, you got ugly. That's for betraying me!" he spat. He ripped the knife free and went to stab again, but Otaktay swung wildly and slapped Ace so hard he flew halfway across the mesa.

I could've gone for the knife, but instead, I crawled and brought myself back face-to-face with Otaktay. I pressed my palms to his leathery cheeks on both sides and turned his head to me. Black blood leaked out of his back like crude oil. It seeped through his razor-sharp teeth, glistening in the moonlight.

"Otaktay, you can stop Ahusaka from going down this road," I whispered. In the corner of my eye, I saw the Piasa thundering ever closer to Revelation. "Everything Dufaux did to you and your people . . . Don't justify him. Don't give him the credit."

Otaktay swallowed audibly, then coughed on the blood. It bubbled and gurgled. His gaze drifted. He didn't have long.

"Look at me." I squeezed his jaw. "Show Dufaux that you're better men. That you and Dyani raised Ahusaka to be better. Not a son by blood, but a son by choice. Save him. Save your family."

He blinked. Then, as he focused on me, I saw human eyes beneath the demon. He pushed me out of the way, extended a palm over Ahusaka's head. Ice flowed from his fingertips. The skin around the boy's temples froze, and the echoing screeches of the Piasa grew strained. It didn't click for me what Otaktay was doing until it was done.

Thoughts of what put me in that coffin sprang to memory.

With Ahusaka's mind temporarily frozen, the link between man and beast was severed. The Piasa faded away in a cloud of crackling lightning from front to back until it was no more than a shockwave. Then, gone entirely.

Otaktay rolled flat onto his back, eyelids stuck open. Dead.

TWENTY-SEVEN

I tapped Otaktay's leg just to make sure it was true. He was limp as a fish.

But he hadn't been alone. Rancid, foul breath escaped his lips, and then darkness enveloped me. The mark on my chest seared from within, far worse than when Shar beckoned. Worse even than when a Nephilim was nearby. It was almost like I was being peeled open, layer by layer.

"*You just had to go and ruin my fun, Black Badge.*" Otaktay's mouth moved but that clearly wasn't him. An ethereal voice slithered around me. I know that's not a way to describe a sound, but that's what it seemed like to me. It was that same voice I'd heard in the quarry, only fuller now, more real, embodying the shadows.

I stood, I think, and backed away, I think.

"What are you?" I asked.

"*More powerful than a Hand of God can ever be.*"

"Wanna test that theory?" I hastily reloaded, never taking my eyes off Otaktay's talking corpse.

"*Where is she? Where is the angel who tugs on your strings, puppet? Show yourself, Shargrafein. I know you're there.*"

"*I could have guessed it was you, Chekoketh.*" Shar's disembodied voice arrived just on cue. I looked around for her but saw no one. Nor did I see any reflections bearing her likeness. "*What do you want?*"

When she spoke this time, I realized she was using my lips to do it. It felt . . . violating.

But either way, there it was. The answer. This was indeed the work of the trickster demon, *Chekoketh*, who went by many names. I wasn't surprised at all, but where was the trick? Or was it simply chaos he was after?

"*The Piasa would have made a fine recruit for Lucifer's army,*" Chekoketh said. "*I was so close.*"

"*There will never be an army,*" Shar replied. "*Your master lost and will always lose. The White Throne stands forever.*"

"*For now.*" He yawned. Good God, it was unnerving enough watching that dead monster's mouth move to speak, but to do something as human as yawn? "*No bother. I was growing tired of this family affair anyway. So much drama and revenge. Only the weak let tragedy befall them.*"

As I tried to make sense of all the darkness around me, the shadow seemed to form a face in front of me. Or maybe eyes. All I knew is that they were like infinite chasms of dread, and I felt like I was gonna be sucked through.

"*Goodbye, Mr. Crowley,*" Chekoketh said. "*See you very, very soon.*"

The shadow faded away, and I blinked. The Yeti was gone. In his place lay a dead native man wearing tattered rags stretched beyond repair. Otaktay, in his true form. Ahusaka sat beside him, cradling his knees. He wasn't crying, but his eyes were wet as he stared down at the man who'd helped rescue him and did what Dufaux falsely claimed to have done for the Piasa Tribe—gave him a life. How many families could one person lose before breaking?

He looked up at me, heartbroken, and his next words shook me to my core.

"Kill me."

I swallowed the lump in my throat, then shook my head. "No." I sat down beside him. "I ain't gonna kill you, kid."

"Please. I deserve it. I could hear everything you were saying while my mind drifted . . . and I still would not stop."

"You would've," I said.

"You don't know that."

"I do."

I didn't. Just like I hadn't known if Rosa was gonna pull that trigger or not. But sometimes, it's best not to leave things to chance when you can affect the outcome.

Ahusaka sniveled and muttered something in his language. "What do I even do now?"

I put my hand on his shoulder, causing him to flinch. But it felt right to do. I think Dale would've wanted me to show Ahusaka this kindness, offer him mercy for being led astray. And even if he didn't, it was what *I* wanted.

"First, you lay your family to rest," I said. "Then, you go anywhere but here."

He regarded the two bodies, then joined me in gazing out across the expanse. The storm was clearing, but energy still crackled along the route the Piasa had flown.

"You do not want to turn me in?" he asked, bewildered.

I knew by returning to Revelation Springs empty-handed, I'd forfeit any bounty still on the table—not that Dufaux was likely to pay it to me, anyhow. But he could keep his gold. Ahusaka had lost enough. He deserved a proper goodbye to his family. And the two dead before me deserved to be buried or whatever his tribe did to properly send off their dead.

"No," I told him. "I don't have that kind of authority. But you're alive. Do something with that, or don't. I'm tired of telling people what to do."

I stood, dusted off my coat, and retrieved all my belongings.

Maybe you should kill him, a voice whispered in the back of my head. Was it mine? Chekoketh's? Maybe even Shar's? That tickle across my chest was there.

No matter who it was, it wasn't my place to end this boy's life. Not unless Shar outright demanded it, and to my relief, she hadn't.

I strolled away, content with my decision, my feet dragging over loose rock and hailstones. I only made it a few steps before I heard

Ahusaka sobbing and whimpering. I glanced back. What I would've killed to have a family I cared for like that, who'd shake Heaven and Earth just to get revenge for me.

All things considered, Ahusaka didn't know how lucky he was.

"Head east of here," I told him. He glanced up, eyes fully glazed over now. "When you reach a boulder that looks like a big old chair, head due south directly. You'll find a valley along the Devil's River; follow it until you see a waterfall. It'll seem like nothing, but step through it. Ask for Mutt on the other side."

"Mutt?" he pronounced, holding the last letters like he was trying to feel them out.

"That's right. Tell him you're a friend of James Crowley."

I knew they were different tribes with essentially nothing in common, but Mutt's people wielded powers that would get them killed by normal folk too. Since only the chiefs of the Piasa Tribe could do what Ahusaka could, maybe he'd find kinship there. A new family. Or at least those willing to give him a chance and help him hone his abilities.

And of course, a part of me was being selfish like men always seem to be. Mukwooru had asked me to spare the Mind-drifter if I could. Keeping her in my good graces had already proved a boon, so I'd do so again. Perhaps that was why Shar seemed to have no problem letting him live.

Or maybe, just maybe, she wasn't totally full of shit, and she believed, like I did, that Ahusaka deserved a chance to atone for his sins. He was a Child of God after all. Now he's got the chance to grow up right.

"Why do you help me?" Ahusaka asked, his brow furrowed. I understood why he'd be wary of a man like me.

"Let's just say I shouldn't be casting stones," I said.

"What does that mean?"

I smiled. "If I've learned one thing, it's never question when a man offers help. Go where I said or wherever you like. Just stay away from Revelation. Live free, kid. Free of vengeance and hate. The next steps are up to you."

I left him behind. An intangible weight seemed to lift off me, as it always did after a job well done. But always a tinge of sadness too. I'd walk away, be dispatched after a new target in this godforsaken West, and eventually forget what happened here. Twenty more years down the road, even a hundred, I'd still be around, and all this would be . . . dust and vague memories.

Something stirred me from my usual ruminations. Ace wasn't where Otaktay had flung him. The bastard was gone.

I sighed and shook my head. "Slippery son of a bitch. You may as well be Chekoketh."

I should've been angry, but somehow, it was sort of nice knowing that somewhere in the world remained a man I truly despised. A man to remind me that I remain mostly human, with those base human emotions that cause so much turmoil.

Scaling down the mesa, retrieving the rifle on the way, I whistled for Timperina. She arrived shortly after. I checked her for injuries, but besides some scratches from hail and a wet coat, she was in fine shape.

She whinnied as I loaded up.

"I know, you would've helped more if you could've," I said, patting the side of her thick neck. "I was onto something earlier. We ought to get you wings."

She snorted.

"Right." I chuckled. "You hate heights."

We reached the flatlands and I heard a distant scream.

"You hear that?" She tapped her hoof. I spurred her, and we took off, snaking our way out to the badlands.

Another scream echoed before I saw anything, and this time I recognized it. I'd heard it before when she was a child, clinging tightly to her mama while Ace Ryker threatened their virtue and their lives. And I'd heard it again in Dead Acre, not long ago when a necromancer mistook her kindness for love.

Clearing a low hill, I spotted Rosa. Only, despite screaming, it was her who was still standing. Ace writhed on the dirt, holding his blood-drenched face.

"You bitch!" Ace shouted.

Rosa hit him again with what appeared to be a gnarled tree branch. It splintered and flaked from dryness, but I'm sure it still hurt like the dickens. Pretty sure it broke his nose too.

"That ain't a nice word to call a lady, Ace," I said, hopping off Timp's back. "You didn't make it far, I see."

Rosa spun and lowered her makeshift club. "James! I couldn't help it. I followed you here just in case, I . . . What was that . . . in the sky?"

"Strangest storm I ever saw. But we got the Trio. They're all gone. Won't be a threat to anyone again."

I didn't like lying to her about Ahusaka's fate, but he deserved a clean slate. I'd tell her the truth one day if it came up, when we weren't in the vicinity of hundreds who'd happily hang him.

Ace, on the other hand . . .

"Got a mean swing," I said.

"I saw him running, untied," Rosa replied. "Thought he'd escaped."

"He did." Just like that, I wasn't so worried about having a nemesis alive in the world. Oh, the things we convince ourselves just to feel all right. "I suppose I owe you thanks for following."

I strode slowly toward them, reloading a pistol. My reserves of silver were nearly empty, but I put the rest in my cylinder, making a show of it.

"You dirty, rotten, liar," Ace said through a mouthful of blood. I raised my firearm, training it on his black heart. "I came back for you, Crowley! I could've run, and you'd be dead! Whatever crazy redskin voodoo Otaktay did to get that big, he would've crushed you."

"I guess you think that makes us even or something?" I asked. "You did it for revenge, not for me. I was getting through to him."

"Like it matters? If they're dead, then you won. You gotta let me go."

"Do I?"

Ace glared up at Rosa, his eye already bruising, nose cracked off to the side. "I should've made everyone watch while I—"

She hit him again.

"Enough," I told her.

"You can't let him go," Rosa said.

I didn't have an answer. I really did want to keep my word. Ace wasn't lying. The Frozen Trio was defeated, and he had a hand in helping. Fair was fair . . .

"He's coming with us," said another voice.

From the darkness behind Ace emerged three men, each with a revolver in hand. The one in front—the speaker—I recognized. The bounty hunter, Anton.

Timperina snorted and I heard her hooves stomp closer. I raised a hand for her to stay back.

"I knew you were involved in this," I said to Anton.

"Took you long enough, you roughneck son of a bitch," Ace said.

"Sorry, boss," Anton said. "We were tracking, but we lost you both in that storm."

"Well, you're here now."

Ace started up that manic-sounding laugh I knew all too well. Couldn't forget it, no matter how many years had passed. Rosa went to strike him again, but Anton rushed forward and stayed her hand.

"Uh-uh-uh," he said. "Ain't nobody ever taught you your place, woman?"

Ace rose to his hands and knees, cackling uncontrollably. Strings of blood dripped from his lips, and he spit out a loose tooth.

Then, he slowly got to his feet. I think he wondered if I'd actually pull the trigger, but I didn't. Not yet. Not until I knew one of his goons wouldn't pop off and kill Rosa.

"Put it down, Crowley," Ace said. "It's over." He grabbed the stick in Rosa's hand and tried to pull it but she held tight. He yanked harder, scraping up her palm as it came free.

"*Cabrón!*" Rosa cursed before she spat in his face.

He lifted the club to strike her. I drew my second Peacemaker. He didn't have to know it was empty.

"Don't you fucking touch her, Ace," I warned.

He grinned that damn grin, wiping the gob of bloody saliva off his cheek.

"Been twenty years,'" Ace said, circling her. Not even caring that he put his back to me. He let his thumb trace the neckline on Rosa's once white but now brown and stained shirt. "Never waited that long for anything. You better be worth it."

He shoved his thumb into her mouth and she bit down. He yanked it back, then sucked it.

"Feisty," Ace said, laughing. "I like that."

"I swear to God, Ace," I said. "Leave her and go, and you and I can kill each other some other day."

He circled her again. Ace's goons had their weapons wavering between me and Rosa. With her between us, it was all too dangerous.

"I told Crowley here that I found love down south, and he didn't believe me," Ace said. "But one thing is for certain. I could find it here with you, no problem. Your mother was a sight. You're a . . ." He chuckled at his own joke before even saying it. "A *revelation*."

Rosa snapped and went to hit him. He caught her arm and started wrenching it back. His hand slithered along her side. Timperina started whining and tapping her hooves, like she always did when she got nervous.

"Would you shut that horse up!" Ace barked, then returned his attention to Rosa. "What's this?"

He snatched Rosa's bag and started rifling through. Pulling the cursed harmonica out, he said, "What's this?"

Rosa must have found it in the brush or something. I never should've let my own guilt get the best of me and let it out of my sight. Or at least, I should have buried the thing.

"Ace, I'm warning you for the last time!" I yelled.

Ace brought the bone instrument to his lips. Unlike myself, or anyone else who had handled it, he smirked. Then he played a few notes. I cringed, remembering what I'd done with it. I hoped hearing it again wouldn't spring Rosa to remember.

"Nice quality," Ace said as the sound echoed.

I couldn't help but wonder why Ace was showing no signs of overwhelming gloom. He just continued speaking like nothing was wrong. Was he so damn evil that not even hellish magic could affect him? So numb to feeling remorse or grief or worry about anything?

"I can play you a tune on Crowley's instrument while you . . ." He snickered at Rosa. ". . . play mine."

In that instant, Rosa's hand moved to his stomach and slid down toward his privates. Her eyes twitched. She was resisting, but his desires were taking control as the cursed harmonica's notes carried.

"Look who's woke up!" Ace exclaimed. "Anton, quit messing around and kill Crowley so we can have fun."

"I'd have thought you'd want that honor, Ace," I said.

"No, I wanna watch this time." Ace dragged Rosa off to the side and out of the way. "No hard feelings, Crowley. I just can't trust your word anymore."

"James!" Rosa called to me, snapping out of her trance. "James!"

"Do it," Ace said as he retreated.

Anton looked around at the others. Then they unloaded full cylinders into my chest and body. I didn't return fire. I just waited, trying not to let Timperina's sad sounds get to me. Even after all these years, she doesn't understand my nature. Likely never will.

When the dust and the gunpowder cleared, I stood tall. They all gawked at me. At least one of them swore. Another said something in Spanish. Anton, however, was stunned silent. Probably realized then how I'd managed to best him in five-finger fillet.

I didn't feel bad about cheating anymore. Nor did I have any second thoughts about giving Ace the fate he deserved. He couldn't walk away. Never could. And hurting Rosa crossed way too many lines.

Ace looked over my way, and horror passed over him.

I cracked my neck.

"My turn."

Quicker than they could think, each of Ace's men had a hole in their foreheads. They stood momentarily as if their brains hadn't yet told their bodies they were dead. Then, one by one, they dropped like flies.

Ace's face went stark white. "What the fuck are you, Crowley?"

With him distracted, Rosa rose quick and kneed him in the man parts. He doubled over and she backed away. I walked toward him. Timp followed close behind me, poor girl trying to make sense of things.

"Some say a ghost. A specter." I kept stalking him while he simultaneously clenched his privates and shuffled away, never taking his gaze from mine. "Others might think me a god. All you need to know . . ." I reached him now and grabbed him by the jaw to raise him up to a standing position. ". . . is I'm your worst mistake."

I pistol-whipped him across the face. He hit the ground and groaned.

"Oh, Crowley," he cackled up blood as he tried to sit up. "Don't you know, you can never beat me—"

From beside me, Timp's hoof shot forward and cracked him in the jaw, way harder than I could hit. Ace's head hit the dirt and his hands fell inert to his side, the bone harmonica still clenched in one.

"Just a horse, huh?" I said.

Rosa ran to me and threw her arms around me.

"*Gracias*, James." She kissed my cheek. "*Gracias*."

Timp nuzzled both of us at the same time.

Rosa pulled back and looked me in the eyes. "I guess I owe you two again."

"Nah. Let's call it even, Rosa Massey." I held her at arm's length and smiled. Threw Timp a wink over her shoulder for good measure too.

When we finally parted, Rosa patted my chest and all the bullet holes in my jacket, concerned. "How did you—"

"I got metal vest under this," I interrupted her, gently grabbing her hands and guiding them away from my person. "A bit medieval. Real expensive. Took a gamble that it'd work and . . . I guess it does."

She punched me in the arm. "*Idiota*. You shouldn't have gambled for me."

"Always."

Her gaze stuck with mine for a short while, then she cursed and gave Ace a swift kick in the ribs.

"Wow, that feels good!" she exclaimed, doing it once more.

"Better than you killing him, right?"

"I suppose." She looked down at her hand. It was bleeding.

I took it in mine for a careful and perhaps overlong examination.

"You should get that wrapped," I said in a low voice. Then I looked up into her eyes. Again, we stood there a while, locked in on each other. Just stood there.

Rosa cleared her throat. "I will." She pulled her hand away, but not unkindly. Her eyes lingered a moment longer, and she returned them to Ace. "So, what do we do with him now?"

"I won't take Dufaux's bounty, but someone somewhere will pay a hell of a lot for the infamous Ace Ryker to die. I can think of a few Vanderbilts already. The money might help those people fix up Revelation. Maybe could get you a ticket to wherever you want to go."

Rosa pursed her lips and spat on him for good measure. "Better to leave him out here to rot in Hell."

"Don't worry, Rosa," I said. "There's a higher authority than us to take care of that . . ."

TWENTY-EIGHT

Picklefinger was on his front porch, mopping up blood. Chops's mostly. That deputy had given me a hard time, but I could hardly blame him. Especially after feeling his final thoughts. In a place like this, where an outlaw would sooner sling hot lead than spend a night in the clinker, these lawmen had to be hardened.

I slid down from Timp's back and lightly hitched her.

"Quite a mess," I said.

Picklefinger turned at the sound of my voice but went right back to work with a monosyllabic, "Yep."

He showed his back to me momentarily and I thought I heard a sniffle.

It was okay. He deserved to be upset. Even being mad at me was totally acceptable. Someone had to take the blame. As a matter of fact, I'd spoken to Sheriff Gutierrez about just that thing. Apparently, after the whole ordeal up the hill, Dufaux vanished like a ghost. The coward couldn't even face his own judgment.

However, this town wouldn't be content without someone taking the fall.

Enter, Ace Ryker.

The bastard hadn't been responsible for everything, but no one needed to know that. Ahusaka could go free, and the Frozen Trio could be dismissed as disciples of the notorious outlaw Ace Ryker.

"Just thought I'd apologize about the window," I said. "Windows, I guess."

After all, it had been my idea to hide out at his place during the gunfight.

Picklefinger turned back to me now. He stopped and leaned on his mop. His eyes were glassy. "Already did that. It's me who owes you a debt."

I thought I'd be getting the cold shoulder or worse from him, but a debt?

"Doubt that," I said.

"No, I do. This whole town does," he said. "Received this in the post this morning," He produced a letter folded three times, business-like, and handed it to me.

I read it out loud.

The infamous murderer Ace Ryker has been apprehended and given full responsibility for being behind the Frozen Trio attacks and the direct murder of Sheriff Culpepper of Elkhart. The Hero of Revelation Springs has chosen to remain anonymous and has generously donated the many bounty rewards on Mr. Ryker's head to be used toward citywide reparations.

"Sounds a mighty fool thing to do," I said, handing it back. "Had I been that 'hero,' I'd have already been settling down in an estate with some cows and a fence."

Picklefinger nodded and offered a knowing smile. "Right. Brain-dead son of bitch, that one."

"Glad to hear it, though. This place took quite the hammering."

"Safe now," he said. "Thanks to you." Then, his demeanor changed, and his head dipped. "Heard about your friend. The deputy."

"Dale," I said.

"Dale," he repeated. "Seemed a fine man."

"Lots of good men died here. A damn shame."

Picklefinger nodded. I moved toward Timp, ready to get on with the day's morbid events.

"Oh!" Picklefinger exclaimed. "I got something for you."

"You don't have to—" I started saying when he pushed his mop into my hand. He disappeared inside. I followed.

"James!" came a call from my right.

Rosa Massey was looking radiant in a pale-yellow dress as she sat inside at a table, nursing a Sazerac. She wore a leather corset and a belt to match, her five-shooter hanging at her hip. No one was gonna mistake her for some fancy mogul's wife under that wide-brimmed white hat.

After everything, we turned Ace in to the sheriff and then spent the night at camp where nobody would be a bother. I'd slept in. No visions to shake me, just pure, relaxing silence in the dark. By the time my weary self awoke, Rosa and the others had apparently already made their way into town. Should've guessed where I'd find her.

"You finally got that drink," I said to her.

She smirked, tapping a ring against the glass. "I did."

"Was it all you've been waiting for?"

"A bit of a light pour."

"What did I hear?" Picklefinger asked as he came shuffling back out. Rosa snickered but stayed silent. Then I noticed what was in his hands.

"Well, I'll be damned," I said. Picklefinger was holding my Stetson.

"Here you go," he said, dusting it off.

I examined it, spotting a couple of new holes. I'd forgotten about how I'd used it to distract the shooter atop the Town Hall. I'd considered it a loss.

"I almost forgot about that," I said. "Got this hat—"

"From John B. Stetson himself," Picklefinger said, finishing my sentence.

"Oh, you'd heard?"

"Only every time you've come through," Picklefinger commented. He reached over the bar—which was a feat in itself with his belly—and grabbed a bottle of absinthe. He tipped his own hat to Rosa and poured a bit more in her glass. "Strong enough for you, ma'am?"

She took a sip and coughed. "Plenty."

Picklefinger gave me a look that conveyed something two men understood without words. Yes, Rosa was beautiful, but more than that, she was a friend. As a Black Badge, I didn't have the luxury of following such whims. But I knew a good woman when I spotted one, and Rosa was that and more.

She downed her Sazerac, then placed a hand on my arm and said, "Bram's waiting for me. You coming?"

"Wouldn't miss it," I told her. "Be just a minute."

She nodded and hurried off to meet up with Mr. Stoker and his crew.

I donned my hat and stood there in the shot-up saloon, looking around. It wouldn't have been a bad life, tending bar at a place like this. Bringing people good times and the occasional fight. It wouldn't be long before my next mission from the White Throne came. And in those brief periods of respite, I liked to imagine how things could've been.

"Hey Crowley, one more thing," Picklefinger said.

I blinked, and the daydream vanished as quickly as it came.

"What's that?" I asked.

He once again reached into his pocket. When he pulled it out, he held a small, flat box made of gold.

"Do yourself a favor," he said, handing it to me. It verily shook when my hand grasped it. "Shave for the lady, will you? You look like hell."

He smiled and I did my best to do the same. Once again, I was holding a mirror, and Shar's presence inside practically guffawed at my failed attempt to be rid of her. At least it was gold this time.

Nothing's ever easy.

"I'll do that," I said. "Thanks."

I headed back outside.

Picklefinger moved to the door. "You ever find out who that generous bounty hunter was, you tell him Picklefinger and the whole city of Revelation Springs thanks him, you hear?"

"I'll be sure to do that."

"And you've got yourself a room here anytime you need it."

"I know," I joked. "Nicest one too, I expect." We shared a laugh. I waved over my shoulder. "See you around."

"Stay out of trouble."

The sound of his mopping started up again and I felt that infernal itch that was Shargrafein demanding to speak with me.

So, I slipped down between Picklefinger's and the Miner's Guild, in that same alley where Dale and I had been arrested. Nobody had re-filled the trough he'd flopped around in yet.

Checking from side to side, sure no one was gonna pop out and start gabbing, I opened the mirror and was met by the swirling, smoky visage of my angelic handler.

"Are you sending mirrors to my acquaintances now?" I asked, eager to get the first word in.

"Don't trouble yourself with trivialities," she replied.

"Yeah, yeah. You see everything, except for the things you don't."

She ignored my jab.

"The White Throne is pleased that you uncovered the Fallen One behind these transgressions. But Chekoketh grows bold. He does not act without purpose."

"You heard his purpose. He wanted the Piasa."

"Perhaps . . . But his motives are always unclear. Misdirection, deceit . . . such are the tools of his master."

I sighed. "If he's already in your head, he's already won. Just like Ace."

"Do not compare him to that rotten Child," Shar admonished. "I sense darkness coming. All this movement. I fear the scions of Lucifer will soon attempt once more to open a Hellmouth."

"And I suppose you have no idea when?"

"Do not patronize me. Or do you forget our last conversation? You've done well here, Crowley. Let us focus on what is to come, and not what has come to pass."

Yeah, I remembered. Her making me feel the decades of pain I'd missed. To watch, with open eyes, as my body rotted away to how it *should* appear. As I was reminded of the "gift" Shar and the White

Throne had bestowed upon me by making me a Hand of God. A Black Badge.

"We will root out this evil," Shar said. "Never forget who you serve."

"As if you'd let me?" I sucked through my teeth. "So where to next, my glorious and incorruptible boss?"

"The marshlands in the southeast call. A terror rises there that will put all the Children of the Crescent City in danger."

Great. The Crescent City. Nothing was ever uncomplicated in that place. On the gulf, crowded with sinners and practitioners of dark arts, where it was easy to blend in because the city was filled with so many people who didn't.

"That's all you got for me?" I asked.

"For now," Shar said. Then she added, "Leave fast. Spare not a moment," as her face started to swirl away.

"Sure thing." I snapped the mirror shut and stuffed it into my satchel.

I headed out of the alley with every intention of taking my time to leave. Like I'd told Rosa, I wouldn't miss what was happening next for all the tea in China. I'd suffer eternity in Hell not to miss it.

I retrieved Timperina because she deserved to see too, and walked her to where Rosa, Bram, and Irish stood at the outskirts of the town square which was still an awful mess.

"Where's Harker?" I asked.

"Oi, the fecker cou—"

"Mr. Harker doesn't have the stomach for such affairs," Bram said, cutting Irish off. "Says the public square is no place for a man to die, no matter his crimes."

"Easy to say when it's not you who's been wronged," Rosa argued.

She approached Timp, who gave a soft snort. Timp nuzzled right up to Rosa and damn near begged for a pat. This lady must've been some kind of magician.

"You're a good girl," Rosa said.

"It seems she's come to like you," I said.

"I'm hoping she's not the only one?"

I smiled but was gratefully spared the need to respond when the gathered crowd began booing and hissing. What did she mean by that? Dammit, Rosa, don't make things harder.

"Here he comes," I said out loud, eager to focus elsewhere.

A slow processional led Ace Ryker from the jailhouse. He cursed up a storm while folks spit at him, kicked dirt, and worse. Most times, the deputies would've stepped in to put some kind of space between the condemned and the congregants, but not now. They welcomed it like Christmas morning.

The harmonica was in his pocket. Left there as a last rite, upon my personal request to Gutierrez. Ace would die with the instrument of a monster on his possession and then be buried with it. That hellish thing, able to compel others to act against their will, would be lost to the world.

I'd waited a long time for this justice and, apparently, so had Rosa. Just wish it hadn't been at the expense of so many more lives, and that a certain Reginald Dufaux had the gumption to take the fall with Ace instead of running like a coward.

Dale deserved a crowd this size for a celebration of his life. Hell, even Chops deserved something. I suppose taking joy in a worthless clump of mud like Ace Ryker finally getting his dues would need to suffice.

Ace stumbled and fell. They had his legs chained without much slack. He was a runner and Sheriff Gutierrez wisely wasn't taking any chances after already losing him once—an issue I cleared for Rosa when we turned Ace in. Not surprisingly, the sheriff understood why a man like him could be so easy to hate. Plus, Rosa turned her charm on and that was a weapon as powerful as the White Throne sometimes.

A couple men jerked Ace upright and gave him a shove toward the gallows, then helped him up the steps, though I think most of us would've been fine watching him try on his own.

All in all, the short walk from the jail to the gallows set up in front of Town Hall took far longer than necessary. But that's how these things were done. People usually traveled from far and wide to be entertained by capital punishment like this, but with the mass departure Revelation Springs had experienced, there might've been a hundred people there. Locals only. The people who'd hate him most for messing up their town.

Part of me was glad Ace didn't get a better audience. Had he been caught right after murdering that Vanderbilt woman on the train, there'd have been a mass crowd. He'd have loved it.

But legends fade as time ticks on, and this was all he deserved.

Gutierrez dragged him to the center of the stage and raised a hand. Everyone watching took a while to hush, but they managed. Mayor Stinson stood off to the side, scowling, wringing his hat as if he wanted to be the one to pull the lever that'd send Ace to dance at the end of the rope. The town reverend was beside him, looking somber.

"I wish they'd burn him alive," Rosa said.

I glanced at her sidelong. Her eyes glinted with anticipation. "Remind me never to cross you."

Mayor Stinson stepped forward and addressed us all. It was good to see him up there, like a changing of the guard. With Dufaux out of the picture, perhaps this man would rise up to bring Revelation Springs into a new era of greatness. Or maybe he'd become equally corrupt. Who knows?

"This man, known as Ace Ryker, is accused and convicted of armed robbery, evading the law, murder, and the murder of a lawman. He is also convicted for the murder of Beatrice Vanderbilt, and likely hundreds of others over the course of his *career* as an outlaw. For these many crimes, and many only God will know, he will hang at the end of a rope until dead. Reverend Peters will now address you as our Lord's mouthpiece."

"In the second book," the reverend started, "Moses ascended the mount and communed with our Lord. Upon that holy peak, he was given ten rules. Ten simple rules by which all mankind should live. Ten rules that any decent human being ought to be able to follow without even a thought elsewise. However, today, we've gathered to watch a man die who couldn't manage to skirt by with a single one left unbroken."

He wasn't wrong.

"However, all men were created as sons and daughters," Reverend Peters went on. The next words came out like they hurt. "Each one of us deserves an opportunity for forgiveness."

The crowd hissed again. Someone threw their shoe at Ace and the heel drew blood.

Ace swore, but Sheriff Gutierrez shut him up with a heavy right hook.

"That's enough!" the mayor ordered. "We will have civility!"

"You ain't Dufaux!" someone yelled. A couple of locals laughed.

"No, I'm not. But where is he? All this wreckage and he's nowhere to be found. He abandoned all of you, but I'm still here."

That got people to start whispering.

The reverend looked at Ace and shook his head. Can't imagine what it would be like to have such closeness to the Maker that anyone could pity Ace, but this man surely found that grace somewhere in his heart.

"Thank you, Mayor Stinson," the reverend said. "May God reward your kindness."

Sheriff Gutierrez was in the midst of lowering the hangman's noose around Ace's neck. Ace bit at his hand.

"Mr. Ryker," the reverend said, "these are your last moments on this side. Now, I won't presume to speak for our Lord, but the Good Book tells us that repentance is the key to salvation. When upon the cross, our Savior promised the condemned that—should he make right the things on this Earth—he would be given passage into the Kingdom beyond. Yes, that he would be in Paradise, even in that very hour!"

The crowd booed at the thought of Ace receiving anything other than Hell's wrath. Ace laughed too. Son of a bitch was gonna do that all the way to the gates. To his credit, Reverend Peters kept his composure through it all.

"If that thief on the cross, sentenced to death, could find forgiveness in those final moments, you too have a chance to receive Heaven's free gift. With your last words, Mr. Ryker, will you confess your sins before God and this crowd? Will you repent and find God's forgiveness?"

Ace sucked in through his teeth. He watched the reverend, then looked out over the crowd and spotted me. Oh, if looks could kill . . .

"Yeah, I'd like to pray," Ace said. "If you'll allow it."

People booed again.

"We will have respect for our Lord!" Reverend Peters shouted. "Now quiet!"

The crowd eventually listened.

Reverend Peters smiled at Ace, nodded, and stepped backward.

Ace rolled his neck and closed his eyes. His hands were tied behind his back, ankles chained, noose in place. He took a deep breath. Others may've bowed their heads and closed their eyes, but I watched him.

"Dear God," he said. Silence hung in the air. Then he opened his eyes, looked right at me with his cold blue eyes, and said, "Fuck James Crowley and the horse he rode in on."

The crowd gasped while Ace laughed like the maniacal piece of shit he was. Sheriff Gutierrez threw the lever, the floor fell out, and Ace Ryker dangled from that rope, neck snapped, face twisted in that evil grin I'd come to know too well.

And that was how two decades of nightmares ended.

I looked to Rosa. She stared quietly as the body swung, rope creaking and straining the wood it was tied to. Eventually, Bram took her shoulder and said, "Time to head on, lassie. You've seen what you needed to see."

He wasn't alone. Eager as the crowd was to watch this affair, they dispersed just as quickly. That's the thing about hangings. It's exciting to anticipate a wicked man leaving this Earth, but once they're gone, it's just a helpless body, swinging. It feels wrong to keep jeering and carrying on. Death, no matter what, becomes a solemn affair.

"Feel any better?" I asked Rosa.

She pursed her lips. "Not really."

"Me neither." I sighed. "But what's done is done, and the world will be a better place for it. It doesn't change the past. Nothing can."

She looked up at me. There were no tears in her eyes, but there was sadness there all the same. "What now, James?"

"Now, we press onward down the path laid before us. But first, I got a friend that deserves to be buried back in Lonely Hill, right beside a sheriff he made proud in the end."

I'd promised that to Dale, and I felt like keeping it. Besides, I'd stopped a Yeti and uncovered Chekoketh's role in everything. That would buy me some leeway with Shar, at least for a bit.

Angels . . . what a pain in my ass.

EPILOGUE

Blue eyes snapped open.

Ace Ryker screamed, his chest feeling as if a hot brand had been pressed there. Like he was some kind of beast of burden. A cow or a goat or something.

Ace Ryker, one of the Wild West's most notorious. Ace Ryker, leader of outlaws. Hanged before Revelation, broken nose after being bashed in the face by a woman and a horse.

He convulsed, eyes streaming tears. As his vision became clearer, he saw another pair of eyes staring back into his.

At first, he thought them to belong to that bootlicking traitor, James Crowley, but they immediately disappeared into a puff of smoke, leaving him staring up into darkness.

The pain in his chest suddenly vanished. He was lying on his back, the surface hard, but he felt no discomfort in it. This hadn't been the first time he'd been out of sorts when waking, but something was different this time. Numb.

For starters, he was sober as a priest on Sunday, and Ace Ryker was never completely sober. This wasn't the result of some blackout bender. Wasn't the bed of some painted lady neither. Apart from the eyes, which he'd clearly imagined, he was completely alone.

Then, his own memories replayed in his head . . .

Hanged before Revelation . . .

Hanged?

Am I . . . Am I dead?

He quickly disabused himself of that notion on account of his thinking and breathing.

Or am I?

Thinking, yes. But as he considered the latter, his lungs neither burned nor begged for air despite his lack of taking it in.

He sat, bolt upright like a gunshot.

Where am I?

Is this Hell?

He was more than convinced he'd done nothing in life to grant him passage to Heaven. Wasn't even a question. Though, there was no fire. No brimstone or sulfurous stench. He heard no weeping or gnashing of teeth.

All those preachers and Bible thumpers, full of shit as he'd expected.

He raised his hand to his face and felt nothing. How bad was his nose broken? He could almost feel that bitch's wallop . . . Rosa. It was her hand that had done it. He should've chased her and her mama down that night he'd failed to kill Crowley.

"Chauncy Ryker." The voice spoke his name—his true name—as if it knew him. He hadn't heard that name in decades. Not since before he shot his piece of shit moneybags of a father, stole an inheritance that was rightfully his to begin with, and took off running.

"That ain't my goddamned name!" Ace snapped.

"Blasphemy!" the voice bellowed and the whole room shook. Stones clattered off the walls and broke against the floor.

Fear overtook Ace like he'd never felt. He stuttered and said, "Just c-call me Ace."

"Ace then," the voice said, no small amount of mockery in its tone.

Ace rose to wobbly legs, nearly falling over as if he hadn't walked in years.

"Who are you?"

A soft *drip, drip, drip* echoed from somewhere in the distance, the only response.

Ace reached for his LeMat revolver, but it was gone. All his things were gone. What was more, he was naked as the day he was born. Was this some kind of . . . rebirth? What did the preacher call it, being born again? Maybe this was his tomb. Like Jesus.

"Shit," he said. "There's no way any God would make that mistake twice."

Here, in the darkness, unarmed as he was, he knew he was at the mercy of whoever spoke. Ace called out again but only heard his own voice bouncing back at him.

He took a few tentative steps toward the sound of dripping water, but his feet were numb too. It was hard to stay upright. He'd reached the point where any normal person would start to panic. But Ace embraced a challenge. Always had.

Now that the voice was gone, he felt nothing. No fear. No anxiety. Well, that wasn't entirely true. He felt something.

Curiosity.

Following a snaking path brought him to a small pool and the source of the pinging drips. Approaching it cautiously, sure some big tentacular beast was gonna burst out and gobble him whole, a glint of light off to the side caught his eye.

His gun.

His clothes.

And on top of it all, Crowley's strange bone harmonica.

He changed course, heading for his stuff. Soon, he was dressed again and checking his revolver. It was full. Though, he had some innate understanding that the bullets wouldn't be needed. Not here. Not now.

He spun the instrument around and sneered. Just holding it, all he could think about was bashing Crowley and his woman's head in over and over again. Until he stuffed it in his pocket.

"Hello?" he called again, shuffling back toward the water.

He leaned over and gazed upon his reflection.

All was as he'd always known it except his nose, flat and crooked off to the left side from where he'd been struck.

It didn't hurt, but he looked like a damn frying pan. His hair, still blond with gray begging to be seen. A small bush covered his chin. His clothes were adequately disheveled, but he didn't need a mirror to see that.

His eyes though . . .

They didn't look the same either. Leaning in for a better view, Ace nearly leaped from his skin when his reflection became a smoky mist and those eyes—which were not his eyes—remained.

"*Ace*," boomed that same formless voice.

Ace stood proudly before whatever this was, though all he could manage was a, "Huh?"

Within the water, smoke swirled, mesmerizing.

"Congratulations, sinner," the smoke said. "Your debt has been paid and you have been chosen."

"Chosen? By who? Speak sense dammit!"

"The White Throne."

Despite the strangeness of his predicament, Ace waved off the notion. "Sorry, but there ain't no kings and queens round these parts."

Water shot up in a geyser, reminding Ace of his last memories in Revelation Springs. And there, inside a cavernous mountainside, the sound of thunder accompanied it.

"You can be returned." The reflection was now within the geyser, which sprayed like a solid pillar now.

That's when he recalled the words, truly heard them this time. This presence had called Ace a sinner, said he'd paid his debt.

"Wait. Returned from where?" he asked.

"The coldest pits of Hell."

"Cold?" Ace shook his head. "Sounds like you need a refresher on the Good Book."

Another thunderclap and a brief memory returned.

Frost covered every inch of Ace's naked flesh. A cold unlike any-thing he'd ever felt permeated his very soul as if his heart was encased in a block of ice. A figure stalked toward him through foggy, cold smoke. Something evil. Pure, unadulterated, fucking evil. It held a rod of some kind, something splintered and long.

A second later, Ace was dry heaving before the pool again. The geyser had disappeared but the whole of the surface was filled with the vague face of a man.

"Who the hell are you!" Ace yelled.

"You may call me Kjeldgaard."

"I don't wanna call you nothing. Let me out of here!"

"As I said, you've paid a debt, but I could send you back. It would be no less than you deserve."

"I . . . Why can't I remember? Where am I? Wh—"

"All in due time," the thing said. Still, Ace saw no mouth, no true features, just a hazy human shape in the water. "For now, all you need know is that the White Throne has use of you. Count yourself blessed. A Child, you are, no more."

"So, you're what, God?" Ace asked.

"Never even jest," Kjeldgaard said. "I am but a servant of the Most High. An angel of the fourth order."

Ace laughed. "You're serious."

"Always."

"And what am I? Don't tell me I'm an angel too?"

"Not remotely. You have been resurrected as a Hand of God, to face the powers of Darkness for the glory of the White Throne."

Ace had to stifle a laugh. How many men in his life he'd heard claim such grand ambitions and power? He'd shot and killed most of them.

"Right . . . so I died?" he said.

"Sentenced to hang some time ago."

That thought was an unpleasant one. How much of his life went missing, with not even more than a hazy memory of time apparently spent in . . . Hell.

"Sounds like you're leaving out some details, *Angel*," Ace said.

"Your essence was restored, but not as you once knew it," Kjeldgaard said. "Your life is not your own, Mr. Ryker."

"Is that a fact?" Ace said. "So am I your slave, then? Because you might as well send me back to Hell. I don't follow orders, Kill Guard. I give them."

"Not to me. Do your job and you will be given a measure of freedom and avoid eternal damnation."

Ace didn't like how the angel had said that word, *freedom*.

"Freedom?" he asked.

"In a manner of speaking."

Ace clicked his tongue. "Okay. Suppose I buy all this. What job are you talking about, and how much does it pay."

"You were sentenced to hang by one of our own."

All the memories came flooding back.

"Crowley?" Ace scoffed, remembering how he'd talked about serving a "higher power" of sorts and called himself a Black Badge. "He's with you?"

"Not me, but he is among us. And he has gone too far. It is up to you to eliminate him . . . before he destroys the world."

Ace stuttered over a response. *Destroys the world?* Sounded like a bit much for a self-righteous shit-shoveler like James Crowley. However, in the end, Ace only heard one thing.

"So, I gotta kill Crowley?" he asked.

"For the second time."

A grin spread across his face, from ear to ear. "Oh, my new friend. Now that's something I'll happily do for free."

ABOUT THE AUTHORS

Rhett C. Bruno is the *USA Today* and *Washington Post* bestselling and Nebula Award–nominated author of the Circuit Saga, the Children of Titan series, the Buried Goddess Saga, *Vicarious*, and *The Roach*, among other works. He is currently a full-time author and publisher living in Delaware with his wife and daughter.

Jaime Castle is the *Washington Post* and #1 Audible bestselling author of *The Luna Missile Crisis*, the Buried Goddess Saga—which includes the IPPY Award–winning *Web of Eyes*—and more. Hailing from the great nation of Texas, he lives with his wife and two children and enjoys anything creative. Castle cohosts *Keystroke Medium*, a popular podcast devoted to reading, writing, and everything in between. His office looks as if Marvel and DC vomited on his walls and he refuses to clean it up.